# 'Til Shiloh Come

## An Arkansas Family in Time of War

### The Shiloh Saga…Volume V

*Written by*

# Patricia Clark Blake

SCOTCHWOOD HILL

**Published by:**
Scotchwood Hill
3101 Scotchwood Drive
Jonesboro, Arkansas 72405
patriciacblake.com

**Cover Design:** Martha Rodriguez
**Photograph:** Simon Bratt
Shutter Stock.com

**All Scripture quoted:** King James Version ©1850,
1611bible.com/KJV
-king-james-versopm-1850.

**Copyright:** ©2020. Printed in the United States of America
*'Til Shiloh Come:*
*An Arkansas Family in Time of War*

**ISBN**: *978-0-9998416-3-1*
**LCCN**: *2020922956*

# DEDICATION

This final novel of the Shiloh Saga is written
in memory and honor of
my extraordinary, loving parents
*H. Gene and Gladys Clark.*


My endless gratitude goes to
*God, Jesus Christ, and the Holy Spirit*
Whose gifts and grace
created whatever value you find in these pages.

# Other Titles by Patricia Clark Blake

*In Search of Shiloh:*
*A Journey Home Through*
*Arkansas—VOL. 1*

*Beyond Shiloh:*
*The Story of an Arkansas*
*Family—VOL.3*

*The Dream of Shiloh:*
*An Arkansas Love Story*
*VOL. 2*

*Shadows Over Shiloh:*
*Unrest in Arkansas*
*VOL. 4*

*'Til Shiloh Come*
*An Arkansas Family in Time of War*

# CHAPTER 1

*Except the Lord build the house, they labor in vain that build it:*
*Lo, children are a heritage of the Lord: the fruit of the womb is*
*His reward.*
*Psalms 127:1,3*

"No, Roy. You're barely eighteen. You can't go to war."
Laurel MacLaine squared her shoulders. Her green eyes met the
brown ones of her adopted son. "Whatever are you thinking? You
know how we feel about secession."

"I never want to go against ya, Mrs. Mac, but it isn't for
you to say. I done talked to Mr. Mac. I don't see I got no choice. I
ain't no coward, and my friends already joined the militia over in
Greene County."

Laurel turned her back so Roy would not see tears
beginning to fall from her lashes. As she did, she glimpsed the
intricate sampler, bordered with native leaves and varicolored
wildflowers. The motto, worked in storm-blue, satin-stitched
letters two inches tall, proclaimed what she felt. 'No War Will
Come to Shiloh.' Laurel had finished the beautiful needlework
within two weeks of Mac's return from the Second Secession
Convention—the failed convention. The sampler was more than an
adornment for her home. This embroidery carried her most ardent
prayer. Arkansas may have gone to war…joined the Confederacy,

1

but Laurel MacLayne swore she'd not allow that reality to cast a shadow over her home.

For most of the first year of the war, Laurel's prayer had been answered. Nothing much had changed at Shiloh since Mac returned home. Until that morning, her life had been filled with the routine of homesteading. Tirelessly, she worked beside her husband, Patrick, as they planted, harvested, and preserved the bounty of Shiloh. She nurtured her children among the treasured family heirlooms brought from Washington County and Maryland. Her children's needs filled her days. Their schooling, storytelling, reading from the Bible, and singing lullabies to her infant daughter added to her already busy routine. Laurel thrived in the attention of her husband who had not been away from home since June. If truth be spoken, Laurel had not been happier at any time since she came to start a new life on Crowley's Ridge. Her life had been blissful in the cabin Mac had built for her home.

Laurel drew her sleeve across her face to erase the traces of tears. "Roy, you are right. You are a young man now. I can't tell you what to do. Just know I care about you—Mac and I love you as our son. I don't want you in harm's way. Please think about what you are doing. Pray…and listen for the Lord to help you make the right decision."

"I'm sorry, Mrs. Mac. I hate hurtin' you, but a man's gotta do what he's gotta do. If he don't, he ain't a man. I'm beholden to you and Mr. Mac for the life you gave me and Cathy." Roy hugged his adopted mother, an act he'd rarely done. With red cheeks, he walked to the back door and stopped. "You both been mighty good to us. Guess I better get back to work."

"Lord, help me. I can't let it come to Shiloh." Since Mac had returned home after leaving his role as a state legislator and a delegate to both secession conventions, Laurel refused to acknowledge the war. When her husband began any discussion that he thought necessary to prepare for the difficult times to come, she changed the subject or left the room. She'd used this tactic to cope with any situation she found beyond her control. Since she was fourteen, when anything threatening came up, she avoided it, denied it, or ran from it. Laurel knew this old defense strategy well. She could do it again. She would. She didn't want the war. Certainly, she didn't start the war. This crisis would not destroy her family.

At bedtime, Mac took his infant daughter from his wife, laid her in the cradle that had once nestled him and even his father. The carved white oak had darkened with age, but the treasured antique remained beautiful. As she slept, Leah Ann's tiny hands clasped the edge of her quilt.

Mac added three more logs to the fire before he undressed for bed and then buried himself under the wedding ring quilt given to Laurel and him as a wedding gift when they came to Shiloh in '57.

Shortly, Laurel pushed open the door with her foot as she walked with a lamp and a copy of Hawthorn's *The Scarlet Letter,* which she had been trying to find time to read for a month.

"You want to read tonight, Laurel?"

"I look for any opportunity to read a few pages. You know that."

"I thought we might talk a while."

"We can do that."

"Well, change into your nightclothes and come to bed. It's cold. I need you to keep me warm."

Laurel stepped into the bathing room and pulled a long-sleeved winter nightgown over her head. Then she returned to sit on the bed to take down her hair. When she reached for her brush, she found Mac had already picked it up from her bedside table. He pulled it slowly down her back, loosening her tawny locks.

"I love your hair, Wife."

"I'm glad."

"Our new baby girl is a beauty. She's gonna look like you. Her hair is already like yours. Look at those little curls. I can see a hint of gold in her brown hair."

"Babies' hair always changes, Mac. She's too little to know what she'll look like."

"No. She's gonna be a little Laurel. Wait and see."

In a tone of voice that sounded almost prayerful, Laurel whispered, "Thank God you are home, Patrick. That makes me happy."

"What brought that on? I've been home for five months."

"Nothing special. I just want you to know I'm blessed that you are home with me…you and our entire family."

"You are very serious tonight, Laurel." Mac turned her to face him and looked into her eyes. "Roy told you he's going to enlist in the militia, didn't he?"

Laurel turned her back to Mac and spooned against him. "That fire feels wonderful. You were so smart to build a fireplace in our bedroom."

"Darlin', you didn't answer my question."

"Roy said he was thinking about it. I told him I didn't want him to go and asked him to pray about his decision. Now let's not talk about it anymore."

"Did he tell you he'd talked to me?"

"Yes. Mac, Andy's boots are too tight for him. Do you think we can order him a new pair the next time we go to Greensboro?"

"Of course, we'll get Andy new boots. They'll make a fine Christmas present for him. You aren't going to talk to me about Roy, are you?"

"I thought we'd finished that conversation. Is there anything else I don't know that he told you?"

"He wants to marry Annie Clark."

"That's not news. Those young'uns have been trying to get Eli Clark's blessing since Annie turned sixteen. He told her she's not old enough."

"Roy wants to get married now."

"I hope he waits. He's too young."

"They are both of age."

"I know they are, but they're still children."

"They love each other," Mac said.

"That's nothing new either. They've been crazy for each other since they met at school." Laurel moved close to Mac and yawned. "Husband, hold me close. I'm tired to the bone."

Mac reached out of the quilt and turned down the lamp wick. Goodnight, darlin'. I love you."

"That's not news either, but I'm glad to hear it."

The weather that first week in November turned bitter. The winds blustered out of the north, and powerful gusts tore scores of dead leaves from the trees. The nights were especially raw. Temperatures fell below the freezing point nearly every night since October had given way to the new month. At least, the area around Crowley's Ridge had been dry Memories of the disastrous ice storm of 1858 had not faded. Both Cathy and Roy remembered too well the night they lost their Grandmother Dunn.

The family settled into the winter routine. Family time centered around the fireplace in the early evening after supper, followed by night chores, and then early to bed. The house was quieter since Roy returned to the Dunn place to care for his livestock. On that Wednesday night, the MacLaynes retired about 8:30. Both Gracie and Cathy had the sniffles, and Andy said he was bored. After herding cattle into pastures near the shelter that day, Mac was ready for sleep, perhaps more than the children were.

Later, pounding on the front door of the cabin jarred the window panes and woke the MacLayne household. Leah Ann's startled cry jolted Mac to his feet. The room was pitch dark.

"MacLayne, you come let me in." A brusque call came from outside.

Mac pulled on his trousers and put a match to the lamp sitting on the bureau nearest the bed. Laurel drew a shawl around her and rushed across to the cradle to soothe her screaming daughter. "What's wrong, Patrick?"

"Hanged if I know, but I intend to find out." He passed into the main pen of the house, carrying a single lantern.

"MacLayne, I said open this door." As Mac passed through the shadowy room, he caught a glimpse of the two frightened faces of his sons, who stood at the loft rail above. Cathy and Gracie were hugging each other, peering through a crack at the door. All the children were startled as the intruder continued to smash his fist into the door.

"Stop pounding on that door. I'm comin'!" Mac shouted. He turned to his children before he opened the door. "Young'uns, get back to bed. It's too cold to be up tonight. I'll see to this." He pulled the latch back and opened the door. "Eli, why in thunder are you poundin' on my door at this hour of the night?"

"I come to get my girl."

"Annie's not here. Why would she be? Have you lost your senses, man?"

"She ain't here? Let me talk to Roy Dunn then."

"Roy's not here either. You ought to know as well as anyone that he stays over at his place most of the time. He's been there for a good spell. What is goin' on?"

"I just come from there. Ain't no one at the Dunn place. Not Roy nor Annie. I can't find her anywhere."

"Eli, come over here and warm yourself by the fire. The temperature has dropped since we went to bed. I didn't realize how chilled the night had gotten."

Laurel came into the room, carrying Leah Ann, wrapped in her cradle quilt. "Mac, what's wrong at the Clark place? Can we help?"

"Eli here is lookin' for Annie and Roy. Says he's been over to Roy's place." Mac lit a second lantern from the mantle and stoked the embers into flame. "Here take this chair and tell me what ya know."

Eli Clark's eyes sank to the floor. His shoulders drooped, and he slumped into Mac's armchair. Light from the glowing coals in the fireplace cast shadows across the room. "I'm gonna shoot that boy." The angry words fell across the silence.

Cathy began to weep.

Andy shouted down from the loft. "You ain't gonna hurt my brother, mister."

Mac picked up another lamp from the table and lit the wick. He lifted it above his head so he could see the faces of his sons, who had not obeyed him earlier.

6

"Mark Thomas. Andy. Did I not tell you to go back to bed? The night is cold, and y'all can both catch a chill. I'd best not have to tell you again."

"Yes, Papa." Mark Thomas scampered back to his bunk.

"Oh, all right." Andy shuffled back across the floor to his place in the loft.

Laurel handed her two-month-old daughter to her husband. "Let me go see about Cathy and Gracie. I need to cover the boys, too. I'll be back to get her in a few minutes."

Mac drew Leah Ann to his bare chest, realizing at that moment how Eli must feel. "Now, Eli, tell me what you know about what's happened."

"Mac, those young'uns musta run off together. I've been lookin' for Annie since sundown. Wasn't quite dark when I came in from the field with Steven. We did the chores in the barn and went into the house. Wasn't no supper laid out. The fire just embers. That ain't like Annie. She always has a hot meal on the table for her brother and me."

"When did you last see her?"

"Round noon. We came in for dinner like we always do."

"Did she say anything to you then?"

"No. She was still spiteful over our spat last night."

"What did you argue about last night?"

"Tarnation, MacLayne, I don't argue with my young'uns. I just tell them how it's gonna be, and they know I mean business. Anyway, when she asked me about the hundredth time to set her weddin' date with Roy, I told her we'd think about it when the spring plantin' was done."

"Spring plantin'? Eli, we've just finished the harvest. What'd she say?"

"I wasn't listening much…something about Roy bein' right. She started cryin' again and went to her nook behind the fireplace and pulled the curtain. She wouldn't eat dinner with us. Steven and me went back to the hayin' after we ate."

Laurel stepped down from the loft ladder and walked over to take the baby from Mac.

Eli spoke again. "Those two done run off together. I wonder where they can be?"

"Eli, you know you have no one to blame but yourself, don't ya?" Laurel asked. "You told those young'uns they could get married when Roy was able to support a wife and after Annie turned sixteen."

Eli interrupted her. "I never gave that girl my blessin'."

She continued. "Annie is closer to seventeen now, and Roy's homestead is doing well. He's made a fine profit on his egg and milk business since he has taken up homesteading full time. You know those two have been in love since they were mere babies. They did what you asked them to do."

"My Annie is too young to leave home."

Mac sat on the raised hearth near the warm fire. "How old was Annie's ma when you carried her to your homestead? That wasn't a little way across a county line. You brought Rebecca to a different state away from her entire family."

"Was a different time then. I wasn't a whelp of a kid either. I was more'n twenty-four years old."

"When we were canning tomatoes the other day, Annie told me her mother was only fifteen when she married you and moved to Arkansas to help you set up your homestead."

"That's the Lord's truth, Mrs. Mac, and now my Rebecca lays in the churchyard, worn out before her time. I want better for my daughter."

"Is that the main reason you are out traipsin' in this cold tonight, Eli?

"What are you getting' at, MacLayne?"

"Could it be you don't wanna lose your cook and housekeeper?"

Streaks of crimson covered Eli Clark's face. He broke eye contact with Mac, dropping his gaze to the floor. "What's that girl been sayin' bout me?"

Laurel stepped between the two men. "She spoke nothing bad, Eli. She said she wanted to marry Roy last summer after her birthday, but you said everyone was too busy. She wanted your blessing so she waited. She told me you depend on her more and more since you lost your wife. She was hurt that you were saying things against Roy, hinting that he's not good enough for her. The last time she was over, she said you asked her to wait another year. She cried in my arms that afternoon."

"I love my girl. I just can't lose her. Steven and Annie are all the family I got left now. I may be a selfish old man, but I'm worried. You suppose they're all right? It's too cold out there for them to be travelin'. They ain't doin' something stupid, do ya think?"

"I expect they eloped, Eli. I don't know what else we can do but wait until they come home."

"Suppose yer right." The two men began to walk toward the door. "Sorry I woke your household, Mac. Laurel, I didn't mean to scare yer young'uns. I'm headin' home now. What time do you think it's getting' to be anyway?"

As Mac opened the door, the antique mantle clock he'd brought from Maryland struck the first of eleven chimes. "Eli, be patient. Don't lose your temper when you find them. When Annie and Roy get home, we'll work all this out."

Eli Clark stepped off the porch into the pitch dark. Mac replaced the bar on the door and turned to his wife. "Nothing we can do tonight, Wife. Let's go back to bed."

Before they left the room, Andy called down from the loft. "Papa, you ain't gonna let Mr. Clark shoot Roy, are you?"

"Son, no one's gettin' shot. Mr. Clark is just spoutin' off. You get to bed. I'm telling you for the last time."

"Good night Mama and Papa."

When he closed the door to their bedroom, Mac stoked the wood in the fireplace into a hotter blaze. He knew Laurel wouldn't sleep now. He returned to his place, awaiting her as she put the baby into her cradle once again. When she returned from covering Leah Ann, Mac pulled her close beneath the now cold quilt. They spooned together for some time.

"Laurel, speak your mind. You won't sleep until we talk this out."

"Where do you think those young'uns have gone off to? They wouldn't go to Matthew because he wouldn't marry them on a whim."

"I wish I knew. I'd not worry much except the weather has turned off so cold. They must be on the road somewhere."

"Can they get married anywhere close, Mac?"

"As close as Jonesboro or the bootheel of Missouri--any place within three hundred miles around us that they can find a preacher or a Justice of the Peace. They are both above the age of consent. I know Roy's too smart to try to make the trek to Tennessee. The state line to Missouri is less than twenty-five miles."

"Why'd they run off? I'd have given them a lovely wedding here at Shiloh."

"You know as well as I do. They didn't want the hassle. Eli should have kept his promise, but he wanted Annie to stay under his roof."

"I'll not sleep. I'm worried to distraction."

"No need frettin' over something you can't change. Nestle those tawny curls on my shoulder, and let's keep each other warm."

"You know it's perfectly comfortable here in our room."

"Maybe I just wanted a little attention. Rest here. I'll bet those young'uns will be back tomorrow, and then we'll get things back to normal."

Laurel prayed, "Lord, take care of Roy and Annie." She nestled closer to her husband. "Mac, do you ever think back to those days when we were newly-weds? Were those good days for you?"

"Laurel, it's not like it's been so long ago. You know your preacher grudgingly spoke those words over us on March 17, 1857...Today is November 6, 1861. It's been four years and two months, such a short time, we've lived in this cabin as man and wife...that September when we were truly married, that first night I made love to you...when I realized what a true marriage could be. I'd not change any of our memories."

"Our lives have changed in these years, Mac."

"Indeed they have…. It's so much better than I ever imagined it could be."

"If our lives will only stay this fine. How can we keep the chaos away from Shiloh? The thought of how much we could lose frightens me beyond any nightmare."

"We are doing all we can to buffer our family, but the future is always uncertain. We will rely on our faith and each other, Wife. Everything will be all right when it's over. God's will be done."

"You are my anchor, Patrick. I would never have learned to live in faith if you had not stood with me these past five years."

"We're a good team, Laurel--you and me and the Lord. Regardless of what is to come, we'll depend on His grace to see us through. After all, we live at Shiloh…the two of us and our young'uns. What else could we need?"

# CHAPTER 2

*Whoso findeth a wife findeth a good thing*
*and obtaineth favor of the Lord.*
*Proverbs 18:22*

Prayers went out. Every MacLayne made trips to the porch to stare down the road too many times to count. They jumped to every sound outside. Roy and Annie did not return on the second day. On the morning of the third day, Eli Clark made another unannounced visit to Shiloh.

"Ya seen them young'uns, MacLayne?"

"No, Eli. I told you I'd send word the minute we saw them."

"I just come from the Dunn place. Roy ain't back, but someone's takin' care of his stock. I didn't see no one, but the place is kept to a tee. All the chores are done—and done right. This elopement wasn't planned on the spur of the moment."

"Roy's always tended to business. Should bring you some peace knowing he'll do the same for your daughter."

"I wash my hands of the whole mess. Annie ain't no daughter of mine. I'm through lookin' and frettin' about that girl."

"You don't mean that, Eli. You don't disown your only daughter because you're angry."

12

"Been neglectin' my homestead long enough. I got work to do. Good-bye, MacLayne."

His neighbor to the north pulled his hat around his graying head, tucked his face into his coat, and walked away. Brisk northerly winds sent dead leaves across his path. Mac shivered that cold November morning. "Lord, let tomorrow find Roy and Annie in their own home." He returned to his cabin, knowing Laurel awaited him with more questions than he had answers. A long day lay ahead.

Φ

The sun cast red and gold beams through the autumn landscape along Crowley's Ridge. Every noise on the road or whinnying of a horse caught her attention. Laurel stepped back onto the porch, holding the newest MacLayne against her shoulder. She stopped next to Cathy, who was just coming in from the hen house.

"Mama, do you think Roy and Annie will come home soon?"

"Darlin', I don't know, but I'm sure they'll come to tell us they're married as soon as they can."

"I'm so mad at them. I wanted to be at the weddin'. It's not fair."

"Well, we need to hear their story before we judge, don't ya think? Could be more to it than we know, Cathy."

"I know you're right, Mama, but I'm not gonna see my brother's weddin', not if they eloped."

"I wish they were home too. At least we'd know what happened, but it's suppertime. Here, Cathy, take the baby and let me go finish the meal. Your papa and the boys will be finished in the barn soon. It's near dark now."

The aroma of bread baking scented the warm cabin. At the hearth, Laurel pushed the pot of beans back over the fire to heat and then pulled the golden rolls from the hearth oven. She slathered them with newly churned butter and set them near the heat to stay warm while she emptied a jar of creamed corn into a second pot. Finally, she placed the nearly ready yams among glowing goals.

This was her favorite time of day. The farm work was done, and her family would soon sit around the table to share their day. Laurel's spirit soared during these times. She hardly felt she was an individual, only a part of the unity that was the MacLayne family. She knew the war existed somewhere beyond Shiloh, but it seemed so very far removed from her home. Mac had promised he would not take sides, and he would remain with her.

Leah Ann whimpered from her cradle but promptly fell back to sleep. Laurel smiled. *How wonderful to have a baby girl.* Her birth had been the easiest of her children, and Mac had been at her side the entire time. She vividly remembered the tear that stood on his lashes when she asked if they could name the new baby for their mothers. Leah Ann MacLayne. Yes, life was good at Shiloh.

The back door flew open, and the males of her household trampled in…tallest to least, though Andy was quickly gaining on his father's stature. Mark Thomas, now just passed three, strutted across to the door and pushed it with such force, plates rattled on the shelf. Leah Ann screamed at the bang.

"Mark Thomas, thank you for closing the door but please do it more quietly next time."

"Okay, Mama." He bounded across the room to look at his howling sister. "Gee, Mama, she can sure scream." The family laughed at his ironic announcement. He had no clue he'd caused the howl.

"Family, it's time to eat. Wash up, y'all." Laurel finished placing flatware on the table as her family gathered. "Wash both sides, Mark Thomas."

Mac stood at the head of the table and bowed his head. "Father, we are beyond blessed. Our family is home and warm and about to be well-fed. We ask the same blessing for all in our community. Lord, we ask you to watch over Roy and Annie. Bring them home to us soon. Bless this fine meal. Amen."

Midway through their family time, Andy jumped from the bench he shared with Cathy. "Someone's here, Papa. Want me to go let 'em in?"

"You sit down, Son. I'll see to it. Mac rose just as a gentle knock came from outside. He pulled open the door. Roy and Annie stood hand-in-hand on the front porch.

"Good evenin', Mr. Mac."

"Hello, Roy...Annie. We've been expectin' y'all. Come on in. Come on over and sit by the fire. You've gotta be cold."

"We are, Mr. Mac. Since sunset, it's got right chilly outside," Annie remarked.

"Annie's pa's been here, ain't he?" Roy asked. "That's why you been waitin' for us."

"As a matter of fact, yes. Eli Clark came by on Wednesday night. Said he was worried because he wasn't able to find Annie. He came back this mornin' about nine. You got something you wanna tell us, Son?"

Roy had not turned loose of Annie's hand one moment since they entered the cabin. "Yes, Sir. I am happy to tell you Annie is my wife, Mrs. Roy Dunn. We got married on Thursday mornin' up at Chalk Bluff, right across the state line. I wasn't sure if we could marry without her pa's signing here in Arkansas, but we're legal in Missouri. A girl only has to be twelve there."

"Congratulations, Roy. Annie will make you a fine wife if her pa doesn't shoot you on sight." Patrick MacLayne smiled broadly at his adopted son.

"Did he say that?"

"He did, Roy," Andy added, his eyes the shape of small eggs. "He had a gun, too."

"That's enough, Andy." Mac turned back to Roy. "Have you two gone to the Clark place yet?"

"We rode by there, but no one was home."

"I suppose they are still out lookin' for y'all." Laurel rose to bring the blackberry cobbler to the table.

"Mrs. Mac, I hope no trouble comes, but we tried to do things the right way. We did whatever my pa asked us to do, but he always wanted more. Lately, he started telling me that someone else would make me a better match."

"Mr. Mac, I ain't never been disrespectful to Mr. Clark. I don't know why he turned against me. I love Annie. I'll be a good husband to her."

"I know you will, Roy. Don't worry. We'll help you work things out with Eli. You and Annie come over here and eat some supper. I doubt you had a good meal since you left home."

"Thanks, Mama. I am right hungry. Come on, Annie. Sit with me here on the bench."

Andy jumped to his feet. "I'll go put your horse in the barn. Y'all gonna stay the night, ain't ya?" He dashed out the back door without waiting for an answer.

"Well, Son. You've made your decision now. I know you love each other, and I know you can take care of Annie. I just wish you had come to us and let us give you a proper weddin'."

"Mr. Mac, there just wasn't no way," Annie said before tears began. "I couldn't have Roy goin' off to the war and us not belong to each other. I couldn't stand it."

Silence spoke louder than any words spoken that day. The clock on the mantle marked the passing moments. Tock…tock…tock…tock.

"Roy, you didn't enlist in the army, did you?" Mac looked Roy squarely in the face.

"Yes, sir. The local troop, the Greene County Roughs that's headquartered in Gainesville."

"And then you eloped to Chalk Bluff? Does that make good sense to you?"

"I didn't see it made any difference. Jefferson Davis already issued a conscription law. Everyone between eighteen and thirty-five can get called up. Just a matter of time 'til our governor does the same thing here in our state. Anyway, Annie wanted us to get married. We've been waiting since last April. Her pa promised us."

Laurel sat down at her place. "Roy, darlin', don't you see that Annie will have to keep your homestead going alone if you are called into service."

"What choice did we have, Mrs. Mac." Roy looked up with confusion on his face.

Mac answered, "You could have waited."

"I wouldn't let him, Mr. Mac. My pa would have tried to push me into marrying someone else. Mrs. Mac, you know Roy and me have wanted to be together since we went to school together. We did the best thing for us."

"Have you thought about how hard it will be to live at the Dunn place alone if Roy gets called into the war?"

"No, but I will do whatever I have to do. That is what a family does, just like you and Mr. Mac. You take care of each other."

"Don't cry anymore, Annie. A bride needs to wear a smile when she's a newlywed." Laurel returned to her task of sharing the steaming blackberry cobbler among the eight members of her increasing family.

They ate quietly until Andy came through the back door. "Pa, the Clarks came back. I saw him and Steven at the end of the road. Leastwise, I think it was them. It's gotten real dark outside."

The sound of horses' hooves brought their attention to the door. "I'll get it, Laurel. Everyone, finish your supper so your mother and Cathy can clear the table. Andy, when you're done eatin', take Mark Thomas and Gracie into the second pen to play. Your mama's already laid a fire in there so it will be warm. We need to talk in here."

The urgent rap on the door resounded like the thunderous beating they'd heard on Monday night. Mac opened the door to Eli and Steven Clark. Behind them stood Matthew Campbell, Mac's best friend, and minister to both families.

"Well, Annie's here now."

"Yes. Eli, come and get warm by the fire."

"What do you have to say for yourself, MacLayne? You told me those young'uns weren't here."

"They weren't until about half an hour ago."

"Where have you been for three days, Annie Rebecca Clark? You been out shamin' our family and yourself with this no-account boy?"

Roy jumped to his feet, but Mac laid a heavy hand on his shoulder. The young man stepped back. He pulled his bride back against him. Her cheeks looked to be on fire and tears flowed freely.

"Mr. Clark…"

"Roy, I'll answer my pa." Annie stood and turned to face her father and brother. "Papa, that was so mean and not one word of truth. You know me better than that. Roy Dunn is a good man, and he is my husband." She lifted her left hand to show him the simple gold band she'd worn two days.

Eli took steps as if he intended to attack Roy, but his son and Brother Campbell stepped between the men.

"Pa. Annie said she got married. They ain't no shame in that," Steven Clark pleaded.

"You mind your own concerns, boy. She didn't get my okay to marry Dunn."

"She didn't have to, Eli. The age of consent in Arkansas is sixteen without parents' signature." Matthew Campbell explained. "A girl can marry at ten if her family will sign the papers."

"You mean we didn't have to go to Missouri to get married, Brother Matthew?"

"No, but it's legal if you have a license."

Annie pulled the folded paper from the pocket of her skirt. "We got this certificate that the preacher in Chalk Bluff filled out for us."

"Well, congratulations, Mr. Dunn, and blessings to you, Mrs. Dunn. I hope you have a long, happy life together."

"Thank you, Brother Matthew."

"Well, I ain't offerin' no congratulations. Annie, I wanted better for you. You come tomorrow and get your belongin's outta my house. You ain't my responsibility no more. You're a Dunn now, so let the Dunn boy see to you from now on."

"Eli, you don't mean that." The minister stepped forward to ease the dispute in the room. The concern on his face was clear to everyone. "I've known you more'n fifteen years, and you've always been a kind, loving father to your young'uns. You're a pillar of our church."

"Stay out of this, Matthew. Don't want no trouble with you. Come on, Steven. We've got chores waitin' at home."

Annie laid her hand on her father's arm, but he snatched his arm away and turned his back. Over his shoulder, he called back. "I mean it…get your stuff tomorrow.

Her brother looked back and mouthed to her, "I love ya, Sis."

Roy enfolded her in his arms and let her cry. "Annie, he's just mad right now. He'll settle down, and then we'll work it out."

"I never knew my pa to back down from his word in my whole life." Her tears continued.

"Come on, Annie. Let's go home. We've caused enough concern here for one night."

"Roy, wait a minute. We need to talk."

"Mr. Mac and Mama, thank you both for standing with us. We gotta long ride home. I've got stock to care for, and Annie and me need some time alone. We'll talk after church next Sunday."

Laurel rushed across the room to embrace Annie. "Daughter, I am so happy you are part of this family. Please don't fret. Roy is right. Your pa is a good man. He'll see things better in a few days."

"Thank you, Mrs. Mac. Goodnight." Annie tried to smile through her tears.

Preacher Campbell spoke, "Well, you two didn't let me do the honors at your weddin', but at least you can let me ask a blessing over ya before you go."

Roy's resolve broke at those words. He walked into Matthew Campbell's arms. "Thank you, Brother Matthew. Please do that for us. We'll feel married when our preacher says a prayer for us."

The young couple knelt before the hearth, and their minister laid his hands on their heads. He spoke the words that traditionally end a Methodist wedding ceremony. Then he added, "God bless you both, Annie and Roy Dunn. Don't ever forget that you are God's children. Live always in His presence. Amen."

# CHAPTER 3

*But by the grace of God, I am what I am: and His grace which
was bestowed on me was not in vain: but I labored more
abundantly than they all: yet it was not I, but the grace of God
which was within me.*
*I Corinthians 15:10*

Laurel tossed and turned all night. More than once, she
roused from a restless sleep. Dreams of her father came to her in
waves, each scene reminding her of life lessons he'd taught during
her growing-up years in the Boston Mountains. *Don't waste what
the Lord's given you, Girl. Tomorrow that may prove a
treasure…Get your house in order today; there may be no other
opportunity…Hold close to those you cherish, Daughter, for they
are here today.*

Such dreams should have brought her comfort. Laurel's
memories of Mark Campbell were dear to her, but that night she
was agitated and frightened. She moved nearer to Mac and brought
the quilt over her ears. For a time, she rested.

Just as the sun pushed its way over the ridge, Laurel sat up
and cried out. "Please Papa, no more. Roy is enough."

Mac shook her. "Laurel, wake up. Who are you talking to?"

She pushed herself back against the carvings of the four-
poster headboard, drawing the warmth of the quilt around her
shoulders. "I was dreaming…. All night my papa came to me,

retelling me the lessons of my childhood. Trying to tell me something…warning me about…I don't know what he wanted to tell me."

"Darlin', your papa didn't know Roy. How could that have been a lesson from your childhood?"

"What about Roy?"

"You cried out, 'Please, Papa. Roy is enough."

"I don't know. Dreams go in the blink of an eye. I remember something about troubles that come in threes. I remember my papa used to say that when bad news came."

"My poor darlin'. Roy's announcement about the enlistment yesterday bothered you more than you let on."

"Of course, it bothered me. We just talked about that, Mac. I said I'd do whatever it takes to keep this family safe and then that boy ran off and eloped…but not until he enlisted in the militia."

Mac pulled Laurel to his shoulder. "Roy is a man, Laurel. We can't prevent him or any of our other children from growin' up."

"I won't have it. Mac, our life is here together, all of us together. All my life, it's what I've dreamed of. I can't let anything take it away. This is the best year we've ever known--the harvest, the young'uns, our time together. I want everything to stay just the way it is for the rest of our lives."

"Laurel, we are at war. People get killed every day. How can you think we are livin' in Eden? I'd give my right arm to turn back time before that fraud of a convention. If I could change the secession vote, I'd do it. If I could have prevented this war, I'd gladly give my life."

Laurel looked into the shadowy eyes of her husband that early November morning. "Don't you ever say that to me again!"

"Wife, we don't live on an island where the rest of the civilized world can't touch us."

"Don't talk about war anymore!" Laurel pulled away, rose from the bed, and ran to the window. She stood for a brief time and raised her head. She pulled back the curtain to reveal the first rays from the sun.

"Come thou fount of every blessing…Tune my heart to sing Thy grace." Mac watched as Laurel swayed across the room toward Leah Ann's cradle. "Streams of mercy never ceasing…Call for songs of endless praise…Teach me some melodious….

Mac broke into her song. "What are you doin', Laurel?"

"Did you know Leah Ann smiled at me last night when I put her down?"

"What?"

"Look here at your beautiful daughter. When she's asleep like this, she reminds me of an angel. Our family is perfect. We've got three beautiful daughters and three fine strapping sons. We're safe here at Shiloh. I'm happy here. Nothing will take away the blessings God has given us. Nothing."

"Roy is already in the army. He'll go to fight when the governor calls the militia out to protect the state."

Laurel changed the subject away from the war again.

"I am a bit worried about Gracie. That cold is hanging on."

"She'll be fine, or we'll take her to the doctor." Mac shook his head, rose, and dressed for another day.

Φ

The Saturday night routine varied little at the MacLaynes. Mac sat, feet stretched toward the fire as he read the copy of the most recent Arkansas Democrat-Gazette he'd found on a bench in front of McCollough's store. He had received no paper from Maryland or St. Louis in the mail this week. Since secession, the mail delivery from areas beyond the state was erratic, when they came at all. The lack of communication from beyond the community was only one of the things that weighed on his mind. Because of this, Mac sought out every opportunity to find news or reports of any kind to tell him about what was happening beyond northeast Arkansas.

Unlike his wife's naïve view, Mac hadn't seen Shiloh as Eden since the state has left the Union. He was too much of a pragmatist to sit back and hope for the best without making preparations to safeguard his family. He began to stockpile things he knew would be scarce as the war spread. He also took steps to convert his money to gold as he was able to do so. Since his return from Little Rock, he had started to sell off his thriving herd of cattle. Knowing that beef would be confiscated or sold for a fraction of its worth or stolen by invading armies, Mac had systematically reduced his herd from the sixty-five animals down to only six, which he'd scattered across his many acres of pasture land. Even his two prize bulls, brought back from Missouri at a king's ransom, no longer grazed in the pasture nearest the barn. Bringing those animals to the homestead had cost so much more than money. The tiny granite cross and lamb under the giant oak in Eden was a constant reminder that he had not been home when Laurel had miscarried their first child. Since selling nearly all the livestock, Mac found himself restless and bored without enough work to occupy his time.

As much as he wanted to shelter Laurel and their children, he knew no person in Arkansas nor the nation would survive the conflict unscathed. Mac would continue to prepare for the worst while he prayed daily for the chaos of war to pass them by.

After supper that evening, Mac searched for something to do. Andy didn't want to play checkers. Laurel occupied most of her evening by bathing the girls and washing their hair so they would be ready to go to church the following morning. Mac missed Roy. After he finished reading every word of the Gazette for the second time, he dozed off in his armchair in front of the blazing fire.

The two MacLayne sons sat at the hearth while Andy read to his little brother from the third-level reader he'd finished the last school term. Cathy stitched on a Christmas gift she planned to give her mother. Bright-eyed and alert, Leah Ann cooed from her cradle.

The mantle clock began to strike out the hour of eight. Before the last note chimed, several riders trotted into the yard. Two sets of footsteps plodded across the front porch.

"Papa, who'd come here at this hour on a Saturday night?"

"Don't know, Son, but go on with your readin'. I'll see to our visitors." A heavy rap followed. Mac walked to the door and pulled the bolt back.

"Evenin'. Y'all chose a cold night to come callin'."

"Are you Mr. MacLayne?" a pale-faced corporal asked. Mac nodded. "Thank goodness. At last, we got to our last assigned homestead." The two young men dressed in makeshift militia uniforms looked as if they were ready for a costume party. Neither looked old enough to be a soldier.

"Well, Corporal, I asked why you came at such a late hour."

"We got our orders. The captain of our local company has been charged with requisitionin' pack mules for Arkansas troops, sir." The taller of the two boys thrust forward a wrinkled, stained document, obviously much handled that day. "We were told you have two mid-size, well-trained mules. We have been authorized to pay you twenty dollars Confederate for the pair."

Laurel re-entered the main pen holding Leah Ann. "You can't take our stock. We are neutral…"

"Laurel, I will deal with this matter. Please put the baby to bed. Andy and Cathy, y'all get ready for bed, too. We have church in the mornin'."

"Yes, Papa." Cathy took Gracie's hand to lead her to their room.

"But Papa, I wanna…"

"Andrew, get to the loft." Andy shuffled his feet toward the ladder as Cathy closed the door to her room.

"Mr. MacLayne, we're tuckered. Our unit's been working at this task since early this mornin'. Can we just have those jacks so we can get on home before it gets any colder?"

"Maybe we don't want to sell those animals. Farmers need mules to plow in the spring."

"Sir, we were told to pay you the twenty dollars and take the animals. The captain made it clear that all jacks from the families on the order were to be brought back to camp."

"I'm sorry to tell you that I don't have that pair of mules anymore. The liveryman in Jonesboro has had his eye on them for some time. I sold them to him last Saturday and for a much better price, I must say. 'Course, it didn't come close to the five hundred dollars that a miner offered me once over in Calamine."

"Sir, we don't have orders to negotiate a different price with the farmers. We were ordered to collect a dozen jacks. Without yours, we only have ten. Don't you have a couple more we could take?"

"No. Sorry to say I don't. Never like those stubborn animals much. I always preferred horses, but with winter comin' on, I saw an opportunity to get some work off my hands."

The young recruits looked with disbelief at the tall man at the door. No one sold their good plow stock. "We need to look for ourselves. We are ordered to bring in a dozen mules."

"Barn's at the back. I'll meet you there. You'll find my saddle horse, a big black stallion, my wife's mare, and a near-grown colt that belongs to my son, Andy. However, I tell ya, I don't take to anyone callin' me a liar to my face."

"No, sir. No disrespect. We didn't say you lied."

"We are just trying to carry out our orders, Mr. MacLayne."

"Nevertheless…"

"Sorry. We meant no offense," the second soldier interrupted.

Mac watched the six soldiers ride away a few minutes later. They drove the ten mules they'd confiscated ahead of them. They were two short of their quota. He returned to his cabin to face his wife.

## φ

The cabin was quiet and dark when Mac returned from the barn. He closed and barred the door before he walked the few steps to the second pen. There he was welcomed by the site of a substantial fire, providing both light and heat. He turned toward the carved four-poster where he watched Laurel turn down the wedding ring quilt on his side of the bed. He smiled and went to take her in his arms.

"So, you decided to sell our mules?"

"I did," Mac said.

"I suppose you figure we have no more use for two excellent plow animals on this homestead."

"Laurel, I heard about the confiscation of animals this afternoon when I was in Jonesboro. I decided it was time to prepare this farm for wartime."

"I told you I won't talk about the war inside these walls." Mac sat on the side of the beautiful bed, carved as a wedding present for the Widow Parker some seventy years ago—the only marriage bed the MacLaynes had ever owned. He pulled his hands through his chestnut-colored hair and silently asked God to help him open this long-delayed conversation with Laurel.

"It's time for us to have a serious conversation about this family. I've avoided the conflict as long as I can. Tonight was the second intrusion of the war in so many days. I couldn't keep either one from our door. Laurel, we have to deal with what's happenin' around us. As long as I have breath in my body, my family will not fall victim to this damned war."

She turned to face him with more green fire in her eyes than he'd ever seen. Her shoulders squared and her chin jutted forward. She was ready to challenge him. "What, pray tell, can you do to stop it? If we let it be a part of our world, it will take everything. Shiloh will disappear. I won't let it consume us…not that ugliness out there. I won't let it take my home and my family. I refuse to acknowledge it. It's the only way. Don't you see?"

Mac understood. She planned to deal with the war as she'd dealt with every other problem she'd faced in her entire life— denial. She wanted to hide from life as she had since the age of fourteen. He almost wished it were possible to wrap her and their loved ones up and hide them away until the nightmare passed.

"Not again, Laurel. That's a child's approach to life's problems. I won't let you put our children and yourself in danger— unaware or unprepared."

"We will be fine here at Shiloh if we don't let the outside intrude. Patrick, I can do anything I have to do if you are here with me. Tell me you won't go to war."

"I told you I'm not going anywhere. As long as I have it in my power, I am staying right here to take care of you and our young'uns. I know my life is here with you. The only time I feel complete is with you. If it is God's will, we won't be separated again."

Laurel spoke through her tears. "Thank God! I was so afraid. Mac, I won't let – I mean, if you left..."

"Laurel. Stop. You aren't thinking straight. You know I want no part in this war."

She slumped into his arms. He gently lifted her. He walked to his armchair where he sat holding her. "Wife, will you let me explain how I intend for us to deal with this war we don't want? We didn't start it, but we have to survive it." He waited for a reply but got none. "Look at me, Laurel Grace." He drew her face up to meet his storm-blue eyes. Fear, hopelessness, and defeat marked her visage as he'd seen only three other times in their lives together: her father's funeral in Hawthorn church, the day he found her in the empty Lutheran church in Bolivar when she'd run away from him, and the day after Easter in '58 when she told him Campbell had died at birth. Mac wiped her tears on the hem of her nightdress, pulled her into his shoulder, and began to recite the twenty-third Psalm.

"The Lord is my Shepherd. I shall not want..." When he finished, he lay his head against the back of his familiar chair. The fire snapped and leaves rustled on the trees outside their window. In the distance, some animal, perhaps a red wolf on the ridge, howled.

Laurel raised her head and spoke in a whisper. "Mac, tell me how we need to prepare for this life we don't want."

"Are you ready to listen, darlin'?"

She nodded, wiped her sleeve across her face, and gently kissed his mouth. "Yes."

Mac spent the next hour outlining his plan for their homestead's survival. The details and timeline for implementing this plan showed the deep thought and extensive time he'd put into the strategy. In each part of the plan, Laurel could see Mac's careful attention to safeguard their family and his plan to rebuild after the war.

"First, we've already begun to prepare. When we built Cathy's room, we built our stash, so we can stock food and household things we'll need. All that canned food, extra bags of grain and potatoes, and salt beef will help keep us fed. Every time I can get it, I plan to buy salt to store. We will try to keep enough milk cows and chickens to provide for us…that will be one of the most difficult parts of our plan. Next week, we have to start teaching our children what they can and cannot say about our home. An empty stash is no good."

"Mac, as long as you are here with me, we can grow enough food to feed ourselves."

"Women and children are always the innocent victims of war, Laurel. Armies come and take what they need. They don't consider how families will survive without the crops they grow."

"You don't think the war in the east will come across the Mississippi!"

"It already has, darlin'. And news in the paper isn't good now. When I came back from the last secession convention, I started work to prepare for what will come. I hope I've done it for nothin', but I'll not leave our future to chance."

"That is why you sold our mules?"

"I'm afraid that was a bit of a lie. J.F. took the mules out to the wilderness area for a couple of days. I did tell Snoddy I'd sell him the mules for $50.00, but I asked him for thirty dollars in gold and the rest in Arkansas currency. Laurel, I started selling off the cattle at the same rate. I won't take less than half in gold or silver and the rest in currency. We'll stash the gold and silver. For now, we will spend the paper money while it still has some value."

"What will happen to the value of our state money, Mac?"

"When the South loses the war, and we will…Confederate money will be worth nothing. Our land and whatever we have laid back will be our security so we can rebuild afterward. We'll make due on our labor, harvests, hunting, and faith until we can start again."

"You've thought about this a lot, haven't you?" Laurel looked intently into Mac's storm blue eyes.

"I have. When I was at Annapolis, we learned about war and military tactics. I've seen first-hand how greed grows through the workin' of politicians in Little Rock. Too many have one motivation—how can I line my own pockets. Look at what Digby did to the Flannagan family for so little as one hundred dollars. Pa told me Peggy and her kids had nothin' left until we gave her the stake back from Digby. That let her buy the Widow Parker's place."

"Thank you for being so patient with me."

Mac kissed his wife. His lingering, warm lips on hers helped to bring some calm, some hope that Shiloh would remain. Yet that one nagging issue still haunted him.

"Laurel, what is the most important thing you've learned since we met back on the porch of your father's cabin in Washington County?

"Gracious me. So much. I don't know where to start."

"I need to know only one thing. If you have learned that lesson, I know you can survive anything that is to come."

Laurel was quiet. She sat for several minutes before she tried to respond. Leah Ann began to cry. She rose to feed her. Sitting in her rocking chair, Laurel pulled the crocheted blanket over her nursing daughter. Mac watched her and whispered a silent prayer of gratitude and moved this image into his memory.

As she rocked, Laurel began her answer. "The most important thing I've learned from you is that when I know I am loved I am never alone. Mac, you taught me the meaning of grace. We don't feel God's presence until we know He loves us. I didn't know true intimacy with you until I knew you loved me."

The first smile Mac had shown that day lit the space between them. "Thank you, Lord. Darlin', I never have to fear for you again. He took her left hand, raised it to his lips, and kissed it tenderly. Then he enclosed her hand in his much larger one. Mac felt the warmth of her touch. He sensed a gentle throb as her precious lifeblood coursed through the veins at her wrist. They were one, more than at any time since they'd known each other.

"Wife, I love you today and have since the day we met. Truly, I didn't know it for a while, but I know it now. I'll love you until the Lord takes me home. We will never be apart. Oh, we may be separated by time and space now and again, but we will be one forever."

# CHAPTER 4

*The Lord by wisdom hath founded the earth, by understanding*
*hath he established the heavens. By His knowledge the depths are*
*broken up...My son, let them not depart from thine eyes:...So shall*
*they be life unto thy soul...Then shalt thou walk in thy way safely,*
*and they foot shall not stumble.*
*Proverbs 3:19-21,23*

The second Sunday in November, the war pushed its way
into life at Shiloh once again. The MacLaynes stood together on
the front porch of Shiloh Church as Roy and Annie drove into the
churchyard. Broad smiles lit their faces as they anticipated the
well-wishes of their church family at their first appearance as man
and wife. Annie's hand lay firmly on Roy's arm as he helped her
from the wagon seat. Roy was dressed in his militia uniform, and
she wore the pale blue wool merino she'd made as her wedding
dress.

"Mornin', Mr. and Mrs. Dunn." Brother Campbell greeted
the young couple. All gathered began to clap and cheer. Annie's
cheeks flushed as her church family welcomed them. "So glad you
were able to be with us at the Lord's house today. Not a better way
to start your married life together."

Mac clapped Roy on the back, and several men standing nearby laughed with Matthew Campbell and Mac as they greeted the new groom. The group moved into the church, animated and jovial, but as they stepped inside, Roy backed into Eli Clark, who stood in the aisle. The laughter stopped.

Roy extended his hand. "Mornin', Mr. Clark."

"Huh…what are ya dressed up for, boy?"

Annie stepped to Roy's side and said, "Papa, Roy's been called to serve with the Greene County Roughs. He enlisted when Captain Anderson called for recruits."

"I don't believe I spoke to you, Girl. The scowl on Clark's face told the story. His anger toward his daughter had yet to cool. He turned from her and went to sit in a pew next to his son. He'd hardly gotten seated when he turned and pointed back toward Roy and Annie. He shook his head and turned away a second time.

The congregation continued to file into the log sanctuary. Shortly before Matthew Campbell walked to the pulpit, Captain James Anderson marched to the front pew. He too was dressed in his full militia uniform, complete with his gleaming military saber. Murmurs filled the room as two other uniform-clad men followed close behind. Counting Roy, four members of the Greene County troop had chosen to worship at the Shiloh Church that morning. Ignoring the reality of war would be more difficult from this Sunday forward.

Matthew Campbell stood tall behind his pulpit. He asked the congregation to bow for the opening prayer. "Father, Thou art a great and loving Creator. We give You thanks for this beautiful Sunday mornin'. As we come to worship, let us be mindful of the blessings You've poured on us this harvest season. We also ask You to be with those of our church family who feel called to serve. Please keep them safe and return them to us soon. We ask You to join us here and lead us in joy-filled worship. Amen."

Laurel looked at Mac. Roy would be gone from them very soon. How could this be happening? He had only eloped with Annie last week. He had responsibilities at home now. Mac took her hand and patted it quietly. He smiled at her. He saw the tears in her eyes. He put his arm across her shoulder and pulled her close. "Laurel, all is well. God will take care of Roy."

A tear traced a path down her cheek, and she wiped it away with the back of her hand. No. She wouldn't let her family be pulled into harm's way. She would talk to Roy and convince him his place was at home with Annie. If she and Mac could stay neutral in this conflict so could her children. The war was not their concern.

Laurel was so distracted by the thoughts running through her mind, she paid little attention to the worship service. When it ended, she couldn't recall one hymn they'd sung or the scripture her uncle had preached on that morning. As the service ended, Matthew Campbell stood behind the pulpit. "Church, Captain James Anderson has asked to address us before we are dismissed. Please be seated."

Anderson stepped up to the pulpit. "Brothers and Sisters, the Greene County Militia leave on this coming Tuesday to march to Camp Borland in Randolph County. These brave young men will begin their thirty-day enlistment. With God's providence, we will win a major victory in the east to end this conflict with no more bloodshed. The commanders of our troops asked that we provide training to prepare our soldiers to fight if we must do so. Our unit will be back home before Christmas, God willing. Pray for our men and the Confederacy."

Matthew Campbell blessed his congregation with the benediction. Then he added, "Please protect the young men of Shiloh church and all those of our community who we commend to Your hands. Amen.

Mac helped Laurel to her feet. "Can you give me a smile, Wife?"

She turned and feebly complied with his request. They turned to make their way to the door, but before they reached it, Captain Anderson called out. "MacLayne, I'd like a word with you."

"Yes, James. What can I do for you this mornin'?"

"Do you have time to talk, just the two of us?"

"Might as well speak your mind. Laurel won't let it rest until she knows what you said to me anyway." Laurel linked her arm to her husband's. More than one stayed to hear the Captain's words.

"MacLayne, you're needed in our local militia. You're a community leader. You served in the legislature, and you've got the respect and education we need in our officers. You'd make a fine leader for our young men."

"Thank you for your confidence in my abilities, James."

"I have been authorized to offer you a rank equal to mine and a unit of your own."

"As I said, I thank you for the compliment, but I won't take sides in this conflict." Parts of the congregation murmured. Others gasped.

"I'd heard you voted against secession, but since our state has been dishonored, and our sister states of the Confederacy have already been attacked, surely you can't hold with that government in Washington."

"I hold with my family. I intend to safeguard them every way I can."

Red splotches marked Captain Anderson's face from his collar to his balding head. His voice took on an edge that Mac had not heard before. "Why, you cowardly traitor. I can't be hearin' you right."

"You are, Anderson. I will live out the days of this war here at Shiloh with my wife and young'uns. I don't believe that's cowardice. To serve a cause I don't support would be dishonest and immoral. When y'all elected me, I told you I'd not support secession. I voted against it in the legislature and both secession conferences last spring. Nothin' has changed." Mac turned to walk away when the captain clasped his shoulder and turned him back.

Mac threw back his arms. "I don't want trouble. This isn't any place to bring up political differences."

"Political differences…why you." Seeing a brawl as eminent, Matthew Campbell stepped between them.

"Brothers, remember where you are. In God's house, we are family. Conflict has no place here."

"Matthew, I'm sorry. I want no trouble. I told Anderson I'll remain neutral. He doesn't want to accept my decision."

"Think you're better than your neighbors, MacLayne? You were the only homesteader who didn't give up his mules to the foraging team last night. Everyone else gave their livestock for the good of the Confederacy."

"I don't believe Arkansas should be in the Confederacy. Anyway, I promised those mules to Snoddy at the livery in Jonesboro. Either my word is good or it's not." I showed your boys there were no mules in my barn."

"That is enough. I want no more discussion about the war in this church." Matthew used his more authoritative, preacher-voice.

"Well, Campbell, just which side are you on?"

"I'm on the Lord's side. I intend to stay there and keep this church a sanctuary, a safe place where everyone is welcome to worship. Shiloh will remain a sanctuary for all believers."

"We'll see about that. This is a Methodist Episcopal South Church, I believe." The captain pulled his hat down and started toward the door.

"James, let tempers cool. This is a southern church, but our name doesn't say Confederate or Union. We have loved and respected each other for years. Mac and you are the same men you were before secession. We don't have to let this thing divide our church."

"Maybe we didn't know each other as well as we should have." James Anderson walked out and slammed the church door.

Dinner that day was a quiet, tense affair. The entire MacLayne family, less Patrick's father who had started eating most of his Sunday dinners at the Flannagan's cabin, sat together, asked a blessing for the meal, and ate the substantial meal Laurel and Cathy had prepared. Yet the silence would be the memory of their family dinner that Sunday.

Laurel sighed as she and Cathy began to clear the table. Mac stood and told the children to find a place to play in another room so that he and Laurel could talk with Roy and Annie.

"I don't wanna go, Papa," Andy said. "This is family business. Cathy and me are family as much as anyone. Let us stay so we know what's said here."

Patrick looked at this firstborn. His mouth dropped at Andy's comment, but the boy's tone and his decision to disobey spoke in place of words that could have conveyed disrespect or rebellion.

*He's right. This is family business so everyone has a place at the table.* Mac studied Cathy and Andy who stood across the table from him. *How they have grown up in the past four years. Neither is a child any longer.* Mac shook his head, almost in disbelief. "You are so wise in your youth, Andy. We will talk this out as a family. Everyone sit down."

As everyone found a seat, Mac went to the head of the table. "No easy way to break the ice. Roy, you owe us an explanation. In the past couple of weeks, you've kept us in the dark and caused considerable concern for the whole family. If you knew that your unit would be called to duty so soon, why did you decide to elope after you waited more'n a year? I'm afraid I don't' understand."

"Mr. Mac and Mama, I am sorry we caused y'all to worry. That wasn't our plan, but I ain't one bit sorry that Annie and me got married."

"Son, you know we have nothing against your wife," Mac said.

"Roy, we love Annie and are happy to have her as part of our family, but why now when you knew the militia would be called out to serve so soon?" Laurel spoke softly.

"Mrs. Mac," Annie broke in, "Pa was tryin' to keep me from Roy. Pa told me not to invite Roy over to our place. I love Roy. We tried to do things the way Pa asked, but he wouldn't set a date for our weddin'. I told Roy I wouldn't wait no more. It's my fault."

Roy stopped her. "That's ain't so, Annie. I wanted you with me out at our place since I moved there more'n a year ago." Roy stood and faced Mac. "I got tired of bein' alone. I wanted a wife— Annie." Silence stood between them for several seconds. "Maybe

35

it wasn't the right time, but is it ever? Did you marry Mrs. Mac at the right time and place? When you love someone, you can only stand being apart so long, and then you do what's in your heart—not what your head says is sensible."

Patrick had no reply. He understood what Roy said. He thought back to all the times he'd been separated from Laurel during the past five years. He remembered the ache of being separated from her, especially in those few times when he thought the loss could be permanent--memories of Laurel lost in the wilderness on Crowley's Ridge, his finding her in the Bolivar Lutheran Church, afraid she'd refuse to speak to him, her laboring to bring Mark Thomas into the world, and the nightmares of the gunshot that nearly took his life. Yes. Mac knew that emptiness and understood why Roy eloped with Annie.

Finally, Mac spoke. "Roy, I know what you felt. But did you stop to think that Annie will be alone on your homestead when the militia is called up? Do you want her there taking care of your animals, defending herself if intruders come, and having to raise a garden and the food crops for the animals? She could be alone for weeks at a time, especially since her pa is so angry with y'all"

"Mr. Mac," Annie broke in again. "I told Roy that we had to elope last week. I didn't intend to wait one more day. I didn't give him a choice."

"She told me if I wanted her to be my wife, I had one time to choose. I'd marry her before the end of October, or she would look for someone who loved her enough to make her a wife. I wouldn't ever let another man take my place with Annie."

"All right. I see. But Roy, I am your mother. I don't want you to go to this war. Let's get you out of the militia."

"I can't do that, Mrs. Mac. I gave my oath. I promised to serve with Captain Anderson and my friends from Greene County. We grew up together, and our troop is tight. I didn't know we would have to report to camp this week, but I'm glad now. We only have to serve for thirty days. Our whole enlistment will be done by Christmas."

"Son, this war will not be over by Christmas."

"It could be, Mr. Mac. Those Yankees don't care nothin' about our slaves."

"Our slaves? Roy, we don't own other people."

"I know, but our honor has been attacked. I have to support the Southern cause and the honor that is the Southern way of life."

"Roy, you know I don't hold with the secession decision our state made. I cannot support the Confederacy. But you have to follow your conscience, just like I have to follow mine. We love you, Son. Nothing will change that."

"Mr. Mac, will you and Mama help me look after Annie for that thirty-days we have to serve?"

"Of course, we will do what we can." Mac and Laurel hugged the newlyweds. A warmer, normal feeling returned to their home, at least for that night.

After the hugging helped ease the tension in the room, Andy said, "Papa, I am glad that you ain't mad at Roy no more. But why was Mr. Anderson yellin' at you when we left the church? I thought he was our friend."

"Truthfully, I was surprised by his harsh words, too, Andy."

"He can't call you a coward. Everone around here knows you ain't afraid of nothin' or no one."

"I'm proud you think I'm never afraid, Andy, but it's not true. There are lots of things that scare me, but that's not the reason I won't fight in this war."

Cathy burst out, "If you think this is wrong and a bad thing, why are you lettin' Roy go fight with the Rebels? I don't want my brother to go away."

"Young'uns, I think that is enough questions for one night."

"But, Mama, I wanna know. If Pa is against the Confederacy, why is he lettin' Roy go?"

Mac rose from the table where he had been sitting. He rubbed his hands through his hair. "Come here, Cathy." He pulled the young lady into his lap. "You and Andy have asked me some mighty hard questions tonight. I guess you have a right to know. I hate that our country is divided and fighting. I think Arkansas took the wrong side. I don't believe we have the right to enslave another person. Our wealth, if we ever have any, needs to come from our sweat and hard work. I also know that our break with the government in Washington will cause extreme hardship in Arkansas for generations to come. I can't fight for something I don't believe in. I love Arkansas, but the leaders of this state didn't make a wise choice."

Laurel moved around the room, picking up one thing after another, repositioning a candlestick, or slightly altering the wick of the lantern. Her agitation was obvious. "Mac, let's not talk about this anymore. I don't want Roy to go off with hard feelings."

"Laurel, we wanted to clear the air this evenin'. Let's do just that. If our young'uns want to know something, they deserve an answer. They can ask me anything that's botherin' them."

"Papa," Cathy asked another question, "how can Roy go off to war if you think it is wrong?"

"Cathy, sweetheart, Roy is a man. He has to make his own decision and do what he believes is the right thing to do. I can love him regardless. I am proud of him because he has enough courage to follow his beliefs, even if I disagree with his reasons. Roy is family. Nothin' changes that."

"Are you goin' to war, Papa?" Andy asked with a touch of fear in his voice.

"I plan to remain here with your mama and y'all. I don't want to take sides. Your grandpapa and I will keep our farms goin' and try to keep as much hardship away from Shiloh as we can. When the war is over, we'll welcome Roy back home and go right on building a good life right here."

Mark Thomas climbed up into his father's lap. "Papa, read me a story. No more sad talkin'." The toddler ended the family discussion.

"Yes, young'un. You are right. It's time to start gettin' ready for bed. Go over and bring Papa his Bible, Mark Thomas, and I'll read you a story about a time a city fell just because God's people obeyed and blew their trumpets."

φ

An hour or so later, after Laurel had seen her children safely tucked into their beds, she stepped through the door to her private sanctuary into the waiting arms of her husband.

"I'm beat, Wife. I don't remember a longer, more difficult day I've ever lived." He cupped Laurel's face in his hands and brought her lips to meet his. She melted into him.

"Please hold me, Mac. Shut out the ugliness of this war and keep it from doing lasting harm to our family."

"I will try my best, Laurel. That is the best I can promise. I will try, Darlin'."

"You won't go away from me, will you, Patrick?"

"I don't know how many ways I can tell you. I won't go to war. I'll stay at Shiloh as long as the Lord allows."

"If only we could stop Roy from going."

"We have to let him do what he thinks he has to do. We have to let him grow up and respect his opinions. Thank God, he only signed that thirty-day enlistment with Anderson. Maybe he'll get this military business out of his system and decide to stay home and take care of his wife."

"I pray that is so."

"Come here, Wife. I need some attention. I've had a bad day. I got insulted at church, grilled by my children, and lost my best helper on this homestead to a war I don't believe in." Mac blew out the lantern on the bureau.

"Mac, we will be all right. I have to believe it."

"We will be fine. We live on the promises of a good Father. Our part is not easy—to keep our faith in the shadow of so much threat. We will do it because we love each other and this family." Mac lowered his face to Lauren's again. His warm tender lips found Laurel's.

"I love you, Patrick MacLayne."

"And I am blessed with that gift every day of my life."

# Chapter 5

*I am for peace: but when I speak, they are for war.*
*Psalms 120:7*

The Greene County Militia deployed that Wednesday, November 13, 1861. Captain Anderson's order mandated the new troops to ride west toward Camp Borland in Randolph County. The officers in charge spread the word that the unit would receive training on the chance they would be called to serve in one of the state infantry units. The troops were instructed to tell their families they'd have little chance of seeing action while they served out their thirty-day enlistments.

Mac planned to see Roy off that morning. He left his home as the sun rose over the ridge because he wanted one last word with the young man. He didn't want him to go without the assurance that nothing had changed in their relationship and that God was with him. Mac also feared that the new bride couldn't cope with her husband's leaving.

A bit of snow spit in the blustery wind that morning. Mac stepped on the porch of the Dunn homestead and knocked on the door. Annie, her face streaked with tears, pulled the door open. He stepped inside the near-freezing cabin. "Why have you let the fire burn out? You can't stay warm without a fire, Annie."

"Roy built a fire before he left." She strangled and coughed as she tried to speak. "I never paid it no mind…." Her words were broken by sobs. "He had to be at camp before sun-up." Again, the desperate young woman broke down. "Captain Anderson told the unit they had to ride out as soon as they could see."

Mac hugged her and then pulled the quilt from the unmade bed to cover her. He squatted in front of the fireplace and began to revive the fire. "Annie, can you keep this homestead goin' without Roy bein' here?"

She shrugged. Silent tears rolled unchecked down her face. The look of defeat on her face spoke more than any words could. Mac knew the seventeen-year-old was not up to the challenge of living alone in the isolated, single-pen cabin…not even for thirty days.

"I want you to pack your clothes, Annie. Bring anything you think you'll want. You're goin' home with me."

"I can't do that Mr. Mac. Roy's countin' on me to take care of our place. I've got stock to tend. Besides, we have customers who want milk and eggs twice a week." Her words were cut short with more tears. "I can't let Roy down."

"Please stop cryin', Daughter. Let me take you back where you'll be with family while Roy's gone. When he gets home, we'll talk to him. Surely, he'll stay with you when he understands."

"I can't leave our stock. They'll freeze in the winter without someone here to care for 'em."

"I'll see to the animals. Let's go back to Shiloh."

Annie became a member of the MacLayne household that day. Mac sent his tenant farmer, J.F. Clarke, to stay at the Dunn place. J.F., like Mac, felt no call to service, and Mac was grateful he wanted to stay. He was a loyal tenant and with his help, Mac could care for all the family at Shiloh.

Near the end of the month, Mac made a trip to Greensboro. He wanted to buy supplies for the pantry and also the stash if anything were available. He grabbed up flour, yeast, cocoa, and sugar anytime he could find them in the general store. He also stored extra lamp oil in the stash along with other items that could not be raised or made on the homestead. Freighters didn't make rounds as regularly as they had before the war.

But more than stores, Mac wanted news from the outside world. Having Roy with the militia made Mac more anxious to know what was going on in Arkansas and on the greater war fronts in the east. That day, Mac found no newspaper to answer his questions. However, at McCollough's mercantile, he learned that the Greene County Militia and other local units had been given only part of the truth about their placement at Fort Borland. The unit had been sent to reinforce Arkansas regulars in defense of the river system in the north and central section of the state because the Black, Current, Arkansas, and White Rivers all played a critical role in transporting supplies to Confederate troops throughout the south.

Rumors spread that Arkansas was in imminent danger from the Union troops who were coming from Missouri to attack a major Confederate military depot near Pittman's Ferry in Randolph County. The thirty-day volunteers had been assigned to support the command of Colonel Borland, who had been assigned to protect this important source of supplies for the Rebel armies.

Mac understood then why the rushed deployment of the militia from Greene, Poinsett, and Craighead counties. Roy and his friends in the Greene County Roughs had received little training, but the threat of a large invasion army made the recruiting of volunteers imperative, regardless of their readiness for battle. This was news he certainly would not share with Laurel or Annie. Thank goodness, Roy had only enlisted for a short thirty days.

The next week proved to be another difficult one for Mac and Laurel. Life outside the boundaries of their homestead was different. Laurel couldn't put into words what she felt, but an uneasiness plagued her whenever she left Shiloh. On her last trip to Greensboro with Mac, she noticed people whom she'd considered friends shun her when they met in the mercantile. At best, they offered a nod or a faint smile instead of a friendly conversation as had been their habit in the past.

Even at church, some of the members treated the MacLaynes more like unwanted visitors than a cherished part of the Shiloh church family. No more arguments like the one between Mac and Captain Anderson arose, but that was because Brother Matthew had made it clear that war talk was not welcome in the sanctuary. His admonition didn't prevent the chill from going outside the church walls. Then on Sunday, the preacher announced the school committee decided not to open the subscription school at all that session. They had already postponed the winter session because so many local men had gone with the militia to Camp Borland. He announced the loss of the teacher, Mr. Tucker, who planned to return north. When Mac questioned the decision, the split in the congregation became clear.

"Why are we not providing a school for our children this winter, Matthew?" Mac asked candidly after the service was dismissed. "I don't recall anyone talkin' to me about this. I have three children who will be at a loss for schoolin' now."

"Mac, a few of the fathers came by the house the other night and told me they were concerned about Mr. Tucker. He's from Pennsylvania, ya know, and he's apt to go back north. We went to talk to him, and he said he'd decided to return home to Philadelphia."

"Did y'all tell him he wasn't welcome here?"

"No. No, he said that he would probably join the Union army." Matthew shifted from one foot to the other, clearly ill at ease.

"Uh-huh. So why don't we just look for another teacher?"

Matthew sat down on the front pew next to his friend. "Well, there was some concern about the cost. Taxes are goin' up, and men are losing income when they join the army. Seems like a lot of problems can be avoided if we just close the school for this season."

"Pa and I will come up with the salary…."

"Mac, that's only one problem. With so many men gone, we probably can't find a teacher."

"Laurel would probably consider…"

"The school committee decided not to ask her."

"Laurel would have her hands full with Leah Ann bein' so young, but…"

"Mac, Laurel is a fine teacher. One of the best we've had, but some of the men in our church family are not sure where your loyalty lies. That question gets brought up every time a local unit deploys. Last Wednesday we got word that Rafe Winston, the oldest boy of Jack and Mollie Winston, died at Camp Borland over near Pocahontas."

Mac stood. "You're sayin' I'm the problem? Because I won't join the Confederate army, I'm now the enemy?"

"No, Mac. You know I'd never say that. I know no better friend or brother in the faith than you. I'm only tryin' to tell ya what the congregation is talkin' about."

"Matthew, why don't they talk to me? Isn't that the way brothers in the body are supposed to handle disagreements?"

"You know it is…but emotions are just too high right now. A troop of Arkansas soldiers was in that battle on Wilson Creek in August. Some died. One was a brother to Sister Lawrence. Recruiters are around gatherin' boys to fill Arkansas's quotas in the Confederate units. Parents are watchin' their boys sign away three years of their lives to the war."

"I guess I'd know that, Matthew. Roy enlisted, and he's at Camp Borland at this moment. I didn't like his choice to join the Rebel cause."

"I know, Mac. I got no answer for you. I want our church family to stay intact. I may be able to keep the war outside these doors, but I can't keep it away from our people once they leave."

Mac looked into the tormented face of his best friend. "I'm sorry I let my temper get the better of me. I guess war comes in many forms, doesn't it, Matthew?" Mac pulled his pastor and friend into an embrace and slapped his back in support. "I'm sorry, Preacher. There will be no further problems with me. Laurel and I will come up with some plan to school our kids this year."

"Thank you, Mac. Before you go, there is one more thing I've been aimin' to tell ya. A radical group of …well, I don't know what they are really…bullies are trying to put an end to all Union support in this area. Some of them are out of the Boothill, and some are locals. They are supposed to have some special commission from the governor to root out folks who don't want to support the war efforts. Believe it or not, you ain't the only one in this area who wants no part of this war."

"What's happened?"

"So far, not much. A bit of name callin'…like what Captain Anderson did to you a couple of Sunday's ago. A little bit of vandalism around, but you know how things can get out of hand. I just wanted you to be aware."

φ

November 28, 1861, was a special day because the MacLayne family would celebrate Gracie's sixth birthday with a party. All her new family attended: the Campbells, Thomas MacLayne, the Flannigan family, and both J.F. and James Clarke. Her raven curls bobbled up and down her back as she danced across the room from person to person who had come to wish her a happy birthday. The radiant smile on her dimpled cheeks told of the security and acceptance she now felt. After her ordeal in Utah where she lost both her parents in the Meadow Mountain massacre, Gracie had spent many months crying out in nightmares and backing into corners to feel safe. Thankfully, she now knew home and love again.

Thomas MacLayne rose to speak. "Family, before we get down to the business of celebrating Miss Gracie's big day, I want to invite all of you to my house on Christmas Day. I know we usually have our celebration here at Mac and Laurel's place, but this year, I want my family and friends around when Mrs. Peggy Flannagan and I will make our weddin' vows to each other." Cheers, laughter, and hugs transformed the family lunch into a scene of chaotic joy. Everyone knew they'd been spending a lot of time together, but no one thought a wedding was planned so soon.

"That's enough of this. Thank y'all for your approval and acceptin' our invitation, but this day belongs to our precious Gracie. Let's celebrate her birthday," Thomas said.

The beautiful little girl squealed When she opened the new Sunday dress Laurel made for her. Andy carved her a new comb with wide tines that didn't pull her tangles, and her granddad, Thomas gave her a new first level reader of her very own.

"Oh, Granddad, I ain't never had a book that was just for me. Thank you. I love it."

Andy teased, "Ya can't read so why do you need it?" Gracie punched her big brother on the shoulder.

"Gracie, all MacLaynes read. We seem to take to readin' pretty quick. I'll bet you will too."

"But Granddad, my name is Gracie Wilson. What if I can't learn to read?"

"That's not gonna happen, Sweetheart. Your mama is a fine teacher. I know you'll be reading me a story from this book soon."

With this opportunity laid before him, Mac walked over to pick up the birthday girl. "I didn't give you my present yet. Let's go to my chair."

"What is it, Papa?" He sat and placed Gracie on the arm of the chair. Laurel walked up and stood behind her and hugged her neck.

"We want to adopt you," Mac told her.

Her entire family clapped and cheered. Gracie looked around the room with a confused look on her face. She clasped Laurel's hand. "Mama, what does that mean?"

"Darlin', that means no one can ever say you don't belong to us. You are a special part of our family already because we love you, but we want things to be official. You know we adopted Cathy and Roy. I adopted Andy, too. We want you to be a-forever-part of this family if you want to be our daughter."

"I always belonged to you, Mama. You told me my mother gave me to you when I was born. You are my godmother."

"All the more reason we want to make this legal," Mac said. "Do you want to be our little girl from now on, Gracie?"

"Yes, but how do you do that?" The somber tone of her voice made the family laugh.

Andy piped in, "It's easy, Gracie. Papa will write you into our family page in our Bible. You'll like bein' in the book. Ma put me in the book when Papa got shot. She made me her forever son."

"I wanna be in the book, too, Papa," Gracie responded. Mac nodded to Andy.

"Son, go get the book, the ink well, and my pen. Let's make Gracie an official MacLayne today on her birthday."

When Andy returned, Mac opened the family Bible to the center. Directly under the record of Leah Ann's birth, he wrote:

Gracie Laurel Wilson was adopted into
the family of Patrick and Laurel MacLayne
on Thursday, November 28, 1861.
Her name will now be Grace Laurel Wilson MacLayne.
Witnesses:
Thomas MacLayne, Matthew Campbell, and Andrew MacLayne.
Shiloh, Craighead County, Arkansas.

Gracie clapped her hands when Mac pointed out her new name. She twisted around and threw her arms around her mama's neck. "I love you."

"We all love you, Gracie MacLayne."

CRASH…the window shattered into scores of pieces as a rock thumped on the floor. Ellie Campbell cried out as a large, jagged piece lodged itself into her arm. Smaller pieces crunched on the floor as people moved around in the chaos.

Mac ran to the door and jerked it open, only to hear the hooves of several horses beat the ground as the intruders rode away from his homestead—the night sky too black for him to recognize any of the men. "They were sure ready to run. I don't have a clue who did it, but I saw at least five horses, maybe six before they reached the bend. Is anyone hurt?"

"Ellie's got a pretty bad cut, but Laurel and Matthew are seein' to her. Who'd do such an ignorant stunt?" Thomas MacLayne red splotched face spoke of the concern for his family.

"Young hoodlums, probably. Andy, bring me that rock. Let me see if they left us a clue." The rock about the size of a small melon had scratches on one side that said 'Leave Shiloh, Yankee Scum.'

Andy said,"That message can't be for us. We ain't Yanks."

"Don't fret about it, Son. Probably just a bad joke. Family, let's not let this stop our celebration. We have a new family member. Cathy, please bring us that fine chocolate layer cake you baked for your sister's birthday."

*ϕ*

Roy returned to Shiloh on December 15. The anticipated attack of Union troops failed to materialize in Pocahontas, so the Greene County Militia was discharged. Unfortunately, the return home proved to be a nightmare for the twelve men who were returning. The snow, rain, freezing temperatures, and impassable roads between Fort Borland and Greene County delayed his return to Annie and his family.

After trudging through the cold, sleet, and drizzling rain, Roy and three of his fellow soldiers found refuge in an abandoned barn near Fontaine. In short order, they cleaned a space on the dirt floor of the barn and built a fire of planks from the stalls and part of a broken ladder that no longer reached the loft. When they'd assured some heat for the night, they devoured the hardtack they'd been issued, but they had no coffee to brew or bread to fill their stomachs. Pulling apart hay bales left behind by the homesteaders, they lay on their makeshift beds, wrapped in the course army blankets.

By dawn, the cold rain gave way to even worse conditions. Blustery winds and heavy snowfall convinced the four soldiers, who wanted nothing more than to be home, to remain sheltered another day. A long hungry day awaited them. Finally, on the third morning, the sun burned away the clouds, and the piercing winds morphed into an almost spring-like breeze. The temperature rose above freezing. The winter landscape around Cache River began to turn into ugly, muddy trails across the lowest part of their journey to Greene County.

Roy and his friends continued until well past dark. The moon-bright night, now free of the cloud cover that had only two days ago laid down the blanket of white, provided light that allowed Roy to identify the Dunn homestead. The house was outlined by the moonlight, but he couldn't see light shining inside.

"Wiley, that's my place. Do you see any light?" Roy asked.

"Dunn, don't be a fool. It's late. Your wife probably went to sleep hours ago. That'll be a blessin', boy. She'll already have your bed warm." His companions laughed, as they climbed the three steps to the porch. Roy opened the door.

"Annie. I'm back, Sweetheart."

A large dark shape arose from the bed in the corner. "Well, Roy, I ain't Annie, but I can tell ya where she is."

"J.F., what are doin' sleepin' in my bed?"

J.F. Clarke struck a match and turned up the wick in the lamp to provide a scant light in the room. He set the lantern back on the table. "You boys hungry? I got some beans I can heat up and part of a pone. Not a feast, but it will fill empty guts."

Wiley spoke up. "You bet we are. I'm about starved. Thank you, sir."

"Set yerselves down, and I'll get ya a bite." As he worked, J.F. asked. "Y'all wanna stay here tonight and get started on home tomorrow? Roy, don't you worry none. Annie is with the MacLaynes. I've been stayin' here to take care of your stock. Been able to fill most of your orders for milk and eggs, too.

"Thanks, J.F., but why did Annie go off and leave our home here? When did she go to stay with Mr. Mac and Mama?"

"She'll do a better job tellin' ya about her doin's than I can. Let's talk about it tomorrow."

The next morning, Annie ran into Roy's arms before he got through the door. The tears on her cheeks were not the lonely, mournful ones she had shed too often during Roy's absence. "Thank you, Lord, for Roy bein' home. I've been so worried about you. Your enlistment was over on the tenth. I didn't know Fort Borland was so far that it would take four days to get back to Shiloh."

"Darlin', the weather caused us to hold up for two days. I tried to get back. I wanted nothin' more."

"We're happy that you got home before Christmas, Son." Mac pulled his son into a strong embrace and pounded his back. "The whole family is so glad your enlistment is over."

"Roy, we'll be happy now. We can celebrate Christmas and you being back. I hope you never go away again." Cathy said.

49

# Chapter 6

*He that hath the bride is the bridegroom:*
*but the friend of the bridegroom,*
*which standeth and heareth him, rejoiceth greatly because of*
*the bridegroom's voice: this my joy, therefore, is fulfilled.*
*John 3:29*

Christmas came and Christmas went. The MacLayne family downplayed the festivities of the holiday in anticipation of a family event that seemed so much more important that year. The highlight of the holiday was the wedding of Thomas MacLayne and Peggy Flannagan. On the afternoon of December 25, 1861, the entire family gathered in Thomas's main room. Peggy and her daughter, Maureen, had decorated the room with holly and evergreen and several beeswax candles. The spacious room was filled with Peggy's three children, Mac and Laurel's family, Matthew and Ellie's family, and the Clarke brothers. The couple stood before a fully engaged fire at the stone mantle. In her hand, Peggy held a horseshoe that Mac had given her and a small linen handkerchief made by Laurel. Both gifts fulfilled special Irish traditions so important to Peggy. Matthew Campbell walked to stand before them and spoke an opening prayer. As the setting sun spread a panorama of red, orange, gold, and gray behind Crowley's Ridge, he asked them to speak their vows to each other.

"Peggy, I promise you my loyalty, my friendship, and my love, as long as the Lord allows us to live on this earth."

"Thomas, I promise to serve you, keep only to you, enjoy your company, and love you as long as I live on this earth."

"Peggy, I also ask you to let me adopt your children. I will never try to replace their pa, but I will care for them and support them if they will have me."

"Thank you for that gift, Thomas."

Thomas placed a golden ring on Peggy's hand.

Matthew spoke. "Peggy, Thomas told me he had Mr. Leser in Greensboro to craft this special ring for you. The three symbols represent the things he promised you. The hands are for friendship, the crown is for a lifetime of loyalty, and the heart is the promise of love. He said you told him of the story of the Claddagh and how your village of Galway was the birthplace of this special symbol. With the givin' and receivin' of this ring, I pronounce you man and wife. What the Lord has joined, let no man divide. God bless you both and this new family you begin today." They knelt before him. He laid his hands on their heads and prayed, "Lord, bless these two as they have declared their love. Please abide here in this place as they work to build a Godly home. Amen."

Thomas took Peggy's hand and helped her to her feet. He bent and kissed her, a soft gentle kiss, to mark their union.

Laurel stood at Peggy's side. *Lord, Peggy is a beautiful bride. She does love my father-in-law—a real love, just a different kind.* A gentle smile touched her lips. She remembered the eighty-year-old couple she and Mac met on their journey to Shiloh. She had been amazed at their lifelong love then and at the gentle, quiet connection she saw in Thomas and Peggy. This love was based on companionship, common interests, and respect. This relationship she saw was every bit as strong and real as the overwhelming passion she and Mac shared. *Lord, as we go through the rest of our days together, let our love grow into this kind of Union.*

She walked behind the smiling couple. Thomas pulled his son into a strong hug, and Mac kissed Peggy's cheek. Laurel took Mac's hand. "I love you, Patrick. I want to be at your side through eternity." She looked into his storm-blue eyes and kissed him.

Peggy Flannagan MacLayne prepared a Christmas wedding feast that would long be remembered by her family. Peggy had spent days preparing a traditional Irish wedding banquet. At the center of the table sat the golden goose with stuffing that she'd baked at her cabin the night before the wedding. Also, she had prepared twice-baked potatoes, roasted pork loin, fried cabbage with sausage, and an apple cake from an old Irish recipe. On the sideboard sat two small casks, one with poteen for the men and the other filled with aged cider, a bit diluted so that even the children could toast the new couple. Laurel prepared some of the favorite Christmas dishes loved and expected by her family. She baked yams with cinnamon, sugar, and butter. Of course, she baked the hot-cross buns.

"Pa, cut that goose and let's eat," Mac spoke up.

" I'm hesitatin' to do that, Son. You know the significance of the cooked goose, don't you?"

"You mean it's more than just good eatin'?"

"When an Irish lady brings a cooked goose to a wedding feast, it means that there is no turnin' back." Laughter rang around the table. Peggy blushed. Thomas bent down to kiss his bride. "Not that I'd ever want to. And family, thank you for comin' to share this happy day with us."

After the dinner was finished, Mac asked Laurel and Annie to provide drinks to everyone present. "I want to offer a toast to my father and his new wife. I had to do some readin' to find one that was suited to this occasion, but if all of you will raise your glass," Mac lifted his small glass of poteen. "Peggy...Pa, may your mornings bring joy; your evenings bring peace. May your troubles grow few as your blessings increase. May the saddest of days in your future be no worse than the happiest day of your past. May your hands be forever clasped in friendship, and your hearts joined forever in love. God bless you."

"Thank you, Patrick." Thomas hugged his smiling son.

"And now, I'd like to have you see my passing of the dowry if you'll be my witnesses." Peggy took the deed to her homestead, the small cabin and parcel of land that had once belonged to the Widow Parker. She handed the document to her new husband. "Thomas, I humbly pass to you all my worldly goods. I am pleased to be your wife."

"Peggy, I didn't expect…"

"Thomas, it is the Irish way. It's the final pledge that a wife makes to her husband to show her confidence in his care for her."

"I am humbled to accept your dowry, Peggy. Thank you."

"Now, husband of mine, if you will hang this horseshoe, a gift from your son, over the door of *our* home, I will declare this to be my home also."

Thomas pounded a nail into the door frame and hung the horseshoe. He stepped down and embraced his new family.

On the way back to Shiloh, the family shared in animated conversation about that Christmas day—everyone except Roy. He wasn't unpleasant, but his behavior was not that of the Roy who had ridden off to Fort Borland a short six weeks past. He fidgeted and flinched at the slightest touch. His part in the lively discussion was curt or nonexistent. When they returned to their front room, Laurel engaged him.

"Roy, are you feeling well?"

"Yeah, I'm fine, Mrs. Mac."

"Aren't you happy to be home?"

"Of course, I am. I'm fed and warm and with my girl."

"And?" Laurel knew there was much more that needed to be said.

Roy snapped back. "And what? I said I'm fine." Roy walked away.

Before the week passed, Roy and Annie returned to Shiloh early one evening. Tears streaked Annie's face, and Roy's grimace spoke louder than words. As a result of their first argument, both the young people sought the solace of Laurel and Mac. They'd hardly reached the yard when Annie jumped from her horse and ran to the house in search of Laurel. Roy sat on his horse at the porch railing, muttering under his breath.

Mac was walking back to the porch from the woodshed. "Roy, come on in out of the cold."

"No, Mr. Mac. Annie don't want me in there. She told me she needed to talk to Mrs. Mac. I only came because I didn't want her to ride home in the dark."

"So, you just gonna stay out here in the cold until she's done talkin'? Looks like snow this New Year's Eve."

"Will you go out to the barn with me while I unsaddle the horses?" Roy's voice choked as he asked.

"I'll help you care for them after I carry in the wood for the fire."

Roy picked up an armload of firewood, but he entered the cabin as if he carried the weight of the world on his shoulders. Annie turned her back to him. Mac stacked the firewood near the hearth and added extra logs to the fire. Andy stormed in from the back door with Mark Thomas at his heels.

"Papa, this is the best Christmas ever. This is the best present I ever got. Our family's had such a fine time together, and now I shot my first rabbit. Golly! How fun."

Roy rubbed his chin.

"Hey, Roy, how do you like my rabbit?' Andy held up the huge swamp rabbit by the hind legs.

"Okay, I guess." Andy's grin died at the curt remark. Mac stepped to intervene, but before he could speak, Cathy came from the kitchen.

She said, "You're so right, Andy. The best part is havin' my brother home again." Annie sobbed and dropped to sit on the hearth. Roy walked over to take her in his arms.

"Annie, I can't stand to see ya cryin'. Please quit. We'll talk this out."

She shrugged away from his arms and continued to sob. Laurel walked over to the young woman and took her hand. "Let's go into the other room, Annie. You can tell me what's brought on these tears, Darlin'."

"Annie, don't go. I'll tell ya, Mrs. Mac. She's been cryin' since Captain Murray came over this mornin'. He asked me to enlist with the Greene County Roughs. Most of my militia troop has joined that group since our troop disbanded."

Laurel's jaw dropped. "I don't understand, Roy. You finished your enlistment. Those thirty days have passed already. Haven't you fulfilled your military obligations?"

"They mustered us out before we left Randolph County. I'm not signed up right now, but this war ain't over." Roy looked down.

"Roy, they can't make you go back again, can they?" Cathy's quivering voice told her mother that more tears were near.

"Are ya goin' back, Roy?" Andy's question came as Cathy spoke.

"I don't know what I'm gonna do." Roy's raised voice brought Mac near. "Mr. Mac, can we get out of here for a while? I wanna talk to you." Roy walked to the back door and stopped. "I'm sorry. I love y'all. Annie, I love you, but I gotta get away for a while."

φ

Mac followed. As they stepped inside the sturdy, well-built barn, Mac lit the lantern, which hung on the peg at the door. The orange glow from the kerosene cast a dim light across the floor. Midnight whinnied a greeting as Mac brushed his hand down his muzzle. Roy dragged a three-legged stool toward the milk cow and placed a bucket under the heavy utters. Streams of milk splattered against the pail.

"I'll do that, Roy." Mac walked up behind the young man.

"Gives me something to do...helps me think." Roy continued the task he'd begun.

"What's become of your herd, Mr. Mac? When I left you had three cows, a dozen hogs, a flock of chickens, a herd of sixty or more heifers, and those two prize bulls. Don't see much here."

"Sold most all the stock, Roy. You'd be wise to do the same. The armies, both sides, will begin takin' what they need when the spring comes and bigger battles are waged."

"You sold all your stock? You worked so hard to raise that herd."

"I kept enough to feed us. No sense in lettin' the rest of it be confiscated. I got a good price for what I sold. I took payment, part in Confederate money but mostly in gold. We need local currency to do business here right now, but as the war goes on it will become useless. That's why I took the lion's share in gold."

"Mr. Mac, I know you don't hold with the Confederacy, but are you gonna support the Union against our state?"

"Roy, I never made it a secret to anyone that I didn't want secession. But no, I don't plan to take either side. I am gonna stay here at Shiloh and try to make sure my family won't suffer from the war."

"Mr. Mac, men are gonna be called out to join the army. They passed the conscription laws, even in Little Rock."

"I'm past thirty-five already, son. I won't volunteer. I can't bear arms against my country. I chose Arkansas to be my home, but this state made a bad decision when we voted to secede. Our state will pay for this mistake in judgment for decades to come."

"Don't you think the Confederacy deserves our loyalty and that Mr. Lincoln and the North have insulted our honor and our Southern way of life?" Roy stared at Mac.

"Son, I never want anything to come between us. You are a son to me, as much as Andy and Mark Thomas. I'm not happy you chose the Confederate side of this conflict. Yet, your courage to stand by your convictions makes me proud. I pray God will take care of you and see you safely through this war."

"Do you think God is against the South, Mr. Mac?"

"The God I know doesn't hold with any war. War brings destruction, poverty, and loss to everyone involved. There is no glory. From the years I spent at Annapolis, I learned that women and children are usually the people most hurt by war. They have the least to do with the reason the war is happening, and they stand to lose the most. I plan to do everything I can to prevent that loss at Shiloh. Are you returning to the militia, Roy?"

"Danged if I know. Sorry. Most of my friends already joined the Greene County Roughs. Captain Murray is pullin' together a whole unit that will be attached to the 25th Arkansas Infantry—regular army. I don't know if I should re-enlist and go with my old unit or refuse to go. I could tell the captain I have a new bride to take care of."

"Do you want to go back, Son?"

"I don't want to, but I know I'll have to serve. They don't care if the troops are married or have kids. If I have to go, I know I'd rather be with men I know, people from my old unit."

"You have to decide, Roy. Whatever you choose, we'll love you and pray for your safety."

"I'm thinkin' I'll stay around through spring. Me and Annie will get our garden out and the animal feed we'll need. Then I can decide." Mac clapped Roy on the back and picked up the full milk pail.

"Follow your heart, Son. Do what you believe God is leading you to do. That is all any man can do."

"I got no idea what God's will for me is. I'm not sure I even thought about it. Grandma always took us to church. You and Mrs. Mac have tried to set Cathy and me an example, but I'm not sure I understand much about following God's will."

"Roy…" Silence followed. Mac's eyes darkened and a frown came over his face. He hadn't realized Roy doubted his faith in God. Mac felt true fear for the young man he'd taken under his care four years ago.

"Roy, do you believe in Jesus?"

"I believe there is a Jesus. I've seen how you and Mrs. Mac believe in Him. Lots of people say He's important."

"Roy, Jesus is so much more. We need to talk about this, Son. I'll never rest if you join the regular army, and I let you go off alone."

"Are you sayin' you'll go with me?"

"No, Roy, not me. I need you to go with Jesus. That is how important He is…to people who know Him. He never lets them go anywhere alone."

"Goin' alone is one thing that makes joinin' up so hard. That month they sent us to Pocahontas, I hated being alone. That was the worst. Of course, I missed Annie, but dang it, I even dreamed about Cathy."

"I know that feeling. It's the way I felt last Christmas Eve in Little Rock until I went to the Christmas Eve service at that little Methodist church near my boarding house. Jesus was right there by me. Because I felt his presence, all of you were there. I felt your thoughts and prayers."

"I don't want to die alone, Mr. Mac. I am afraid I'll not make it through this war."

"Roy, no man knows if he'll live one more day. I nearly died in my front room while I was playing checkers with Andy."

"I remember that night. Are you afraid to die, Mr. Mac?"

"No, I'm not afraid of death. I don't want to die because I cherish my life with Laurel and my kids, but I know that God is going to be with me regardless. I don't have to fear death."

"I wish I knew everything is gonna work out."

"Roy, when you go in tonight, please pick up my Bible. Promise me you'll read the third and fourth chapters of the Gospel of John. Maybe you can read it aloud with Annie, and y'all talk about what it says. We'll go talk with Brother Matthew if you want."

"I'll read it. Thanks for listenin' to me. I guess I wanted someone to hear me. Annie can't because it makes her cry. I tried to tell her about seein' my friends die over at Fort Borland. She got scared. I told her we didn't get shot at or anything like that, but she still cried. Mostly they got sick. Measles, bad food, not enough blankets, sleeping on the ground in the cold…all that stuff happened at camp. Made me think about lots of stuff I never thought of before."

"Will you let me pray with you before we go in, Roy?"

"You can always pray for me, Mr. Mac. You've been doin' it since the day we met."

Mac knelt with Roy in the barn. He laid his arm across the young man's shoulder. "Gracious Father, thank you for the bond I share with Roy. He's been a blessin' in my life. Lord, as we begin a new year tomorrow, I ask you to speak to him and let him feel You with him. Help my son understand your precious gift of grace. Lead him to Jesus. Amen."

# Chapter 7

*Therefore, if any man be in Christ, he is a new creature:*
*old things are passed away and behold, all things are become new.*
*II Corinthians 5:17*

Roy was true to his word. He and Annie lived and loved at
their homestead through the spring. Roy worked until sundown
each day, preparing his land for planting. Annie gradually turned
the Dunn cabin into a warm, cozy home as she hung curtains,
crocheted delicate doilies, and used Roy's family treasures to
decorate the walls, tabletops, and mantle of the single pen cabin
where he'd grown up. In the place of honor at the center of the
mantle hung Roy's Grandfather Dunn's Enlistment Charter from
the American Revolutionary War. Roy had never known a day
when this precious document had not hung in this cabin. This
ancient parchment and a letter in the family Bible were proof of
ownership of the homestead where he and Annie dreamed of
building a home for the third and fourth generation of the Dunn
family.

Each evening, the young couple cuddled together on the old
settee that had been Roy's grandmother's prized piece of furniture.
They nestled together under a quilt, pieced at a quilting bee by the
ladies of Shiloh church. Roy read the scripture from the gospel of
John aloud to Annie. When he was finished, the newlyweds

59

discussed the meaning of the words as they understood them. At every opportunity, Roy discussed the word with Mac and Brother Matthew. The more he read and learned, the more peace Roy felt, even though the talk of the war never faded from conversations around Shiloh.

News of a major Confederate loss at Pea Ridge in the western part of Arkansas rekindled Roy's anxiety. Through Mac, he knew that Arkansas had twice become a battleground, not just a supplier of men and supplies. Arkansas soldiers shed blood at Sugar Creek three weeks before the major battle in Washington County. More than two thousand men died near Elk Horn tavern around Pea Ridge in the vicious two-day battle.

Part of Roy's old unit, now a part of the Greene County Roughs, merged into the Eighth Arkansas Infantry. When he read the death toll in the newspaper he'd brought from Mac's place, he headed to the barn to saddle his horse intending to ride to Gainesville to re-enlist. Before he reached the corral, he saw his sweet wife with a hoe in hand tending the early shoots in their garden. He recalled the promise he'd made to Mac and Annie. He would wait until all the crops were planted and the food for the new year was up. He would make sure that Annie would be able to survive without him.

Wars have a way of interrupting human plans. In mid-April, Governor Rector activated the Conscription Act in Arkansas. The Trans-Mississippi Army sorely needed replacements to defend Little Rock from Union attack. Jefferson Davis, the Confederate president, ordered all males between eighteen and thirty-five to enlist for three years to fight off the Northern invaders.

"Annie, I gotta go talk to Brother Matthew. Too much is happenin'. I have to decide if I'm gonna sign up. I sure do wish Gran Dunn was here. She'd tell me what's the right thing to do."

"I'm sure she was a wise woman, Roy, but this decision is between us. You're supposed to be buildin' a home with me, not your gran or with Brother Matthew."

Annie's pallor and the streaming tears told Roy she expected him to stay with her on the homestead. He walked to her and pulled her into his arms. "Annie, are ya sorry we got married?"

"No. No." She jerked away. "I'm sorry this stupid war interrupted our life. We can make a good life for us here at our farm."

"I believe we can, darlin'." Annie relaxed a moment. "But how can I sit out the fightin' when I know my friends are dyin'. Ain't it my duty, too? Southern honor's bein' trampled on by the Yanks."

"Go on and talk to Brother Matthew. I don't want you to leave me, but I don't guess I got much say about it."

Roy kissed his pretty blonde bride and smiled into her brown eyes. "I'm one lucky man, Mrs. Dunn. I got me a smart wife and a good farm. Don't cry anymore. Maybe we'll get up tomorrow and the war will be over." He laughed. She didn't.

The next morning, Roy found Brother Matthew at the Shiloh church where he often spent his early mornings. "Do you have a while to talk to me, Brother Matthew?"

"Course I do, Roy. What's on your mind?"

"The governor's called us to re-enlist. I gotta make a decision sooner than I planned to. I want to fight for my home, but I gotta think about Annie."

"I can see you are worried. Have you prayed about it, Son?"

"I've tried. I don't know what to do. What do you think is the right thing, Brother Matthew? How can you know what God wants you to do?

"No easy answer to that question, Roy."

"Do you think He's for us, or are we on the wrong side?"

"You can't convince me He's taken sides. He hates violence and loss. I know he hates the abuse in slavery, too. Some of His children wear blue and some gray, and He loves 'em all."

"Why is it that brothers in the faith can fight against each other? I don't understand."

"I don't have an answer that makes sense of it, Roy. No man can tell you what to do. This is a decision you have to make for yourself. I will remain neutral. I'll offer my help to any who needs me. That is all my conscience will let me do."

"I can't support a cause against my home. My grandpa was a true Virginian before he brung us to Arkansas. He didn't bring slaves with him, but our family back there still holds their family land and slaves. My uncles and cousins are already in those battles in the east."

"I expect that's true, and if you refuse to join the Confederacy, you'll feel like a traitor to them. But what hangs over the mantle in your cabin? Why did your grandpa treasure that parchment to the point that he framed it and hung it the place of honor in his home?"

"I know, Brother Matthew. My grandpa Dunn was a patriot. He loved bein' a part of this country."

"And what about your family here? You know Mac will not join the Confederate ranks."

"We talked about it…a lot." Roy paused and his eyes scanned the sanctuary of the Shiloh church. "I love all of the MacLaynes. They've been good to me and Cathy. Mac told me nothin' that can happen in this war will come between us. He said he ain't never gonna choose sides."

"I pray the time won't come when we're forced to do that very thing." Matthew pounded another nail into one of the pews that had broken the previous Sunday. "Roy, have you decided to make a commitment to the Lord? That concerns Mac and Laurel most. Mac told me that when you were deployed to Camp Shaver, you felt alone. That was the part that scared ya the most."

"That's true. We didn't see much action or even get fired on, but I hated feelin' alone. I needed someone with me, and no one was there."

"That had to be a bad time for you." Brother Matthew patted Roy's shoulder.

"If I don't go back to my old troop, won't it be even worse? I won't know one soul."

Matthew rose from his knees where he'd been repairing the old log pew. "I can tell ya from my experience, Son, I'm never alone. When I'm most tired, sick, or scared, the Comforter is with me. That is the promise. Have you finished reading John's gospel?"

"Just did. Mac asked me to."

"Remember, John wrote that Jesus would send the Comforter to be with us. That is what I feel when I'm most in need. Jesus with me."

"How do ya know you're truly making a real commitment? I don't wanna do it just because I'm afraid of goin' to hell."

"Roy, you know what it's like to experience hell already. Being separated from God's love is hell. All you have to do is look in your heart. God is there. I've seen it in you. You love your neighbor. All that's left is for you to believe that Jesus has the power to save you."

"I believe He can do anything but have I learned enough to be a good believer?  What if I ain't done enough yet. Will I ever know?

"Roy, did Mac ever tell you his redemption story?"

"Mr. Mac?  He's always been the same Mac I know now, ain't he? What has he ever done to need to be redeemed?"

"Son, every man falls short of God's will for him. Some more than others. That is true of Mac, too. You know about Andy." Roy turned to look into the eyes of his preacher. His wide eyes and slightly opened mouth showed he understood. "Roy, go speak to Mac. Let him help you make this decision. He'll be happy you shared this with him. Once he tells you about his past, I know you'll have no trouble knowing what to do." Matthew put his arm across Roy's shoulder and prayed for some time. "Lord, move into the life of this young man, so he never feels alone again. Amen."

Two days later after Sunday dinner-on-the-grounds, Roy asked Mac to walk with him. That early April day on Crowley's Ridge showed colors of spring. Hundreds of shades of green dressed every tree. Daffodils and lilies bloomed across the valley. The bawl of a new calf broke into the song of birds and the laughter of children as father and son walked across the field toward Big Creek.

"Mr. Mac, I'm gonna ask you to tell me somethin'…if I'm outta place, you don't have to tell me. Brother Matthew asked me if I was ready to commit to Jesus yet. I told him about questions that I can't answer. He said to ask you to tell me your story."

Mac stopped and looked at Roy. "You know most of it already, Son. I've only been a believer since '53, not quite ten years. My mama tried to raise me in the Catholic church, but I'm afraid it didn't mean much to me as a boy."

"I want to know how you knew if you really believed and not just said it. If I'm gonna do this, I wanna be like you, good and honest. You don't make mistakes, like me. You got the courage and strength to safeguard our family. I gotta be that kind of man for Annie and our kids."

Mac looked into the eyes of this young man who had opened his heart to him. He was dumbfounded. How had Roy gotten that image of him?

Roy shuffled back and forth as time passed. "I'm sorry, Mr. Mac. Maybe it's not my business." He turned to leave.

"No, wait, Roy. You have every right to know. Your words humbled me, is all. I was tryin' to find the right way to answer. Your words are the best compliment I've ever been given."

"I didn't say it to be flatterin' ya. I was tryin' to tell you why I'm considerin' what you and Brother Matthew been talkin' to me about. When I look at you, I know what kind of man I wanna be—not like my pa in prison. Since we were born, he never gave one single thought to how me and Cathy would grow up."

"I wish I deserved that compliment, but Roy, if you had known me when I came to Shiloh, you'd not have liked anything about me."

"That's not possible, Mr. Mac. I ain't never met a better man than you."

"I was not the man I am now. My father sent me to Arkansas to start a new life after I murdered my best friend in a duel."

"Duels ain't murder. I know you fought fair."

"That shot was just the last incident in seven wasted years. I was a drunk, used women for my pleasure, spent time gamblin', and wasted the time the Lord gave me to build a decent life. My idleness and sinfulness make me cringe with shame when I look back. And Roy, I didn't have an excuse. I was raised by loving, godly parents. I broke every commandment the Lord spoke. I even abandoned my son."

"That don't make no sense. You're not like that. Don't say stuff to make me feel better about my pa."

"It's the truth. This is my story, as it happened. You know yourself how some of these things impact our family yet today. You know Laurel is not Andy's mother. I didn't even know he'd been born until he was more'n six years old. He lived poor, had no schoolin'. He lived as an orphan before my father found him in Tennessee. I left his mother to die alone without a second thought." Mac continued to recount for Roy the disgusting seven years he'd rambled across Tennessee and Kentucky.

The young man sat in silence, at times shaking his head in disbelief. "I don't get it. You couldn't do all that, Mr. Mac. That ain't you."

"No, Roy, not the man you know. When I finally realized the pit I lived in was hell on earth, I couldn't do one thing to get myself out. Thank the Lord, He'd already planned my redemption. When my pa sent me to Arkansas, God planted me right here at Shiloh. I met Brother Matthew and a fine old circuit rider. They introduced me to the Lord who killed the old Mac and taught me to be the man I am now. This Patrick MacLayne is a new creature."

"Does Jesus talk to you like we're talkin' now?"

"No, not out loud. Mostly I feel assured when I read my Bible and pray. The most important proof I have is that I'm never alone. Not once since I surrendered have I been alone."

"I wish I felt like that. I hate bein' alone. That and Annie are the two things that have kept me from goin' back to my old unit."

"You will have to make that decision, Roy, but when you decide to follow God's will, He will show you the things you need to do."

"I ain't got no choice anymore. I'll be conscripted. I guess I'll go with the Greene County Roughs because I know most of 'em. It's just a matter of when."

65

"Even if that's true, you don't have to go alone. Think about what you've told me, Roy. Pray about it and continue to read the scripture. You'll always be in our prayers. You didn't let Laurel and me legally adopt you as we did Cathy, but you're no less our son."

"I know, Mr. Mac. I'm blessed to have you be a real Pa to me."

The following Sunday, Roy made his confession of faith at the altar of Shiloh church. At his left side knelt Brother Matthew Campbell and at his right was his earthly father, Patrick MacLayne. Tears flowed freely down the faces of the three men.

"Brother Matthew, can we go down to the creek? I wanna be baptized today." Hope showed on Roy's face.

"The creek's mighty cold. We can wait 'til summer, Roy. The Lord'll understand."

"I can take a little cold. When I have to go back to the Roughs, I ain't goin' alone."

The congregation followed them to the creek. Roy walked to the edge of the clear, cold water and sank to his knees. Matthew Campbell took the pewter bowl from the altar, filled it with water, and poured it across Roy's head and shoulders. "Roy Dunn, I baptize you in the name of the Father and the Son and the Holy Ghost. Amen." The pastor laid his hands on Roy's streaming hair. "May the Holy Ghost work within you that being born through the water and the Spirit, you will be a faithful disciple of Jesus Christ. Amen."

Roy stood, his arms lifted in praise and his face graced with the broadest smile his family could ever remember. Annie ran into his arms, laying a tender kiss on his lips.

Mac approached. "Roy, if I'd known your plans, I'd a brought you a dry shirt."

"I didn't know either. The Lord laid it on my heart that it was time. So, I just did what he led me to do." Mac pulled him into a strong hug. Laurel wrapped her arms around them.

She said, "It's been a fine day at Shiloh church. Let's go home to Sunday dinner."

φ

As Laurel thought back to that fine Sunday, she realized how many blessings she'd experienced since the war had started. She stopped for a minute to thank God because so many people she knew marked times of grief, not joy. She was surrounded by her family, all of whom were safe and well. Only her brother and his family remained far from her care, and the last letter from Samuel spoke of his desire to return to Arkansas as soon as he could safely travel with his wife and three children. Roy had even lost his restlessness, and he didn't talk about re-enlistment anymore. Laurel walked through her budding orchard with a sense of joy and peace, singing to herself a hymn of thanksgiving. God was in His heaven, and all was right in the MacLaynes' world.

The following week, though, the chaos of the war again broke the peace of Shiloh. Mac refused to ignore the war. Laurel asked him not to go into town so often, but he went, using the slightest excuse. He felt compelled to know what was happening beyond the sanctuary of Shiloh.

Some news relieved his anxiety about life in the Confederacy. From a Little Rock paper, Mac found the legislature in Richmond had passed a bill to develop a postal system for the South. They had been without regular mail service since secession. While that was good, in the same issue of the Democrat-Gazette, he read the same body enacted the Conscription Act to be implemented by all Confederate states. The new law required all men from eighteen to thirty-five to enlist for three years. These men were to report at once. Roy would now be required to re-enlist. His choice to volunteer was out of his hands. Mac dropped the paper into his lap. Roy would now join the Green County Roughs so he could stay with people he knew.

On April 21, 1862, Mac and Roy rode together to Gainesville. Roy found the camp of the Roughs at the edge of town. He met with the assistant of Captain Murray, the commander of the unit, who welcomed him to join his previous unit that had merged into the Roughs.

"Well, Dunn. I was wonderin' when you'd be back. Came to your senses, did ya?" Sergeant Carnes remembered him.

"Just knew if I was gonna serve, I'd rather be with my old unit."

"I sure hope some of 'em come back to serve with ya."

"What do you mean by that, Sgt. Carnes?" Mac asked.

"Ain't ya heard? Our boys left out of here last week of March. Our troop has been called up to join the Arkansas infantry to reinforce the Army of Tennessee. Two weeks ago, they saw some heavy action at an attack at Pittsburg landing over in Tennessee. The reports comin' in from the officers are callin' it the Battle of Shiloh. We lost lots of men there, but so did the Yanks."

"No. We didn't hear about that fight yet." Mac shook his head. "So are ya sayin' the Roughs are comin' home now?"

"No, sir. They ain't. Captain Murray's been ordered to send more recruits over to Memphis to join up with the unit by May third."

Roy's jaw dropped. "So soon?"

"Need troops pretty bad. They'll be glad to see you, Private Dunn. You've got some trainin' and a little action behind ya. Most of the recruits are green as spring corn."

"Do ya think I gotta stay today, sergeant?"

"Don't see no reason for it. You can report back on April 29th. You'll have a little time to get ready to march out on the 30th."

Roy walked away a sadder man. He and Mac went down to the local cafe to get a bite to eat before they rode south to Craighead County.

"Battle of Shiloh...ain't that odd?" Roy mused.

"I didn't expect you'd have to go so soon. At least you have a few days to get your place in order. How will Annie take this news?"

"We talked about it a lot. She says she'll keep our farm goin', but I don't think she can. I saved up our tax money, but Annie will be alone. She's smart and knows how to care for the homestead. But she is nervous and worries a lot. She won't be able to live out there all alone."

"Son, do you want me to take her back with me to Shiloh? We could bring your animals over, too. I got the space now. I'm not sure I can spare J.F. full time to take over your place."

"I'll let ya know. I'll talk to Annie tonight."

"Are you all right about goin' back, Roy?"

"I am now, but pray for me, Mr. Mac."

"I will, Son. I always do."

They finished their meal and stood to leave as a group of ten men tromped in and plopped into chairs at three different tables scattered across the room. "Hey, Woman, you're slow as molasses. Git yerself over here and wait on us!" The voice of an unshaven, dirty ruffian bounced off every surface in the room.

"You tell her, Sarge." A boy who hardly looked old enough to be out without his pa screamed.

"Hold your tongues. I'm doin' the best I can." the middle-aged woman brought out several cups and a pot of hot coffee on a tray. A bear of a man with dirty blonde hair stood up directly in her path, causing her to spill the coffee on her dress and bare arms. "Ouch...Oh."

"Clumsy waitress. You got that coffee on my boots. You get down there and clean 'em up."

Mac walked between the woman and the ruffian who'd caused the accident. "Excuse me, but you owe this lady an apology. She tried to serve you, but you caused the accident." Mac stood his ground.

"Who do you think you're talkin' to?"

"I don't believe we've met," Mac answered.

"Look, you stupid dirt farmers," a man who looked vaguely familiar intervened.

"It's every gentleman's business to take care of womenfolk. Why don't you and your pack go on down to the saloon? It's just down the street."

"Maybe we want some vittles," the first man answered.

"Get what you want down the street. Y'all move on before this spat grows into a brawl."

"Come on, Captain Duncan. I'd rather have a little more fun than this place can give us." A boy who looked to be about Roy's age spat on the floor.

After a second look, Mac recognized Robert Duncan, the bully from Laurel's past. They'd not seen each other since Mac's meeting with Digby in Little Rock. When he'd settled the Flannagan's land fraud business, he'd caught a glimpse of him across the dining room of the Anthony House.

"Captain Duncan? When did you join the Confederate army?'

"Ain't exactly the army, MacLayne. Our troop serves under the governor of our state. Our unit is a Partisan Ranger company out of Missouri, but part of our territory is the Boothill and this part of Arkansas. We are a special unit that helps out our Rebel troops from time to time."

"I haven't heard about any special Partisan Rangers assigned to Arkansas."

"Maybe you ain't heard everything, MacLayne. Our job is to scout around and harass the yanks anytime we find 'em. Looks like we found one," Duncan bragged. "We can raid anywhere from the border Missouri counties to Jonesboro to Black River. We don't need special orders."

"Outlaws, in other words," Mac said.

"Bet some of your neighbors don't think so. I'll be seein' ya now and again." The Partisan Rangers sauntered out and slammed the door behind them.

"I'm sorry they caused you problems."

"I appreciate you for standin' up for me."

Roy and Mac bent down to help her retrieve the shards from the coffee cups that lay across the floor.

"I'll get that mess." She smiled at Roy.

"No problem. Glad to help."

Roy's time at home passed long before the MacLaynes were ready for him to go. He'd been right that his new bride would not be able to cope with her husband's leaving and the problems it would create for her. Mac convinced Roy to close up his cabin and move his animals to the MacLayne homestead. Annie would share Cathy and Gracie's room. Once again the MacLayne cabin was full.

Mac, Laurel, and Annie drove Roy to the recruiting camp in Gainesville on March 29th. The older couple went back to the small cafe where Mac and Roy had encountered the Partisan Ranger unit during the last trip. Neither wanted dinner, but Roy and Annie needed some time to say their good-byes.

"Mac, I still believe we could get Roy released if we asked. Surely if we explain his circumstances--his new wife, an orphaned sister, the only employee of his business--they'd make an exception.'

"No, Laurel. In a matter of a few weeks, Governor Rector will enforce the Conscription Act in Arkansas, too. Roy did the only thing he could do, volunteer. At least, this will let him choose where to serve instead of having to take any random assignment."

"Perhaps he'll get to stay close. The Roughs are supposed to be a local militia group."

"Wife, stop worryin' about it. Roy is in God's hands now. Thank the Lord, Roy is going with the assurance that he'll not face the war alone. I can let him go now."

The lady who owned the diner came to take their order. "I remember you. You helped me a couple of weeks ago when those ruffians tried to start that ruckus in here."

"Yes, I was here. This is my wife. Have you had a repeat of that incident?" Mac asked.

"Wasn't much of a spat," the waitress said to Laurel. "Your husband just asked the people who called themselves Partisan Rangers to stop causin' problems and told 'em they'd like the town's saloon better, so they left."

Laurel looked up into her husband's eyes, which he turned away at once. Mac hadn't told her the whole story. "I know there is more to this than you're tellin' me, Patrick MacLayne."

"No. I can't think of anything important that I left out."

"Then why did you look away?"

"You are too observant, Laurel Grace. I didn't want to tell you that the run-in was with Captain Bob Duncan. He's back in the area."

Laurel sat for some time without replying. "What could Bobby Duncan want here?"

"Nothin' to be concerned about. He got sent here. He was takin' orders. You know that soldiers have little choice of their type of service or the places they are sent."

"I hope you're right." Laurel brushed off the bad news.

Annie and Roy came in to share a final cup of what the waitress was serving as coffee. Roy stood. "I gotta go report in, folks. Thank you for lookin' after Annie for me. I hope to be home for Christmas. I heard that we may get a furlough by then."

Mac rose and shook his hand. "God keep you, son. Take good care of yourself. Remember you're not goin' alone."

Laurel pulled Roy into her arms. "I love you, Roy. I wish our oldest son wasn't goin' so far away from home. Memphis is a long way. Try to write to us as often as you can." Laurel choked before she finished speaking.

Finally, Roy took his young wife in his arms one last time. "I'll miss ya so much, Annie. I love ya. Stay with my folks, and I'll be able to rest knowin' you're taken care of."

"I will, Roy. I love you, too. Please be careful and hurry back to me." Roy kissed her, turned his back, and walked through the door. Laurel held her daughter-in-law and let her cry.

Mac spoke. "Family, it's time to go home. We've done what we came to do." He opened the door and led them to the wagon.

## ⌀

The following Sunday, the war intruded once again. Dinner-on-the-grounds after the service had become a time of isolation for the MacLaynes and the Madison family. They were the only pro-Union families that continued to worship at the Shiloh church. Two other families had moved north, and one family had signed the loyalty oath to the Confederacy. Brother Matthew worked constantly to keep dissension outside the sanctuary doors, but beyond the church, emotions ran high. The more bad news came of young Rebel soldiers being killed or maimed in battle, the more anger was repressed among the people who had once been friends.

At times the conflict came to a head and the incidents were no longer rare. In the early days, snubbings and forgotten invitations to community events were common behaviors. A few people refused to greet them. Laurel and Mrs. Madison were not invited to community social activities, like quilting bees, candling days, and workdays when hogs were slaughtered and soap was made for the new year. Neither was invited to a wedding party for a new bride, a girl who had been one of Laurel's students at the subscription school. When the Sunday dinners were held, Brother Matthew visited each group. He didn't want any group to feel he was biased.

In mid-summer, children of the church brought the dissension to a point that it could no longer be denied or ignored. About three o'clock that afternoon, Andy stumbled to the quilt under the hickory tree where his family sat with the Madisons. His torn shirt and bloody nose silenced the talk. Both his eyes were swollen and black. He moaned as he held his right arm next to his chest. No one doubted there had been a fight.

"Are you all right, Son?" Mac rose and began to look at his son's injury.

Laurel cried out at the same time. "Andy, what's happened to you?"

"Nothin' Mama. I done took care of it."

"Well, Son, tell your papa exactly what you took care of."

"Let's wait 'til we get home, Papa. Okay?"

"Come over to me, and let me see to your scrapes and cuts." Laurel didn't make it an option. She placed a wet cloth on his nose to stop the bleeding. She cleaned the small cuts and scrapes on his chin, knuckles, and his neck. When she picked up his hand to clean the palm, he cried out.

"Ouch, Mama. That hurts bad real bad."

"Andy, can you move those fingers?" Mac frowned as he stepped close enough to lay his hand on the boy's shoulder.

"I can, maybe, Papa." Andy did move his left hand, fingers, and arm, but when he tried to do the same with his right arm, he couldn't. He screamed in pain and again nestled his arm against his chest.

"Mac, I believe his arm is broken. We'll have to get him over to Greensboro to see Dr. Edwards tonight." Laurel began throwing things into the family basket to prepare for a quick trip home. She was about to place the basket into the wagon when a man, a boy in a bloody shirt, and several on-lookers approached her and Mac.

"MacLayne, your boy beat my son down by the creek. That bully broke my boy's nose."

"I don't think your son was an innocent victim here, Richard. Andy has two black eyes, a bloody nose, cut and scrapes. Worst of all, we think he has a broken arm."

"I wanna get to the bottom of this. If he started this brawl, I want you to punish him."

"I'll handle the discipline in my household. You do the same." Mac walked Andy to the front steps of the church and set him down. "Son, why did you get into a fight with that Barton boy?"

"I didn't wanna fight him, Papa. I was mindin' my own business, fishin' with Sean. Nate walked up to me and snatched my fishin' pole. I told 'im to give it back. He wouldn't."

Mac looked at the boy who reminded him of himself at that age. "Andy, that's not much of a reason to fight, especially on Sunday. Do you think it was something else that caused the fight?"

Laurel stood with Leah Ann on her shoulder, watching over her brood. "Andy, just tell us what happened. Tell us all of it."

"I didn't start a fight when he took my pole. I didn't hit him until he called my papa a bad name and said he was a Yankee coward. He said Papa was scared to fight in the war." Mac's face blanched. His son had become an innocent victim.

Nate Barton yelled, "I didn't say that. You're a liar, Andy. Papa, I didn't say nothin'. I promise."

"Papa, I never lie to you. I did hit him, but I didn't smash his face 'til he started after me."

"I know you're tellin' me the truth, Son." He helped the boy stand. "Let's get you over to Dr. Edwards."

"Wait a minute. What do you know about this kid? He lived on the wrong side of the blanket most of his life."

Mac turned around and threw his fist into the face of the man who had insulted his son. "That boy never lied to me. He's not judged me for my life, which he has far more reason to do than you. He hasn't learned to hate just because I hold different politics than others. Don't you ever insult my son again! He is MY son."

"You've not heard the end of this. I'll call in the sheriff."

"You do what you feel is the right thing to do. Andy is an honest boy. He seems to have gotten the worst end of the brawl, which I believe your boy started. Your son is three inches taller and a good twenty pounds heavier. Perhaps he's the one being a coward and a bully. I think they've both been punished enough."

"My boy's right. You're a danged Yankee coward. You won't even work this out with me."

"I thought I already did. You didn't strike me back." Once again he began to help Andy to the wagon. "Come on, Son. I need to get you to the doctor."

Mr. Barton stepped toward Mac to take up the challenge, his fist raised and clenched. Matthew Campbell walked between the two men. "Enough. Richard, we're brothers in the faith. What you said in front of my nephew is low, to say the least. You owe the MacLaynes an apology. We can work out this dispute between the boys. I don't think he'd spoken those words to Andy had he not heard them at home."

"Me, apologize? I didn't do nothin' but state the truth. MacLayne don't have the backbone to fight for his home or his state."

"Brothers, can't we sit down and talk about this when tempers cool?" Matthew held up his hands. "For the good of our church, let this end. Let's go in for evenin' services."

"Laurel, help the kids into the wagon. We'll take them home, and I'll drive Andy on to Greensboro. Mac turned. "Matthew, I…well…perhaps…Nevermind. I'll talk with you later. Andy needs a doctor."

# Chapter 8

*If any man among you seems to be religious,*
*but bridleth not his tongue,*
*but deceiveth his own heart, this man's religion is vain.*
*James 1:26*

Laurel awoke at midnight to find Mac sitting in his chair near the window. His Bible lay open in his lap. Only a low-light from the lamp cast a modicum of orange light across their bedroom. "Mac, why are you up and tryin' to read in that feeble light?"

He looked over his shoulder toward the tall, four-poster. "Sorry, Wife. I didn't mean to wake you. Couldn't sleep. I should have walked away from Richard yesterday. I can't believe I lost my temper at his ignorance."

Laurel stepped onto the torn-rag rug covering the walnut plank floor. The night was not unbearably cold, but the rug felt good to her bare feet. She stopped by the armchair and drew Mac's face up to meet hers. "You were protecting our son. Not one man there expected any less."

"I expected more, Laurel. I've gotta talk to Matthew in the mornin'. I have to make things right with Richard and all the others in our church family who have turned their backs on us."

76

"Attending Sunday worship's not as special as it was before. I feel it, too. I'm not sure what we can do to change anything."

"I'm gonna try, but it's not good for our church and not good for our family."

Laurel saw the hurt in Mac's eyes. Shiloh Church was much more than a building to her husband. The loss of fellowship and the growing isolation tore at Mac's peace of mind and sense of belonging, both of which he treasured. She pulled him to her and held him as she would hold one of her hurting children.

"I want you to talk to Matthew as soon as you can. And your father, too. Seein' you hurt like this breaks my heart."

"Too much is at stake, Laurel. For one thing, I feel guilty that I hit Richard. He shouldn't have said those despicable words about Andy, but my putting my fist in his face didn't take away Andy's slight. I have to ask both of them to forgive me. Something even worse though...." Mac closed his eyes and laid his head back against his chair. Laurel saw him clinch his mouth to stop a quiver. He slammed his fist against the arm of the chair. "I may choose to remove our membership from the Shiloh congregation—for the welfare of all concerned."

Laurel gasped. She never expected to hear those words from her husband.

When Mac finished morning chores and choked down a biscuit and a cup of coffee, he rode to Matthew's cabin, a mile north of the church. Everyone in the community knew Matthew claimed Monday as his day of rest.

"Good to have a visit this beautiful mornin', but I'm guessin' this ain't a social call."

"Can we talk?"

"Let's do it at the fishin' hole. Grab some canes, and we'll go to the creek. May as well catch us a few fish while we mull over what happened at that slug-fest with Richard, don't ya think?"

Seated on a flat outcropped rock above the creek, the two friends tossed out their lines and promptly turned their attention elsewhere. Matthew tilted his hat to the side so his view of Mac was unobstructed. "All right, Mac, what's got ya so upset that ya made a beeline here today?"

"You already said it—a slug-fest at church on Sunday in front of my entire church family. I thought I'd become a better man than that."

"Maybe a blow to the face wasn't the best way to deal with Richard, but what happened is understandable. Andy didn't deserve those hurtful words. I'd probably have hit 'im, too."

"Matthew, you know as well as I do that was just one example of my old nature tryin' to surface. I've let it happen too much since this stupid war began. Can't keep my temper in check, and I'm too short with my young'uns. I'm furious with Roy for goin' back to fight, but I didn't tell him that. Havin' Annie in our house is a daily reminder of his goin' to the Confederate army. Worst, I feel slighted that people of my church family have turned against me."

Mac looked up into Matthew's face. "Any of that seem unnatural to you?"

Mac's face flushed and his mouth gaped open. "You're supposed to be makin' me feel better, Brother. No. It's not unnatural, but it's a worldly reaction. I can't change one thing about any of it except how I react. I tried to give it over to God, but I slip more every day."

"Mac, I want us to talk with Barton to see if we can get past what happened after service. You ain't the only one in the wrong here. Let me see if I can get Ransom Wiley to meet with us, too. He's not taken a stand on either side, so he'll make an unbiased witness. I'll get word to you when we can get together."

"I appreciate you, Matthew. You've saved my life more'n once over the years we've known each other. I couldn't ask for a better friend."

"Mac, stop kickin' yourself. We all fall at times. You know what you have to do to deal with the bad that is happenin'. If you can't fix it, give to the One who can."

"Thanks, Matthew. I hope our meetin' with our brothers from Shiloh will put some of this behind us."

Mac untied his horse and trotted home. The moment he walked through the door, he heard groans from the loft. He climbed the ladder to find Laurel trying to spoon laudanum into Andy's mouth.

"Here, Son. This will ease your pain." The boy continued to writhe back and forth, holding his splinted arm.

"Andy, stop. Let your mama give you the medicine."

"My arm hurts real bad, Papa. Worse than it did at Dr. Gibson's last night."

When the boy swallowed the milky-colored liquid, Mac drew back the blanket and looked at the bandaged arm. The top slat had dislodged in Andy's sleep. Mac recognized at once that the break was no longer aligned.

Watching the doctor manipulate the broken arm the previous night had been a nightmare for Mac. The need to lengthen the ligaments and straighten the muscles called for the doctor to pull and bend the arm several times. He'd explained it was the only way to assure the bones went back together in good alignment. Even with some pain medicine, Andy screamed, called out for his papa to help him, and moaned until the bones meshed. As much as Mac hated to see his son go through that agony a second time, he knew the doctor would have to repeat the procedure if Andy's arm were to heal properly. However, he wouldn't drag his son in the back of a wagon over the four miles to Greensboro again. He sent J.F. for the doctor.

That afternoon, Dr. Edwards came to perform the bone setting a second time. He sent all the children out of the house. The procedure was not a pleasant thing for anyone to witness. "Andy, I have to hurt you again, but I gotta get those two ends back in place. Grit your teeth and scream if you need to. I won't take but a couple of minutes."

After manipulating Andy's arm, rolling the bones into the right position, and pulling the bones back to meet each other, he placed his entire arm between two sturdy slats and wrapped several lengths of white linen cloth around the length. Then he wrapped the arm against Andy's torso so that it would not move at all. "Son, I know that don't feel good, but we gotta make sure that bone stays together 'til it starts to mend. I'll let it loose in a couple of weeks and put the shorter splints on again. We can't have you with a cripple arm, so for a couple of weeks, you'll be a little uncomfortable. Are you hurtin' now, Andy?"

"Not so bad. I'll try to be more careful."

"Well, it's gonna hurt off and on. Tell your mama. She'll give ya a little pain medicine, but not too much or too often."

"Thank ya, Ed."

"Mac, keep him down. That break is a bad one. It seems nearly straight across and clean. Nothin' to anchor the bones together. That splint has to do the job. I don't want Andy to end up with a useless limb. Keep him in bed for about three days."

"We'll do it, Ed. Thank you again." Mac handed the doctor a twenty-dollar gold piece for his fee.

Dr. Gibson looked at it and flipped it in the air. "Not too many of these floating around Greensboro these days. A federal minted coin, gold no less."

"I've got some Confederate shinplasters if you rather have 'em. Your service is worth more than those things."

"Mac, be careful where you show these around. There are already too many folks around here suspicious of you."

"I know, but my son is worth your care. I paid that much for a wagon wheel once."

𝜙

On Thursday of that same week, Matthew met with Richard Barton, Ransom Wiley, and Mac at the Shiloh church to talk. Before he started, he prayed for the men and read them a piece of scripture from Matthew. "Brothers, I believe what we came here to do is what the Lord would have us to do. We had a problem here on Sunday. I asked Ransom to be our unbiased witness. First, how are the two boys doin'?"

"Nate'll be okay in a day or two. His tooth is loose, but I don't think he'll lose it. His nose is swollen, but the bruises are healin'."

"Dr. Gibson says Andy's arm should mend fine if we can keep him still to let the healin' start. Right now he's got the arm bound to his side. He's got some pain, but Laurel's seein' to him, and he seems to be gettin' better," Mac spoke slowly with a calm, quiet voice.

"Sorry about your boy, MacLayne. I wish they'd not gotten into a fight," Barton said.

"I wish that too, but they did. That's the problem—not the boys' scrapin' but that they had something to fight about. They were friends before the war."

Richard Barton flinched and squared his shoulders. He turned his back to the other men. Shortly, he turned back and spoke, "MacLayne, feelin's are runnin' high around here."

"That's not hard to see. Good example right now. When did I stop bein' Mac to y'all? MacLayne sounds hostile when I've been your friend for so many years." Mac's fiercely clenched knuckles belied his calm voice.

"The kids let things get out of hand. You know that."

"I'm not talkin' about kids. Kids react to what they hear from their parents and friends of their parents. Furthermore, it wasn't Nate that commented on Andy's legitimacy in front of the entire church. Regardless, I am sorry I hit you. I know better. Violence never fixed anything. That is the first reason I am here today. I ask your forgiveness for that attack."

"Mac, I am right sorry I let my tongue get the better of me. I lost my temper with you callin' my boy a liar, but I had no call to say that about your boy. Let my temper overcome my good sense. I'd never hurt a boy like that on purpose."

"I'll accept your apology if you never speak those words again—in public or in private. That's where kids get hurtful things to use against other kids."

"Look here. I said I'm sorry. I can't take back what's said. I don't need no lecture."

Matthew intervened, "Men, do you need to take a few minutes to let things calm down?"

"I'm calm, Matthew," Mac replied.

"Let's just get this over. I've got things to do. Surely Ransom and the preacher do, too."

Ransom Wiley spoke for the first time. "It seems this problem is more about you two than those young'uns. What's at the bottom of this spat?"

Richard Barton bluntly stated his gripe. "Neighbors have to stick together to defend our honor and our homes. MacLayne has turned his back on Shiloh. He insulted Captain Armstrong in this very church. He won't support the cause." He approached Mac until his face was within inches. "MacLayne, you ain't the man we thought ya was."

Mac moved behind the pew to put some distance between himself and Barton. "Richard, I stood before this body on many occasions and swore I'd not support secession. I told all of you that I owned no slaves. The MacLaynes never have. Before y'all ever elected me to the state assembly, I made it clear where I stood. I worked every minute I was in Little Rock to prevent Arkansas from leavin' the Union. I've not changed one whit! I don't believe in the Confederacy. Arkansas will suffer for years because of the decision we made. If I went against my integrity, I'd be a hypocrite. I'd rather be dead than to live a lie. I'm the same man you've always known. Can you say the same?"

Wiley turned to look at Barton. "Richard, Mac's said his piece. You got anything else to say?"

"MacLayne thinks he's right. It's mighty hard to live with someone when ya don't know if they'll have your back. Can ya trust someone who won't support his state or community? I'll try for the good of our church." Barton extended his hand to Mac. "Can't say my feelin's will change, but there'll be no more words from me or my boy. We don't have to agree on everything to sit in the same church, I guess."

Mac refused to take his hand. "I love this church. My life has been changed here. Matthew, I'll be in your debt 'til the day I go to be with the Lord. I never dreamed I'd say this, but my family and I will worship elsewhere for the time bein'. Laurel and I love this church too much to be the cause of the dissension."

"Wait, Mac. That's not the answer," Ranson said.

"I didn't mean for ya to go, MacLayne," Barton mumbled.

"We'll talk later, Matthew. This isn't about you. We'll always be friends. God keep ya, brother, and Shiloh Church. I think I'll go talk with my pa for a while. Sometimes I need to be the son."

Φ

Keeping Andy down was not the only thing that occupied Laurel in those first days after Roy's departure to Memphis. She worked almost as hard to keep her daughter-in-law occupied, hoping to take her mind off her husband's absence. She allowed the younger woman to care for Leah Ann part of each day and gave her a few of the household duties. This freed up some time for Laurel to begin school with her children, the Flannagan's, the Campbells, the Randalls, and the two Madison boys who lived to the east of their place. Being in her home, she had a smaller group than the class she'd taught at the Shiloh church. The church had opted to keep the school closed that year, but Laurel would not allow her children to miss a year of learning. Because the subscription school would remain closed, she offered the same opportunity to any of the children in the community who wanted to attend.

No other families took advantage of her offer, and she knew why. They would not allow their children to be in the care of a traitor's wife. She ignored the snub. Her tireless work to prepare for the new term gradually converted the front room of the cabin into a classroom. Laurel felt grateful she could use her gift. For the rest of the week, she poured her energy and time into putting her abilities to the service of the eleven children she would teach that term.

The Saturday before the first class, she went to her Uncle Matthew to ask for the books, slates, maps, and charts she'd collected for the subscription school. They were being stored.

"I wish I could give you those things, Laurel, but the school committee told me to store all the school property until after the war when we can re-open the school."

"Uncle, you can't be tellin' me that our congregation would rather horde those things than have them used."

83

"Please understand. Some of the families are very angry right now. Two families had boys killed in action at the Battle of Shiloh. The Estes lost a nephew at the Battle of Pea Ridge a couple of months ago. Then the words got out that Mac pulled y'all from the church. Maybe in a few weeks…"

"In a few weeks, half the school term will be over."

"I'm sorry, niece. I'm tryin' to keep peace in the congregation. I was able to keep the anger outside for a while, but now that's…"

"I've felt the rejection, too. These same people who called me sister when I came here as Mac's wife now treat us as we are lepers. I watched my husband give up his place in this body to keep the peace. What else do we owe because Mac feels compelled to follow his principles?"

"I know both of you have been hurt. I wish I could help."

"You can. Give me half of everything you've stored. I bought most of it with half my salary for two years."

"Laurel Grace, that'll only cause more problems."

"I need those things to serve my students. Tell the school committee I want what's mine, or I want the money they owe for my salary now. I am starting school next Monday. Any student in this community is welcome to attend."

"I'll convey your message, Laurel Grace."

"I'm sorry to cause you problems, Uncle Matthew. You know I love you and respect you, but my students need those books. And maybe it is time for you to stand up to the people at Shiloh and help them remember what the Lord says about supporting all the members of the family, not just the ones they agree with."

"I try to do that every week. I hate the division this war has brought to the church, both here at Shiloh and across the nation."

*Φ*

Laurel convened the first day of school on May 4th. The main room of the cabin was crowded, but she made a place for the eleven students who would be enrolled that term. The only non-family members of the class were the Madison boys. They

84

belonged to the only pro-Union family with children young enough to attend school.

Mac had devised a rough chalkboard from leftover timbers from his father's house. He smoothed them and painted them black. He constructed a large, sturdy easel in which to stand the blackboard in front of the hearth when it was needed. Laurel had gotten half of the school materials that she'd asked for, mainly because cash was hard to come by since the war started. She was so glad they had relented and gave her the books because freight took so long to come from St. Louis. Laurel wasn't aware that Matthew's intervention had caused a huge rift between him and the school committee, but she was overjoyed at having the materials she needed to teach her students.

The first week was no different than any school day the students had experienced in the subscription school in previous years. They read, worked math problems on their slates, and practiced penmanship on scraps of paper that Laurel was able to provide. The two first-level students began learning to recognize and copy their ABC's. Naturally, they loved recess time when they played without conflict and insults. Because none of the students from the Confederate families attended, they didn't have to deal with ugly talk about the war. Best of all, no one was on the wrong side. Laurel looked forward to the three months before summer gave way to fall when the older kids would be needed to help with the harvest. She would dismiss school then until late October or early November.

Some did not intend for her school to be a success, though. Captain Duncan and his special unit of Partisan Rangers returned to Greene and Craighead County. He told locals he'd received orders from his commanders to stop Union activity in northeast Arkansas. Rumors told another story. According to the local gossips, some men from the Greensboro area had asked the rangers to pay a visit to the MacLayne's homestead and set things right with the woman who'd taken most of Shiloh school's property.

Two weeks after school began, Duncan's troops made a late-night call to the MacLaynes. In the darkest part of the night, they sneaked into the barnyard and defaced all four sides of the barn. They'd painted slogans reading:

"Beware...a Yankee lover is here teaching
Yankee brats treason. Beware!"

Red streaks ran from each letter down the length of the barn, giving the words the appearance that they'd been written in blood.

The following morning when Andy and Mac went to do morning chores, they found the profane messages.

"Papa, look what someone did to our barn." Andy's eyes bulged. "Who'd do this?"

"I know where it came from, son. Let's get to our chores. I'll take care of this later."

Without a doubt, Laurel was the target of the message. She was the one who had defied the school committee and demanded the books. She had dared to open a school after the school committee had ordered the subscription school closed. She was a woman who had dared to stand her ground with a group of men.

"Mac, what can we do to cover this mess up before the other students get here?" She had run to the barn when she saw the huge letters from the window in the kitchen. The students would see it as soon as they approached the MacLayne property.

"I can't get it covered that fast. After you call the students to order, I'll come and explain it to them. You know they'll carry the story home. I want them to know what to say."

"Surely, this is not meant to be a threat to the children."

"Don't worry, Laurel. I'm not leavin' the place today. This was aimed to scare you into closing the school."

"I'll not do that."

"Some of the parents may decide to remove their kids."

"I hope that doesn't happen, but if only our three remain, we will still have school this term."

Mac had been right. The following day, the two Madison boys did not come to school. Mary and the Randalls arrived a bit late and in the care of their fathers. Laurel convened the classes as

86

usual while Mac took Matthew Campbell and Warren Randall to the barn where he showed them the vandalism.

"Mac, do you think whoever did this will try to hurt the children?" Matthew asked.

"It wasn't whoever, Matthew. That unit of Partisan Rangers from over the state line is responsible. They come here under a special mandate to harass the Union army in the area and to steal supplies from them. They say they are allowed to carry out punishment on Union supporters wherever they find them. I'd like to see those orders. I think we need to bring in the county sheriff to get some proof that they are sanctioned to be here at all. We haven't been brought under martial law by any Confederate mandate I know of."

"My kids were pretty upset when they told Susan and me about the messages on the barn. Nancy said she didn't think she felt good enough to come to school," Warren Randall, Matthew Campbell's son-in-law, expressed his concern.

Mac replied, "I'd never put my kids in harm's way. Rest assured that I'll be here watchin' over all the family. They'll be as safe here as at home."

"Mac, I appreciate your wantin' to keep the school open. Laurel is set on givin' our kids their schoolin'. Perhaps we ought to keep 'em home a few days 'til we know they'll be safe."

"That's exactly why those hoodlums wrote that message on my barn. They want to close down all semblance for normal life until we do what they tell us. My tenants and I will stand guard until we know those bushwhackers are out of the district. We have to stand together to show them they can't dictate our way of life, not now—not ever," Mac said.

"You're right. We'll keep the school open for now. I'll help keep an eye on things around here, too. Susan couldn't take the loss of another child since we lost Martha in that 'flu epidemic in '61." Warren agreed they were doing the right thing.

"Son-in-law, your havin' that new baby has given my girl a new lease on life. The Lord's been good to us."

"Congratulations, Warren. I hadn't heard there'd be a new Randall."

That night as Laurel and Mac spooned together under the yellow summer coverlet, they found it impossible to sleep. They wanted...no, needed to talk about the events of the past two weeks.

"I don't understand why they chose us to attack, Mac. We aren't Union sympathizers. We've made it clear that we won't take sides."

"If you think hard enough, you know the reason, Laurel."

"No, I don't. Surely we offer no threat if we won't take sides."

"The leaders of the Confederacy don't see it that way. They are leading people to believe if a person doesn't agree with them, he is the enemy. There is no middle ground."

"How do you know what the Confederate leaders are saying?"

"All you have to do is read the papers, Wife. Last month in the Democrat/Gazette, an article about the Conscription Act laid out the rules. All able-bodied men from eighteen to thirty-five who live in the Confederate States are subject to enlistment. Anyone who refuses can be arrested and punished as the military sees fit. For most, that means they will be executed as traitors. All the property of those men will be confiscated and sold by the state to support the war effort. The head of the Confederacy wrote the bill, and the Confederate legislature enacted it. Now Governor Rector is approving the use of the bill in Arkansas."

"My dear Lord. How can they do that to law-abiding citizens?"

"You forget, Darlin', that we no longer live under the same constitution where those laws were written. And we are at war. Armies make up the laws they want and need in war times."

"Thank God, you are too old to be pulled into the army. I can survive anything that comes if you are here with me."

"As long as He allows, I'm not goin' anywhere. I love you more'n ever."

"Wasn't it wonderful news about Susan and Randall's new baby?"

"Yes. Randall seemed real pleased."

"Mac, do you want to have another child?" Quiet fell over the room. "Never mind. I don't know why I said that."

"No, Sweetheart, I want to answer you. This family means everything to me. What's come through providence and those we've born through our love are a blessing. Right now, though, no. I don't want to bring any more children into this unsettled world."

"That's how I feel, too."

"But Laurel Grace…I don't see that I'm willin' to give up one of the greatest joys of my life to prevent it. Doubt if I could if I tried. Can we just leave it in God's hands?"

"You're too wise, husband. I share your feelings exactly. More children during this unsure time could be a hardship. Yet, well…I…You…"

"Why, Mrs. MacLayne. If the lamp were lit, I'll bet I'd see bright red in your cheeks."

"Don't tease, Mac. Southern girls were not taught to talk about such things."

"I don't care if we talk about making love as long as we don't stop making love. You have been an enchantress far too long for me to let you go now."

# Chapter 9

*He hath put forth his hands against such as be at peace with him:*
*he hath broken his covenant. The words of his mouth were*
*smoother than butter, but war was in his heart:*
*His words were softer than oil, yet they were drawn swords.*
*Psalms 55:20-21*

Toward the end of the month, Laurel planned a family supper for her Uncle Matthew and his family. She and Mac had not attended church since the Sunday of the run-in with Richard Barton. They conducted a simple service each Sunday in their main room or under the grand old oak at Eden. Mac sorely missed the fellowship he shared with his best friend. Furthermore, Laurel had no intention of losing contact with her family. A quiet family supper would provide the perfect time for the two families to reconnect and enjoy the company they'd always shared.

"Laurel Grace, that was a feast. Thank you for askin' us tonight. I've been hopin' we'd find time to talk...Mac, you and me."

"Sounds serious, Matthew. Are you removin' us from the membership at Shiloh church?"

Laurel dropped the pewter plates she'd just picked up. "Mac, how can you say that?"

"Wife, I was makin' a joke. Hey, young'uns, will y'all go outside to play 'til dark? There's a nice breeze tonight."

"Oh, Papa! You always send us away when the talkin' gets good." Andy kicked his foot against the floor. "I ain't got no one to play with, just girls and babies."

"Poor Andy. Why don't you give that horse of yours some attention? It's rare for a boy your age to still have one, ya know. If Sparky was two hands taller, the army would've taken him already."

Once the six children traipsed outside, Mac settled again at the head of the table with his wife, his best friend and his wife, and Annie Dunn. Opportunities to talk from the heart rarely came among this group. Mac reached to take Laurel's hand. "What did ya wanna say, Matthew?"

"I had a visit from the bishop after services last Sunday. He's making the circuit to visit the local pastors across the state. He asked about the mood of our people and if we'd had any serious changes at Shiloh church. He also asked if we'd been carryin' out the tenets of the Methodist South Church."

"Wasn't a very pleasant visit, was it, Brother?"

"Uncle Matthew, what did you tell him?" Laurel asked.

"I told him the truth. Shiloh has changed some. I told him I preach the gospel of Jesus every week, just like I did before the war. I also told him I have no intention of changing my message."

Ellie Campbell wiped a tear from her lashes. Matthew bent to kiss her cheek. "Ellie, we already talked about this. I know I'm doin' what the Lord is callin' me to do."

"I'm all right, Matt. I agree with you," Ellie said.

"What are you talkin' about, Uncle Matthew?" Laurel stood with her arms crossed.

"Let me finish my story, Niece. The bishop asked me if there has been any disruption among our people. I knew from the sound of his voice someone from our church had been talkin' to him."

"And?" Mac stood and stepped to put his arm around Laurel's shoulder.

"I said we dealt with some stressful times, but I had stopped the fuss from comin' into the church. Then I asked him what kind of story he'd heard about Shiloh."

"Our brothers and sisters have been complainin' about me, haven't they? Did they tell the story straight, or did he get a biased version?" Mac asked.

"You know how rumors are—told from the side of the teller. He knew about the confrontation with Capt. Murray and Capt. Anderson. He'd heard about Andy's broken arm in a fight during the dinner-on-the-ground. Mostly he was upset about the brawl between two members of the flock. Someone reported to him that I always favored you in a conflict. They told him you are a Union loyalist."

"Sorry you got caught in the middle of all this, Matthew."

"You didn't do nothin' wrong, Mac."

"Did he censure you, Uncle Matthew?"

"No, Laurel. He complimented the work we're doin' here at Shiloh. Before he rode off, though, he did ask me to put the dispute in the church to rest and reminded me the word South is part of our church name."

"Our leavin' was the right thing. As much as I miss Shiloh Church, we'll not return, Brother."

"Mac, that's not the answer. You're not the only family involved. The Madisons and that elderly Jones couple stand with the Union. A couple of others ain't said, but they don't support either side. I'll not ask anyone to leave God's house."

"What else can ya do, Brother Matthew?" Annie spoke for the first time since the conversation started. "Can't our people understand we don't have to be mad at each other? Like Roy and me...he's fightin' with the militia. By now the troops probably got sent to fight with the Arkansas regulars. Mrs. Mac and Mac didn't throw me out of their house. They told Roy that no matter if he was a Rebel or a Yankee, they'd love him anyway and welcome him home when the war's over."

"Bless your sweet soul, Annie. If everyone could feel with your heart and see with your eyes, we could sit down and solve this problem without soaking this country's soil with blood." He walked over and hugged the young wife of his latest convert. "Ya know, Roy has a lot to do with the decision I've made. When he came to talk with me, he said the worst part of the war was being alone. Now he never has to feel that way again. But how many other of our young soldiers face that fear?"

Matthew bowed his head, praying for several minutes. Finally, he stood, walked behind the chair where Ellie sat, and laid his hands on her shoulders. "Ellie and me talked long and hard about what I should do. Mac, I believe the Lord is callin' me to serve as a chaplain to the soldiers and the wounded. This is how I can help."

"No. Uncle Matthew, you can't mean you'll leave Shiloh!" Laurel's voice quivered.

"I can't minister there right now. I hate the split. We were a family before this war. Now I can't have one service where brothers and sisters aren't at odds with each other. They are unkind, angry, and bitter toward people they used to love. My sermons fall on deaf ears."

"Aunt Ellie, talk to him. Shiloh needs Uncle Matthew."

"Laurel Grace, I've supported Matthew all these years because he has always followed God's call. I don't want him to go away from home and me, but he will do what the Lord is asking him to do. It's not my place to speak against what he knows he must do."

"Please understand. Laurel, I love these people. They're good folks, all of 'em. I can't condemn them because I know what is causin' the hurt. Some of them have lost sons, husbands are bein' crippled, and for some, the only way of life they've ever known is threatened. I'll not leave Shiloh all together. Our homestead is here, and I still have to earn a livin' for my family. I can serve as a chaplain to any soldier who needs me, whether Rebel or Yankee. I am called. I can't turn my back when God asks me to do something."

Mac took three steps and embraced his best friend. "Please don't put yourself in harm's way, Brother. I'm sorry that I contributed to your problems."

"Mac, you are the best friend I've got. I respect your decision because I know you stand on principles. You have to be true to yourself. You have always been the man God has meant for you to be since the time you came to know Him. Stand with your convictions, Mac. He'll see you through."

"I'll miss you. I'll keep watch over Ellie and Mary while you're gone. I'll find a new hand for the homestead so John can stay home."

The kids came rushing into the house. "Can we come in yet, Papa?"

"You can always come in, Son. This is your home."

"Ellie, I think we need to head home."

"Matthew, please pray for us before you go." The family joined hands around the table. Matthew prayed—first praising God for his love and then thanking Him for the fellowship of those in the room. Then he prayed for Roy's safety and for all the soldiers who fought but did not know the Lord. He closed with a plea for peace to come soon.

## φ

Summer at Shiloh proved to be hot and dry. The intemperate weather paralleled Mac's mood. For three months, he'd encountered obstacle after obstacle as he worked to expose the vicious activities of the bushwhackers. Since the rock-throwing incident, attacks against Unionist families had escalated. In mid-June, a hog was mutilated in its sty at the home of the elderly Jones couple from the Shiloh congregation. The meat was unfit to eat after laying many hours undressed in the mud and insects. With the help of Mac and Laurel, they managed to save some of the fat to use for tallow in candling.

The next weekend a worse loss came to the Madisons. Their corn shed was burned to the ground. Thankfully, the new crop was not ready to harvest, but they lost the building and a quarter of the previous year's crop. Madison had planned to fill the shed to provide for his family and then sell the surplus to pay taxes. Two days later, the Confederate army came to confiscate corn and meat to supply the army. The Madisons faced a year of need, thanks to the bushwhackers.

Mac investigated similar incidents in the area. A fire near Buffalo Island burned the kitchen of a clapboard house. Fences were pulled down in the Greenfield area, and a small herd of milk cattle was stampeded from a farm near Lorado. The bushwhackers visited the MacLayne homestead three more times. The last time they trampled the oat crop meant as winter feed for Mac's livestock. He found the tracks of a horse with a misshapen shoe at the edge of his fields. He had seen that same track at both the Jones place and the Madison farm. The last vestige of their visit was another terse message painted across the fence nearest his house. This one read 'Go North, Traitor.'

After the senseless destruction of the oat field, Mac decided to take the matter to the county lawman. He didn't know if he would get much cooperation because the men responsible were exploiting the sanctions granted by the Partisan Ranger Act. That law was meant to help provide supplies to the Confederate army. Supposedly, they had a commission from the army to harass the Union families and any Union troops they came upon, but because of a lack of accountability, they raided, stole, and destroyed at will. Their attacks on the MacLaynes were acts of vengeance, not southern loyalty. Mac hoped the county sheriff would intervene because he knew he would be compelled to take matters into his own hands if the constant harassment did not stop. Mac wouldn't tolerate acts that put his family in harm's way.

Mac decided to go to Jonesboro to make the report and to request the sheriff's help. On the first day of August, Mac set aside the day to ride to the county seat.

"Papa, can I go?" Andy pleaded.

"Andrew, you'll miss school if you go with your papa. Don't you think you should stay?" Laurel never wanted her children away from her with the troops around so often.

He ignored her question and addressed his father. "I'd sure like to go with you. We never get to spend the day together, just the two of us. Sparky would love a good stretch of his legs. Can I go?"

"Get permission from your teacher. If she'll let you miss school, I'll take ya with me."

"I wanna go too, Papa."

"Mark Thomas, the ride is too far. When you get older, I'll get you a pony, but for today you stay home with Gracie and Leah Ann. You need to be the man of the house while I'm gone for the day."

"With just those girls?"

"That's why they need a man to stay with them, Son."

The four-year-old puffed out his chest. "I'll take care of 'em, Papa. Don't worry."

Mac told Laurel of his plans. He explained he had several errands to tend to, including the purchase of a pane of glass to repair the window. Laurel grudgingly gave her permission for Andy to go along. Before 6:00 a.m., the two were trotting down the Old Military Road together. The heat and humidity were tolerable this early in the morning. Even a gentle breeze blew through the trees.

"Golly, Papa, I ain't been to Jonesboro since—well, I don't know if I ever was there before."

"You'll find it's not much of a town yet. Lots of buildings goin' up now, but it's not near the size of Greensboro."

"Why is the sheriff there if it's a tiny town?"

"Andy, you know that Jonesboro is the county seat."

"I know. I just think he should be where most of the people are, don't you?"

"No, Son. Jonesboro is where the local government stays. Someday, that town may be as big as Greensboro or even Gainesville. Look over there? That's our new courthouse, just finished this spring."

Andy looked around Courthouse Square. The muddy streets and patchwork of buildings in the center of the community were far from impressive. "Should have put the county seat at Greensboro. At least, we got a good Main Street and some mercantile stores."

"Jonesboro will grow, Andy."

"Where we goin' first?"

"Let's see if we can find the sheriff."

After a short ride around the courthouse, they came upon a small rough timber building about half the size of the main room of their cabin. A sign hung from the porch that read Sheriff A.E. Armstrong. Mac and Andy dismounted and tied their horses to a hitching rail just outside the sole door. Inside, they found the county sheriff.

"Sir, my name's MacLayne. This is my son, Andrew. We live at Shiloh over near Greensboro."

"I've heard about you. You were the state representative during the last two legislative sessions, weren't ya?"

"Yes, but now I'm home, farmin' and raisin' cattle. I've got a concern I'd like to talk to you about if you'll give me a minute."

"Speak yer mind, Citizen. I've gotta minute to spare."

"Have you heard about the bushwhackers that have been raiding around the northern part of the county?"

"Been some talk, but I ain't had no contact with any group like that. Rumors have it that it's a bunch of boys pullin' pranks."

"I'd not call what they've been doin' pranks. I'm pretty sure it's not kids. A group of bushwhackers, who call themselves Partisan Rangers, have decided to run all the Unionists out of the area. Some of those men are from the bootheel of Missouri, but at least two of them are familiar to people in our community."

"I've got no word of any group like that. Nothin' official. You got any proof?" Armstrong looked up from his paperwork for a minute.

"Someone threw a rock through a window at my home back in the fall. My pastor's wife got a pretty deep cut when a shard of the glass pierced her arm."

"Yep. Sounds like somethin' a kid would do. Throwin' rocks don't seem like much of a threat."

Mac pulled the stone from his saddlebag. "This one seemed to be a threat to me and my family." He handed it to the sheriff.

He read the scratched-in words. "You a Yankee supporter, MacLayne?"

"I'm on no side. I voted against secession three times. I will not support a cause I don't believe in. I have no plans to support either side. I want to remain on my homestead and take care of my family."

A smirk fell across the sheriff's face. "You ain't gonna take neither side, ya say? You must not be very popular around here right now."

"I don't want to be popular. I just want to take care of my family until this conflict is over. Then we'll go on buildin' a decent life at Shiloh. What's wrong with that?"

"You're some kind of fool, MacLayne. Feelings against the Union are runnin' pretty strong. Most of the local boys enlisted in the county militia units. Some of those units have joined with battalions of state forces. Craighead, Poinsett, and Greene counties have already sent local units to Pocahontas to train."

"I know that all too well. My oldest son served his thirty-day enlistment with the Greene County militia. As we speak, he's with the Roughs. Last we heard, they'd been sent to reinforce the Eighth Arkansas Infantry. That bein' said, are you gonna do anything about that pack of hoodlums attacking the citizens of this county? None of them are combatants, and not one family is providin' support for the Union."

"Sure, I'll look into the matter, but I'm pretty sure it's just a gang of kids like I told ya. Kids' pranks sometimes get outta hand."

"The next time these pranksters decide to come to Shiloh, they'll be met with gunfire. My family won't be victims." Mac walked out of the office and slammed the door. Blotches in shades from frostbite to flame ran up his neck and into his cheeks. He clenched his fist until his knuckles blanched. "Come on, Andy." He jumped into the saddle.

"You doin' okay, Papa?"

"I'm fine, Son."

Andy jumped onto Sparky's back, but before he could turn his pony toward home, a cadre of soldiers blocked the street. The larger group was dressed in gray or butternut homespun. A smaller number of men in blue uniforms held guns on the Confederate soldiers. Behind the marching group, three more Yankees rode ahead of a band of thirty horses being wrangled by a few more Yanks. Bringing up the rear was a file of three supply wagons.

The officer in charge yelled his orders. "Troop, halt." People came out of the few buildings near the courthouse and a few houses. Some walked over to the ground in front of the partially painted courthouse. "Guard these prisoners. Shoot anyone who attempts to escape." The captain disappeared into the two-story building on the square.

Andy's eyes took on the shape of small eggs, and his mouth fell open. "Papa, what's goin' on?"

"Not sure, Son. Let's wait here out of the way and watch for a few minutes."

Within five minutes, the captain returned. "Troops, move the prisoners inside. The judge said the jail is too small for this large a group. We'll house these two dozen Rebs in the courtroom until they can be moved to Memphis." Slowly and at gunpoint, the captured Confederates filed into the new Craighead County courthouse.

"How we gonna feed all these horses, Captain Porter?" A private who looked only a year or two older than Andy asked.

"Men, take the horses and those confiscated supplies back to our camp. I'll get orders from Col. Eggerton as to their disposition. Return south down that same road we used to come here. Remain at camp until sun up. The eight of you, stay here to guard the prisoners." The men scurried to carry out the orders.

"Golly, Papa. I think these folks have been fightin' and those Rebs got caught. I guess they're prisoners now…right here in our courthouse. I can't believe we saw the war right here in Jonesboro."

"I'd been just as glad if we'd never seen it, Andy. Let's get back to Greensboro. I've got a couple more errands to do." Mac kicked Midnight into a gallop back toward Greensboro.

The eight-mile ride back to Greensboro gave Mac time to lose the animosity he felt about his visit to the county seat. He tried to smile as he pushed open the door of the Davis General Store. A couple of acquaintances nodded but left almost immediately.

The owner, J.T. Davis, stood behind the counter, organizing a few items on his nearly empty shelves. He muttered to himself. "Hang it all! How's a man gonna stay in business if he can't get his orders when the freighters come?"

"You all right, J.T?"

"No, MacLayne, I ain't. I got less than a quarter of my order this month. I'll not have enough goods to get me through 'til the next shipment."

"Ya can't expect things to be like they were before the war."

"What do you want, MacLayne? Did you just come in here to tick me off?"

"I came in here to buy a pane of window glass."

"You won't find glass anywhere in this county. I can order it from St. Louis, but it may or may not come. Mail's not real steady now. We ain't getting' much from northern ports anyway. I can try New Orleans, but that will take months."

"Well, order it from both places, then. I've gotta replace a broken window at my place. We can live with it now, but this winter, my house will get mighty cold,"

"You got money to pay for it? Last I heard, a windowpane could cost twenty dollars or more."

"Don't think I've ever failed to pay you, Davis. I do have the money, though. You're actin' like you don't want my business. Did I do something to you?"

"Look, MacLayne, I don't want no trouble in my store. I'll order your glass if you'll pay half down."

"I believe I asked you a civilized question, Mr. Davis. Have I done something to offend you?" Mac gritted his teeth.

"There's a lot of talk around town that you are a traitor to the Southern cause."

"You've known me since I came here, more'n seven years ago. Not one thing is different about me now. I don't know who said I am a traitor, but he's a liar. I am not. I never supported secession, and I don't now. I didn't when y'all elected me to the General Assembly, twice."

"Is it true you refused to give up your mules to help the militia?"

Andy peeked around his father to look at the man behind the counter.

"I'd promised those animals to someone else. I didn't have any more to sell the militia," Mac said.

"I heard you insulted Captain Anderson at Shiloh church a couple of weeks ago." Davis pointed his finger toward Mac.

"That's a bare-faced lie. Papa was the one who got insulted," Andy shouted.

"Andrew, don't get involved in adult business."

"Rumor has it you refused a place of honor as an officer in the militia."

"I refused to serve in a cause I can't support. I won't do it."

"You don't make no sense, man. You let Roy go."

"Roy is a man who has to make his own choices. I didn't want him to go. I pray every day he comes home safely. Mac turned to leave the store, his frustration back again. "Just forget that glass, Davis. This war won't last forever."

Ø

Andy told and retold the story of the Rebels' arrest and lock-up in the Craighead County Courthouse. His friends' reaction bridged the gamut from awe to jealousy that he'd seen the Jonesboro incident. Some of them called him a liar and a show-off making up tales to impress the other boys in the community. The ugliest remarks from his pals did not stop him from telling his story to anyone who would listen.

The following week, Mac returned to Greensboro to have Midnight reshod. He no sooner stepped into the stable where the blacksmith worked over a glowing horseshoe than he heard about the "Battle of Jonesboro."

"Barney, there wasn't a battle. I was there with Andy that afternoon."

"That's not what I heard. A couple of Rebel soldiers opened fire. Seven Union soldiers died right there in the square."

"Rumors sure grow. No one fired a shot that day. The Yankees locked up a couple of dozen Rebs, and then they drove the supply wagons and horses they'd took away from 'em back to the camp."

"Yes, but the next morning at dawn, the Rebs that escaped the first skirmish on the southern side of Jonesboro gathered a troop and broke those prisoners out of the courthouse. They shot it out at the crossin'. You know that low spot below the square that's a good deer huntin' place. Total surprise. Our boys took the day, and killed seven of the Yanks to boot."

Mac shook his head. "I guess Andy and I missed the action. He'll be peeved when I tell him."

That evening when Mac told Andy the rest of the story about the "Battle of Jonesboro", the boy sat quietly. The excitement that had danced in his eyes when he'd told the story to his friends was missing.

"Well, Son, now you have more to tell your friends."

"Did those men we saw the other day die? Seven of those Yanks?"

"When I talked to the constable, he said that ten men had died in the raid the second day. Three Confederate soldiers died, too."

"Golly—they died. Those men I saw. I don't think I want to tell that story anymore. What was the shootin' about in Jonesboro? We don't have no guns or ports or railroads…nothin' worth capturin'."

"War was the reason, Andy. They are enemies in war."

"No. I ain't gonna tell that story no more. I know lots of better things to talk about than that."

# Chapter 10

*Children, obey your parents in all things:*
*for this is well-pleasing unto the Lord.*
*Colossians 3:20*

Laurel dealt with her share of problems on the home front. True, the concerns she faced were not likely to show up in *The True Democrat*, which Mac devoured when he could find a copy. Yet, these issues seemed more urgent and demanded her attention. Some of them were aggravated by the war, yet most would have surfaced as a part of a family's routine regardless.

She spent a great deal of her time with Annie. When Roy joined the Arkansas Eighth Infantry with several of his friends from the Greene County Roughs, Annie fell into a low mood. She cried nearly every day and often isolated herself from the family. Only when Laurel drew her into a useful task did the young woman show some semblance of the happy, energetic girl she'd been at Christmas. At that time, Roy had been home, and the two of them worked on their homestead. Routinely, Laurel made it a point to give Annie chores to do each morning to keep her from crying.

In addition to the work in the garden and orchard, Laurel continued to teach her students. While the Madison boys had not returned since the last vandalism attack, the Flannagans, Susan's two children, Mary Campbell, and Laurel's own kept her more than occupied. This term they were fascinated with geography. Mac fed their curiosity with stories from the newspaper accounts and gossip about local troops. When the Battle of Pea Ridge happened in March, the kids asked questions about the western parts of the state. Laurel could easily talk about the place she grew up and enjoyed sharing part of her youth with them, but when places like Shiloh, Tennessee; Norfolk, Virginia; New Orleans, Louisiana and Fair Oaks, Pennsylvania, made their way into the newspaper, Laurel found her evenings filled, studying to be able to answer their questions about the eastern and deep southern parts of the country that were just as unfamiliar to her. Because she had to use those same newspapers to study as she rocked the evenings away on the front porch, she learned much more about the war than she wanted to know. On occasion, she called on Mac to talk to the students about his youth in Maryland and about Washington City. Cathy always asked about the places where her brother Roy had gone. Thankfully, these battles all happened far from Shiloh. Laurel gave praise that her children were not witnessing the ugliness of war.

Andy didn't seem interested in the stories of the battles. Since the skirmish that occurred in Jonesboro, he found other things more worthy of his time. The Mississippi River and steamboats captivated him. When he poured over the newspapers Mac brought home, he searched out stories that mentioned paddle-wheelers, the multi-decked steamboats that had become the workhorses for supplies during the war. Laurel breathed a sigh of relief that her son had lost interest in the conflict that none of them could avoid.

About the middle of June, Annie's depression worsened. She lost her appetite and picked at her food at every meal.

"Annie, aren't you gonna eat tonight?"

"I'm sorry, Mrs. Mac. I know that stew is good, but I'm not hungry. Not one bit."

"Something is botherin' you besides not bein' hungry." Laurel laid her hand on the young woman's forehead, checking for fever.

"I miss Roy." Tears streamed. "It's not fair. And he don't never write to me." Laurel sat next to her and let her talk. "I don't even know where he is…"

"That has to be hard--not to know."

"He don't care a whit for me. And my pa…. I feel like everyone threw me away." Waves of sobs stopped her from continuing. "I feel so bad. Every day I throw up almost anything I eat. That's why I don't wanna eat. It's better than throwin' up."

"Let's go out and sit on the porch a spell, Darlin'. The air is nice this evenin', and we'll rock a while." Laurel led the way outside. "Now stop cryin', Annie. How long have you been feelin' sick at your stomach?"

"The last couple of weeks, it's been worst. I hate to complain. I know I been so much trouble for this family already. Anyway, since I stopped sellin' eggs and milk, I got no money for a doctor. I'm sure this sickness will go away."

"Annie, did you miss your time last month?" Laurel stood next to her and laid her arm across her shoulder. Color rose in Annie's cheeks.

"May have. I didn't think about it. My mama always warned me that bein' upset causes…well, she said nerves make girls…you know."

"She was a wise woman, Annie. Did she ever tell you that having a baby also makes a woman queasy for a few weeks?"

"She didn't tell me much about babies. We didn't expect her to be gone when I needed to know such things. Now, I ain't got no family at all. My pa disowned me when I eloped with Roy, and he won't let my brother talk to me. Roy deserted me to go fight in a stupid war."

"Calm yourself. You've got a family who loves you right here in this house. In a couple of weeks, we'll know if we should go see Dr. Gibson. And you do need to eat. For a while, bland things may sit better with you. I'll make you some oatmeal if you want or have a piece of warm bread with butter. You may need to avoid milk early in the day."

"Mrs. Mac, do you think I could be havin' a baby? I don't think I can, not alone."

"Annie, you won't be alone, ever. You are a part of this family. The Lord will take care of you until Roy comes home. And he does love you, Annie, very much."

φ

After Independence Day, Laurel drove Annie to Greensboro to see Dr. Gibson. He confirmed what she already knew. Roy and Annie would become parents in the winter. Annie's reaction to the news was a mixture of fear and excitement, joy, and dread. She had not written a letter to tell Roy, wanting to be sure of her pregnancy. Receiving a brief letter from Roy on the first of July buoyed her spirits because she knew he was safe. He continued to serve with the Eighth Arkansas Infantry, and his unit was east of the Mississippi River, not too far from Memphis. Of course, the letter had a date of early June. Before he closed the letter, he told her he was safe and busy. He said he felt good, knowing the Lord was with him every day. In about every other line he wrote he missed her and loved her. His letter closed with a plea for her to write to him and to ask Mac, Brother Matthew, and Andy to write, too.

Laurel suspended school after the Fourth of July. Of course, mid-summer brought ripe vegetables from the garden that Laurel had to can. That added workload with a teething daughter and a pregnant daughter-in-law simply would not allow time to teach. With no school to attend, the children of the MacLayne household had excess time on their hands to get into all sorts of calamities. Praise to the Lord, Edward Gibson was beyond the age of conscription, and he'd decided to remain in Greensboro. Local folks were lucky they had such a good doctor to see to them, as this was rare in 1862. Gracie was the first to require a trip back to Greensboro to see Dr. Gibson.

Laurel and Mac found themselves on emergency trips to town more than once. Gracie refused to accept the fact that she couldn't do everything her big brother was able to do. Like most not-quite-seven-year-olds, she didn't know how to fill her time. The excess of playtime allowed her to put herself into dangerous situations more than once that summer.

The first incident occurred when the MacLaynes planned a family outing with Thomas and his family. Mac drove Laurel, Annie, and his children to their favorite swimming hole at the creek. Thomas MacLayne with Peggy and her children met them under the shade of centuries-old oak trees where they laid out quilts and spread a feast. Andy, Paddy, and Sean rigged an ivy vine to reach the deepest part of the creek. They would take turns swinging out, letting go of the vine, and dropping feet first into the cool, blue water. Cathy and Maureen joined them. Mark Thomas and Gracie were playing in the wading end of the pool, well within easy reach of their parents who watched from the bank. Even Annie had removed her shoes, hoisted her skirt, and walked in the ankle-deep water of Big Creek. The MacLayne adults relaxed, talked, and enjoyed each other's company and the frolicking of their children on the beautiful summer day.

But the laughter and the shenanigans from the young'uns ended that pleasant afternoon when Gracie climbed the tree faster than Andy could stop her, grabbed the vine, and swung over the creek. Then she cried out. The strength in the sassy little girl's wrists couldn't hold the vine long enough to get her feet straight beneath her. She landed flat on her back. The impact knocked the breath from her, and she sank to the bottom of the creek. Laurel screamed. Mac ran to pull Gracie from the water. Andy also reacted immediately. He swung out, dropped, and dove into the swift stream to rescue his sister. Andy's quick reactions and his strong swimming skills took him to her before his father had reached the bank.

As Andy pulled her from the creek, Gracie sputtered, coughed, and spit up water. He carried her to the bank where she looked up into her father's face. The little girl threw herself into his arms and hugged his neck so tightly that Mac choked before he could ease her embrace. He set her on the ground and held her at arms' length. "Why did you do that?"

"Andy did it. So did I."

"Gracie, you have to wait until you are older…big enough to hold onto the vine. You scared your mother and me."

"I'm big enough to play with Andy and Cathy. I ain't no baby."

A stern look on Mac's face ended Gracie's tirade. "I'm sorry, Papa." When the little girl started to take a step away, she fell. A dislocated hip joint resulted from her ill-timed fall. Thank goodness, a doctor was nearby.

About a month later, Mark Thomas showed his too confident nature, too. Laurel sent Andy out to carry in a few small logs to add to the fireplace to increase the fire so she could cook supper. Her youngest son insisted he help his older brother carry in wood. Laurel smiled at his gesture and allowed the four-year-old to help. Mark was never one to follow when he could lead so he ran to the stack under the lean-to. Andy followed but not in much of a hurry.

A scream pierced the quiet afternoon in the barnyard. "Ouch..ow..ow!" Mark Thomas continued to cry out. "Mama…Mama."

When Andy reached the lean-to, he found Mark Thomas pulling the tail end of a snake that had wrapped itself around his arm. The snake had sunk its fangs in Mark Thomas's forearm. Laurel ran around the corner of the shed in time to see Andy pull the scared snake off his brother and hurl it into the cornfield. She grabbed the little boy and pulled him into her chest.

"He bit me, Mama. That snake done bit me. Andy, kill that dang snake. It bit me." Mark Thomas began screaming again, so loudly that he agitated the horses in the corral nearby.

"Hush up, Brother. You're scaring Sassy and Sparky."

"I told ya, I got bit."

"Well, you caused it." Andy rolled his eyes.

"No, I didn't do it. I'm gonna die now. Snake bites are bad."

"Andy, what kind of snake bit your brother?" Laurel asked.

"Oh, Mama, it wasn't nothin' but an old king snake. You know they keep the mice and rats away from the place. That snake wouldn't of bit him if he hadn't jerked it up by its tail."

Laurel nearly laughed from the relief she felt, but she knew how Mark Thomas would react to laughter. She also remembered an encounter with a snake once in her life that had not been quite so funny. She couldn't laugh at his fear. "Come on in, Mark Thomas. Let's go clean up that bite. Even good snakes can cause bad infections, and I don't want my boy sick." She picked him up, kissed his dirt-streaked face, and carried him to the cabin. She'd have a humorous story to tell Mac when he returned from Gainesville that night.

The most serious incident that took the MacLaynes to the doctor gave no reason to laugh. The day in early August was hot, humid, and miserable. Andy saddled Sparky so he could ride to his grandfather's place. He and Sean planned an afternoon of frog gigging and fishing. Gracie told him that she intended to ride along. Taking care of a little sister was not how Andy intended to spend the day.

"No, Gracie. Sean and me got plans. You stay at home with the girls. You can't do boy stuff."

"I wanna go, Andy.

"I ain't takin' ya." Andy searched his pockets. "I gotta go back to the house and get my knife. Got to have a knife to gut frogs and clean fish. You stay away from my stuff." He ran toward the cabin.

Gracie kicked the dirt. She looked back toward Andy. She saw Sparky prancing, just waiting for a rider. She shook her dark, curly head and climbed the side of the stall. She untied the reins and climbed from the top rail on to Sparky's back. Her legs hung to the pony's side as her feet were far from the stirrups. She jerked the reins back and kicked Sparky's sides as she'd watched Andy do often. The bewildered pony took off in a run. Gracie floundered atop him as she could find no way to keep her balance.

"Mama, help me," Andy yelled back as he ran toward the horse. "Gracie done untied Sparky. She's gonna fall." Andy ran faster, but he didn't have to run for long. Before the horse reached the road, Gracie lost her balance and fell. When Sparky reached the fence line, no longer confused by the erratic jerking on his reins and the random kicks into his flanks, he stopped. Gracie lay in the dirt, not moving. Laurel and Andy reached her at nearly the same time.

"Don't try to pick her up, Andy. Let me look at her before we try to move her. She could have broken her neck or her back." The unconscious girl sprawled with her legs and arms in unnatural positions.

"Andy, go see if you can find your Papa. He's at J.F.'s cabin out in the west section. Hurry, son."

During the wait for help, Laurel watched the little girl carefully. Gracie roused briefly a couple of times, but she never fully awakened. She whimpered in pain. At times, she moved her legs and tried to raise her head. Laurel felt sure she had not broken her back or neck. She knew only this beautiful little girl of her best friend needed a doctor. When Mac arrived, he took Laurel and Gracie to Greensboro in the buggy. The ride seemed to last an eternity. Laurel held her closely, trying to buffer the jolts caused by the rough road. Mac pulled up to the hitching post in front of Dr. Gibson's office.

"What ya got there, Mac?"

"Gracie decided to ride a horse this afternoon, Ed. We've told her over and over not to get on a horse without one of us. Sparky didn't take to the idea much. From what we can tell, she's got a pretty bad bump on her head and at least one broken bone. She's so headstrong."

"Lay her there and let me look and see."

Mac laid the frightened youngster on the bed and stepped back. The doctor spent several minutes looking into Gracie's eyes and checking her reflexes before he told Laurel and Mac that the blow to the side of her head had caused a concussion.

"She'll have to stay down a few days. Watch her pretty close for the next two days to make sure nothin' worse comes from that knock on the head. That break is more of a concern. That bone came close to comin' through the skin. See this bulge? Gonna have to set it and splint that leg mighty snug to keep it in place." He walked to a small cabinet in the corner and returned to talk to Gracie. "Young lady, they tell me ya think you're all grown up. Well, I hope so. I'm afraid I gotta hurt ya some more to get your leg back where it will grow straight. Can ya take a little more?"

Her lip trembled. Her wet lashes flickered before she closed her eyes. "Yes, sir. I ain't no baby." Dr. Gibson turned his face to the MacLaynes to hide the near laughter caused by the comment of the "grown-up" six-year-old. "Miss Gracie, you may not be a baby, but for the next few weeks, you do everything your mama and papa tells you to do." After giving her a small dose of laudanum, he began the procedure to reset and splint the broken leg. Gracie didn't cry out, but her whimpers told her parents how much she wanted to. When he finished, the little girl succumbed to the strong painkiller. "Folks, this will take a while to heal. You may have a chore on your hands to keep this one down. If she does well, we'll try a crutch after a couple of weeks."

"Thanks, Ed. You've always taken care of this family," Mac said.

"We are so grateful, Dr. Gibson. You've come between me and disaster too often. Bless you."

"Laurel, when are you goin' to start callin' me, Ed? Mac's never called me Dr. Gibson. Anyway, it's my pleasure to serve. I'm only doin' what I swore to do when I took up my trade."

"Not everyone here in town is willin' to associate with us right now. I appreciate you takin' care of Gracie."

"I know, Mac. I've heard the talk. I also heard that the Partisan Rangers have paid a few visits to you folks."

"Just annoying pranks. The worst thing they've done to us so far is breaking a window. I can't seem to buy any glass to replace it."

"They've done far worse to others. You know they ain't gonna stop. They'll only get bolder and put y'all at more risk."

"What else can we do, Ed? If we leave and go north, we lose all we've worked for. We love our homestead. We love this community."

"We aren't goin' anywhere, Dr. Gibson. Mac and I will defend our home. He is not goin' to war. We are stayin' on our land," Laurel said.

"That what you're plannin' to do, Mac?"

"Since I'm over conscription age, I think I can stand my ground. I'm not breakin' the law. We paid the taxes, even the extra

111

ones added by the war. I just can't fight for the Confederacy. I don't have it in me to fight against my country." Mac sat on the bed next to Gracie.

"Mac, I hope you can keep to your convictions. I pray those bushwhackers will leave you be."

Laurel turned, concern written across her face. "Dr. Gibson, have you heard threats against my husband?"

"Just uneasy times, Laurel. I've always respected Mac. I don't care that he's decided to stay neutral. Lots of folks don't feel the same way is all. Too many men dying and too much loss in many families already. Tempers are runnin' high."

"What can we do about it? Mac has explained that we aren't takin' sides."

"Just be alert. Be ready for those hoodlums who call themselves the Partisan Rangers." Dr. Gibson returned to his patient.

Gracie roused and whispered. "Mama, my head hurts real bad."

"I know, Sweetheart. The doctor is makin' it better."

"Take her home. Keep her still and in bed for a few days. Give her a half a spoon of laudanum if the pain gets too bad, but be sparin' with it. Very hard to come by some medicines now, especially laudanum. If she don't need it, stop it. Not good for her anyway." He handed Laurel a small bottle, not quite half full.

Mac paid the doctor his fee in Confederate bills. "We're beholden for your care and your friendship."

*ϕ*

The second week in September, Annie received a second letter from Roy. When Mac handed her the envelope with the address written in Roy's script, she brought the dingy paper to her lips and kissed the seal.

"Thank you, Lord. I didn't think he'd ever write to me again."

Annie danced across the porch to one of the rocking chairs. She pulled open the letter and squealed with excitement. "Mrs. Mac, Mr. Mac, Roy says he'll be comin' home for Christmas. Their unit is being sent back to Greene County as the home guard."

"Such a blessing, Annie," Laurel replied. "Is there other news?"

"He said he hasn't gotten any letters from home. He don't know about our baby!"

Mac tried to reassure her. "Annie, surely by now he's gotten our letters. See the date is nearly a month old."

"Oh, my goodness. Roy has to know that we're having our baby. And maybe he'll even be home when our little one comes. Home for Christmas…. Thank you, Lord."

Annie hurried into the room she shared with Cathy and Gracie. She began to write a letter to Roy. She would post it as soon as anyone from the family went to a town where the mail was posted. Where did Roy say they were now? South of Memphis headed for Mississippi. She smiled as she wrote, 'All my love, your wife.' She prayed quickly, "Lord, please let Roy be heading for Arkansas very soon."

For the next week, Annie walked on clouds around the homestead. Even the short one-page letter had revived her hope to have her husband returned to her in time to be present at the birth of their first child. Even severe discomforts caused by her growing torso on her slight frame didn't take the smile from her face. Both Laurel and Mac breathed a sigh of relief that Annie had moved out of her depression and was now looking forward to becoming a mother.

# Chapter 11

*Better is it that thou shouldest not vow,*
*than thou shouldest vow and not pay.*
*Ecclesiastes 5:5*

Fall, 1862, on Crowley's Ridge was breathtaking. Perfect amount of rain and sunshine that year mixed to create an array of leaves with splashes of red, gold, orange, brown, and various green hues in Mother Nature's perfect bouquet of autumn. The color cascaded down every hillside and through the fenced pastures. Laurel used every excuse to be out in the glory of fall. This year, she was reminded of home in the Boston Mountains more than at any time since she'd come to Shiloh. She had a taste of homesickness she'd not experienced since Mac had made her his wife.

She intended to reconvene school the first week in November. Harvest had been a boon, and families worked long, hard hours to preserve the Lord's bounty for the coming winter. Haying was nearly finished so the older boys were now free to return to school if their families had the mind to send them. Laurel offered the opportunity to anyone in the area. She wanted to get in as much school as she could arrange before the worst of winter set in. Also, Annie's baby was due early in January. Annie would have her hands full with a new life and certainly would not be able to deal with Mark Thomas and Leah Ann, too. Laurel smiled to herself at the thought of having a new baby in the house. After all, her baby was a healthy toddler now.

Laurel continued to worry about Annie. The young woman's perpetual mood changes tended to the low side unless she could get some word about her husband. Roy's letters were sporadic, to say the least. He mentioned letters he'd sent, but they'd never arrived at Shiloh. Everyone knew the mail system would not be dependable until the Confederate government was able to mandate stable mail routes and provide payment to the men who carried the mail between post offices. The local postmasters seemed to be the only stable part of the entire system.

Since Roy enlisted in June, Annie received three letters. Mac had gotten one letter. News of heavy fighting in Kentucky and Tennessee reported in newspapers added to their anxiety. From local hearsay, everyone in the community knew that the Arkansas Eighth Infantry had been embedded into the Van Dorn Army of the West. Roy's unit had fought in both Kentucky and Tennessee.

On October fourth, Annie received a long-awaited letter from Roy. When Mac handed her the thin note, Annie pulled it to her face and kissed the seal as she did with every precious letter. Tears smeared the ink on the outside of the letter.

> Darlin' wife,
>
> I miss you. If I could just hold you for one hour, I'd know some peace. How's my beautiful Annie? I wish I knew you're okay. Why don't you write to me? Or Mr. Mac? I want to hear from y'all.
>
> If I didn't feel the Lord here with me, I couldn't stand it. I'm not alone here in Mississippi, but, Sweetheart, I am lonely for you.
>
> Yesterday we fought a long fierce battle against thousands of Yanks. I think the town was named Iuka. We put them to runnin' for sure. Some of the fellas said to celebrate. I just felt sick. All the young men, some in blue, others in gray was layin' around, life gone outta their eyes. Hundreds of 'em. I

hate this war. I hate the killin' because I have no good reason to shoot at those Yanks. If they'd just go back up north…

Enough of that…tell Cathy to study hard at school. She needs to stay away from the boys 'til I get home. Tell her that her big brother loves her.

Annie, I got some good news. Captain Murray said we're ordered home. We'll be leavin' the Arkansas Eighth behind about the middle of November. We're comin' back to Greene County. We'll have to serve as the home guard for about six months.

I ain't got no more paper. I'll be home soon. Wife, remember I love ya. I always will.

God bless ya, darlin'
Roy

P.S. Please write to me.


Annie kept the most personal parts of the letter to herself, but she shared most of it with Cathy and her family.

"Thank you, Lord," Mac prayed.

"Roy will be home for Christmas, Mrs. Mac." Annie threw herself into Laurel's arms.

"Yes, Roy will be headed home in about a month. Perhaps he'll not have to leave us again." Laughter rang around the room.

"Mama, I gotta make my brother a special Christmas present. I'm so happy we'll all be together for Christmas." Cathy's smile spoke for them all.

When Laurel convened school on November 1, her class was back up to twelve students. The two Madison boys had returned and a daughter of a neighbor enrolled, too. Her mother, Mrs. Gillian, was a confirmed Confederate woman with two grown sons in the Greene County Roughs. Her daughter was about Cathy's age.

"Mrs. MacLayne, I hope you'll let Beth come to your school. I heard you folks are traitors to the cause, but I don't believe it."

"My husband is neutral. We don't support either side of the war because we don't believe in secession."

"I heard too that your boy Roy is in the Roughs already."

"Yes, that is so. Roy chose the Confederate side."

"Well, my girl wants to learn. Before the war, she talked about teachin', 'course she's got behind now because our school's been closed since '61."

"Beth is welcome here, Mrs. Gillian."

"Can we barter the fee?  Money is rare at our house, but my husband and me are willin' to trade whatever we got."

"I'm not asking for tuition. I may ask Beth to help around the homestead from time to time." Laurel said.

"She's a good worker. I know she'd be glad to help. If the weather turns bad…"

"Keep her at home if it's dangerous to get out, or if it turns durin' the day, I'll keep her here with the others. "

"Thank ya, Mrs. MacLayne. My daughter will be happy when I tell her. I don't care what the neighbors say. You're a fine woman."

"Mac and I are the same people we've always been. We've not changed. I look forward to teaching Beth."

As Laurel and Mac settled into their sanctuary that night, she told him of the pleasant conversation, she'd had with Mrs. Gillian that morning.

" It's about time someone from this community started usin' some common sense. Maybe it's a sign and others will begin to understand that neutral doesn't mean traitor."

"You've been hurt by the reaction of the Shiloh community, haven't you, darlin'?"

"Of course, it hurts. I thought this place would always be my home. These people welcomed me here when I was a sinner, low as they come. I spent ten years in their midst, and now I'm worse than a leper."

"Patrick,I wish I could change things."

"I'm most upset because of how the women have shunned you. You've been nothin' but a blessin' here."

"Don't fret about me. I'm happy. You and most of our kids are here around me and safe. That is all I need. More than I've ever had."

"It's not what you deserve."

"I'll not ask for more, Mac. The Lord gave you to me, Patrick MacLayne, to love me and make me a beloved wife. He's allowed me to become the mother of your children. I know he'll see us through."

"Your name suits you. Since I met that scared little girl in Washington County nearly six years ago, you've become as beautiful as any spring day filled with laurel blossoms across acres and acres of meadow. And grace flows from you like living water. My dear Lord, I love you, Laurel."

Mac pulled her into his arms and kissed her tenderly...then with a ferocity that took her breath. Mac's plan to talk to her about the newest conscription laws was completely forgotten.

The following morning after Laurel stoked the fire, she picked up an old copy of the True Democrat Mac had found in Jonesboro the previous day. She started to wad the paper up when a headline caught her eye.

## REVISED CONSCRIPTION ACT TO BE ENFORCED ACROSS THE STATE

Laurel searched the top of the paper, looking for a date. They rarely found a paper less than two weeks old. Before she could read the article, Mac came in from the barn, carrying a pail of milk and about half a dozen eggs.

"You found out what I planned to tell you about last night, didn't you? I meant to talk to you about it before you enchanted me and swept that bit of news right out of my head."

"This is serious, Mac. Don't treat it as a joke. The first line says the governor changed the age of conscription to seventeen to forty."

"I saw it. I wanted to talk to you about it."

"Talk about it? Mac, this headline says the act is being enforced across the whole state. You aren't forty, yet."

"That's not the issue, Laurel. As more and more men are lost, the age will go up again."

"Can you be drafted into the Confederate army?"

"Not gonna happen, Wife. I'm sorry you found this. I've got several things I need to talk to you about. The legislature in Richmond has been busy passing several laws that we need to talk over."

"Mac, this can't happen. We're not takin' sides. We've paid our taxes. There must be something we can do...pay that exemption fee."

"Laurel, don't get upset. We'll talk later. The kids will be here for school soon. Our kids will be in and ready to eat. I don't want them to hear about this when I can't explain it."

She set about preparing breakfast for Mac and the children, but the chore was not on her mind. Before she sat down for Mac to bless the meal, she'd overcooked the oatmeal and overfilled Mac's coffee cup. Hours would pass before she would find a quiet moment to speak about her greatest fear. And he made matters even worse.

"Laurel, I'm gonna ride over to Gainesville. I want to talk with Jim Bush. He served in the General Assembly for Greene County after I could not run in '60. He was opposed to secession, too."

"I want you to stay at home. What if you run across soldiers who are arresting civilians who haven't volunteered?"

"The army takes time to carry out new orders. We'll hear about any group that is here lookin' for men who have failed to report. I need another opinion. Matthew is out on his circuit."

"I think you oughta stay home."

"I can't hold up in the stash until the war is over. Don't mother-hen me, Laurel Grace."

"Please be careful."

"I will."

"Lord keep you. Please come back early so you can tell me more about what you've learned."

Mac kissed her and walked to the barn.

On his ride across the countryside to Gainesville, Mac tried to analyze the options he had. Foremost, his promise to Laurel seemed to be the stumbling block to every plan he devised. How many times had he spoken those words to her? *No, Laurel Grace. I'll not go to war. I'll never leave you alone again. As long as it's God's will, we'll be together.* Was it God's will that he join the army? If so, he'd have to enlist in the Union army. He had no desire to leave Shiloh. For so many reasons, being conscripted into the Confederate army was not an option for him. He didn't believe in slavery. He resented the cotton aristocracy being exempt from service if they owned twenty or more slaves. Arkansas's financial future was dismal for years to come and burdened even more by war debt. Mac believed in the Union and the hope of a free nation where he could raise his family and prosper through his hard work.

He hated feeling isolated in the community he loved. He was angry that his stance for his beliefs put his family in danger. Roy's safety plagued his thoughts daily and filled his prayers every night. Now he faced an even worse fear. If he broke his pledge to Laurel, would he lose the woman he'd come to love more than life itself?

Mac found Jim Bush sitting on a fence rail overlooking a newly-cut hayfield. Several well-fed steers grazed there. "Mornin', Jim."

"MacLayne. It's been a while. What brings you over to this neck of the woods?"

"Wanted to talk, if you have a while."

"Surely do. What's on your mind?"

"Jim, I know you voted against secession when we served in the house in '60. I heard you voted against secession at the first convention. How's this affecting you now?"

"At times, folks have been downright mean. Others don't seem to care one way or the other. You havin' problems over your way?"

"Minor stuff...bushwhackers who tell us they've been sanctioned by the governor have done some minor vandalism. Closer to the state line, they tried to burn out one family they called traitors. Some of our neighbors give us the cold shoulder."

"The local lawman ought to do something about those outlaws. Their only rules come from the man they elected as captain. He says act in the name of the Confederacy, and they follow orders. I doubt the Rebel army sees much of what they are stealing from our local folks. Most of 'em act out of spite and greed."

"You had trouble with bushwhackers over this way?"

"We did for a while, but a few of my neighbors and I confronted that pack one night and scared 'em off. We were told they'd joined up with a pack in the bootheel. Thought maybe they'd gone back up to Missouri."

"What have ya heard about the conscription laws they're proposin'? When the governor announced the first round of conscription in the spring, my oldest son enlisted in the Greene County Roughs. His wife is scared to death...our whole family, to tell the truth."

"Must be hard, having a son in the Confederate army."

"No worse than having a child in any army at war."

"But Mac, you're so against the Confederacy."

"No, not the Confederacy. The split in the Union is what I can't support. You've been in the legislature. You know what's gonna happen to Arkansas without federal support and funds.

"Can't take their money without their rules, too. Hope this war won't go on much longer." Jim Bush wiped his forehead.

"What are you gonna do about the new conscription law, Jim?"

"Not one thing. I turned forty on my last birthday in August. I'm stayin' on my homestead."

"And what will you do when enough of our young men get killed off, and they raise the age to forty-five or fifty?

"Guess I'll cross that bridge when I come to it. You at that bridge now, MacLayne?"

"I am, Jim. I'm thirty-nine."

"You're in a hard place. You got a big family to take care of, don't ya?"

"I do. My wife and I have six young'uns, both ours and adopted. Roy is servin' now. Thank the Lord, my pa is near-by, so I know he'll help see to my family."

"You could leave the state for a spell until you have your next birthday."

"That's not gonna help. Before the next year passes, they'll raise the age again. Too many young men are dyin' in those huge battles in the east. You can't pick up a paper without seein' those terrible numbers—on both sides."

"Man, I haven't looked at a paper since I left Little Rock after the secession convention. I don't wanna know what's happenin' outside Greene County, I guess. It's bad enough local."

"Only a month ago, more'n a few Greene County boys died in a little skirmish in a town in Mississippi—Iuka. Our Roughs are deployed with the Army of the West fighting under VanDorn and Sterling. Roy wrote to us about that battle in his last letter."

"Well, if I have to go, I guess I'll go with my state. I hope it won't come to that."

"That's my prayer, too. Take care, Jim. I need to get back across the way to Shiloh. By the way, you don't know where I can find a pane of glass?"

"It'd be a miracle to find one in this county. I hear they've got the most regular supply deliveries in Greensboro."

"Yeah, the wagons come pretty often, but they are half loaded and carry only staples. The stores haven't had any glass in nearly a year. Bless ya, my friend. Take care of yourself."

Mac turned Midnight back toward Craighead County and walked him a good part of the way. He was in no hurry to face Laurel. Telling her about the change in the conscription law could not be delayed any longer. As he rode on southward toward home, Mac prayed continually. Yet, he felt no answer to his repeated plea. *God, show me how to explain to Laurel what I have to do.* The despondency he felt was akin to the depths of his despair after he killed his best friend in a senseless duel. The scowl on his face reflected this inward pain. As he rode on through one of the many "tree tunnels" crossing the path back home, he heard a familiar voice, one that he'd missed sorely in the past months.

"Wilt Thou not regard my call? Wilt Thou but accept my prayer? Lo, I sing, I faint, I fall! Lo, on Thee I cast my care! Reach out Thy gracious hand…"

"Matthew! The Lord has answered my prayer." Mac jumped from Midnight and approached the fallen log where his best friend sat. "What are you doin' out here?" Mac embraced his friend and pounded him on the back.

"Singin' to the Lord, brother. I love that old hymn, *Jesus, Lover of my Soul.* Can't think of a better way to rest."

"I don't think I ever heard you sing that one at church."

"It's personal praise, I guess. The church don't much like the word choices Wesley used, I guess. Speaks for me many a day."

"I'm so glad to see you, Matthew. I've missed you—hearing you preach, but mostly havin' you here to talk to when I can't work out my problems. How've you been?"

"Too busy. I spend a couple of weeks at a time making a circuit around the camps, hospitals, and even a skirmish site or two. So many young men are dyin' out there, callin' for a touch from anyone."

"I don't know how you stand it."

"One day at a time, tryin' to ease the fear, pain, loneliness...Hang it all, Mac. Too many of these men are dyin' and don't know the Lord. I'm able to help so few."

"But Matthew, if you weren't out there servin', some of them wouldn't have anyone to ease their passin'. Thank the Lord for you and others who are doin' the work you are tryin' to do."

"Thank ya, Mac. But I doubt that greetin' was to say thank you for becomin' a chaplain."

"You know me too well. Matthew, I've got to go home and tell Laurel that I am leavin' to join the Union army. I see no other way for me. She's gonna despise me. I told her I'd not leave her alone again."

"She won't despise you. Laurel loves you to the core of her bein'. To tell ya the truth, I've been concerned about you too. Lots of talk around the camps about the new conscription laws. Some of the bigger camps are beginnin' to send out officers to bring in the men who have not volunteered."

"The stories have been in the Little Rock papers pretty often. The True Democrat has an article just about every time I can get my hands on one."

"Let's saddle back up and get on the trail. I wanna sleep in my bed tonight. I ain't seen Ellie in more'n three weeks."

"We'll have to ride hard to get back by sundown. Lorado is a piece from Shiloh."

"Well, we can talk as we go." Matthew pulled the reins to turn his horse, and they rode across the meadow together.

"You shoulda known not to make a promise like that to Laurel, Mac. We never know what the next day will bring."

"I know, but I've been away so often since we married. I can't believe she stayed with me this long."

"But look how much she's grown since y'all came here. Laurel can handle any crisis that comes. She's not that frightened, helpless spinster you married, in case you haven't noticed."

"I know. She isn't timid or helpless anymore, but she looks at separation as if I am rejectin' her. I've been away during some horrible times in her life."

"And she survived every one. She knows you aren't her strength, brother. Do you know it?" Matthew's candid remark brought silence. For some distance, only the rhythm of horse hooves broke the quiet of the Crowley's Ridge sunset.

"Matthew, how can I tell Laurel so she understands? I don't want to leave Shiloh, but I have to go. It's the only way I can safeguard our family."

"I got no words, Brother. Ellie and me had a conversation when I left our church appointment. We prayed about it long and hard. She cried a while, and then she kissed me and said I had to do the Lord's work."

"I'm not bein' called to preach, Matthew."

"You don't know what the Lord will put in your path. Go home and read the fifth chapter of Ephesians...I mean read it over and over. Read Hebrews 4 and study I Peter 3. Look at the advice he gives about the wife. If you can grasp those words, you'll know how to approach Laurel. Remember, Brother, you don't have to do this alone."

"I'll try, Matt. Thanks…here's my cut-off home. You gonna preach this Sunday?"

"Maybe to a few at my place. The Shiloh church has a new lay pastor. Some of the members don't like me ministering to just any soldier who needs me."

"Only those who never really knew you. Bless you, my friend. Visit me whenever you're home."

"God keep y'all, Mac." As the two friends took their separate paths, the sun glowed red setting behind the ridge.

# Chapter 12

*But though He cause grief, yet will He have compassion according*
*to the multitude of His mercies. For He doth not afflict willingly*
*nor grieve the children of men.*
*Lamentations 3:32-33*

Mac sat before the blazing fireplace, holding his sleeping daughter. He took in every feature of Leah Ann's beautiful face—a rosy blush on her baby skin, her long eyelashes splayed across satin cheeks as she slept, and the fine tawny curls twisting their way down the side of her face. *This must be the image Mark Campbell saw all those years ago when he held Laurel as an infant.* Mac adored this little girl, the spitting image of his beloved wife.

Only when Laurel called his name did home become a real place to him again.

"Patrick, you haven't heard one word I've said. What are you thinking about?" The tone of her voice showed her irritation at his inattention.

"Sorry, Darlin', I was lookin' at our precious daughter as she slept. She's changin' so fast. Every day she gets to look more like you."

"Let me put her in the crib. She's been sound asleep the whole time I've been getting the other kids to bed."

126

"No. I want to hold her a while longer. Babies grow up in front of our eyes, and they are not babies anymore. I missed all those years with Andy and too much of the time with Mark Thomas. Let me watch this one as long as I can."

"What's brought on this nostalgia, Mac? I don't know that I've seen it before."

"Circumstances of life, I guess."

"That's been on my mind all day. It's been a miserable day. Keeping my attention on the school activities was next to impossible. Tell me about those two newspaper articles you seem so worried about."

"I'll tell you in a few minutes." Mac paused, stood up, and carried Leah Ann to her bed in the corner of their room. "Laurel, when I went to talk with Jim Bush, I thought he'd tell me that he shared the same worries I have. We've been of a like mind in votes in the General Assembly on about every issue—especially anything that dealt with secession bills."

"I was pretty sure the meetin' didn't go as you'd hoped. You've been far too quiet since you got back."

"No. I was surprised. Jim said he was gonna ignore the war because he was past forty. Then he told me if he was forced to serve, he'd go with the state."

"You must have been disappointed." Laurel laid her hand against his bearded cheek.

"I can't make any sense of it. Guess it doesn't matter anyway, but it wasn't what I hoped for when I rode over to Gainesville." Mac shook his head. "The only good that came from that long wasted trip was meetin' up with Matthew over around Lorado."

"Uncle Matthew is home?" A smile lit her face.

"Yes. Said he wanted to be home with Ellie and Mary for a spell. He's only gonna make one more circuit before Christmas."

"Has Uncle Matthew seen much call for his work here in this part of the state?"

"Too much, according to him. Sickness is rampant in the camps, some wounded men, and far too many who need the Lord.

He feels compelled to continue even though he hates being away from his family."

"I miss his preaching and singing."

"Matthew is gonna preach at his place on Sunday. We could go if you want. It'd give us a chance to visit. Do you want to go?"

"You know I do. Now I want you to stop the petty talk and tell me what you've learned from the papers." Mac went to his bureau and took out several newspapers he'd found over the past few months. The St. Louis Dispatch didn't have any news about the laws in Arkansas, but several of the broadsheets from Little Rock, Batesville, and Helena carried detailed accounts of the major battles happening in the east. The papers also reported the staggering numbers of deaths and injuries being inflicted on both sides.

"Mac, this is horrible. So many young men."

"That's the reason the conscription laws have been changin', Laurel."

"When did all this happen?"

"The first law calling men to service happened last year, nearly as soon as the war started. The Confederate legislature passed a law, but each state was required to pass its laws. State's rights is a major issue for the Confederacy."

"So Arkansas didn't have to conscript men to serve?"

"Well, I guess the state could have refused, but it wasn't likely since we voted to secede."

"So that is the main reason Roy re-enlisted. Thank the Lord, you didn't have to go."

"I didn't have to go yet. Laurel, there are three laws now that have been passed by our legislature that will change everything. I want you to listen to me—if you understand, we can make this decision together when the time comes. I fear we will have to make it."

"I don't understand, Mac. You promised me that you were not going to serve. Surely, you don't think they can make you go. Isn't taking care of your wife and children a good enough reason?"

"Let me tell you about the laws. Then we'll leave it with God. We don't have to do anything for a while."

Mac went on to explain the three laws that loomed over his family. He didn't tell Laurel these laws would eventually make it impossible for him to remain at Shiloh. He showed her the articles that supported all he told her. The Conscription Act of Arkansas, The Alien Enemy Act, and The Sequestration Act had all been ratified by the General Assembly, and each made Mac's situation worse. As long as he was "too old" to be conscripted, he would remain with Laurel and protect his family. When the age changed to forty or forty-five, his presence would become a threat to their welfare. Any man who refused to serve the Confederacy was considered a traitor—an enemy to be eliminated without trial.

"But Mac, you don't know the age will be raised."

"It will, darlin'. But for now, I'm watchin' things. I will stay as long as God wills it. Perhaps I'll never have to go.

"Maybe the war will end. We can't continue to lose so many men. Their sacrifice will devastate this state.

"It won't do any good to worry over something we can't control. Right now all we can do is leave it in His hands and go on with life the best we can--cherish each other and our kids every day." Mac pulled his tearful wife into his arms and held her for several minutes. He tilted her head toward his and kissed her. "Every day...Laurel. We have to live every day."

No day passed that Annie didn't read Roy's letter. The cheap writing paper began to separate in the folds from its frequent handling. Her conversations with Laurel and Cathy took on a liveliness that had been missing since Roy's deployment. Hope bubbled up in her voice. "Mrs. Mac, I want to make this a special Christmas for Roy. When do you think the Greene County Roughs will get back to stand home guard?"

"Sweetheart, we've not heard any more than you have. Surely won't be long now. It's only seven weeks 'til Christmas."

"Do you think Roy will be upset to see me like this?" Annie laid her hand on her well-rounded torso. "He's not seen me since I found out about the baby."

"Knowing Roy, he'll be so excited with the news, he'll never see past your pretty face. You know he wants to be home as much as you want him here."

"Oh, Annie, it will be so wonderful for our family to be back together again. As a big brother, Roy can be a pain, but I miss him somethin' terrible," Cathy said.

"I know but having you here with me has been so good. You're gonna be the best aunt to this baby."

They turned back to the stitching of tiny gowns and soft blankets. The newest member of the Dunn family would be well-provided for.

Mac pushed through the backdoor, shaking the rain from his hat. "This rain was a drizzle when I left Greensboro, but I began to wonder if I was gonna get home before the flood kicked in."

"Come on over near the fire and give me that wet coat and scarf. The last thing I want is a husband sick with the grip."

"I'm comin'. I can't believe how cold it got all of a sudden." Mac shivered.

"Did you get the news you were looking for, Mac?" Laurel continued to remove the water from the heavy coat. "Were there any newspapers in town?"

"I found one Little Rock paper, but nothing from St. Louis. No mail came from Maryland either. I did find something else of interest. A traveling photographer has come to town. He's been making his way to the battlefields in the western part of Tennessee and Mississippi."

"Just what's so interestin' about a photographer?" Andy asked.

"I asked him to come to Shiloh on Saturday to make family photographs of us, Papa's household, and Matthew's, too. I hope Matt's back from his circuit before then." The words fell out so quickly and upbeat, Laurel was surprised. A broad smile graced her face.

"Isn't it very expensive, Mac?" Laurel asked.

"Whatever it costs, it's something I've wanted for a long time. I remember how your papa loved to look at that portrait of your mama that hung just above his bed…and that was just a drawing."

"Yes. Papa did love that picture of my mother, but the extravagance in a time like this…"

Mac cut her off. "No more quibbling. I am gonna have these photographs done. Please plan for what everyone will wear on Saturday. I want Annie, Andy, Cathy, Gracie, Mark Thomas, Leah Ann, you and me in one big group. I got a family I'm proud of. I wanna be able to show folks."

"Not me, Mr. Mac. Not like this." Annie looked down.

"Not to worry, Annie. You can use my wool shawl and stand behind the chair."

When Saturday came, a strange-shaped wagon, much like the one Mac used to bring her back from Bolivar, pulled into the still muddy yard. A middle-aged, graying native of Ohio pulled his team of two ancient horses to a stop near the back porch.

"MacLayne, O'Rourk is here. Where can I shelter me animals, Man?"

Mac, followed by Andy, Cathy, Mark Thomas, and Sean Flannagan, hurried out to greet his guest and show him the way to the barn.

"You did say ya had a large family. Is this all of 'em?"

"Not quite. And two more families will join us tomorrow. We are happy to have ya here."

"Think the others can make it here in this foul weather? Taking a photograph seems a trivial thing to most folks."

"They'll be here."

"Well, tell me what kind of pictures you'll be a wantin'. I'll need to prepare the glass slides tonight. I'll want to have plenty to do the job."

Mac went on to explain what each family had requested. "Mr. O'Rourk, before you get too involved, come join us for supper. My wife lays a fine table, especially when we have company."

That evening and the following day turned into an early winter party. Matthew and his family had not visited as often as they did before the war because he was gone so much with his chaplaincy work. Mac sought out an empty corner where he and Matthew could use this opportunity to catch up on the conversations that had always been so important in their friendship.

Sunday became a full day of activity, too. The extended family who'd crowded into the MacLayne house for an overnight stay were no worse for the lack of comfortable beds. Matthew convened church services in the MacLayne's main room shortly after breakfast. The family sang their favorite old hymns before they listened to a stirring message on gratitude. The family partook of communion that Sunday morning, along with their visitor, a ritual they had sorely missed since the war had taken Matthew Campbell from the pulpit of Shiloh church. He closed the service singing the words of Psalm 121. The beauty of the words and the gift of Matthew's beautiful voice left the little congregation silent for a time. "Now, go in peace. Amen."

The family didn't have far to go. Peggy, the recent bride of Mac's father, Laurel, and Annie prepared a fine Sunday dinner. All ate their fill of rabbit stew, fresh-baked bread, fried potatoes, and brown beans. The huge amount of food disappeared within minutes. Peggy then placed a tall cake on the table. She had created it from a bit of flour, some honey, as sugar was scarce, a dash of cinnamon, and several egg whites that she had beat into stiff peaks. She called it Angel Food.

Shamus O'Rourk then went about his business, taking photograph after photograph until everyone had gotten exactly what they wanted. Even Annie sat for a portrait. She said it would be a present for Roy at Christmas.

$$\phi$$

Would that every memory could be so sweet. About noon on the first Saturday in December, Captain James Anderson knocked at the door of the MacLayne home. When Laurel opened the door, the color drained from her face. *Why was this leader of the local Confederate troops standing on her porch? Was he there to confront Mac again?*

"Good afternoon, Mrs. MacLayne."

"Captain Anderson." Laurel acknowledged his presence. "Is there something you need from us, Sir?"

"Is your husband home today?"

"Yes. He's around the homestead somewhere."

"Can you ask him to come in, please?"

Laurel called to Andy in the loft. "Son, will you go out to the barn and corral to see if your papa is there. If so, tell him we have a visitor."

"Yes, Mama." He ran out the backdoor.

"Mrs. MacLayne, does Annie Dunn live with you?"

"She does. Annie has been staying with us since Roy left with you to go join the Arkansas Eighth Infantry. Roy is our adopted son."

"I'd heard that." Anderson stood silently until Mac and Andy entered. "You're still here, MacLayne."

"Where else would I be, Jim? I told you I was gonna take care of my family. That's exactly what I'm doin'. Did you come over here to see if I lied to you? You can see, I didn't."

"We'll see how much longer you can shirk service to the Confederacy, MacLayne. The new laws are bein' enforced here in Arkansas now. Just a matter of time before they come and ask you to take the loyalty oath and show your support for the Confederate cause."

"We'll have to cross that bridge when we come to it. I prefer not to talk about such matters in front of my wife and kids."

"Doesn't matter to me. I didn't come here today to talk about you. Is Annie Dunn here?" Captain Anderson shuffled from foot to foot.

"She's resting. Annie's approaching motherhood has been tiring for her. She naps most days in the early afternoon," Laurel explained.

"Is she doin' poorly?" A frown came over the gray-clad man.

"No more than any other first-time mother-to-be who is only seventeen years old. Her baby is due within twelve weeks. Of course, like any other woman, she misses her husband."

"I need to speak to her. I'm afraid I have bad news." At that comment, Cathy broke into tears, and Andy's face lost its color.

"I'll bring her in, Laurel. Will you see to the other kids?" Shortly Mac walked with Annie toward the fireplace where the Captain stood. "Jim, this is Annie Dunn, Roy's wife."

"Good afternoon, Mrs. Dunn. I come as the bearer of bad news, I'm afraid." Annie's knees buckled, and Mac pulled her closer. "Roy was killed by Yankee fire at the Battle of Corinth on October 4th. He was a gallant soldier, carried our standard into the midst of the fray at Battery Hill. He was the fourth of our brave men to hoist the flag against the invaders. The day before, Roy saved the lives of four of his fellow troop members by downing a Yankee sniper nest with his excellent sharpshooting. Roy Dunn died a hero's death, Mrs. Dunn. You can be proud of him. Greene County will always honor him."

Annie shed no tears. Her stoic face gave no hint of any emotion. "No, you've made a mistake, Sir. Roy's comin' home for Christmas. He wrote me a letter…"

Cathy screamed out, "You let them kill my brother." She doubled over with sobs. Laurel sat with her on the floor, letting her pour out the grief too great for a thirteen-year-old orphan to bear. Roy had been her last family member remaining.

"Damn, Yankees…I'm gonna get.."

"Andy, son. Not now. Angry words only hurt when we grieve." Mac picked up the shocked girl who continued to tell everyone her husband was coming home any day. He carried her to the bedroom, and Laurel followed with Cathy.

Mac returned to the main room. "Is there more?"

"The Roughs returned home yesterday with reports of our losses. We got hit hard. Three officers, includin' me, are out today takin' the news to the families. Please express the condolences of the troop and our respect to Mrs. Dunn."

"Where is Roy's remains?"

" In a country cemetery not too far from Corinth, Mississippi. I'm sorry, MacLayne."

"We appreciate your sympathy."

134

"I can't say I like your politics. A man should stand with his own, but I have a great deal of respect for your takin' in those Dunn kids like you did. Mighty generous of you."

"Not generous at all. Roy was one of the best workers I've ever known. He supported his grandmother and his sister before the ice storm in '58. Roy was our son. We love him."

"Again, I am sorry Roy's gone. He was a fine soldier--a tribute to our county and state. I hope things go well with you, MacLayne. I do." Captain Anderson put his hat on and left the cabin.

"Papa, I'm sorry I lost my temper. I didn't mean to say that bad word. I know better. I can't believe Roy's gone. He's dead, just like my ma and my grandpa. People I love are always dying and leaving' me." Andy broke down in his father's arms.

"Andy, Roy's not gone—not really. Roy believed in the promise of resurrection. He's in Heaven now. Someday we'll all be together again." Mac picked up Mark Thomas who stood pulling on his shirt sleeve. He sat in his armchair near a warming fire, holding his sons, thanking God they were too young to be pulled into the fray. He began to sing in a quiet tender way,

> *Jesus is fairer—Jesus is purer*
> *That makes the wounded heart to sing—*
> *Jesus shines brighter than all*
> *The Angels band can boast...*

# Chapter 13

*My grace is sufficient for thee: for my strength is made perfect in*
*weakness. Most gladly, therefore, will I rather glory in my*
*infirmities that the power of Christ may rest upon me.*
*II Corinthians 12:9*

December was cold and wet. The dreary weather matched
the mood at the MacLayne home. Since the news of Roy's loss,
grief and tears happened more often than not. Annie came to terms
with the reality of her husband's death at Corinth after a few days.
It was then that Laurel began to worry if Annie would carry her
baby to term. Annie seemed unable to control her emotions at all.
One day she would cry, great jerking sobs, for what seemed to be
hours. On other days, she would hide in the bedroom, away from
heat and family for an entire day. She refused to eat many times.
No one could coax her into family gatherings where she could be
comforted.

Cathy became somber and angry at the loss of her brother,
as well. In the five years since they'd lost their grandmother in the
ice storm of '58, she and Roy had developed a strong bond. Cathy
tried at times to comfort her sister-in-law, but more often than not,
the grief overtook them both, and they cried together.

Laurel lengthened the school days and added things to their
days' work they'd not studied before. Keeping the children

136

occupied seemed to bring back some semblance of the home life they'd known before. Laurel asked Cathy to teach the youngest students their alphabet and how to write their letters. When she was busy, her mood lifted and hints of the happy girl she'd been before the news of Roy came to light.

On the afternoon in early December, Mother Nature gave a helping hand. Snow began to fall shortly after the noon meal. The acorn-sized flakes, dancing outside the windows near the table where the students were studying, provided too much distraction. Before the hour was up, the students were begging to go outside and play in the first snowfall of winter.

"Well, first your papa has to take the Flannagans back to granddad's place. We don't know how bad this storm will be."

"This ain't no storm, Mama. It's just snow."

"Andy, we'll study until your papa gets home and then we'll have a long recess." Laurel put the older children back to their books, but Mark Thomas bounded around the room in his three-year-old exuberance, pleading to go out and make snow angels. By the time Laurel allowed them to put away their slates and books, nearly two inches of snow had fallen, covering the yard, nearby fields, and the road to Shiloh. At four o'clock, Mac drove into the yard, and before he could stable his team, Andy, Gracie, and Mark Thomas stumbled out the backdoor imploring Mac to let them stay outside for an hour or so. Even Cathy joined them.

"Are you sure you want to be out here? It's mighty cold," Mac said.

The reply came in squeals, hoorays, and laughter.

"Well, if your Mama said it's all right, you can stay out until the sun sets over the ridge or until you can't stand the cold any more...whichever comes first. Stay close by, though."

Mac brought the team into the barn and began to carry firewood to the back porch. As he worked, he smiled at the antics of his children. He looked at Cathy and saw a real smile on her face. So much joy, the first since...*Oh, thank you, Dear Lord, for the gift of the snowfall. What a beautiful day. Bless you, for giving my children back their childhoods, at least for a few hours.* Mac went to the cabin and called Laurel to the window to watch the frolic outside.

"It would be so wonderful if we could encourage Annie to go play with them, too. She's been as low today as she's been since the day Captain Anderson told her Roy died a hero's death. What a cruel thing to say to her."

Mac laid his arm across his wife's shoulder. "Only time can heal that hurt, darlin'. Perhaps when the baby comes, Annie will see her blessings and put her grief aside."

"I pray it is so. She is so young to feel so dead inside."

At dusk, the snow-covered kids ran through the back door. They weren't laughing anymore. "Papa, where are you? We need you now!" Andy screamed out, not finding his parents in the kitchen. Tears streaked Gracie's face, and Cathy pulled her against her side to stifle her sobs.

"Andy, what's all the yellin' about? Are y'all frozen now? Ready to call it a night?"

"Papa, we can't find Mark Thomas! We looked everywhere. He ain't nowhere in our yard or the barn or no place."

"Andy, calm down. He can't be far. Y'all didn't leave the yard, did ya?" Mac knelt in front of his shaking son to meet him eye to eye.

"Not exactly, but we was playin' hide and seek. Mark Thomas wanted to be IT, so we hid and then he came lookin' for us...well, he was supposed to come but he didn't."

"We called him, Papa, but he wouldn't answer us, "Cathy explained.

"Didn't ya think he was awful little to be IT?" Mac asked.

"He wanted to do it. He always wants to do the big kid stuff." Andy defended himself and his sisters.

"I'll get my coat and go get him. He wandered away, I'm sure. Tell your mama where I've gone." Mac hurried outside and began to call out to his three-year-old. Snow continued to fall and the visibility was limited. "Mark Thomas, answer me. Call out and I'll come to get you, Son."

Mac got no reply. "Son, I'm not mad at you. Please call out to me. This is your papa. It's time to come home for supper." He listened, but again he didn't hear his son call to him.

The light was all but gone. He went to the barn and found a lantern. With the feeble orange glow from the kerosene light, he walked to the edge of the woods beyond the corral. The shadows on the ground made tracking difficult, but the faint, eerie light let Mac make out one large boot track in the snow. He knew this was not the footprint of a child. Crouching near the ground, he followed the boot tracks toward the creek. There he found hoof prints from at least two horses. Mac cried out, "Mark Thomas!" *Lord, please don't let us lose another son! Where is our boy?*

Mac's prayer brought clarity to him. His son had been taken. He ran back to the cabin. "Andy, go out and saddle Midnight for me. I've got to find Mark Thomas. I believe someone has taken him."

"Oh, my Lord, no!" Laurel dropped back into the rocking chair. "Who would take Mark Thomas?" She began to cry.

Mac pulled her into his arms and whispered, "Laurel Grace, don't go to pieces. I'm goin' to get our boy, but you have to stay strong to take care of the rest of our family."

"Where will you go? Do you know where they came from or where they went? You can't follow a trail in the dark. With this snow falling, there won't be a trace left by morning."

"I said get hold of yourself….I'm going to get some men to help me search. At first light, we'll set out. I've got a hunch about who's behind this."

Laurel pulled away. "I can't deal with any more loss. Haven't we been dealt enough sorrow to last us a lifetime?" She cried out.

Mac put his hands on her shoulders and held her at arm's length. He shook her roughly. When he spoke, his voice carried authority. "Stop this at once. You are strong enough to hold this family together. Remember, we aren't alone. We never have to deal with difficult times alone unless we choose to. I need you to take care of our children. I will find Mark Thomas. I know you can do this. I know your faith is strong, Laurel Grace. Use it now. We can do what we have to do—together."

"Mac..."

"Promise me, Laurel. I need you to take care of our home."

"I will. Please be careful and bring Mark Thomas back to us."

Mac went to the barn and Andy followed him. "Papa, I'm sorry. I shoulda been watchin' my brother when we was outside."

"Andrew, this isn't your fault. Right now, you have a job to do while I'm gone. Go in and help your mama take care of our family. I'm gonna bring your brother home, but I need some help." Mac mounted Midnight and headed down the road to his father's house.

Within half an hour, Mac dismounted at his father's porch. He knocked but didn't wait for anyone to open the door. Thomas MacLayne met his son in the dining room where his newly acquired family was at the supper table.

"Come in here, son. Want a cup of coffee to chase the cold?"

"Pa, I got no time. Mark Thomas has been abducted. It's gotta be that gang of hoodlums, calling themselves the Partisan Rangers. They've been harassing us and other families that haven't supported the Confederacy."

"Surely not, Patrick. What would they want with a little boy? He's got no value for them."

"Pa, that group is led by an old enemy of Laurel's from Washington County. He also tried to steal a part of Shiloh with a false land claim. We stopped that. He hates me because we stood up to him and his partner. They lost a lot of money when they had to pay Peggy and her children for the fraud they attempted. Robert Duncan swore revenge then."

"Thomas, dear, Mac is right about that Duncan man. His partner and that evil man caused Paddy to die. They ran him off the land. I'd not put anything past that man." Peggy handed Mac a cup of coffee.

"Well, Son, let's get after them. Must be a pack of cowards to go after a little boy. We'll teach 'em to attack my grandson."

"We'll go at first light. Can you help me gather a group of men to search? I'll go to Matthew now. Please finish your supper and then go to some of your help and neighbors."

"I'll go now, Son. I couldn't eat, knowin' little Mark Thomas may be in harm's way."

"Thanks. The coffee helped, Peggy. Pa, tell anyone who will help to meet me at Shiloh church at sunrise."

φ

Midnight galloped down the snow-covered road, taking Mac to see his best friend. He hardly noticed the cold and brutal wind, which blew the heavy snowfall in blankets across the region. He kept his head tucked into his collar and scarf. He prayed as he and his great stallion raced toward the Campbell homestead. Mac hoped against all reason that he'd find his best friend at home.

As he rode into Matthew's yard, Mac called out, "Matthew, Matthew Campbell, I need your help."

Ellie came to the door. "Mac, what's wrong? Why are you out so late and on such a night?"

"Ellie, I gotta talk to Matthew. He's not a circuit somewhere, is he?"

"No. He's in the barn. He just brought in the last of our stock out of the storm. Go on around back, but first, tell me what's happened."

"Someone's taken Mark Thomas from our place. I think the Confederate Partisan Rangers did it. My boy's been gone since before supper. He must be scared out of his wits."

"My sweet Laurel. How much more can she deal with? She must be beyond her limits."

"Just pray for us, Ellie."

Mac pulled the reins to turn Midnight back toward the barn. He saw the light glowing through the partially opened door. He jumped down and ran into the barn.

"Matthew, I gotta have your help. Someone's abducted Mark Thomas. We have to find him."

"Slow down, Brother. Give me the details while I saddle a horse. We'll gather a posse and we'll begin a search."

At daybreak, seven men joined Mac and Matthew at Shiloh Church. Two neighbors, who'd been quite cold to Mac since the confrontation with Colonel Anderson back in the early fall, came to help search.

"Thank you for comin', Granville and Jacob. I know y'all aren't too pleased with me right now, but I'm so glad to see ya both here."

"MacLayne, we'll put our politics aside until we find your son," Granville Stephens said.

"Ain't no real man gonna make war by usin' a baby to bargain. No, sir. Mark Thomas is a child of our community. We aim to get him back home." Jacob Meadows slammed his fist down on the pulpit. "That group has been causin' trouble for too many of us—not just Yankee sympathizers."

Matthew clapped the man, who was a member of his former congregation, on the back. "Bless you, Brothers. What's the plan, Mac?"

Mac outlined a search pattern they'd start as soon as the sun rose. Matthew divided men into search teams of three. He poured each man a cup of coffee. Then he asked them to join him in prayer. By the time the first glimmer of light showed through the windows on the east side of the church, each team rode away. They searched every abandoned cabin, barn, and shed in the area. They walked into caves and lifted low branches they couldn't see under. The search continued for hours. They had one goal— finding Mark Thomas and returning him to the family who loved him.

Yet, at the end of a long cold day, no sign of the Partisan Rangers or the missing three-year-old had surfaced. At nine o'clock, Mac returned home. He and the others were near exhaustion and frostbite. Before he could return to the search, he had to talk to Laurel. He dreaded this task as much as he worried about the welfare of his youngest son.

When he opened the back door, he found the cabin quiet, the lights extinguished for the night. All the MacLayne children were asleep. Only Laurel sat alone in the main room, rocking in front of the blazing fire. Her head was bowed. Mac knew she was praying.

"Laurel, I don't mean to interrupt your prayers..."

"Did you find Mark Thomas yet?" Laurel looked into Mac's face.

"Not yet. We covered a big area today. Talked to people around Greensboro and in the Shiloh community. We didn't get any leads. We're headed back out at sun up. I came home to ask how the kids are doin' and you...are ya holdin' up?"

"As well as you'd expect. Andy's been quiet all day. He thinks he caused all this. But he's been a big help with the girls. He found things to keep them occupied so they didn't fret so much." Laurel walked across the room and took Mac's hand.

"We'll find him, Laurel. I promise you we'll bring him home."

Laurel cried out her answer. "Mac, don't make promises you can't keep." Despair marked every word.

"Laurel, you are strong enough to deal with this. You need to believe we are going to find our son. God won't allow us to lose another child."

"I hope you are right." She turned her back to her husband. He pulled her back and put his arms around her as she began to cry. His embrace was all that kept her from falling apart. "Mac, I'm not sure I can deal with anymore."

"Laurel, let's go to bed to rest. Tomorrow we'll need all the strength we can muster. But first, come and pray with me. I believe God will return Mark Thomas to us. I know he will."

Mac lifted Leah Ann from her cradle near the fireplace. He laid her in the crib and covered her well. He stood looking down at his newest child for a time. Finally, he rubbed his thumb across her rose-toned cheek. "Papa loves you, Little One." He moved to sit on the side of the old four-poster and pushed his boots off. He lay down fully dressed. "Come over here, Wife. I need to be held for a while."

After midnight, the entire household awoke to a loud thump on the front door. Following the second crash on the porch, the MacLaynes heard a loud Rebel cry.

" Yee-haw! You, Yankee scum. We don't want you here. Leave the county before your family pays for your treason."

Then the sound of several horses faded away down the road toward Greensboro.

Mac ran to the door, rifle in hand. By the time he pulled the bolt and stepped out to the porch, the intruders had disappeared into the starless night. Laurel stumbled out behind him. She tripped over a potato-sized rock. She fell to her knees and picked up the stone. Around it was tied a note scribbled on an end page ripped from a book. Mac helped her up, and they went into the house to find a light so they could read the note. Once inside, they found their entire family had been awakened. In the main room stood Annie with Cathy, Gracie, and Andy. Concern was etched on each face.

"What happened, Papa?" Gracie stammered. "Are they comin' back?"

"No, Sweetheart. That's just a pack of cowards, trying to act important. You are fine here with your papa and me." Laurel hugged the trembling girl.

"Come over to the fire, young'uns. It's right cold in here. Andy, will you put some wood on the fire?

"Yes, Pa."

Leah Ann began to cry. Laurel took her daughter and brought her to her shoulder. Mac pulled Cathy and Andy into his chair with him. At that moment, ending the chaos and fear was the priority.

Cathy finally asked, "Mama what's on that piece of paper in your hand?"

"I haven't been able to read it yet. Annie, can you turn up the lamp, please?"

Laurel struggled to make out the nearly illegible scribbling on the yellowed end page. "The best I can make out, this note says Mark Thomas has not been hurt in any way. The bushwhackers say they got no plans to hurt him. They said another message will come to tell us where to find him. I can't make out the rest of the note."

Laurel passed it across the room to Mac. When he was able to decipher the rest of it, he didn't tell his family what he read. He saw no reason to cause more fear than they already felt.

"Come on, kids. Back to bed. Cover yourselves well and try to go back to sleep. I'll have Mark Thomas back tomorrow."

"We love you all. Try to rest." Laurel kissed the girls good night and sent them back with Annie to their room. "Annie, please watch over Cathy and Gracie for me. If they start to cry or seem to be having bad dreams, come and get me. Good night, Annie."

"I will, Mrs. Mac. You try to rest some, too."

At dawn, Laurel awoke, shivering. Mac's place next to her was empty. She rose, pulled her shawl across her shoulders, and after checking on Leah Ann and pulling the tiny quilt over her, ran into the second pen. She had to find her husband. Fear gnawed at her. Mac was not one to sneak away. Still in her nightdress, she ran to the barn, hoping to find he'd started morning chores early because he couldn't sleep. Even before she was fully inside, she saw that Midnight's stall was empty.

"Dearest Lord. What is he doing?" Surely, he'd not left without telling her where he was going. She grabbed the top rail of the stall to prevent a fall as her knees buckled. She screamed. "Mac!" All the ugliness of the past two weeks had taken its toll. Laurel had nearly convinced herself that she couldn't go on. The report of Roy's death in battle, the Partisan Rangers butchering one of Mac's prize bulls and leaving most of it to rot in the pasture, Annie's false labor episodes brought on by her grieving, and now Mark Thomas being taken all seemed punishments. Yet, Laurel couldn't point out any misdeed she and Mac had done to merit all this pain. What was the purpose of it all?

"Enough, God. You have to help me. I am beyond my limits to deal with any more loss in my family. Relieve this burden, please." Almost at the moment she whispered the prayer, the words of Romans 8:28 came to her…not once but three times—each time in connection with the image of her son, her daughter-in-law, and her husband. Laurel stood up, and she scolded herself for her weakness. "Bolster yourself, Laurel Grace. You have children who

145

need your care. You can't change anything. It's in God's hands, and he promised to bring good. Go fix breakfast. That is something you can do."

So near Christmas, many things waited to be done. She needed to bake bread. She had yet to finish several Christmas gifts for her family. She went to the fireplace to stoke a fire to begin breakfast when she found a note, written in Mac's strong, precise hand.

*I have gone to bring Mark Thomas home. The note we got yesterday told me where to find him and to come alone. If I obey, no harm will come to him. I'll return by mid-day with our son. Don't be afraid or angry. I have to follow my instinct to do what I think is best. I love you.*

*Patrick*

Laurel dropped the note, and it fell into the embers. The corner caught fire, but she quickly pulled it out and crushed out the flame. She could not lose this note from Mac. Fear told her these could be his final words to her. Again, the words from Romans ran through her mind. She brought the note to her lips and then place it in her Bible. Mac would be home in a few hours. She had much to do to prepare a hot, filling dinner for her family. Goodness, Mark Thomas would be famished.

## φ

Midnight's long, powerful strides carried Mac closer to Gainesville. He knew the old deserted homestead on the east side of Greene County where the Partisan Rangers had taken up residence. The ramshackle cabin bore signs of long neglect and abuse. The barn behind the old house was as bad. The property had been left to rot for more than ten years. Since that time, only outlaws and occasional bands of the Confederate army had used the space to shelter themselves and their stock when they were moving through the area.

Of late, Duncan's unit had been a bane to Mac and other loyalist citizens of Northeast Arkansas. The local constable knew they'd commandeered the place but was unconcerned. They used the central location to raid around their assigned territory that ranged from Chalk Bluff at the St. Francis River to the west limits of Randolph County and south to Poinsett. They made frequent "inspection tours" where they harassed individuals, stole what they wanted, and captured any black people they encountered, freedmen or slaves. The twelve men in the unit had a license to terrorize at will, as long as they didn't cause dissension among the people who supported the Confederate cause. When they wanted to rest, they returned to the abandoned farm. From there they would plan and launch the next attack.

Mac did not attempt to approach the relic quietly or to take the group by surprise. His sole thought was to return his son to Laurel. He would do whatever they asked to prevent more harm to Mark Thomas.

"Duncan. I'm here. What do you want from me?" Mac called out in the still of the morning.

Awakened by Mac's call, three men whose dress indicated they weren't ready for the day, peeked out the door. The glare of the morning sun prevented a clear view of the rider. Duncan pushed a man aside and stalked out to meet Mac. Mac clenched his jaw. He gripped the reins tighter. He had to harness his anger, or he would pummel the smirk from Duncan's face.

"Well, MacLayne, you came real fast, didn't ya, Yankee lover?"

"I am not a Yankee. I want my son." Mac looked toward the decaying barn.

"That cute little boy ain't in there. We got 'im real comfy up in the house. Me and the boys had a good time playin' with the kid.." Duncan's laughter sent chills down Mac's spine.

"If you hurt him, you'll not live the month out."

"Don't be gettin' nasty, MacLayne. I done told ya, we ain't gonna hurt that young'un if you act sensible."

"Tell me what you want from me. I'll try to get whatever you ask for."

"Why, my troops don't need nothin' from you. We got permission to take anything we need…for the war effort."

"If you don't want anything I have, why take a toddler? He can be of no use to you."

147

"Oh, he can. He's gonna help me get revenge on two people I hate most in this world. High and mightly legislator MacLayne and his harlot of a wife, that Spinster of Hawthorn, ya know, that whore you married when no real man would have her."

Mac laughed, long and loud, slapped his knee, and continued for what seemed like hours. The crimson on Duncan's face told the story.

"What in the name of Jefferson Davis are you laughin' at? What's so dang funny to you? I can still…"

"Still what? Beat up a three-year-old? Take your revenge on a child who's not a quarter of your size? Yes. I'd say that's about what you're capable of doin'."

Members of Duncan's unit standing near the barn chucked under their breaths.

"Shut up, MacLayne. I'll shoot ya down."

"If you want your revenge, take it out on a man. I got no gun."

"Don't ya tell me what to do."

"Tell me exactly what my wife and I did to deserve you takin' our three-year-old?" Mac took two steps toward Duncan causing him to step back. "Tell your men how Laurel harmed you, or would you like me to tell that story for you?"

"Shut up, I said." Duncan's face again became the color of flame. His eyes narrowed into slits. "You don't know what she was when I knew her. I tell you she was a harlot—always was. All the boys in Washington County talked about her."

"You're a liar, Duncan. She was fourteen years old when you tried to have your way with her. You weren't very good at that either. Laurel had never known any man when I married her."

Again, strong laughter came from the barn. Duncan sputtered. "That's just what she told ya. She ruined my pa's life."

"She did or you?" Duncan swung his fist at Mac, but Mac dodged, causing Duncan to lose his balance. Mac knew he may be risking more danger to himself and Mark Thomas, but he felt compelled to defend his wife's character.

"You ain't no better'n her. You got me locked up in that stinkin' prison in Little Rock for nearly two years."

"You should've been hung. Mr. Flannagan died because of what you did. Duncan, you are always trying to push your shortcomings off on someone else." Mac stepped closer and clenched his teeth. "I want my son, now."

"Go get that brat, Ryder. I got nothin' else to say to this lyin' Yankee before I beat him to death." Two men who'd joined Duncan grabbed Mac's arms. "Now, MacLayne, I've got a score to settle with you."

"Look, Duncan, call to your man and tell him to keep Mark Thomas in the cabin. He doesn't need to witness your vengeance. I can hold my own, but I doubt I can whip ten men by myself."

"Fine with me. Martin, take that whelp back to the kitchen."

"I appreciate you for sparing him. Do what you will." Mac stood erectly, waiting for Duncan to land a blow. Mac gasped and took a moment to regain his breath when his opponent slammed his fist into his abdomen. He regained his footing and made no voluntary moment while Duncan continued to pummel him. After several minutes, when Mac could no longer stand on his own, the men holding him let him slump to the ground.

"Now take that Yankee brat and get out of here. We have much more important work to do today." Duncan kicked Mac in the back. "And before we head out to our duty for the Confederacy, be warned. You got thirty days to leave Arkansas. If you're still here when we get back, we'll burn you out. The South will be a better place with the MacLayne clan gone to meet their maker, all of 'em."

Within ten minutes, Duncan's men sent Mark Thomas to the barnyard. He walked over to his father, sat in the dirt beside him, and started to cry. "Papa, get up. I wanna go home. Wake up, Papa. Wake up."

Mac was roused by the small boy's voice. "All right, Son. Can you help me up? I think Midnight can get us back to Shiloh."

Early in the evening, Laurel and her uncle Matthew rushed to the porch. She'd heard Mark Thomas's frightening call even before Midnight reached the edge of the yard.

"Mama, Mama. Help me. I can't hardly hold onto Papa no more." Mac slumped behind the small boy with both his arms around him and grasped the pommel of the saddle. Mark Thomas held the reins, but Midnight had brought them home with little guidance from either rider. Mac moaned and jerked with each step the great horse took.

Matthew ran to stop the horse. Laurel pulled her son from the saddle. She hugged him so tightly he squirmed to get free. When Matthew reached up to help his battered friend down, Mac cried out from the excruciating pain. He collapsed on the ground.

"What happened to you, Brother?"

"The bushwhackers took Mark Thomas. I had to get him back."

"Can you walk to the house, Mac?" Laurel's voice broke as she spoke.

"I'll get there somehow. Take care of Mark Thomas. Been a hero all the way home."

Laurel's children stood around, stunned to see how badly beaten their father was. She quickly assigned them tasks to take their minds off the image before them, as she and her uncle managed to get Mac into the second pen bedroom. They removed his bloody, torn shirt. The sunken area on his right side indicated several broken ribs.

Matthew spoke, "Laurel, I'm riding to find Dr. Gibson. I'll bring back some law too if I can find someone." He ran from the room.

Laurel set the kettle over the flame of the fire she'd built earlier. She would need hot water to clean the open wounds. She knew she could clean the wounds she could see but had no way to deal with the ribs. Mac's frequent moans and grimaces on his face told her his pain was strong and constant.

"Patrick, my dearest. Why didn't you tell someone so you didn't go alone?"

There was no response.

"How can any human being be so vicious?"

Silence was the only answer. She took the warm water and washed Mac's face. Once the dirt was removed, she found no open

150

wounds, but nearly every inch of his face was bruised. One of his eyes was swollen shut and his lips were split in more than one place. They ran the gamut of colors indicating they were hours old. She continued to wash his chest and back. Again, she found no blood, but the bruising was even worse on his torso and back. The areas above his hips were nearly black, not the red and purple shades she'd found on his face. She was unable to hold back her tears, seeing the result of the horrendous beating Mac had taken to return Mark Thomas to their home.

"Lord, how can this be good? Mac is a good man. He loves you and tries to serve you. Why did he have to take this scourge to rescue his son? Please help me believe."

Laurel didn't have to wait long to hear the answer to her questions asked through prayer. Before the sunset, help came from across the area. Mac's father arrived first. He came to sit with his son while Laurel dealt with her children. Within two hours, Dr. Gibson came to Shiloh with the Craighead County sheriff. Two women from Shiloh church who had not been in their home since the incident with Colonel Anderson at church brought dishes to help feed the family. Neighbors arrived, asking if help was needed with chores. That evening, political differences seemed to have disappeared in Shiloh. Before the time for the MacLayne children to go to bed, two constables from Greensboro and Lorado also had made their way to the cabin.

The law officials wanted the story Mac was not able to give them at that time. Dr. Edwards administered a strong dose of laudanum to ease the pain and put Mac to sleep while he worked to push the broken ribs together and tightly bind Mac's chest. This was Mac's best hope to return to any hope of pain-free movement. Broken ribs had been known to kill if the jagged breaks pushed their way into lungs. Now sleep was the treatment for the injuries Mac had returned home with.

After a good two hours, the sheriff became restless. Dr. Gibson explained Mac would sleep through the night unless the pain increased dramatically. He had no idea when Mac could supply the information they needed to begin a search for the men who had beaten him.

"Mrs. MacLayne, I guess I'll be headin' back to Jonesboro. When your man comes to his senses, send for us and we'll try to find the man who did this," Sheriff Armstrong said.

Rubbing his eyes, Mark Thomas tugged on the sheriff's coat tail. "Weren't one man, sheriff. A whole bunch of 'em was standin' around. Two big ole men held my daddy, and another man grabbed his legs. Captain Duncan did most of the hittin'. I saw him"

The sheriff got down on his knee so he could look the boy in the face. "Are you sure, Boy?" Mark Thomas nodded. "How do you know it was this Captain Duncan?"

"I seen all of 'em. They're the men who had me for a long time. They grabbed me out of our barnyard."

"They took you? Right out of your own yard?" The look on the sheriff's face showed he didn't believe what the boy was saying.

Andy spoke up. "Yes, sir. My papa has been lookin' for Mark Thomas since day before yesterday. At first, we thought he got lost, but then we got those messages."

"Messages? Can I see 'em? Took a kid outta his own yard." The sheriff shook his head.

Laurel retrieved the rock thrown against the front door and handed it to the sheriff. "I don't know where Mac put the message he got last night. He didn't show it to me, but it told him where to go find our son."

"I'll go look in Midnight's saddlebags," Andy said.

The Greensboro constable stood up. "Sheriff, someone told us over at the Greensboro saloon that MacLayne was lookin' for the boy yesterday mornin'."

"Well, why in tarnation didn't y'all come tell me?"

"We sent ya message by the miller who was carryin' cornmeal to Jonesboro yesterday afternoon."

"Sent the miller? Why didn't you come and find me?"

"We sent word, but you wasn't at the courthouse. We got called back when someone shot off a gun over behind the saloon at Greensboro. We headed home quick." The constable squared his shoulders. "We can't be in two places at once, ya know."

"Never mind. Boy, you tell me everything you saw. Say it straight. Don't make nothin' up and don't leave anything out."

Mark Thomas was intimidated by the anger in the sheriff's voice. He walked back to Laurel and wrapped his arms around her legs. "Should I talk to him anymore? He's kinda mean."

She picked him up. "Do you think you can tell the sheriff what happened to you, Son? It takes a brave boy to tell a scary story."

"Yes, Mama. I didn't see it all, 'cause they locked me in the house a while, but I saw a lot."

"Go ahead, Mark." Andy encouraged his brother. "We need to help find those men who hurt our papa."

Laurel continued to hold the small boy as he told his story. He told them from start to finish how the Partisan Rangers had taken him, held him captive, and treated him for the time he'd been gone. "And then my papa asked Captain Duncan to take me to the cabin 'cos he didn't want me to see. But I saw them grab Papa, and I heard him when they hit him. I looked out of the window when I heard them yell and say I could go home with Papa. That's when I saw Captain Duncan kick my papa in the back."

"I don't suppose you know their names?" The sheriff asked.

"I heard Duncan, Ryder, and Johnny Boy. They are the same bad men doin' all that mean stuff around here. Ryder said he killed my papa's bull, and they had a fine meal one night. Johnny Boy said he took the layin' hens from a farm they burned that belonged to an old man and woman. Captain Duncan told my papa to move or they'd come and burn us out and send the MacLaynes to meet our maker. Not sure what that is, but he's a bad man."

"Son, did you say they are in the army?"

"I don't know. They didn't look like no real army. Only one had a uniform. That was the captain. He was dirty and mean. Looked like a mangy dog."

Everyone in the room laughed at Mark Thomas's evaluation of his abductor.

"You did a good job, Son." The sheriff rose to leave.

153

"I ain't yer son. My papa's in there. Our name's MacLayne."

Φ

The swelling around Mac's thoroughly blackened eyes ebbed after a couple of days and the black changed to various shades of purple, red and yellow over a couple of weeks. Unable to stand tall and walk in his usual vigor and confidence, Mac developed an unpleasant moodiness, so unlike his usual nature. He refused to stay in bed beyond the three days the doctor demanded. With tightly wrapped ribs, he got up the fourth morning, expecting to help with chores. In a matter of minutes, he realized how useless his effort was. Andy and Cathy had already milked the cow, gathered the few eggs, filled the wood box, and fed what remained of the livestock. The more demanding tasks were delegated to J.F. Clarke and his brother James. He returned to the cabin and plunked himself down his chair and groaned from the pain of his broken ribs. His bruised ego may have hurt more.

The sheriff and Greensboro constable made frequent visits to the MacLayne homestead during the two weeks following the attack. They kept the family apprised of any news of the bushwhackers. Their frequent visits usually came with copies of newspapers, any mail from the Greensboro post office, and parcels sent from the shopkeepers in town.

About ten days before Christmas, Sheriff Armstrong arrived about suppertime. "MacLayne, we got word yesterday that Duncan's troop of bushwhackers are commandeering supplies in Missouri right now."

"I'm sure they're helpin' themselves to whatever they can get." Mac grimaced as he sat down. "I doubt the Confederate army will see much of what they steal."

"We had a visit from the commandin' officer of the local militia in Greene County named Anderson. He told us that unit is a renegade group, and they have no authority here. The beatin' you got was not ordered by the Greene County Home Guard. They are not targetin' your family."

"Sheriff, I'm under no delusion that Duncan and his thugs are carryin' out legitimate orders. I can't believe any sane person would appoint bands of thieves and murderers to rove the state in the name of the government, especially without any kind of oversight. I blame the governor though. He issued the original proclamation that started these partisan groups." Mac's animated statement stopped abruptly as he doubled over from the pain.

"Careful, man. Takes a while to heal broken ribs. We're watchin' for him. When he comes back to Arkansas, we'll haul him in to answer for what he did." The constable continued. "We're here to protect you and your family."

"I appreciate any help you can give, but my children will not be victimized by that gang again. If that Partisan Ranger unit comes on my land again, I'll meet them with my gun."

"MacLayne, we don't need that kind of violence here in this county."

"I didn't start it, Sheriff. You told me yourself the gang is a rogue operation. They're no better than any other intruder or thief. I'll do what I have to do to protect my wife and young'uns."

The bushwhackers were not the only problem that plagued Mac. The newspapers from Little Rock and St. Louis carried reports of the conscription of soldiers from across the south. The law had been passed more than a year earlier, but due to heavy losses of Confederate troops, local militia had been sanctioned to enlist all able-bodied men between the ages of seventeen and forty-five. Anyone who refused to enroll was arrested and tried. There had been reports of some men being executed for their refusal to serve. In his present condition, Mac knew he would not be forced to enlist, but he would not be laid up forever. With Duncan on the loose, the entire MacLayne family was in danger. He would play the invalid through Christmas, but he must begin to make plans to safeguard his family after the first of the year. Local gossip around both Greene and Craighead Counties carried stories that the militia had already begun searching the area for men who had yet to enroll in the Confederate military.

He could no longer delay the talk he must have with Laurel. Mac had dreaded this conversation more than any they'd had since coming to Shiloh. He didn't want to hurt her He had done that more than enough in their life together. And he'd promised more than once he'd not leave her. He knew she felt that to be a rejection of her. The last time he'd spoken the words, he had pledged against his faith that he would keep his word. Now, he could find no way out. Duncan had threatened Laurel and the children. The Confederate legislature demanded service from all men who lived in the states that had seceded, whether they chose to serve or not. He was being forced to do the thing he didn't know if Laurel could forgive again. He whispered a prayer, asking for courage and wisdom to have this talk with her…an honest, sincere explanation of what he had to do. He also prayed that Laurel's faith in the Lord and her belief in herself would be sufficient to preserve their family.

But this would wait until after Christmas. Providence had kept Mac at home during the entire year of 1862. Surely the angels would allow him sanctuary at Shiloh for at least ten more days.

# Chapter 14

*To everything, there is a season, and a time to every purpose under*
*the heaven: A time to be born, and a time to die:*
*Ecclesiastes 3:1-2*

Christmas day started before the rooster crowed. Mark
Thomas and Gracie bounced out of bed to search for the gifts left
by St. Nicolas. Even though the older kids weren't as eager to get
up, all the MacLayne children found a mound of gifts near the
hearth on their grandmother Campbell's rag rug. Laurel and Mac
had not spent as lavishly on the gifts this year, and some special
things like fruit and nuts were missing, but they had kept the
MacLayne tradition alive. Everyone got a needed gift, something
to promote learning, and one last gift that always brought screams
of joys or gasps of awe. Because the war made things from
catalogs hard to come by, Mac and Laurel had made most of the
presents.

Presents for Cathy and Andy were the exceptions and the
most extravagant gifts that year. Both needed new footwear. Mac
had gotten Andy new boots and Cathy laced-up leather shoes with
the suggestion of a heel. The local leatherworker in Greensboro
had been hired even before harvest time to make sure they would
be ready for Christmas morning. Mac had built beautiful gifts for
Mark Thomas and Gracie. Mark Thomas jumped atop his new

rocking horse and yelled, "Giddy-up, Midnight. Lookee, Papa. I can ride Midnight, just like you."

When Gracie was given her new dollhouse, which was a replica of the MacLayne cabin, she said, "This is for me, Papa? Goodness." Laughter continued for the entire morning.

Mac had carved a rattle from a single piece of walnut for Leah Ann. The moveable bead in the middle fascinated the tiny girl. Laurel's gifts to her family included new shirts, dresses, woolen scarves, and a warm blanket, made especially for the soon-to-be baby of Roy and Annie. Laurel had taken one of her dresses, bought for her days in Little Rock, and resized it to fit Annie. The young widow would need new clothes very soon. Books, games, and puzzles completed the gifts passed out that morning. Some had belonged to another member of the family in earlier days, yet all were cherished.

Laurel prepared their usual Christmas breakfast with cinnamon rolls, even though she had to use a two-week ration of sugar and flour to prepare the feast. It didn't matter. The special day could not be slighted, even in wartime. Mac blessed the banquet, and for the next hour, the MacLaynes shared a grand meal and wonderful family time. Then Mac tucked his family into the hay-filled wagon and headed across Big Creek to spend the day with his father and his family. Matthew Campbell and his entire clan would also be present, which for the MacLayne family held the promise of a blessed day.

This would be the first Christmas holiday the Thomas MacLayne family would spend in their newly completed two-story clapboard house on the banks of Big Creek. They had named their new home Grace Creek. Peggy said her life with Thomas had been built on grace so it was the only name that fit. Since she moved with her three children, she had worked tirelessly to make it a real home. Thomas swore that Peggy had brought life into the place when she came. He had become a father to the two younger Flannagan children and a friend and employer to Paddy, Peggy's oldest son.

Thomas doted on his new wife and lavished attention on his new young'uns. He loved them all, but he made his relationship very clear to them. He told them he never intended to replace their father, never vying for the love or loyalty they owed him. Peggy blossomed under Thomas's attention, despite the differences in their ages. Peggy's practical nature and personal faith grounded her. Thomas appreciated her work ethic and the time she put into their home. She was delighted to be hosting the Christmas celebration for the entire family.

Too much food, excessive laughter, more than a few hugs, every known Christmas carol, and more than ample love spilled out through the day. Even Annie, who missed her husband tremendously and felt the weight of her pregnancy, smiled many times during the happy day. After their lavish Christmas dinner of goose, venison, yeast bread, every kind of vegetable from their gardens, cakes, pies, and puddings, no one could eat another bite.

Afterward, the men settled into Thomas's office, and the ladies settled at the dining room table. The children found space in the front parlor to play games and enjoy the company of cousins.

At the table, Ellie Campbell nestled her youngest grandson on her shoulder. "Peggy, this Christmas outshines any we've celebrated here at Shiloh. Thank you for havin' us all here."

"Been such a blessin' to our whole family to have ya here celebratin' our first Christmas in our home. Thank y'all for bein' with us."

"You've done such a wonderful job makin' Mr. MacLayne's house so homey, Mrs. Peggy," Annie said.

"Why, thank ya, Darlin'. Thomas said what I did makes this my place, too. I feel that now. I have to pinch myself sometimes to realize we have such a fine place to live. Thomas has been good to us…almost bein' a father to my young'uns after they lost their pa."

A shadow passed across Annie's face. Both Laurel and Peggy reacted at once. "Annie."

Peggy continued, "Dear sweet Annie, me and my careless tongue. Please forgive me. I'd no intention of bringin' a blight on this Holy day. Your young husband was a fine man. I know you grieve for him, but Annie, we also have to rejoice that he's with the Lord. We know he is."

159

"I'm all right, Mrs. Peggy. The only thing that lets me go on is knowin' that Roy found the Lord when he came home last Christmas. Do you think I can go rest for a while? I'm really tired."

"Do you want me to go with you, Sweetheart?" Laurel asked.

"No, Mrs. Mac. I want to nap for a while."

In the meantime, the men were having a more somber conversation in the office. Traveling across the upper part of the state and even to some counties in Missouri, Matthew had seen firsthand the loss and death from several battles. While no huge battles had occurred in the region, too many scrimmages were taking place whenever troops from the opposing sides ran into each other. This happened all too often, as supplies became more and more scarce. Both sides needed food, animals, firearms, and ammunition. The armies bought what they could and confiscated what they couldn't buy. Sometimes they simply did without because what they needed was not to be had.

"You know, the only reason I can go back and leave my family for weeks at a time is that I can be with men, some of them just boys, and ease their passin'. This war is carnage."

"Brother Matthew, are you in harm's way out there?"

"No, not really, Thomas. My work starts when the battle ends."

"How does Ellie take to your bein' gone so much?" Mac asked.

"Like you'd expect. She don't like it none, but she knows I feel a call. She's always been a willin' partner when the Lord calls. I couldn't do it if our older kids weren't close to see to her well-bein' while I'm gone."

"Do you think Randall and Mark will be forced to enlist, Matthew?"

"Not Randall. He's blind in that right eye, but Mark is another problem. So far his father-in-law has been able to keep him out by paying the fee to exempt him. As things get worse, I'd bet the governor will have to do away with that exemption. Too many people are protestin' now, sayin' the rich don't have to do their

160

part. If he gets conscripted, I may send him and his wife out west for a while. Mark don't want to fight, but he don't like his father-in-law keepin' him out either. He says it makes him feel like a coward, but his pretty little wife's always been pampered by her wealthy family. He can't bear to hear her cry."

"I hope he won't get forced into the army, Brother Matthew. We can't lose all our young men." Thomas shook his head. "No, we gotta keep our future the best way we can. I ain't lettin' Paddy enlist. He asked me but I told Peggy he's too young, and I need him on the farm. I may send him back to Pennsylvania to Peggy's sister if I have to."

"What are you gonna do, Mac?" Thomas lifted his head to look at his son as Matthew asked his friend.

"I'll do what I have to do to keep my family safe. I'm plannin' to talk to Laurel about all this before the New Year."

"Son, you are goin' to enlist with the Union army, aren't you?"

"Pa, I've got no say. I can't fight for the Confederacy. I think their cause is wrong for so many reasons."

"Patrick, what about Laurel and your young'uns? How can you keep them safe if you leave?"

"I can't find any way to protect them if I stay. Pa, I know you'll be here. J.F. is over the age of conscription. If I desert my family, the community will surely allow Laurel back into their good graces."

"Desert her?" Matthew became livid. "You can't do that to her."

"Patrick, think of the disgrace she'll feel if you desert her. She loves you. You can't break her heart. I won't let you do that to her."

"Pa. I'll explain what I have to do to Laurel. Regardless, I have to do what I have to do. Nothin' is more important than keepin' my kids alive and safe. After Mark Thomas was kidnapped a couple of weeks ago, I knew the war wouldn't pass me over."

"I pray you are makin' the right decision, Son. I will do all I can if you have to go. You've always been the pride of my life, even in those hard times before you came to Arkansas. I never lost faith in you. I'll not question your motives now."

The somber mood was interrupted when Andy knocked on the door. "Papa, Mama says it's time to head home. It's startin' to snow."

"I'll come directly, Andy. Can you help your mama get the younger kids ready to go?"

"Yes, sir."

"Pa, I love you, and I'm so grateful for what you just said. I know I caused some worry for both you and Ma, but I never doubted one minute that you both loved me. I'll come to say good-bye before I leave."

"God keep ya, Patrick."

"Mac, let me pray for us all. I so want this war over."

Later that night when Laurel had settled her children into their beds, she snuggled into Mac's arms as he sat in his chair in front of the blazing fire in their second pen bedroom. The quiet of their sanctuary was wonderful after the hectic, exciting day they'd spent with their family. The only break in the silence was an occasional snap from a pine knot in the flames. Mac began to pull the pins from Laurel's hair and run his fingers through the coils to release her tawny mane. "You are beautiful, Laurel Grace."

"You make me beautiful because you love me, Patrick. Today has been the best holiday we've ever known. Our family is such a blessing."

"I agree with you. You've made this patchwork into a true family. Regardless of how they came to us, you've woven them into the fabric of the MacLayne family."

"I could never have done anything had you not taught me the meaning of love. Before you, I had none to give."

"You always did, Laurel. You cared for your father for years after your mother died. You were a sister to Rachel long before I knew you. All I did is show you that you deserve to be loved as much as you have poured out your love on others."

"I am glad you cared enough to show me, then."

"How could I help it? You captured my heart. I couldn't stop lovin' you if I tried."

"Lord, I am so blessed." Laurel captured Mac's face between her hands and kissed him. "Mac, even in the midst of this uncertainty and the ugliness of this war, I am happy and safe here in your arms." Mac's smile disappeared. "Did I hurt you, Darlin'?"

"No, Laurel. Just a twinge from my ribs." He pulled her to him and kissed her again. "I don't want to talk anymore. I haven't given you your Christmas present yet. Let me up a minute."

Laurel stood and Mac walked to the bed, bent down, and pulled a large, rectangular-shaped package from underneath. The plain brown paper was tied with a green ribbon.

"Mac, what have you done? We agreed not to spend much on gifts this year."

"I didn't spend much. I made most of this." He handed her the package. "Open it."

Laurel tore at the brown paper. She found a mirror in an intricate frame. Every inch of the brown-stained walnut was carved with daisies, ivy, and native wildflowers. Laurel gasped.

"What a beautiful present, Mac. This had to be very expensive."

"No, I told you I carved it in my spare time. I've had plenty of that since I've got no herd to care for. The glass was the hardest thing to come by, but I kept my word. I spent very little. Now, where is my new shirt?"

"Oh, you. I'll have you know I didn't make you a shirt this year. You have enough."

"Well, what did you get me? I know you got me something."

She laid the mirror on the bed and crossed over to her bureau and opened the bottom drawer where she kept her summer nightdress. "I knew it would be safe there. You never look in my drawers where I keep my nightclothes." She handed him a small draw-string sack.

"Well, what is this?"

"Open it and see!" Laurel laughed at being able to pull off a surprise. Mac pulled the strings and found a two-by-three-inch silver case, engraved with his initials. Inside the case were two sepia photographs—one of their family and the other a portrait of her. Laurel had ordered them from the traveling photographer who had done their family portraits back in the fall. These small photographs had become quite popular since the start of the war. Thankfully, the jeweler in Greensboro had been able to engrave the case and insert the photographs. Laurel had bartered several jars of vegetables, pumpkins, and homemade soups for the case. Only the photographs had cost money. She was so pleased with the gift she had been able to give to her husband.

"Laurel, this is the best gift I've ever received—well, except for you and our kids. I love this. Havin' your likeness to carry with me all the time...I don't know what to say. What a blessed gift!"

"The Greensboro jeweler says that lots of soldiers have them so I reasoned that the best husband in the state deserves one. I wanted to surprise you. You always get a shirt."

"Not this year. I'll treasure your gift always."

"I love you, Patrick."

"Don't tell me, Wife. Come over here and show me."

Gold shafts of light streaking across Crowley's Ridge ushered in the year of 1863. When Laurel awoke, she caught her reflection in the detailed framed mirror Mac had given her for Christmas. She smiled. The woman looking back at her little resembled the Laurel who had come to Shiloh in the spring of 1857. Strength, confidence, and contentment showed on the face of this woman, where fear and self-doubt had once been. The mirror image told the story of how much she'd changed—all because Patrick MacLayne loved her.

She pushed the quilt back so she could get up to stoke the fire, but before she got her feet to the plank floor, Mac clasped her wrist and pulled her back into his arms.

"Wife, you can't leave me alone here. It's cold in this room."

"That's why I was getting up...to stoke the fire. It's time to start a new day and a new year. Leah Ann will be cold if I don't put wood in the fireplace."

Mac continued to hold her close to him. "What's on your mind this mornin'? You seemed to be lost when I first saw ya."

"I was admiring my Christmas present and that intricate frame you carved. I didn't expect it. Do you remember that night you told me the only mirror I needed was my image in your eyes?"

"That was when I was married to that shy, helpless little girl I met in Washington County. My wife is not that person anymore."

"That's what I was thinkin' too. How much I've changed in these years we've been together. Not many women are blessed to have a husband who loves so well."

"Thank you for letting me do the lovin'." The tone of Mac's voice and the playful slap on her backside told Laurel that he had no intention of engaging in a serious conversation.

"You enjoy playin' the rogue sometimes, Patrick MacLayne. Time is so rare for us to have a serious talk with our kids around all the time. When we have a few free minutes, you prefer to tease me."

"What kind of serious talk do you want to have, wife?"

"I wanted to ask you about the article from the Little Rock paper you tried to hide from me." Before Mac could answer, Andy burst through the doorway. "Papa, Mama...it's snowin' outside again, and I saw more horse tracks in the snow out by the corral."

Mac hoisted himself up. "Are you sure, son?"

"When I went out to start mornin' chores, I saw 'em plain as could be. Had to be at least four or maybe five riders. Did ya hear anything last night?"

"No, I didn't. Did you, Laurel?"

She blushed remembering the past evening. "No. I didn't hear anything beyond the usual. If there'd been much noise, it would have awakened Leah Ann, and she slept through the night."

"Andy, I'll be out directly as soon as I get dressed. Don't you go back out there alone."

Andy walked out of his parents' bedroom and closed the door.

Mac threw on his clothes. "We've seen the return of our local bushwhackers, Laurel. This madness is gonna stop. Duncan's a madman, and his thugs do whatever he says. I am gonna teach him that I'll do whatever I have to do to keep y'all safe."

"Mac, you can't go alone. Get the sheriff involved again."

"All right. I'll go to Jonesboro as soon as I can get someone over here to protect you. If that scum comes here before then, I'll show him what an excellent shot I am. He'll not hurt one of mine again."

Mac rushed to take Andy to the barn. He wanted to see the tracks for himself. The snow was falling in large, sloppy wet flakes. If the storm continued, the tracks of the night visitors would be covered long before the law could see them. Andy's report had been accurate. At least four men had prowled around the MacLayne barn and corral since the family had retired for the night.

Mac wondered what chicanery they'd been up to. He saw no obvious damage to the property or his livestock. The doors to the smokehouse, corn crib, and chicken pen were still fastened. The fencing he could see remained intact. He shuddered. What had they done? Was there a hidden danger that could harm his family? He carried that anxious feeling throughout the day as he and Andy worked to complete the work that waited to be done.

"Let's go in, Son, and eat breakfast. It's blame cold out here today."

"Papa, what are we gonna do about this? Mark Thomas don't like to come outside anymore."

"Only thing I can do is call in the sheriff. Before I can get him here, all these tracks will be gone. Look real close, Son. You'll have to back me up. See this shoe has a missin' nail. On that track, see how much wider the left hind shoe is than the other three. The rider musta had it replaced by a different smith. Now you remember these things so you can tell the sheriff. I know we'll see these tracks again."

The family settled at the table. Mac spoke grace over their food. He reached for his steaming coffee. He blew across the cup a couple of times to cool the aromatic brew. He was pleased they still had real coffee because they'd stocked several parcels in their stash. He took a swig of the brew and immediately spit it out.

"It's got salt in it."

Gracie dropped her spoon back into her bowl of oatmeal. "Mama, I know you put some honey in this, but it don't taste good."

"Laurel, when did you draw water last?"

"First thing I did when I came to the kitchen. The water pail was empty."

"Those devils in the Partisan Rangers salted our well. From the taste of that coffee, they used a lot of salt. They must hate us pretty bad with the cost of salt bein' what it is." Mac rose from the table and stalked to the peg near the door to retrieve his hat and coat. Before leaving the room, he picked up his rifle.

"I'll get the sheriff. I may have to ride to Jonesboro. Bar the cabin doors, front and back. Don't open them for anyone except family. I'll send J.F. to stay if I can find him this mornin'. I'll be back when I can."

J.F. was tending the remnant of Mac's herd just below the barn. He sent his loyal tenant to watch over his wife and family and turned Midnight toward Jonesboro at full gallop. A cross country trip would have been shorter, but the recent snowfall made the old military road safer. Mac's decision proved to be the wise one. He met the sheriff and two deputies about a mile south of Greensboro.

"Sheriff Armstrong, wait up. I was on my way to find you."

"Well, ride with me, MacLayne. A problem in Greensboro called me over this way. A messenger from McCollough said a man was killed just outside town."

"Who was it?

"No one gave me a name. All the message said was a man who refused to turn over his beef to the army got killed last night. I thought maybe it was you."

"The bushwhackers again. That worthless gang of hoodlums who say they've been appointed by the governor as a special unit. I'd say they've come back from Missouri. They do whatever they want. They don't believe any law applies to them." Mac scowled and red streaks ran up his neck.

167

"What did you want me for?" The sheriff's curt response further added to Mac's anger.

"I want you to protect all the citizens of this county—not just the Confederate ones."

"See here, MacLayne. We're doin' what we can. I only got three deputies. We can't be everywhere at the same time."

"If you'd catch that band of renegades, things could return to normal around here," Mac stated.

"MacLayne, things are pretty peaceful for most of our citizens now. Perhaps you need to take your family north 'til the war is over."

"This is our home. We got as much right to live here in peace and safety as any man. We pay our taxes. We help our neighbors who need us and will allow us to look to those needs. We don't ask anyone to like what we stand for, but we expect them to obey the law." Mac turned Midnight back toward Greensboro to find out who besides himself had been a victim of Duncan and his men the previous night.

When he got to McCollough's store, he found a sizeable crowd gathered around the stove at the rear. Mac didn't have to ask questions because all the conversation centered on the Masters family. He and Laurel hadn't seen them since November when their boys stopped attending school. One of the men remarked that the widow and her three children were in Dr. Gibson's office.

Mac stalked away and down the street to speak to Naomi Masters. He knocked on the door of the doctor's office. Ed Gibson opened the door. The tragedy of the night was written across his haggard face.

"MacLayne, what are ya doin' out on a day like this?"

"I came to see how Naomi and her young'uns are. I just heard about Art."

"She's not doin' so good, but she's tryin' to keep it together for the kids. Those damned raiders shot Art Masters in the back, right in front of those two boys." The doctor shook his head.

"My dear Lord. How can men be so low? They didn't know Art, but they shot him just because he didn't hold with their politics."

"Mac, Naomi is back there, puttin' those kids down for a spell. She drove them here in a wagon with Art in the back. He was still alive when they got here, but before I could get the bullet out, he was gone. Lost too much blood. If a doctor had been closer…" Ed Gibson slumped in a chair behind his desk. "Ya know, I don't like your politics or his either, but hang it all, no one deserved what happened to that family."

"I didn't come here to defend my attitude toward this war. I came to demand that the sheriff protect me and mine and any other family in the area. Who will be next? The Swensons, who just moved here three years ago from Michigan. Maybe it will be those real enemies of the South, Bertram and Heidi Nelms, even if they are seventy years old."

Naomi Masters came from the backroom in her blood-drenched dress. Her eyes were almost as red. She broke into hard, jerking sobs as she collapsed into Mac's arms.

"Naomi…" Mac stopped. He knew no other words to speak to his grieving neighbor. What words would make any difference at that moment? He continued to hold her as she wept.

A few moments later, the sheriff walked through the door. "MacLayne, what are you doin' here?"

"Tryin' to care for my neighbor. Armstrong, this is Naomi Masters. She lost her husband Arthur to that band of bushwhackers last night. You gotta put an end to this violence around here."

"Can you tell me what happened at your place last night, Mrs. Masters?"

She nodded and turned to face him. She stumbled backward, and Mac reached to steady her. He pulled a chair for her to sit in and stood behind her as she tried to recount the horror of the previous night. "About ten of 'em or so…" She choked back tears. "Six on the ground, I counted."

The doctor handed her his handkerchief. "Take your time, Naomi. Do ya need something to drink?"

"I'm cold." The lady shivered, partly from the cold, but more likely from her raw nerves.

The doctor pulled a blanket from a cabinet and draped it across her shoulders.

"Go on, Mrs. Masters. What happened when the group of ten men rode up to your place?" The sheriff asked.

"Horrible screeching... yelling...Some called out for Art to come out to the porch. One of the men said, 'If ya ain't no coward, come out and face yer betters.' I tried to stop him." Again Mrs. Masters fell into tears. "My husband wasn't ever a coward. We don't believe in fightin'. Art was a Quaker. Neither of us wanted to see our country split in two."

Mac laid his hand on her shoulder. "You speak the truth, Naomi. I've never known a braver man than Art."

"One of those awful men said, 'Captain Duncan, can we have us a little fun with that handsome woman.' Art turned back toward the door to protect me. One of them shot him, right there on our porch. Both our sons were standing in the door." Naomi covered her face as her sobs returned. She couldn't continue.

"I think you've got enough to start a manhunt. I'll join a posse to help look for the gang of bushwhackers. If you think murder's not enough reason, add to it the kidnappin' of my son three weeks ago. The next day they assaulted me, and last night that bunch of hoodlums filled my well with salt. We'll file the charges. You go get the men who obey no law except their own."

"Settle down, MacLayne. Mrs. Masters, did your husband take a gun to the porch when he went out?"

She looked at the sheriff as if he'd slapped her. The doctor didn't wait for her to reply. "What difference does that make? He was on his own land, and I told you, they shot him in the back. That man, lyin' over there on my operatin' table was shot dead center of his back. Can't be no defense for that."

"Did he have a gun?"

"No. She told you he's a Quaker. He didn't believe in violence." Mac stormed back. He took a couple of deep breaths. "I said I'd volunteer to serve on your posse. We oughta get a start after those murderers before they head back to Missouri."

"We'll gather at the livery stable at noon. Gather a few more men to help with the search. Tell 'em, high noon. Bring your rifles and warm clothes. We'll be out until we have 'em in jail." The sheriff donned his hat and walked away.

φ

Mac made a mad dash back to Shiloh to gather a few more riders for the posse and to tell Laurel what happened to the Masters family. He sent Andy to bring Matthew Campbell, and he sent J.F. to take a message to his father. He had only a short time to prepare for the manhunt and to explain the situation to Laurel.

"Laurel, come with me to the other room. I want to talk while I gather warmer clothes and pack up my supplies."

"Mac, what are you doing?"

"I'm gonna ride with the posse. We're goin' after those bushwhackers. This community is not gonna take any more of their violence toward innocent people."

"Getting our well filled with salt isn't worth risking your life, Mac."

"Gone way past that, Laurel. Duncan and his mob killed Art Masters in front of his kids last night. He wasn't even armed when they did it."

"Oh, no. Those poor children. And Naomi. She must be lost."

"She's gonna need her friends. Maybe you and Ellie can go help her to get through until she has a chance to lay Art to rest. She's at Dr. Gibson's office. I'll send J.F. over to check on her place."

Mac walked to the main pen to say good-bye to Mark Thomas, Gracie, and Cathy. He held each of them for a short time and whispered in their ears, "I love you. God blessed me when He let you be my child." He then went to the barn to prepare Midnight for the trek. Shortly, both his father and Matthew joined him and agreed to ride with the posse. J.F. was left behind as the protector for three families until the posse returned. Mac stopped on the porch to say goodbye to Andy and Laurel.

"Andy, you're nearly a man now. You can be a big help to J.F. takin' care of our home until I get back. I love ya, Son, and am so proud of you." Then he turned to Laurel. After a brief kiss, he said, "Wife, I'll be back when this problem is solved. Robert Duncan has been a nightmare in your life for too long and in ours for as long as we've known each other. I promise, he'll not bring pain or harm to us again. When the sheriff arrests him, he'll get the justice he has earned." Mac mounted Midnight again, and he rode away toward Greensboro with his father and Matthew Campbell.

A posse of a dozen men gathered at the Greensboro livery stable. Sheriff Armstrong divided the men into three groups to begin the search. Mac, Matthew, and Thomas made up one of the groups led by one of the local deputies. They were assigned to go south of Greensboro to search a couple of abandoned buildings. Rumors from the saloon said the Partisan Rangers hid out in one of those barns from time to time when they were in the county. Duncan's men would know the place well as they had burned it out on one of their first rampages in Craighead County. An elderly couple had lived there and the old man had refused to forfeit his last remaining milk cow to the Rebel army. The cabin was now a heap of ashes and charred timbers, but the barn had an intact roof.

The posse started down the old military road. The deserted homestead was less than five miles, just shy of Buck Snort Hill. The trip could be made easily by mid-afternoon.

"MacLayne, you know this man, Duncan, don't ya?"

"We've met more than I like. He's a bully with a vendetta against my wife that goes back more'n half her life. Since I've known him, he's brought grief, worry, and destruction to my family too often."

"Well, don't go off half-cocked. We need to take him alive to stand trial." The deputy reminded him. "The sheriff said we gotta do this by the book because of that appointment from the governor."

"I got no intention of harmin' him. I want him out of Laurel's life and mine. He's the one who kidnapped my son. He and three of his men beat me when I went to take the boy back home. He won't get that chance again."

"Mac, the deputy is right." Matthew intervened. "We don't want any more reason for the Rebel supporters at Shiloh to turn against you. If they do have some kind of sanction from the governor, some folks will think they have every right to search out and harass people who refuse to support the Confederacy."

"I said I'd not murder anyone, if that's what you're afraid of, Preacher. But he will go to prison for what he's done—or be hanged for killing Art Masters."

"Son, Matthew is right. Do it by the book so everything falls on them, not on you."

"All right, Pa. I'll keep my temper caged if the Lord will help me."

When they arrived at the barn, two young recruits were there trying to build a hot enough fire to work metal to shape a new horseshoe. A tall, black horse with a missing shoe stood tied to a stall nearby. When Mac picked up the discarded shoe, he knew the owner of the horse had been on his homestead the previous night. The cracked shoe had one side much wider and thicker than the opposite side. This shoe had made the tell-tale tracks near the corral that Andy had pointed out to him. "Whose horse did this shoe come from?"

The two young Rebels standing over the makeshift anvil shuffled in their discomfort. Neither of them answered. The deputy pulled out his gun and said, "Get a rope, Matthew. These murderers don't deserve a trial."

"Wait, wait." The youngest looking soldier of the special unit blanched as he spoke. "That shoe came off that horse right there. See, he's missing that left hind one. He belongs to Captain Duncan."

"Where is Duncan?" Thomas MacLayne asked.

"We don't rightly know. Said somethin' about a saloon in Greensboro. Told us they'd be back by midnight. They'd have to sleep off the booze before they could carry out another campaign." The second Rebel spoke up.

"Naw—they'll hold up at the cave for a couple of days." The younger man said.

"Yer a lyin'. I ain't aimin' to get killed lyin' for Duncan. I told him I didn't hold shootin' people. I ain't no killer." The second young bushwhacker retorted.

"Did Duncan shoot someone?" Mac asked.

"He did, just last night. He shot that man in the back. He didn't have a gun. Duncan was just mad because that farmer's barn was empty. We didn't get nothin' to carry back to the troop we'd been assigned to forage for."

"Shut up, Harve. Don't ya see that man's got a badge?"

"Matthew, arrest these renegade Rebs. Tie 'em up back there in one of those stalls. We'll wait around here for a spell and see if anyone else joins them." The deputy sat on a hay bale to begin his vigil.

"Whatever you say, Jim. I hope this is the beginning of the last night we have to deal with this. I want this violence and rage to end." Matthew Campbell motioned for the prisoners to go toward the back of the barn.

Within two hours, a second of the four posses arrived at the barn. Sheriff Armstrong led this group. "Did ya find any sign of those bushwhackers yet?"

"We found two young recruits here. They told us the main body of the troop is due back about midnight. We thought we'd wait 'em out." The deputy reported.

"We found no trace of them toward the west. When we doubled back, we did run across a farm where all the fences around the pastures had been pulled down." The sheriff took a place near the fire at the make-shift forge. "How about let's make some coffee while we wait. Even a brew of that roasted chickory will chase this cold." Thomas MacLayne set about to make a pot. "When we asked the woman in the cabin what happened, she told us a band of ten men used ropes and their horses to rip up the fence posts. They rode off with three horses from her corral. Funny thing. She said her husband was a sergeant in the Arkansas Eighth Infantry, Company F. That group started with Joel Woods. Confederate, not Union."

"That band of thieves would hang if they didn't have the governor's special sanction. Whose place was it anyway?" Mac asked.

"Sam Munson was the name the woman gave. She said he'd recently come home from the Battle in Corinth. Said he lost an eye. They stole from a wounded Confederate veteran."

"Sheriff, maybe that will be enough to convince you that my son is tellin' ya the truth. Duncan needs to be stopped. bolder."

φ

A long anxious afternoon grew into an evening with a dense, eerie fog settling over Crowley's Ridge. The strange rise in the temperatures on this January evening brought conditions more common to spring than mid-winter. The snow began to melt. By eight-thirty drizzling rain added to the gloom. Laurel's unease only increased. Mac had not returned. She set about settling her family for the night. When she went into the girls' room, she noticed a pinched look on Annie's face. A small line of sweat sat across her upper lip.

"Annie dear, are you feelin' all right?"

"I suppose I'm doin' pretty well. I feel warm, and I gotta an ache in my back." She laid her hand just below her waist. "I can't find any easy way to sit or lay back."

"How long has this been goin' on, Annie?"

"Not very long…."

"Mama, she's been kinda hurtin' like that since before supper, but it's got worse." Cathy's wide-eyed concern spoke louder than her words.

Laurel felt Annie's brow, checking for fever. She smiled down at her young daughter-in-law. "Young lady, you ain't sick. I think you're about to become a mother."

While those words always brought great joy to Laurel, Annie didn't smile. A sole tear traced its way down her cheek.

"Don't be afraid, Sweetheart. I am here, and we are sending for Dr. Gibson. Just lie back and rest for now." Laurel plumped a pillow and pushed it behind her back.

"I'm not afraid, Mrs. Mac. I know I can have my baby, but I am scared for us after. How am I gonna raise a baby without Roy? I can't do this alone."

"Darlin', you're never gonna be alone. When Roy married you, he made you our daughter as surely as he was our son. Mac and I will always be here to help you and this little one. Don't fret one thing about tomorrow or any days after that. Let's just think about getting that baby here."

"Mama, are we havin' a new baby in our family today?"

175

"Well, maybe today or tomorrow, Gracie. Pretty soon, Leah Ann won't be the youngest member of this family. Won't it be fun to have a new baby to play with?"

"I love to hold new babies, but where is this one gonna sleep? Do we got another crib?" Gracie asked her practical question. All the girls laughed, even Annie.

"Cathy, please take Gracie and Leah Ann to my room and y'all get ready for bed. I'll come in a few minutes and listen to your prayers. It won't take long to get Annie settled in."

"You want me to give her a bath, Mama?" Cathy asked.

"Not tonight, darlin'. Tomorrow will be soon enough."

When Cathy with Leah Ann in her arms ushered Gracie out of the room, Laurel closed the door. "That should give you a little privacy. Annie, labor can last a while. That pressure in your back will get stronger, but it may not happen for some time. Try to sleep now. I'll be back very soon." She brushed the young woman's hair back and kissed her forehead. "Everything will be fine."

Laurel wished she felt as sure as she tried to pretend. Annie's labor was early, by at least three weeks. Dr. Edwards had declared both Annie and her baby to be strong and healthy, yet Laurel was very concerned with the onset of the labor pains. Thank the Lord for J.F. who sat at the table whittling, as he watched over them. "J.F., please ride over to Greensboro and bring back Dr. Gibson for me."

φ

Some after midnight, the posse heard the pounding sound of several horses approaching the barn. The sheriff directed the two groups of men he'd deputized to find cover and wait until the bushwhackers came inside. About half the men walked their horses inside. In the dimly lit building, the men inched their way back toward the stalls to put the animals away. Three more men entered and the last two stood at the door.

"Look at that star-bright sky, Capt'n. Surely is a beautiful sight." A middle-aged troop member spoke.

"Buck, get in here and shut that dang door. That wind is enough to blow a man's clothes off. Where's those knuckleheads we left here to shoe my horse?"

They didn't answer with Thomas MacLayne standing over them in the dark with his cocked revolver.

"Anyway, bed down. We're headin' out at sun-up. I'm payin' MacLayne one more visit before we head back to Missouri. He don't need that fancy barn. We may even get some nice horse flesh. That stallion of his is mighty nice." Duncan continued. "I got me one more good surprise for that smug wife of his, too."

At that, Sheriff Armstrong stepped from behind several bales of hay. "Get your hands up, Duncan. You're under arrest."

A great commotion broke out as the Rebel troops scattered, trying to escape.

Duncan called out, "Settle down, boys. The sheriff's got no jurisdiction over us. We're carryin' out orders from the governor."

The panic subsided temporarily. "Did he tell you to murder an unarmed man in front of his family?"

"We got a right. He's a traitor to our cause."

"I said raise your hands, Duncan. I'm takin' ya in."

"Not alone, you ain't."

"But I'm not alone. Men, make your guns ready. Cover this band of outlaws until I get that gun from their captain." Before the sheriff finished, Duncan fired. He missed the sheriff but wounded the deputy just behind him. A second shot splintered a plank just above Mac's head.

"Duncan, you low life. You can't seem to do anything right...not harassing a fourteen-year-old girl or shootin' a local sheriff at short range."

"Maybe I'll do better killin' you, MacLayne. You've been a burr under my saddle since the day I met you." Duncan pulled his revolver, which he'd not reloaded. When the gun didn't fire, he threw it and hit Mac in the head. Duncan pushed the door open and mounted a horse left outside. He kicked the animal brutally in the flank and fled south.

The sheriff ordered the posse to arrest the troops who were still in the barn. Then Armstrong, one deputy, Matthew, and Mac followed Duncan. The roads were covered with melting ice. Riding at any speed was dangerous. They followed the tracks as best they could, seeing that Duncan had headed toward Jonesboro. This path led directly down Buck Snort Hill.

As the posse neared the crest of the hill, they had to slow considerably. That was not the case with Duncan. He pushed his horse forward at breakneck speed. Then they heard Duncan cursing loudly. His frightened horse jerked the reins from his hands as the animal slipped on the icy road. Duncan landed amid a clump of icy bushes. He righted himself, pulled a revolver, filled the empty chambers, and began firing toward the posse. The deputy returned fire and proved to be a much better marksman. Robert Duncan's last mark on the community was his crimson blood covering the melting snow on Buck Snort Hill.

"You know, Armstrong, this is almost the ideal form of justice. Duncan caused the death of Paddy Flannagan in this very place about four years ago. Now, he's met his end in the same place. The Lord does dispense His justice in His time." Mac looked one final time at the man who hated him so strongly—and for no real reason. He felt sad. The acts of this madman seemed utterly senseless.

φ

About two o'clock in the morning, Mac returned to Shiloh. He found that he couldn't share the night's events with Laurel as he'd planned to do. His wife was locked in the girls' room with Annie. He peeked in briefly to tell her he was home and then retired to the main pen to wait for the birth of Roy's child. Laurel felt better just knowing that Mac was home, and his presence assured her that she could deal with the birth of the baby, even if the doctor did not arrive in time.

As the night edged toward morning, Annie's labor grew stronger. When the pain increased, the young woman cried out to Laurel and her dead husband. "Roy, I need you with me. Please help me, Mrs. Mac. I can't do this without Roy."

"Try to relax, Annie. J.F. will bring the doctor soon. Sweetheart, you aren't alone. I am right here." Again, Annie called out in her pain. Laurel sat at her bedside and held her hand. "Hold on to me." Laurel sang to Annie, old hymns, even lullabies. She used every kind of small talk, trying to distract her. The pain came in waves, stronger and more often. Laurel realized that she would have to deliver the baby herself.

*Lord, give me the strength and the know-how to serve my precious daughter-in-law. Please let this little one bring back her joy. Amen.*

After the next spasm passed, Laurel hurried to the hearth to get hot water from the kettle, chose a sharp knife from the drawer, and picked up the clean cloths she would need.

"How is Annie?"

"We're in God's hands, Mac. I wish the doctor were here."

"You will do fine, Wife." Mac planted a quick kiss on her cheek.

Laurel returned to Annie's side just as she cried out again. As the sun rose that cold January morning, Annie Clark Dunn gave birth to a healthy, if small, son. He had a head full of almost red hair, so much like his father's. When Laurel had cleaned and clothed the beautiful child, she laid him in his mother's arms. His tiny balled fist lay on his creamy cheeks, and his little bowed mouth made a suckling motion as he slept.

Mac came into the room to look at the new member of the family. "Isn't he the blessed image of his father? What a blessing!"

"Oh, my dear Lord, he's so beautiful, Mrs. Mac! He looks like Roy. I so wish he knew about his perfect son." Annie began to cry. Laurel knew they were mixed tears of grief and joy. She saw love in the new mother's face. Annie would be all right.

"He knows, Annie. Can't you feel his presence here with us? That kind of love is always with us. Roy knows about his son. Rest assured." Laurel bent to kiss Annie's forehead.

Annie spoke in a quivering voice, "Mrs. Mac I wanna name him Roy, after his Papa. You think that's all right? I heard you're supposed to name the first son after the grandfather."

"I think that's a perfect name for your beautiful son, Annie. Roy Dunn, Jr. is a blessed addition to our family."

# Chapter 15

*The Lord is nigh unto them that are of a broken heart, and saveth such as be of a contrite spirit.*
*Psalm 34:18*

Mac's optimism that Robert Duncan's death would return Shiloh to some degree of peace faded overnight. News from the battlefronts in the east was devastating. More than five hundred Rebel soldiers were killed in a battle at Cane Hill in Washington County, Arkansas. The news reported a tactical victory for the Confederacy, but the losses didn't seem to confirm that optimistic report. Within three weeks a major confrontation occurred at Prairie Grove in the same area of the state. This time more than thirteen hundred Rebels died in the rolling hills of the Boston Mountains. A short time later, Arkansas Post in the southern part of the state was besieged in a major battle as Union troops attempted to gain river access to get them to Vicksburg. This battle cost the Confederacy more than five thousand men.

Mac had followed the news of the battles as closely as he was able. He read every newspaper he could find, and he listened to the 'war talk" whenever he went to Jonesboro, Greensboro, or Gainesville. He was not unaware that the Confederate governor, Harris Flannagan, had changed the conscription law to require service of all men between seventeen and forty-five, and he had charged local militia officers with enforcing the laws. Mac knew the danger, but he knew he had enough family and friends to give him ample warning if the local guard began to call on men who had not yet volunteered to serve. He also knew that able-bodied men were the greatest shortage in the Confederate army.

On a cold mid-January afternoon, Mac galloped into the yard, jumped from Midnight's back, and tossed the reins across the top rail of the corral. "Laurel Grace, where are you?" He ran toward the back porch. As he pulled open the back door, he found Laurel and Annie elbow deep in kneading bread for Sunday dinner. "Mac, please close the door. That cold air will kill the yeast."

"Laurel, I want you to come with me, please." The tone of his voice was strange, so devoid of warmth.

"Mac, I need…"

"Please don't argue with me. I want you to go with me. Now."

Laurel brushed the loose flour from her hands. "Cathy, do you mind looking after Leah Ann and the boys while I see what has upset Mac?" Cathy nodded. "Please put the bread in the hearth oven after it rises again. I'll be back as soon as I can."

Laurel walked the short distance and put her hand on Mac's arm. "All right. Where are we off to? Is something wrong?"

He looked at her. Then he averted his eyes. "Let's ride down to Eden so we can be alone. I need to talk to you and want your complete attention." He picked her up, carried her to Midnight's side, and hoisted her onto the saddle. He swung himself up behind her and followed the path leading to the giant oak tree and the glade they'd called Eden since the first day they'd come to Shiloh as husband and wife.

The trip was short, silent, and tense. When they dismounted under the bare branches of the grand old tree, Mac pulled a letter from his vest pocket. He took her hand and walked over to the fallen log where they often sat when they visited the grave of their first son, Campbell'.

"Laurel, I have to ask you to forgive me again. I have to break the promise I gave you when I came home from the secession convention in May of '61. I have tried to keep it. I swear I have tried. This letter makes it impossible now."

"What are you talking about?"

"I am goin' to Helena to enlist in the Union Army or Navy. If I refuse, the governor will have me arrested as a traitor. Everything we've worked for will be confiscated and sold to pay for the war. Without our land, how can we feed the children? How can I take care of you as I told your papa I would?"

"NO. NO. You can't go, Mac. You promised that we would remain together…declaring we're neutral until this wretched business is over. You can't bear arms against our neighbors. Roy died for the Confederacy."

"I don't have a choice, Laurel. If I stay here, refusing to aid the Confederate Army, I'll be arrested. I could be executed, Laurel. If they decide I am a traitor they will confiscate our property. You will be destitute."

"I don't care about that. I won't let you go. We can write to the governor and explain that we intend to remain neutral. We'll pay our taxes."

"Stop it, Laurel. The letter didn't say you are invited to come and fight for the Confederacy. The letter says 'You are ordered to raise a unit of men.' I've even been given a report date of the end of next month to report to Little Rock."

Laurel turned and faced her husband. "Patrick, I can't let you leave me alone again. I've been loyal to you, agreeing to whatever you believed God was calling you to do. I won't do it again. I lost our first son—alone. I spent Christmases alone, explaining to children who love you that you thought your duty to be more important than they are. I nursed three children through influenza—alone. I've kept this homestead going when I was so tired that I could hardly raise my head from the bed. You will stay home and take care of your family." She started to walk away.

Mac grabbed her shoulders and turned her back to face him. "Stop it, Laurel. You're hysterical. Wife, I don't have a choice. If I stay home, I'm putting the family and our home in danger." She jerked away and struck out at him, smashing her fist into his chest. "Listen to me."

"Let me go."

Mac shook her until she stopped trying to pull away. When she stood quietly in his grasp, he pulled her into his arms. They stood together for some time, as the wind blew a few dead leaves around them. "Can you listen to me now, Laurel?" She nodded. "My dear Lord, how I wish I could make you know how much I love you. The idea of leaving you again rips at my heart. If I knew a place where I could hide our family away 'til this war ended, I'd gladly go there with you."

"I've never been happier than these past eighteen months. Most of our family is safe and well. I don't want anything to change. Stay with me. We'll be all right."

"We won't, Laurel. We've already lost Roy. Things have been changing here at Shiloh since the day Arkansas seceded. You're being snubbed by people we thought were our brothers and sisters in the faith, just because I won't join the Confederate army. Did you know that I got into a brawl in Greensboro two weeks ago when a soldier threw a petticoat in my face and asked me if my wife needed a man in her bed?"

"Those things don't matter. As long as we're together, we can deal with this stupid war."

"No, Laurel. We can't."

She screamed and began to run toward the creek. Blinded by tears, she stumbled her way across the dead grass. She saw no beauty in Eden that day. She yelled back, "This war will not destroy my dream of Shiloh. I won't let you toss away the life we've built together. This is not our war."

Mac ran after his distraught wife. He caught her just as she reached the creek bank. When he turned her around, she collapsed into his arms. "Listen, Laurel Grace. Please just let me tell you the choices I have. This order from the governor's office made me an officer in the Confederate army. I can't take a troop of men and lead them to fight in support of a cause that goes against everything I've ever believed in." Laurel nodded as if she understood. "I can't do it. You know that, don't you?"

"I know."

"A second option would be to take our family, load a wagon with what possessions it could hold, and try to find sanctuary in another state, maybe Kansas or Oklahoma. If we are lucky enough to get across the state line, I might be safe. It would cost us everything we've worked for. Shiloh would be lost to us."

"Mac, we can't run with our babies. Leah Ann and Roy, Jr. are too young for such a long journey, especially this time of year."

"Well, Darlin', that leaves me with one last option. This is what I have to do. I am going to Helena. When I leave, my father and Matthew will be here to help take care of you. J.F. is too old to be drafted so he can take care of the heavy farm chores. The story will be spread around Shiloh that I deserted you and the kids."

Laurel stood stark still. Her mouth agape. "Who would believe that?"

"You have to make them believe you, Laurel. It's the only hope we have of savin' our homestead and protectin' our children's livelihood."

The slope of Laurel's shoulders spoke of her defeat. Mac felt as if he'd lost much more than an argument. "Laurel, I am so sorry. This is the last thing I want to do—and the only thing I know to do. Please understand."

She turned and began to walk back toward their cabin. She pulled her apron up to dry her eyes.

"Laurel, come back and we'll ride back to the cabin."

She continued to walk away. He ran to catch her. He pulled her around to face him once again. "Won't you tell me what you are thinkin'? Please talk to me."

"I need some time. Go on back. I'll go home to get supper on the table when it's due." She walked away.

The strained evening meal took its toll on everyone. Cathy and Andy quarreled over the last spoon of cobbler. Mark Thomas refused to eat at all, and because she was a bit feverish, Leah Ann fretted throughout the time they sat around the table. Mac tried to open conversations a time or two, but no one seemed interested in small talk.

"Cathy, will you give Leah Ann a bath before bed? She's been fussy all day. Perhaps she'll sleep better if she's clean and powdered. Thank you, Sweetheart." With the request, Laurel excused herself and started to the barn to feed the animals.

"May I join you, Wife?"

"I'd rather you didn't. I need some time."

Mac stood and watched her go out the door. Andy looked at his father and back at the door. "What's wrong with Mama?"

"Son, I'll talk to you about all this later. Let's get our chores done. It'll be bedtime soon."

*φ*

Mac returned from the corral. He hoped Laurel would be ready to talk, but he found she had not come in to help the children get ready for bed. Annie had stepped into that role, and all the children, except Andy and Cathy, had already gone to sleep.

"Cathy, have you seen your mama since I went out to do the chores?"

"No, Papa. The last time I looked out, she went into the barn with the feed basket." Cathy's eyes showed signs of tears.

"Did ya fight with Mama? Y'all don't never fight."

"No, Andy. We didn't fight."

"She seems riled at ya. I think you better say you're sorry."

"Son, I wish that could fix everything." Mac pulled his fingers through his hair. "Young'uns, it's time for bed. I'll see y'all in the mornin'. Don't be frettin' about tonight. Things will be fine when we have a few minutes to talk. Goodnight."

Mac went outside and walked around the yard until he got cold. He didn't see his wife. Then he went to the second pen to see if she'd gone to bed. Laurel wasn't there either. He ran to the barn to see if Sassy Lady was missing. He found the mare in her stall, finishing her oats. He returned to the bedroom.

He read his Bible for a while and then lay down to wait. Laurel would return so they could talk. He knew she would. But she didn't return. Mac spent a sleepless night, angry at first, and then anxious because of Laurel's unusual behavior. She was too stable to do anything foolish. He knew that; nevertheless, he prayed long and hard for her safe return.

At sun-up, Mac heard Laurel had shut the door when she carried in water pails from the creek. He pulled on his trousers and hurried to confront her. He found her preparing the morning meal as she did every morning.

"Good morning, Mac. How are you this morning?"

"How am I? Where were you all night?" He asked.

"I was here on the homestead. I told you I needed some time."

"Laurel Grace…"

"I don't need a scolding, Mac. You gotta do what you've gotta do. I don't have to like it. I don't."

"Just understand. I'm not doin' this because I want to. This is the last thing I want to do."

"I don't understand. You promised me that you would never leave me to face life without you again. You betrayed me. You lied to me. How can I ever trust you again?"

"Laurel, I told you the reason I have to do this. I can't believe how unreasonable you're bein'."

"I won't argue with you, Patrick. You've made up your mind so do what you believe you have to do. I will stay at Shiloh and take care of my children."

Mac walked toward her, intending to take her in his arms. She stepped back.

"Would you like your coffee now?" Mac knew he'd need God's guidance to cross the chasm. Laurel's cold voice and refusal to look at him spoke more loudly than any tirade she could throw at him. He had to reach her, but he feared time was not on his side.

Later that afternoon, Matthew Campbell raced into Mac's yard. He jumped from his horse, not taking the time to tie the reins to the porch rail. He approached Mac who was working with J.F., digging the new well on the opposite end of the back porch. They had tried one closer to the door, but it proved too near the salted well, and the bad water had seeped through into the new shaft. The second attempt was almost to the depth of the original well, but they had not yet reached an adequate supply of water. Mac knew he could not leave until Laurel had a new well.

"Mac, you gotta get ready to leave here. Last night at a pot-luck dinner over near Herndon, I heard a group of the Greene County rowdies talkin' about the order to round up troops from the Shiloh area. They said they're starting just south of Gainesville on Monday mornin'.

"I need a couple more weeks. I have to finish this well and…"

"You ain't got no more time. John and Mark are packing to leave now. Thank the Lord, Randall has that one blind eye. At least Susan won't have to…" Matthew stopped. "I'm sorry, Brother. That was thoughtless."

"So, I got two days left?' Mac threw his spade to the ground.

"I figure you'll be okay until Sunday. After that, you'll be takin' a chance. Have you ironed out the plan with Laurel yet?"

"I tried. All I accomplished was makin' my wife so angry with me she said I betrayed her and that I'm a liar. Now all she does is spout pleasantries at me."

"Want me to talk to her?" Matthew asked.

"No, she may be your niece, but she's my wife. I'll make her understand—somehow.

"You do whatever you need to do to get ready to leave. I'll make sure that well gets dug."

That night when the household turned in, Mac took Laurel's arm. "Laurel, come to our room. We have to talk."

"No. I will return to the barn loft. I don't have anything to say that won't cause an argument. I'd rather not fight with you."

"I'm not askin' you, Laurel Grace. I'm tellin' ya to come to our bedroom."

She jerked her arm from his grasp. "If that's what you want."

She went to the water closet and changed into her nightdress. Then she sat on the side of the bed and began to pull the pins from her chignon.

"Are you ready to hear me out yet?" Mac asked.

"You can say whatever you want."

"Are you gonna listen?"

"I wouldn't disrespect you by ignoring you. I'll listen. That doesn't mean I'll agree with what you say."

"Laurel, I know it will do no good to try to convince you I am doin' all I can do. What I will say is what has to happen on

Sunday after we go to my pa's. Matthew is holdin' service for us there."

"All right. We'll go to church on Sunday."

"After that, I'll bring you and the kids back home. I plan to pick up my gear and ride as far as Jonesboro, headed toward Helena. The Second Arkansas Union Cavalry is located there. I think I can stay in the state if I enlist there. Perhaps, I can get home once in a while."

"That's nice." Laurel's smug retort brought out the tendons in Mac's neck and the blood vessels at his temples. He'd never been so angry with Laurel.

"You're not goin' to forgive me, are you?"

"Is there anything else you want to tell me?"

"Only one more thing. I love you more than I can ever tell you. I thank God every day he gave me the time to learn what marriage is." Mac's voice broke. Tears streamed down his face. "Thank you for givin' me beautiful children and for lovin' my son. I hate that I've hurt you. God keep you until I can return to you."

"Goodnight, Patrick."

"I want you to share our bed tonight, Laurel."

"I'll sleep beside you if that's your wish."

"Goodnight, Laurel."

Φ

Everything went as Mac had planned. Sunday afternoon about 4:00, Mac kissed his children good-bye and hugged them to him as he prayed a blessing over them. He hugged Annie and held the tiny hand of Roy Dunn, Jr.

"Annie, you're doin' a wonderful job with that little boy. Roy has to be lookin' down at you every day, smilin' at his family. Take care of yourself and help Laurel when she needs it."

"I will, Mr. Mac. God keep you."

"I won't need these things anymore." Mac threw three issues of a recent newspaper and a broadside into the seat of his chair. Laurel had not come from the second pen to say good-bye. Mac hesitated at the back door, looking toward his children. When Laurel failed to come out, he went to the barn to pack his few belongings and supplies into his saddlebags. Finally, he placed his

Bible and a couple of books he'd been reading in the remaining space. In his interior breast pocket, he tucked the silver case with Laurel's picture and his father-in-law's whittled cross. All the time he whispered a prayer that Laurel would come to tell him good-bye.

In the meantime, Laurel went into the main room to comfort her children. She knew Mac's departure would be especially difficult for Andy. She saw the folded papers in the seat of the armchair. She picked them up and when she did the crumpled broadside fell. She'd not seen it before. She quickly scanned the words.

---

# To Arms ✝ To Arms

## Headquarters 3rd Brigade
## 1st Arkansas Military Command

By order of the Governor and Commander in Chief of the Militia and President of the Military Board in Arkansas, every man subject to military duty is required to report himself forthwith to the commanding officer in his county, armed and equipped as the law directs.

Those who refuse to report themselves must be made to comply or be treated as deserters in face of the enemy. Such persons can not be left behind safely!

All suspicious persons will be arrested as sympathizers with the North. If there be such in the land, the cannot be trusted in the rear when the Militia moves forward. All must, therefore, move together or be dealt with as the law directs.

All are entreated by their honor, their homes, and their families to act promptly. Officers will lay aside all other business, and devote themselves to the public service, rally men, borrow, purchase, or seize all arms in the hands of non-combatants, and march to the appointed site for rendezvous.

---

"Oh, my dear Father in Heaven! What have I done?" Laurel ran out the door, praying she could reach Mac before he rode away. She heard the clomping of Midnight's hooves on the road. "Mac...Mac, please wait. Come back. I have to tell you..."

Mac continued to ride toward Greensboro.

"Mac," Laurel screamed as she ran to the edge of the road. "Please, Mac."

Midnight stopped, and Laurel continued to run to meet Mac as he returned to her. He slipped from his saddle and enfolded his wife in his arms.

"I'm sorry, Mac. I was so mean and childish. I didn't listen."

"Thank you, God. Laurel, thank you for callin' me back. Leavin' without tellin' you good-bye was killing me."

"Please forgive me. If I had understood the threat, I'd have encouraged you to go months ago. Why didn't you show me that terrible broadside?"

"I wanted to, Laurel. I wanted beyond all for you to understand why I have to go. I don't know any other way to safeguard you and our family. Lord, I wish I did."

"I know now, Mac."

Mac pulled Laurel into an embrace that rivaled any kiss they'd ever shared. "I'll miss you, darlin'. I'll come home any chance I get. I promise you."

"God keep you safe, Mac, and bring you back to me and Shiloh soon. I love you."

"And I love you." With one final kiss, Mac turned and remounted Midnight. His heart was much lighter as he galloped toward the bend in the rode. There he turned and waved his hat to Laurel, calling back to her, "Kiss our kids for me."

# Chapter 16

*And withal, they learn to be idle, wandering about from house to house; and not only idle, but tattlers also and busybodies, speaking things which they ought not.*
*I Timothy 5:13*

Laurel turned to face her children. They'd followed her as she ran out of the cabin calling to Mac. The four stood gaping at their mother. After a moment, Andy stuttered, "Mama, where is Papa goin'?"

*Lord, what do I tell them? How can I make them understand when I don't understand myself why my husband thinks this is the only way to protect us?* Laurel stooped to pick up Mark Thomas and nodded toward the door. "Come on to the house, young'uns. I don't want to say this but once." She put her youngest son on the bench at the table and motioned for the others to sit, "Annie, please come to the table, if you can. I need to talk to all of you."

Before Annie entered the room, Leah Ann began to whimper from her cradle. Laurel picked her up and brushed her baby-smooth cheek against her own. She walked to the head of the table and sat in Mac's chair. "Annie, please sit in my chair there." Then she bowed her head, praying to collect her wits and to stave off the tears she felt too close to the surface. After a deep breath, she pulled her shoulders back and spoke, looking into the eyes of the children she adored.

"Last night, your papa told each of you good-bye. He said he was going to join the Union army. He didn't want to leave us." Laurel stopped to clear her voice. "Patrick MacLayne is a man of principles. I don't have to tell you that, but it's the one thing you must always remember about your father. He tried all he knew to stay out of this war, which he hates. Laws passed by the Confederate government in Richmond and by Governor Flannagan in Little Rock forced his decision to join the Union army."

"But where is he goin', Mama?" Andy asked again. The uproar from the older children around the table all talking over each other startled the babies. Both Roy and Leah Ann screamed.

The confusion pushed Laurel to the edge, and she yelled "Stop it. Stop all this noise." The clatter ceased except for two frightened infants. "Annie, please try to calm, Roy. S-h-h-h, Leah. Sweet little one, quiet." In a few minutes, Laurel continued. "He is riding to Helena to enlist. He would have remained here with us at Shiloh if the state would have allowed him to remain neutral. When he was pushed to choose, he had to join with the side that he believed in. He thinks Arkansas was wrong to secede."

Annie began to cry. "This is so unfair. We already lost Roy to this war. That oughta be enough sacrifice for one family."

"I agree, Annie, but when wars happen, people are always expected to choose sides. When Arkansas went with the South, the decision put us on the wrong side. Mac either had to deny his convictions or leave to protect us. In his mind, he had no choice."

"What's gonna happen to us, Mama?" Cathy asked. "It'll be impossible for us to take care of our homestead without Papa."

"No, Cathy. We'll be fine. We're capable, and the Lord will see us through. We aren't alone. Your grandpapa MacLayne is just across Big Creek and my uncle Matthew is not two miles away. J.F. will be here to take care of our animals and help with the crops. We have plenty of help when we need it."

Cathy broke into tears. Laurel went to her and pulled her into her arms. "We'll be all right. Why are you so upset?"

"My brother got killed. We don't even know where he is. Now Papa is gone and he'll be in danger. I don't wanna lose someone else I love."

"Cathy, dear, all we can do is pray for Mac every day. Perhaps the war will be over soon and he'll come home."

"But why go now? He stayed home with us all this time, Mama."

"Andy, Pea Ridge, the Battle at Shiloh in Tennessee and the huge loss of men at Prairie Grove hurt the South. The Confederacy needs men. Your uncle Matthew brought news three days ago that Greene and Craighead County militia were conscripting all men in the area."

"We coulda just hid Papa for a few days," Andy replied.

"Your papa left to protect us. If he'd been taken, the Rebels would have tried him as a traitor and hung him if they chose to do so. Being an enemy of the Confederacy, all our property would have been taken by the government in Richmond to help pay for the war."

"How could they do such a terrible thing to a good man like Mr. Mac?" Annie blurted out.

"Kids, listen to me. What I have to tell you is important." She turned her back and walked to her rocking chair, needing a minute to compose herself. She began to rock Leah Ann. "I don't want you to talk about your papa to anyone. If they ask you anything, tell them I won't let you talk about him."

"Why, Mama? Don't we love Papa anymore?" Gracie had tears on her lashes.

"Of course, we love your papa. He's not doing anything wrong, but we have to do what he asked us to do. He wants us to be safe so we have to honor his decision. Just remember, tell anyone who asks that I told you that you can't talk about our family business."

Andy walked to her and hugged her. "We'll keep Papa safe, Mama. We won't talk about him to no one."

"And, if someone says something bad about him, please don't get into a fight. We know your Papa is a good man, and he wouldn't do anything dishonest"

"Yes, Mama. We won't never talk about Papa."

"Mark Thomas, you can always talk to me about your papa." Laurel hugged the tearful boy.

"I'm glad 'cos I love my papa."

"We all do, Son."

φ

Despite the bone-chilling cold of late February and early March, visitors made their way to Shiloh. Thomas MacLayne made a weekly visit to see to the welfare of his grandchildren and Laurel. Rarely did he find a need for concern, but he was always welcomed. Andy especially thrived on the attention his grandfather paid him.

Matthew Campbell came to see Laurel each time he returned from one of his mission circuits to the army camps in his district. On most of the visits, he included his wife and daughter. Laurel told them she was doing well, and the children kept her too busy to worry about life outside of Shiloh. Matthew's frown told her he didn't believe her. Behind Laurel's gray eyes, dark clouds of sadness spoke her true feelings. She was not able to hide the deep circles under her eyes nor the perpetual posture of fatigue that showed in her slumped shoulders and gloomy face. Ellie tried at every visit to talk about Mac's absence, but Laurel evaded any question that exposed the feelings she struggled to control.

Laurel's stoic façade stayed in place as long as those who cared for her didn't press her for too much. She could talk about her children, about the weather, the needs around the homestead, and current events around Shiloh. She could not talk about Mac. She had no intention of opening the floodgates of emotions she had so little control over.

This all changed about six weeks after Mac rode off to Helena. On Wednesday afternoon, Laurel and her older children were in the garden preparing the soil for spring planting. Three of the ladies from the community drove up to the homestead. These women hadn't been very pleasant to Laurel since Mac's scene with Captain Armstrong at the church nearly two years past.

"Good afternoon, Laurel. Looks like y'all are gettin' a nice start on plantin' your garden this year."

"Hello, Mrs. Jeffer, Mrs. Hawkins, and Sally. Yes, the weather's nice, and we have a lot of mouths to feed here."

"Indeed you do," Maude Hawkins replied. "You poor dear. How can you manage such a load alone?"

Laurel knew immediately why these ladies came for a visit. She stood up and held her hoe, almost as if it were a staff. "We manage quite well. My family works together to supply what we need. My uncle and father-in-law are near-by if we need anything. Have you started your garden yet?"

"Well, no, not yet. My husband's been under the weather." She coughed and put her kerchief to her mouth.

Mrs. Jeffers stepped down from the wagon. "Bless you, Laurel dear. We know how hard it must be for you with Mac away."

"He'll be back when he's able. Thank you for your concern. Is there something you need?"

"Oh, no. We're just worried about you and all your precious little ones. We wanted to see if we could help."

"No, Ma'am. We have no needs that you can help with. Would you like some cool water before you return home?"

"Oh, I would." Sally June Hawkins stepped to the ground. "I'd also like to talk with Cathy. We haven't seen each other for ages."

"All right. Cathy, please take the ladies to the porch and give them some cool water from the well. If you'll excuse me, I've got three more rows to string before nightfall." Laurel returned to the garden. She had no doubt these visitors had heard of Mac's desertion of his family. They now had a first-hand account to fuel their gossip from the woman he had discarded.

The most stubborn clot of dirt had no chance of surviving as Laurel crashed her hoe into the ground over and over. She muttered under her breath. "How dare those biddies come here? They didn't bother to come for more than two years."

"What did you say, Mama?"

"Oh, Andy, I didn't say anything. Let's finish these three rows and then quit for the afternoon."

"You didn't like those ladies comin' here, did ya?"

Laurel looked at Andy and grinned. "You've become a good observer of people, Son. No, I didn't like it. Their reason for coming shows me they're not friends."

"They wanted you to talk bad about Papa, didn't they?"

"Andy, some people like to gossip. That is why I told y'all not to talk about your papa's decision to join the Union army. His decision is not anyone else's business."

Within fifteen minutes, the wagon with the visitors headed back toward Greensboro. Cathy returned to the garden. Streaks of tears ran through the dust on her face.

"Cathy, you've been crying. Are you all right?"

"Yes, Mama. I did what you told me. When Sally June went with me to the well, she asked me where Papa went. I told her you didn't want us to talk about our papa. Then she said she already knew. People all over the settlement are sayin' how he deserted us."

"I said, 'Sally June, you're a liar. Our papa loves us, and he'd never run away from us."

"That's a good thing to say, Cathy. It doesn't matter what they say. We know the truth."

"Someone better not say that to me. I'll punch their teeth down their throat."

"Andy, no. Don't let your temper get to you. Remember what we read about gossip in the book of Proverbs the other night. All those verses say how the foolish mouth tries to destroy their neighbors, but knowledge is delivered by the one who does right."

"I remember that, but I doubt I can stand back and let anyone put down my papa."

"Andy, God says it's His role to defend the innocent--not yours. I don't think your papa has done anything we need to defend."

"All right, but I miss Papa so much. Almost ever day, I need to talk to him about one thing or another."

"You can talk to me, Son."

"You ain't no man. It's not the same."

"I guess your granddad will have to do until your papa can come home."

# Chapter 17

*"Likewise the Spirit also helpeth our infirmities: for we know not what we should pray for as we ought: but the Spirit itself maketh intercession for us with groanings which cannot be uttered.*
*Romans 8:26*

The day Mac rode away from Shiloh, he pushed Midnight at a strong pace toward Jonesboro for several minutes until he realized he was running from his frustration. He'd kill his faithful mount if he tried to get to Helena at that pace. The hundred and ten miles would take several days if the weather co-operated, and longer if winter decided to raise her hoary head again. So far, the snow and ice had stayed well to the north, but the cold had been brutal in Arkansas during the winter of 1863.

As he rode near Greensboro, Mac decided to stop at the local jewelry shop. Laurel's birthday in April and their sixth wedding anniversary would all happen before they would be together again. He wanted to have a gift ready for her, even if he could not deliver it in person. She had long admired a golden locket that belonged to her Aunt Ellie. If he could find one, he would have a small picture of himself, made when they'd had their family portrait taken, set in the pendant. This small gesture would reassure her of his constant devotion. Even at an exorbitant cost, he was determined to send the gift she wanted.

Mac found the jeweler behind his work table and gave him careful instructions for the design, along with how and when to deliver the present. Before he could leave the shop, three local rowdies, who'd thrived on harassing Union sympathizers, came into the tiny shop.

"Afternoon, MacLayne. How's things at your homeplace? Had any visitors?"

"Everything is fine, thanks. If you'll excuse me, I've got business in Jonesboro this afternoon."

"You better get it done quick," a tall bald man said.

"Yeah, Charlie did ya hear the local militia are roundin' up all the traitors and deserters over in the Shiloh area this week? I heard they're givin' them a choice…join up or get shot."

"That so, Zeke? What ya think about that news, MacLayne?"

"It's not news to me. Guess it's a good thing I'm neutral. I got no plans to do either of those things…die or join up with the Rebels." Mac turned and handed Mr. Lister the price of the locket. "Thank you, Laban. I'd appreciate you seein' that item gets delivered with this note."

"Yes, sir. It'll be done."

The men jostled him as he left the shop, making him even edgier than he'd been. Undoubtedly, he'd done the right thing…the only thing he could do. If his father, his best friend, and his wife could carry out their part of the deception, his family would survive without further harassment. Surely, the people of Shiloh would rally in support of Laurel when they believed he'd deserted her, leaving their large family for her to support by herself. Except for their unreasonable support of the Southern Cause, they were good people.

Mac was more than confident in Laurel's ability to care for Shiloh and their family. They could ride out the war at the homestead. The good land would support them if the militia raiders left them alone. With him counted as a deserter, the land would no longer be in jeopardy. No Southern gentleman would deny a lady the means to provide for her children. Although Mac believed his plan to be sound, he continued to pray with every mile he rode away. "Lord keep my family in Your hand. Please give Laurel Your strength and wisdom. Bring us back together at Shiloh soon."

At sundown, Mac approached the town square in Jonesboro. He saw Captain Anderson and four of his troops standing on the porch of the newly constructed Craighead County Courthouse. He could not allow this group of men to see him. Mac knew his name was the first one on the list of men to be conscripted. He turned Midnight and followed a back street to the outskirts of Jonesboro. He would forego a talk with Sheriff Armstrong and his plan to seek a room in the boarding house across the street from Snoddy's livery. His best hope now was to find some kind of shelter in the countryside beyond the settlement. Mac loosened the reins and let Midnight pace so as not to arouse suspicion. He headed toward Bolivar.

As the night deepened, Midnight showed signs of tiring. They were nowhere near Bolivar. Mac looked for a place to shelter for the night. He found exactly what he needed. A small one-pen cabin stood several feet back in a wooded area, just off the Old Military Road. The door had been pulled off its hinges, but it lay on the floor. This was an easy fix. He rode to the ramshackle building, dismounted, and lead Midnight inside. After propping the door in place, Mac built a small fire in the crumbling fireplace. It wasn't home, but it would serve for one night. Midnight neighed and Mac fed him.

He heated the small slab of ham and cheese and placed it on the bread Laurel had packed for him. He made a cup of what served as coffee from the chicory in his pouch. He rolled into his saddle blanket and pulled out his Bible. He read the same passage time and again, but he took no comfort from the words. His mind wandered to his children and wife. The words blurred on the page. The peace he needed evaded him as the demons in his mind screamed out that he couldn't deal with the separation. His conscience called him 'liar' and unfaithful in the promises to his wife. He tried to pray, but instead of communion with God, Mac cried out plea after plea. "Father, keep them safe. Let me go home because I hate this war. Don't let me take sides. Pick me up, Father. Tonight, I am a defeated man. Give me the will to do what

I have to do. Please help me. Show me what you would have me do. Please."

Mac took out the small silver photo case and looked at the pictures inside. He whispered a blessing for each child by name. He gazed at the picture of Laurel. "I love you, Wife. Please forgive me." As he returned the case to his pocket words from the scripture that he called his life motto ran through this mind. He opened his Bible once again, this time to Romans, Chapter 8 and he read all the words. Verses preceding the 28th spoke to him, almost as if he could hear the words aloud. *And he that searcheth the hearts knoweth what is the mind of the Spirit because He marketh intercession for the saints according to the will of God. And we know all things work together for the good to them that love the Lord, to them who are called according to His purpose."*

Mac knew his purpose. He would protect his family and maintain his integrity. He could do nothing else and keep himself within God's will. He lay his head in his saddle, rolled himself into his blanket, and slept.

At dawn, Mac rode on, each stride taking him farther from where he wanted to be. But he didn't carry the burden he'd laid down the night before. Shortly before noon, he reached Bolivar and turned Midnight down the familiar Main Street of the town. He stopped in front of the hotel and dismounted. He tried to push open the door to the hotel but found the place locked. He looked up and down the street for someone to ask why Lizzie's hotel was closed at dinner time. Her fine cooking always drew a large crowd at that time of day. He found no one, so he went back to the door and knocked, hard and long. He repeated his call for service a second and third time. Finally, Lizzie came to the door. She hardly looked to be the same woman, he and Laurel had seen in '59 when they returned from the legislative session.

"What do ya want? I'm closed."

"Lizzie, don't ya remember me? I'm Mac MacLayne from Greensboro. Why are ya closed in the middle of the day?"

"Mr. Mac—I remember you. You and Miss Laurel. Now that I can see ya, I recognize ya. What'cha doin' in Boliver?"

"On my way to Helena. I thought I'd get a bit of dinner at the best table in Poinsett County."

"I don't feed the town like I used to…"

"I'm sorry to hear that. What's shut ya down?"

"This danged war. Most of our men are gone. Even if I wanted to keep my business open, they ain't no good meat. Most of the time we're lucky to have cornmeal. The supply wagons don't come regular, and when they do get here, they bring shoddy goods."

"I didn't realize things got so bad."

"Bein' here on the main road between the river and St. Louis, we got more'n our share of raiders and scalawags to take most of what does get shipped to us."

"Lizzie, I'm so sorry you've fallen on hard times. Can I do anything to help ya?"

"No, Mac. I ain't got the heart to work at it anyway. My sweet old man's gone now. He took sick with influenza and got pneumonia. No medicine anywhere. The doctor was gone to the army. Lee's been gone for six months."

"That's a hard loss."

"Well, that's no reason two old friends can't share a bit of a meal. Come on in. All I got is brown beans and cornbread, but I got some hot coffee. I think I can even find ya a piece of sweet 'tater pie."

"Knowin' how you cook, that sounds like a feast, Lizzie. I'd love your company for a little while."

By two-thirty, Mac kissed Lizzie good-bye and continued his southern trek toward Helena. The road took him down the west side of Crowley's Ridge, much farther south than he'd ever been down the ridgeline. Even in the winter, the contrast between the ridge and the flat of the delta awed him. He'd always found the natural beauty of Shiloh amazing, but the further he traveled down Crowley's Ridge, the more he was struck by the paradise God had placed in eastern Arkansas. With such glory in the winter, what must this region look like in the spring?

Mac traveled at a good clip, but Lizzie had told him the twenty-six or seven-mile ride to Wittsberg was not doable in half a

201

day. She'd warned that in the cold, even half a day ride would take a toll on horse and rider. Near sunset, he'd begin to think he should have taken her up on her offer to stay the night. When the temperature dropped more and snow begin to stick to the trees and brush, Mac realized he had to find shelter for himself and Midnight. After a few minutes, Mac drew his horse under a large evergreen tree with limbs bowing toward the ground. He cleared dead pine needles and other debris away from a large area under the tree. He also tied several limbs closely together to make a windbreak to one side. He then gathered small branches to make a small fire. This was not the ideal place to spend a snowy winter night, but they were at least out of the wind. The dense needles of the evergreen kept them dry. Midnight had his night's meal of oats and a handful of dried grass Mac found. Mac gave thanks he'd had a filling dinner with Lizzie for he'd find none this night.

At dawn, Mac again mounted his well-rested horse and trotted down the road to Wittsberg. Surely, he had less than twenty miles to go. He should be able to reach the busy freighter hub town well before dark so he could find a stable for Midnight and a hotel room and a decent meal for himself. When he arrived, he saw that this town, unlike Bolivar, still bustled with people. Several freight wagons in different stages of being filled sat at loading docks. A couple of different livery depots were busy. Loud, tinny music came from dancehalls and saloons, so typical of Wittsberg. But at every loading dock, guarding the supplies were two or three gray-clad soldiers with rifles slung across their shoulders. Confederate troops were everywhere, and they had commandeered supplies and wagons.

Mac continued to ride away from the main part of town, seeking a place where he could board Midnight. If his purpose were known, a run-in with these Rebel troops would be disastrous. He also knew that prime horseflesh was always a prize for the calvary. He had no desire to walk the rest of the way to Fort Curtis.

Eventually, Mac found a small blacksmith shop some way from the supply depots in town. The elderly blacksmith stood bent-shouldered and sweating over his anvil, pounding a glowing horseshoe. He looked up when Mac spoke to him. "Evenin', sir.

You got any space to shelter my mount for the night? We've traveled a long way…from Bolivar. He deserves a good night's rest."

"I do, but the stables back in town would be closer to the saloon, stranger."

"Ain't lookin' for a saloon—just a hot meal and a warm bed."

"Like I said, the saloon is down in the middle of town. That'll be the only place to shelter and eat this time of night."

"If you will take care of Midnight, here, I'll go see if I can find someplace for myself. This horse means an awful lot to me."

Mac found the old smith's word to be true. He had a poor meal and found a shabby, not too warm room above the saloon in the middle of town. When the sun rose the next day, the snow was falling in sheets, and the blustery wind made riding that day out of the question. Mac trudged through the ankle-deep snow back to the small blacksmith shop to check on his horse. In the daylight, he saw the sign above the door that read Schmidt's Ironworks and Livery.

"Mr. Schmidt, if you're able I would like you to stable Midnight again. Until this storm ebbs, we'll have to tolerate Wittsburg, I'm afraid. Can't say I enjoy my stay last night, but my horse looks fine."

"I'll show you the way to a boarding house. Mrs. Grantham is a good cook, and her house is clean."

"That'll be a welcome change. Thank you."

Mac's second day at Wittsburg proved to be more pleasant than the first. With a couple of good meals and a wonderful featherbed to sleep on, he was well-rested and ready to resume his trip when the sun shone the next day.

The seventeen-mile journey to Madison was uneventful, if uncomfortable. The sun shone sporadically through the clouds during the day. The temperature didn't rise enough to melt the icicles hanging from the tree branches. When Mac stopped for the night in the Lee County seat, the town reminded him a great deal of Greensboro. The little metropolis had two hotels, both palaces compared to the saloon lodgings in Wittsburg. On the sixth day out, Mac had traveled almost a hundred miles. He arrived at the town of Marianna, sitting on the banks of the L'Anguille River. A small steamboat was moored at its dock that afternoon, and many fashionably dressed gentlemen and ladies were making their way into the ballroom of the *Delta Princess*. Many of the younger women were accompanied by Confederate officers in dress uniforms. Mac watched for a while as these elegantly dressed couples made their way to the dance floor and swayed to the music of a stringed quartet. He hadn't expected to see such a sight in the midst of a war. He knew his children were not experiencing this kind of life. Perhaps he didn't know as much about the Delta as he thought.

Finally, on February 24, Mac rode into Helena, a thriving port city. He also saw the end of Crowley's Ridge as the dominant feature of the eastern part of the state just stopped as it neared the Mississippi. From that point, the delta dominated the area south. Here he also found no gray-clad soldiers. The Union had dominated this busy river port for nearly two years. Around him, he could see signs of the conflict as both sides fought over this port and continued to do so. The proximity to Vicksburg, a major Confederate stronghold meant the Union could never take their hold on this place for granted. Fort Curtis had been built to maintain that control. A camp for a sizeable guard had been set up all around the redoubts made of earth and strong timbers. Little in the way of comforts had yet been built, but the engineers and commanders worked long hard hours to assure this port remained Union.

Mac arrived too late to seek out the commander of the Union forces in Helena that day. The almost thirty-mile trip was the longest day's ride he'd made since he left home. As the temperature moderated, the roads became muddy and slippery the closer he got to the river. He sought out a room and board for Midnight. He would make his commitment to the Union army the next day.

Troops stationed around Fort Curtis drilled with precision and looked the part of trained military. Their uniforms were intact and clean. All the soldiers wore study boots. Each man carried army-issued weapons. The contrast to the Confederate troops he'd encountered was stark.

When Mac approached the entrance of the fort, he was stopped by the armed sentry. "Halt. What business do you have at the fort, civilian?"

Mac smiled at the official demeanor of the young man who could not possibly have reached his twentieth birthday, the Union counterpart of Roy.

"I've come to enlist if you'll point me in the right direction."

"You sound like a Southron to me…"

"And you sound like a northern boy a long way from home. I don't guess what we sound like says much about which side we support. Can you tell me who I need to see to enlist?"

"I'll call Major Lockwood. He'll decide what to do next. You wait over there by the sally port." The private pointed toward tall wooden gates closed at the entrance. He called out to his superior to handle this unusual event.

Major Lockwood escorted Mac to the post office across the street from the earthen work fort where he started an interview with the southerner who asked to enlist. The Union officer asked scores of questions, some repeated several times in slightly different words. Mac presented the scant paper work he had to support his education and his time in the General Assembly.

"Are you satisfied I'm no spy, Major?"

"Don't think you're a spy, but frankly, I am very curious why you show up here now. This war has been going on for more than two years. Why not ride it out at your homestead?"

"I can't join the Confederate army. I don't believe in secession. I tried to keep Arkansas in the Union but I failed."

"How did you do that?"

"I served in the Arkansas General Assembly two sessions. I went as a delegate to both secession conventions. I said nay every time the question came to a vote."

"That still doesn't say why you're only enlisting now, MacLayne."

"I left so my wife and children could stay on our homestead and make a livin'. If I'd stayed, I'd been hung and my property forfeited as a traitor to the Confederate cause and my state."

"Can you leave your family alone?"

"I can and I did. If you don't want me, I'll try another fort, Major."

"Hold on there, MacLayne. No one said we didn't want ya. Just had to know where your loyalties are."

"They're at Shiloh. I want only to protect my family, but I'll serve the Union as long as I believe the government is trying to preserve the nation. Arkansas can't afford to be a part of the poverty-stricken South once this war is over."

Major Lockwood delivered the oath to Mac and shook his hand. "Well, now we'll have to decide what to do with you. Right now, we don't have any Arkansas recruits at this fort. All our divisions are from Ohio and Missouri. Can you read and write?"

"I can. I spent three years at Annapolis at the naval academy a few years back. May have gone to sea if I hadn't lost most of my hearin' in my right ear the year before I'd have been commissioned."

"Military school? Well, I'll bet we have lots of things for you to do around here. Let me take you up to meet Major General Prentiss. He's the commander of Fort Curtiss. He will be darn pleased to have an educated man on his staff."

Mac followed the captain upstairs to the main office. General Prentiss was indeed pleased with the qualifications of the recruit. "MacLayne, can you shoot? I know you can ride. No second-class horseman owns an animal as fine as the one you rode in on."

"I'm a fair marksman, sir. I helped feed my family huntin' at Shiloh."

"With your military training, I believe we can assume you'll make a good officer. Captain MacLayne, you will ride with the Quartermasters Unit. You'll be assigned a small unit of five men, and you will help supply the troops of Fort Curtis and special needs requested from units near our fort. When you're in camp, you'll bivouac with the 33rd Missouri. When you're out gathering supplies, you'll be on your own until the Arkansas units come back from Batesville. Do you have questions, Captain?"

"No, sir. I'll try to serve with honor and do all I can to help preserve the Union."

"You can shelter your horse with the animals of the Missouri 33rd, too. You'll find the officers housed in the tent row about midway down the meadow. We've been too busy digging redoubt around here to build barracks. Our job is to use this ridge to defend the river port at Helena. The tents aren't the warmest places, but we have plenty of blankets."

"I'll find my place."

"We'll get you a uniform, supplies, and a weapon. We'll bring bedding to your tent. While you're waiting, you'll have time to write a letter to your family."

"I wish I could. I can't endanger Laurel and my kids like that. They live in the middle of no man's land. Neither side has claimed our area. We have little mail service, but a lot of harassment for Union sympathizers. It's better for my family that our neighbors believe I deserted them. I can't risk the mail. It's a nice thought, though."

"Welcome then, and let's get busy and get this war over so you can go home to your family. Where did you say they are?"

"They are at Shiloh in Craighead County. As soon as this war is finished, that's where I'll be, too."

# Chapter 18

*Remember O Lord, what is come upon us…We are orphans,*
*fatherless, our mothers are as widows. The joy of our hearts is*
*ceased; our dance has turned into mourning.*
*Lamentations 5: 1,3,15*

By the end of March, the vestiges of new life cropped up around Crowley's Ridge. The trees spread hints of green on the branches, and jonquils danced in the breeze on every hillside. Laurel saw new life springing up in her garden, the orchard, and the corral where two new calves were born from their nearly depleted herd. Easter was only days away, and for Laurel, that holiday always brought hope and a sense of renewal. In the spring of 1863, she needed that beyond all else.

Little news from the outside world found its way to Shiloh. When Laurel received a letter from Mac around the time of their anniversary, his optimistic reports concerning the Union troops he'd encountered buoyed her spirit. He didn't say it, but she developed a sense that war would come to an end soon, and Mac would return. She knew he was safe and that the units he served with were well-supplied and trained. Perhaps her fears for his welfare were unfounded. The letter had been sent to her father-in-law and had been written in late January, but Laurel counted it the best blessing of the new year.

March 15, 1863

Dearest Wife and Children,

I pray this letter reaches you soon so you know I am well. I reached Helena safely. The ride was not too difficult except for the cold. Midnight served me well as he has done all the years I've owned him.

I was welcomed by General Benjamin Prentiss, commandant of Fort Curtis. Most of the troops here are connected to a battalion in Missouri. I may have to make frequent trips back and forth. That could let me sneak home from time to time. I am enlisted in Company B of the Second Arkansas Cavalry Troop, but I am billeted with the 33$^{rd}$ Missouri until the Arkansas group returns. Because of my schooling at Annapolis, they made me a captain. I'll have a unit in the Quartermaster Corp traveling across the state, gathering supplies for Union troops. I was surprised by the rank.

Kids, I know y'all are working hard to help your mama. I love you and pray for y'all every day. I'll be home as soon as I'm able. You are a blessing to me.

I have to send this to Pa because I am afraid that local postmasters may report suspicious mail to the military officials. I had to reach out to you. I'm about to lose my light as the sun is setting here on the bank of the Mississippi River. I think about y'all especially now because sunset is when our family time together starts. Love to Andy, Annie, Cathy, Gracie, Leah Ann, Mark Thomas, and Roy, Jr. And my beloved wife, Laurel...the back of this letter is just for you. Please tell Pa I'm well.

Laurel pushed the letter into her pocket to read when she had some private time. The letter did set her mind at ease. Mac had given her information where she could contact him if the need arose. He was no longer in danger from the Confederate conscription laws that had hung over them since the war started in 1861.

When she'd bedded the family down and banked the fires, she went to read the part of the letter Mac wrote for her.

Laurel, this part is for you. I ache for you, Wife. I knew I'd miss you, but I didn't know how badly my body would react to your absence. My arms are heavy with the need to hold you. I can't get warm at night without you spooned next to me. I yearn to pull your tawny locks through my fingers and to kiss your sweet mouth. Without your beautiful picture to look at when the need is too great, I'd have to desert this army and return to you, even though I know the consequences.

Never doubt I love you with my entire being. Thank you, Lord, for giving me such a good woman to be my wife.        Your adoring husband,

Mac

She folded the letter and placed it in her Bible. She was blessed by his words. The letter revived her spirit. What the letter could not do was remove the same losses Mac had described. With her husband gone, part of her was missing. In day-to-day living, Laurel dispelled her emptiness. But at night, when she lay alone in the beautiful old four-poster, Laurel knew the void and the yearnings Mac wrote of. She cried herself to sleep.

$$\phi$$

On the last day of March, circumstances shook Laurel's resolve again. Near nine o'clock in the morning, about the time she began school with her children, a troop of six Confederate soldiers rode into the yard between the house and the barn. They didn't call out or knock on the door. The men dismounted and began to walk through the outbuildings and corral, taking stock of what supplies and food had been laid back by the family. Andy ran out to ask what business they had on their homestead.

"You got no right here. My mama already paid our taxes this year."

"Get away, you snot-nosed young'un. I don't have to explain myself to no kid." The corporal turned his back and began giving orders to the men under his command. "Men, I see two milk cows in the stall yonder. I counted more'n a dozen chickens and three sows in a sty back there. Leave them shoats. They're too small to feed anyone yet."

"There's early vegetables…some onions and greens in the garden." One private yelled.

"Don't bother with that. Ain't ready yet. We couldn't make a decent stew from anything there, but go check the root cellar."

Two of the soldiers began to put tethers on the cows and chase the sows and chickens to put in makeshift pens on their wagon. They also took several bales of hay from the loft. As the corporal and his troop readied themselves to depart, the distinct clink of a firearm being cocked drew their attention to the barn door.

"What are you doing with my livestock?" Green-gold eyes didn't blink once.

"Wait a minute, ma'am. We've got a right to collect your taxes."

"We owe no taxes. You are stealing the animals I depend on to provide for my family. You've gathered every animal I own."

"We're only followin' orders, ma'am. Will you send your husband out so we can settle up with him?"

"You've already taken him from this family. Inside the cabin, I got seven mouths to feed. As you said, the garden is far from being ready to harvest. Are my children supposed to starve?"

"Every farm in the state is supplyin' our troops. We'll only take what we need."

"You'll not leave us without. I'll shoot you before my children cry in their sleep because their stomachs are empty. And I don't care what color your uniform is. We paid our share."

"But ma'am, I ain't askin'. I got my orders."

"Go ahead and try. I've already told you, I'd shoot any man who tries to walk away with our animals."

"I don't wanna arrest you. If you shoot me, my men will have to shoot you. Just go back in the house, and let us do our duty."

"Looks like we're at a stalemate." Laurel continued to stare at the corporal. One of the privates took a step in her direction, and she re-aimed her rifle. "To stop someone from getting hurt, I will let you take my livestock, but not what belongs to my daughter-in-law. She's the widow of a Confederate hero. We're told he carried the battle flag up the breastwork at the Battle of Corinth, where he lost his life. His wife needs her livestock to feed her infant, born after his papa died for the Confederate cause."

"Lady, I gotta take..." Laurel pulled the trigger, and the bullet split the fence rail just inches from the corporal's chest.

"I said you can have one cow and one sow. The fattest one belongs to me. You can have four of those laying hens. The rest of that stock belongs to Annie Dunn, Confederate widow. You tell that to your commander. Take mine and leave, or try to take them all. I'll fill your carcass with lead."

"You'd better listen, mister," Andy said. "My mama's a real good shot. She means business when she's riled, and I'd say she's pretty riled with you."

"Private, leave the livestock that belongs to Mrs. Dunn. We'll make do with the rest."

Laurel watched them leave with her property.

"Golly, Mama. I didn't think you'd ever be so brave."

"Andy, it's not brave to do what you have to do. Annie has to have milk for the baby. She also tries to supply her customers when she has any spare eggs and milk. She needs her animals."

"But those Rebs coulda shot ya."

"Son, your papa told ya a long time back that no one was getting shot around here. He didn't just mean that one time. Now let's forget all this. Put the padlock on the door so any more visitors will have to ask before they start takin' our animals again."

Nerves got the better of Laurel when she realized what she'd done. She hadn't thought. Andy was right. She could have been shot. Her knees buckled, and she dropped to the floor of the barn.

"Are ya all right, Mama? Did ya hurt yourself?"

"No, son. Just a bit of delayed reaction to my fright. I'm fine. We have to be more careful from now on."

She pushed herself up and picked up the rifle that had saved Annie's livestock before she walked to the house. Even with her little fit of nerves, her confidence had seen her through the incident. She had stood up to the soldiers, not backing down once, fear never showing. She'd protected her children. Even in the loss of her livestock, she smiled and whispered, "Thank you, Lord."

Φ

Long grueling work filled the month of April. Laurel, Andy, and Cathy spent every day the weather allowed, planting, weeding, and irrigating the large garden at the back of the house. Although Mac had finished the new well, it was less convenient than the old one had been, dug as it was at the opposite end of the kitchen porch. Mac had assured the water would be good by putting it some distance from the salted well. A new chore was added this spring, and it was a time-consuming, laborious task. Late in the spring, the first apples of the orchard had to be pulled and buried. Laurel was no stranger to this routine part of apple growing as she'd done this as a girl in the Boston Mountains. Those first two years of apples must be removed from the trees so that mature, good fruit would eventually grow in the orchard.

On one of the first pullin' days, all the children except Leah Ann and Roy were in the orchard helping to pull fruit. Mark Thomas decided that an apple he'd pulled was just the right size for him. He took a bite into the hard, nearly rock-like green apple. He puckered his mouth and cried out, "Mama, mama, help me. That's a poison apple, just like the one in the story you read to us."

"Mark Thomas, sometimes I think you are too much like your papa. I told you these apples weren't good to eat. You'll try anything once, though, even when you're told not to. Here, let me wash that tart juice out of your mouth. Silly boy, when I tell ya something's not good, please listen to me. I'm only telling you these things for your own good."

"Apples are nasty. I don't want no more apples off that tree."

"You'll change your mind someday. In two more years, we'll love the fruit from this tree. We'll make apple pies and cakes, use the juice for jelly, and have apples all year round."

"I love apples, Mama," Gracie replied. "I'll wait, but it seems like a long time since we had any."

"That's true, sweet girl. We didn't have our Christmas fruit last year, and the freighters haven't brought much to the mercantile for quite a while. But in a couple of years, we'll have our own grown right here at home."

"Do you think Papa will be home by the time we have apples ready to eat?" Gracie asked.

"Let's pray so. We can be grateful though that our grapes are thriving this year. By end of summer, we'll have lots to make juice, puree for jam, and to eat from the vines."

Cathy picked up the basket of small, tart apples they would discard. "Mama, this seems like so much to just throw away. Can't ya do anything with this fruit?"

"No, Cathy, until it's time, we just throw away the culls. Two years will seem like a short time when we have good apples."

"Papa ain't even been gone that long, and it seems like forever." Andy frowned. Laurel understood. Mac had been away from Shiloh for less than five months, and she'd have sworn she'd not seen him in a decade. In the time he'd been gone, Laurel had worked harder, slept less, and mourned his loss beyond anything she'd imagined she could. The separation of time and distance would have been unbearable without the frequent visits from her father-in-law and her Uncle Matthew. But they didn't have news about Mac either.

Easter came early in April that year. Thomas MacLayne invited Laurel and her family to spend the holiday at his home, Grace Creek. He'd planned to have the Campbells join them and hoped Matthew would hold an impromptu Easter service for them. However, Brother Matthew did not return from his circuit by Sunday morning. He'd sent a message to Ellie that a skirmish in the northcentral part of the state had delayed his return. His note hinted at high casualties on both sides. He told her he felt compelled to minister to those badly wounded.

The best part of the day was seeing Thomas and Peggy so happy in their newly established home. Peggy had added touches here and there to soften the austere look of the newly built house.

214

The two newlyweds displayed an affectionate relationship, frequently holding hands and whispering to each other. Her children had settled into the home and seemed to enjoy having Thomas fill the role left by their father. The fact that they weren't exactly children seemed quite irrelevant. Laurel smiled at their innocent attempts to cover up covert glances and private conversations they tried to sneak in when they thought no one was watching. Everyone could see their fondness for each other. Laurel envied their companionship.

Andy sought out the company of his grandfather continually. Even before the Easter visit, Laurel had noticed how frequently Andy mentioned his grandfather or commented on the things his grandfather had said to the family. She'd also found him to be withdrawn and very quiet at home. After school was dismissed, he'd often go off by himself. He was so much more animated with Thomas. She knew Andy missed Mac. All the children did. Mac had given all his children the attention they wanted, but Mac had always made an extreme effort to make up to his oldest son for the time he'd been alone.

That Easter afternoon Andy came to her as she was packing the buggy to return to Shiloh. "Mama, I'm gonna stay here with grandpapa a couple more days, okay?"

"I'm not sure if you are telling me what you are going to do or asking for permission," Laurel replied.

"I knew you'd act like that. I just wanted to go fishin' with Grandpapa tomorrow."

"No, Andrew. I need you at home."

"Oh, all right."

Laurel pushed her concern to the back of her mind. She didn't want to cause a rift. Andy was a good boy. He'd be fine. He was no different than anyone else at Shiloh. He missed Mac. How could she expect more from him when she knew her shortcomings since Mac had left.

"Laurel, before you go, I have something to give you. When I was in Greensboro last week, the jewelry asked me to give this to you before your birthday. He said it was from Mac and had to be delivered before the 8th of April. Today seems to be a good time. Easter couldn't be a better time." Thomas MacLayne handed her a small package with a green ribbon tied into a bow.

Laurel opened the box and found the sterling locket Mac had ordered for her. She opened the silver oval and found the portrait of Mac. He had sent her a ray of hope one more time. Even with the spat with Andy, the day proved to be blessed.

The last Monday in April Laurel began the new school term. All the planting had been finished, leaving free time for the kids. The Masters family move back to Tennessee after the death of Mr. Masters, so the school population was nine, all members of Laurel's family. With the subscription school closed, Laurel offered to take any student in the community, but no one enrolled. Truthfully, she didn't expect many because too much animosity remained between the pro-Union side and the Confederacy. Even though many members of the Shiloh community believed Mac had deserted Laurel, few were willing to cross the community leaders that supported the Rebel movement. Laurel and her family remained isolated from the social life around Greensboro.

And just as well…. In Laurel's present frame of mind, the demands on her time and energy pushed her to her limit, physically and emotionally. She held school with her children, the Flannagans, and the Campbells between eight and noon. She fed them lunch and immediately send them home. She and her children then began their workday on the homestead. Laurel made sure the crucial work of keeping food available for her family was the priority of all. Even J.F. Clarke helped, but his work also included overseeing the forty-acre farm that belonged to Annie and Roy Jr. Thankfully, the abundant rain abundant that year made it unnecessary to irrigate the orchard. Every day was full. If Laurel had been able to sleep, much of the stress and anxiety may have faded. Yet with Mac gone, Laurel the peace that would allow her to rest alluded her most nights.

Another month passed and early vegetables were ready to harvest. Although few of these things had to be canned, they did add to the variety of their stored victuals. Of course, the workload again increased as the harvested garden space was dedicated to their crops of late vegetables, such as turnips, beets, and cabbage.

Laurel planted two rows of chicory plants, knowing that coffee would be non-existent at the mercantile. With a good supply coming from her spring garden, the addition of the fall garden would assure that her kids would have plenty to eat through the winter.

With the additional work in the garden, Laurel asked Andy, Cathy, and Mark Thomas to take on most of the care of the livestock. That was the time Laurel faced her first rebellion with her oldest son.

At the supper table, Laurel broached the problem she'd never thought she'd have to face. "Andy, you didn't brush down the horses as I asked you to do this afternoon. Did something come up I don't know about so you couldn't finish your chores?"

"Guess I forgot." Andy squirmed on the bench, knocking his fork to the floor.

"What caused you to forget?"

Instead of an answer, Andy ducked beneath the table to retrieve the dropped fork.

"Andrew, I am talking to you. I know Sassy is my mare, but Sparky is your horse. The entire task would have taken you less than an hour."

"Sorry. I said I forgot. I'll do it tomorrow."

"Tomorrow is the Sabbath. The horses will have to wait 'til Monday now. What did ya do with your time, son?"

"I just went to Grandpapa's to fish with him and Sean."

"Andy! You didn't ask me if you could go off so far."

"Mama, Big Creek ain't that far. I'm old enough to ride over to see my grandfather."

"That is not the point. What if Mark Thomas decided to follow you?"

"He didn't. I told him he couldn't come with me. I wanted to spend the afternoon with grandpa. Ain't no other man around here to do nothin' with."

Laurel stood up and began to clean the table. Cathy joined her at once. They left the room without speaking.

"Mama, don't be mad at me. I didn't mean to disobey. I forgot that's all."

From the kitchen, she answered. "I understood what you said. Please go get ready for baths now."

"I don't need no bath. Sean and me swam in the creek this afternoon."

"Andrew, I said it's time to get your Saturday night bath. Hair washin' and soap didn't happen at the creek this afternoon. Besides, you need to help Mark Thomas with his bath. He didn't swim in the creek today.

"Come on, Mark Thomas. Let's go get a real bath with soap." Laurel looked up into Andy's storm blue eyes, so much like Mac's. Laurel scowled at Andy's mocking tone, but she held her tongue. She knew cooler heads would be needed to resolve this conflict. Tomorrow would serve much better.

The next afternoon when the family finished their Bible lesson and had eaten Sunday dinner, Laurel asked Andy to walk with her to the orchard. Gracie and Mark Thomas asked to go along, but she gently explained her time that afternoon was just for Andy. She promised to walk with each of them later in the week.

At first, the walk was quiet. Andy shuffled his feet and frequently looked back over his shoulder. Laurel gave him time to open a conversation. He didn't seem to find words. By the time they'd walked the length of the orchard, the young man was fidgeting, pulling at his shirt collar, and dragging his fingers through his hair, so much his father's son. "All right, Mama. I know I didn't do what ya told me to do. I'm sorry. I already told ya, I'm sorry I made ya mad at me."

"Yes, you did."

"Then why did ya make me come out here with ya? What do ya want me to do to make it up?"

"I didn't make you come out here with me. I asked you to take a walk with me. You could have said no."

"You know I couldn't do that. What do you want?"

"I thought you might want to talk. You've been upset lately. Yesterday, you didn't seem yourself...seemed to have a lot on your mind. We've been so busy lately, I just wanted to spend some time with you."

"I ain't upset. We spend time together every day. I didn't mean to make you mad. I didn't think goin' to grandpapa's was a big deal."

"It's not. It's the not askin' me that's a big deal. Not doin' your chores is a big deal. The big problem is that I am your mother and you showed me no respect yesterday. Have I done something to lose your love and respect?"

"No, Mama. I love you. You are the best mother."

"Is that why you mocked me in front of Mark Thomas and the other children last night when I told you to take your bath?"

"I didn't mean no disrespect. I just hate it when you treat me like a little boy. Papa doesn't treat me like a baby. Grandpapa don't boss me around like a little kid."

"Andy, don't raise your voice to me."

"I didn't mean to do that. I never want ya to be mad at me. Papa asked me to be a help to you. I promised I would. And I would anyway, Mama because I love you."

"I'm not angry with you, Andy. I know you love me. I am very glad you are my son. I want us to continue to have the good relationship we've always had. I don't want you to be unhappy. Will you tell me why you are unhappy?"

His eyes filled with unshed tears. He coughed a time or two to clear his throat. He dragged his shirt sleeve across his face. "My papa shouldn't have left me."

"I thought that was at the bottom of all this."

"Mama, it ain't fair. All those years, I was alone. I thought I was an orphan when my grandpa died. And then I got me a family. Since this stupid war started I already lost my big brother, and now my papa is gone, too."

"You miss them both."

" 'Course I do! Sometimes I just gotta have someone to talk to—about man stuff. That was one of the best things about havin' my papa around. Ever since he got me, he's talked to me about important things. Now he's gone. Do you think he'll ever come home again? Roy didn't. He never seen his little boy."

Laurel pulled Andy into her arms. His head knocked her chin, and she was awed by how tall he'd gotten that spring. But that day her son was feeling very small. His words had touched her. Andy's fear was every bit as terrifying as her own.

"Andy, I wish I could promise that nothing bad will happen to your father. I love him, and if I could, I'd bring him back to us today. He left to protect us. You know that."

"I know what he said. I wish we coulda all gone away together. I don't think I can stand to lose my papa."

"We can't do anything but pray for him. Nothing else is in our control. Our job is to keep our family together and keep our homestead going so we can earn our livelihood. We all have to do our part."

"I understand, Mama. I will do my work. I'll help you, and I won't cause you no more problems."

"Thank you, Son."

"I love ya, Mama. I do, but let me go to grandpapa's ever so often so I can talk man-to-man with him. Please."

# Chapter 19

*Favor is deceitful, and beauty is vain: but a woman that feareth the
Lord, she shall be praised. Give her the fruit of her hands, and let
her own works praise her in the gates.*
*Proverbs 31: 30-31*

Near sundown on that May 4th, Laurel was taking down the
last of the bed linens from the clothesline. The playful breeze
whipped the sheets into her face as she walked between the dual
lines and pulled the pins loose. The sweet aroma from the early
roses drifted across the yard. She bent to drop an armload into a
wicker basket at her feet. When she stood up, two powerful arms
covered in Union blue pulled her into an embrace. Glare from the
sun obscured her view as the man captured her lips.

Laurel pushed back and opened her mouth to scream. A
second kiss prevented her call for help. "Laurel, Darlin', what a
wonderful welcome home."

"Mac!"

"Yes, Wife. In the flesh and all is right with the world."

"You startled me. What are you doing here? Rebel troops
have traveled the road out front all day. Aren't you in danger?"

"I don't think so. They're retreatin' from Chalk Bluff. I'll
tell ya about it later. Where are my young'uns?"

"Here and there. Finishing chores mostly. It's pretty close to suppertime. Come on in the house in case any Rebel soldiers are still around."

Mac picked up the basket and took Laurel's hand. They walked to the back porch and into the kitchen where Mark Thomas and Gracie worked together setting the table for Annie.

"Papa! Papa, you're back." Gracie flung her arms around Mac's legs.

The pewter plates that Mark Thomas was carrying clattered to the floor as he pushed Gracie away to reach his father. Mac bent to pick them both up and to plant kisses on their laughing faces.

"Mr. Mac, I'm so glad you're home."

"So happy to be here, Annie. Where's the baby?"

Before she could answer, Andy and Cathy came crashing through the back door, both dirty from evening chores. Andy pushed open the door so fast that Cathy nearly stumbled. When she looked up to complain, she saw the reason for Andy's haste. Both ran across the room to welcome their father.

The hubbub caused by Mac's unexpected return brought much-needed joy and life to the homestead. The family had so much to share that one tale hardly ended before another began. They continued to talk until well after ten o'clock when Mac insisted they turn in for the night. The little ones had been ready for bed for some time and clearly showed it with their feistiness and occasional tears. The four older children wanted to talk, loving the attention from their papa.

"But Papa, I didn't get to tell ya how Mama ran off the Rebs."

"Andy, stop exaggerating. You've had plenty of excitement around here without havin' to make up tales."

"No, Papa. It really did happen," Cathy said. "Andy tells it real good 'cause he was there."

"Your mama ran off a troop of Confederate soldiers?"

"I'm tellin' it straight. Ten or eleven Rebs wanted to walk off with all our livestock. That sergeant said we didn't pay our taxes."

Laurel intervened, "Andy, that's enough for tonight. Your papa said he's tired and wants to go to bed."

"But Mama, it's the best story ever," Cathy pleaded.

"I think I'd like to hear this story." Mac returned to his chair and stretched out his legs to the hearth. "Go ahead, Andy. Tell me what my wife did."

"Well, me and Cathy was doin' night chores, like we do ever night. We heard a lot of horses out by the barn. I went out to find out what they wanted."

"They said they were gonna take our cows, hogs, and chickens and the stuff from our root cellar. Andy called out to mama, and she pulled a rifle out and stopped 'em. She told those soldiers they couldn't steal from a Confederate widow." Cathy was talking so fast a confused look came over Mac's face.

"Did they take the livestock?"

"Course not. Mama shot at the sergeant, and they took her deal. That's why we still have milk and eggs."

"My dear wife, I didn't realize you were skilled with my old rifle."

"I learned from the best."

Mac roared with laughter and shortly, all the MacLayne children were laughing, too. "I can almost see you givin' those Rebs a tongue-lashin'. I remember how well you can do that. You've done it to me more than once."

"Don't say those things in front of the children. I haven't done it in years. Are you ever gonna let me live it down?"

"Maybe in fifty more years." Mac leaned over to kiss her.

"Kids, have you been mindin' your mama and helpin' around the homestead?" Mac asked.

The chatter stopped. Andy's face became bright red. When the silence became uncomfortable, Andy spoke, "Papa, I sassed Mama a couple of weeks ago, and I didn't do some chores she asked me to do. I'm real sorry. Mama and me had a grown-up talk. Now I understand. If you think I need punishment, I'll take it like a man. I know I did a bad thing."

"Laurel?"

"It's true, Mac, but in Andy's defense, he has more than made up for the incident."

"I wanna know more about what happened."

"Tomorrow will be soon enough."

"Laurel, I will meet my unit at Greensboro at 6:00 a.m. tomorrow. And I still have so much I need to tell you."

"Six? Mac, you've only just gotten home."

Mark Thomas walked up behind Mac and pulled the back of his uniform jacket. "Papa, did ya have to shoot anyone in that battle ya just was at?" The small boy rubbed his eyes, but he insisted on hearing his papa's story.

"Come over and sit in my lap, Son. Laurel, bring me my littlest angel to hold for a few more minutes. I'll tell ya about Chalk Bluff. Then it's off to bed with the whole lot of you."

"But Papa, I wanna hear about Helena and the steamboats," Andy said.

Cathy added, "You haven't told us anything about the big houses on the plantations or the ladies in their gowns."

"I like your uniform, Papa. I like the blue more than that ugly gray of those Rebels that have been marchin' by our house all day," Gracie remarked. "What's this?" Gracie ran her fingers across Mac's captain's insignia.

"Enough. I'll tell ya lots more next time. I only have time for one more story tonight." Mac proceeded to tell them about the squirmish he'd witnessed at Chalk Bluff on the St. Francis River.

"Did you get shot at much, Papa?" Andy had so many questions.

Mac continued with his explanation of his role in the Quartermaster's unit and how he and his men had been sent from Helena with four wagons of supplies, medicines, and ammunitions to restock the company of Major John McNeil who had come out of Missouri to preserve the Union hold on the river crossing.

"Was it bloody?"

"Andy, what a question." Laurel tried to end the war talk, but the children insisted their father tell them about the battle he'd just come from.

"The battle lasted almost two days. My men and the wagons we brought arrived at the state line on the thirtieth of April. We had two orders. Get the supplies to McNeil and keep them out of the Rebels' hands."

With eyes the shape of small eggs, Gracie whispered, "You didn't get in the fightin' part, did ya?"

"No, Gracie. I was safe. We crossed the river and stayed at the rear. Quarter- masters know the best way to shorten this war is to keep supplies out of Rebs hands."

"I know you did your job, Papa." Mac smiled and ruffled Gracie's curls.

"The skirmishing went on all day on May 1$^{st}$. We had to ward off a few Rebs who tried to take over our wagons, but we weren't in the main battle. The Rebels were trying to capture Major MacNeil and secure a place where they could cross over into Missouri when they needed to forage or attack a Union division camped in that area. They beat up the Union troops pretty badly that first day."

Mac continued his account. "On the second day, we got reinforcements from a couple of Missouri militia groups and some fire from naval artillery from the river. Marmaduke, he was the Confederate general in charge, planned a sneaky retreat back into Arkansas. I gotta hand it to him—those floating bridges they built saved the day for them. He marched nearly his entire force across that river in one night."

"Papa, if the Rebs did so good, how did we take the battle?" Andy's astute questions made ending the evening difficult.

"Son, the Rebels started at a disadvantage. Of Marmaduke's troops, about a third of them had no weapons. Many of them, these are cavalrymen mind ya, were on foot. They fought like maniacs because they needed that crossing. I don't know how many men they lost, but our side lost more than 120 soldiers, killed, wounded, and captured. It was a sad day."

"Did any of your men get hurt?"

"No, Andy. We delivered our supplies as we were ordered to do, and now we are returning to Helena for our next assignment.:

"Papa…"

"Andy. That is enough. It's after bedtime."

"Yes, Mama."

Mac hugged each of his children, kissed them goodnight, and said 'I love you' to each of them. To Andy, he added, "Don't forget, as man of this house, your main job is to take care of your mama. I love you, Son."

Laurel handed Leah Ann to Annie. "Please put her into the crib with Roy tonight. Goodnight, sweetheart."

*ф*

"You said you need to talk to me, Mac?"

Mac closed the door to their second pen sanctuary. "I do. I need to talk to you, to hold you, to touch your sweet face, to kiss your beautiful mouth…" And he did. Not a sweet gentle kiss, like those he'd given her several times since he'd met her in the yard, but a kiss that spoke of his hunger for her. This kiss told of the loss he felt at their separation. The kiss was filled with the desire to keep her in his arms forever. "I love you, Laurel. Every day that I'm gone, I know it more. There is nothing beyond Shiloh I want or need." Again, he pulled her into an ardent embrace. Come lie with me. Spoon next to me. Tell how you've been."

Laurel lay next to Mac. He nuzzled her neck as she started to tell him about life at Shiloh.

"No, Darlin', don't tell me about his homestead or our kids. Tell me about you."

"I'm not sure what you want me to say. I've been busy. I work all day—teaching the kids, tending the garden…"

"Shootin' at the enemy…but how do you feel?"

"I'm satisfied during the day. I know I'm doin' what I have to do. I worry about you. Not knowing if you're all right or where you are is hard. Some nights I cry myself to sleep because I miss you. At times my arms ache from the need to hold you. I miss you. The only thing that keeps me goin' is knowing the Lord is watching over us."

"I hate this war, Laurel. I never wanted to be a part of it. I believe I'm on the right side, but I didn't want to take sides. I don't hate the Confederates. I can't rationalize why I should be shooting at them any more than I can understand them shooting at me. I should have sold this homestead and taken our family out west."

"We both love Shiloh, Mac. I doubt if you could have convinced me that moving to another place would solve the problem. We'd have just exchanged the problem we know for one we don't know. This is our home. Another place would not be the right thing for us.

"But Laurel, being a part, not getting to talk with you, not working beside you, not reading our Scriptures together, missing all this has been hell on earth for me. If I didn't have your picture and your papa's cross in my pocket every minute, I'd desert. I'd come home, even if they came to arrest me as a deserter."

"No, you wouldn't. Your honor wouldn't let you do that. You committed yourself to this cause when you enlisted. You'll see it through."

"Laurel, I'm not sure I'm strong enough to do this when we can't be together. That's so strange. I thought I was the strong person in this family, but I'm not so sure anymore."

"Patrick MacLayne, you know where our strength lies. You taught me. I hate being away from you, too, but I guess I make it through the days because I know we aren't truly separated. You are with me every minute of every day. You will be as long as I know you love me."

"If that's the case, you never need fear because I couldn't stop loving you if I tried." Mac turned Laurel toward him. He looked into her gray-green eyes. He pulled her chignon loose and ran his finger through the tawny curls he loved to touch. He kissed her with a tenderness that brought tears to her eyes. "Laurel, I want to make love to you. Will you be my willing partner?"

"I have been for more than five years. If the Lord allows, I will continue to be your lover for many decades to come. I love you, Patrick. I love that you want me."

In the beautiful, carved four-poster, Mac and Laurel celebrated their love and marriage, forgetting all outside their sanctuary existed. Their love was an eternal bond, and they were truly one. At dawn, Mac kissed his sleeping wife, her hair splayed across his pillow. He left a small box and a note beside her. He was gone.

When she awoke, Laurel opened the gift and she found a single apple blossom bud. Mac's note read, 'Proverbs 31:10-31...the scripture could have said Laurel Grace.'

# Chapter 20

*Be strong and courageous. Do not be afraid or dismayed...*
*for there be more with us than him: With him is an arm of flesh,*
*but with us is the Lord our God to help and to fight our battles.*
*II Chronicles 32:7-8*

Mac and his small unit of men made the trip back to Fort Curtis at Helena in record time. The nearly empty supply wagons, driven by well-trained ex-freighters, traveled almost as fast as a rider on horseback. Of course, their orders had been to deliver supplies, not to forage for animal feed, meat, or fresh produce, all of which would have been futile at that time of year. Mac had scouted well in advance of the wagons to avoid any run-ins with Rebel troops. If he'd not left his heart at Shiloh, he may have even enjoyed the comradery and sense of purpose he found with the fine men under his command.

This Quartermaster team was composed of eleven men, mostly from Missouri and Michigan. Mac led four two-man teams, who handled army mules as well as any man he'd ever known. Two sharpshooters also served as armed escorts. Mac was in command, partly because of his military training, but mostly because he was an Arkansan, somewhat familiar with northern and eastern parts of Arkansas. Most of the men who served with Major General Prentiss at Fort Curtiss were either from Ohio, Missouri, or Michigan. Prentiss, a native of Illinois, was an army veteran of the Mexican wars. Presently, Mac was the only Arkansan serving at Fort Curtis. His unit was deployed, fighting in Tennessee and Mississippi.

Mac had grown particularly friendly with two teamsters, a pair of identical twins from the bootheel of Missouri. Jonas and Reuben Massey, both corporals, worked as freighters before the war and their route was the Old Military Road from St. Louis to Wittsburg. They knew Greensboro and Bolivar well. Sons of a staunch Unionist from Pennsylvania, the boys had joined the Union army early in 1862. They were great pranksters, both played homemade musical instruments and delighted in teasing their commanding officer—the Yank from Arkansas.

Although Mac's entire enlistment had been served at Fort Curtis, he stumbled over the word 'fort' every time he was called to use it. This large rambling hole on the bank of the Mississippi River didn't look like what he thought a fort was supposed to look like. Even the academic buildings at Annapolis seemed more like fortifications than did the dirt and lumber redoubts built to defend the town and port of Helena. Huge embankments of dirt were laid out in four levels as barricades. The dirt was then held in place with thousands of wooden slabs, as tall as the walls of dirt. He was amazed by how many redoubts had been built in the short time since the war started. The number of man-hours used to erect this fort was beyond calculation. The Union had spared no expense or manpower to assure this vital position on the river would not fall into Confederate hands.

Despite all the effort at fortification, no accommodations for troop housing had been made. All the recruits were housed in three long rows of sturdy canvas tents. General Prentiss said barracks and administration buildings could wait. The redoubts protected the foot of Crowley's Ridge, and that was the Major General's sole mission. He didn't even waste time thinking of names for the impressive barriers he'd ordered. Each battalion was assigned to protect one of the redoubts, either A or B or C or D. Mac admired the Major General's dedication to his goal—keep supply lines open for the Union and closed for the Rebels. The goal was a tenuous one because Fort Curtis was within easy striking distance of Vicksburg, Mississippi, one of the Confederate's strongest entrenched areas which lay only a few miles downriver.

A few days after Mac returned, he was called to the commander's office in the two-story brick house, just outside the fort wall. Mac was surprised because he'd never been called to the commander's office. He hurried to answer the call. In the five months that Mac had served, all his orders had come from Major Lockwood, the aide to Prentiss.

"At ease. Captain. I called you here to ask a question or two about your recent mission to Chalk Bluff."

"Yes, sir."

"You reported a minor injury to one of your men. Did you engage in the fighting on the bluff?"

"No, sir. We were attacked by a party of about four Confederate soldiers who tried to commandeer our supply wagons. We were able to run them off, but Private Stone received a flesh wound in his left thigh."

"Uhm…about what I thought. I figured you followed orders to stay back and protect the supplies."

"We did that, sir."

"The second question came from a report that you left your unit in charge of Corporal Jonas Massey the first night out from Chalk Bluff. The report said you were gone all night. Is that true, MacLayne?"

"It is. When we arrived at my homestead at Shiloh near Greensboro, I secured my men on a back wooded area of my property. After sunset when I knew the camp was secure, I went to visit my wife and children. That was the first time I'd been home since I enlisted in February. I returned to camp at sunrise. At 6:00 a.m. we began the second day's journey. We made more than twenty miles that day and laid over in Bolivar that night."

"You say the men camped on your property? I assume you know that area to be safe."

"Yes, sir. A tenant farmer lives out in that area, and he hides out my prize bulls. The area is heavily wooded. We've never harvested trees or made any attempt to clear the land for plowing. Pretty well secluded from the main roads. Have I done something wrong? I thought I was following protocol."

"No. no. I hope you found things well at your place, Captain. Do you have a large family there along Crowley's Ridge?"

"Yes, sir. Considering that Laurel and I married in '57, we've amassed quite a brood. Counting our adopted son, Roy, who was serving with the Arkansas 25th Infantry when he died at a battle in Corinth last year, we have six children we call our own. The Lord's been good to us."

Major General Prentiss laughed. "Six children in five years. I'm not sure I'd want to be so blessed."

"It's a long story; nevertheless, we'd not give up a one of 'em. Losing Roy was a blow we don't want to repeat."

"You say he was a Rebel soldier, MacLayne?"

"He was." Mac made no apology for Roy's decision. He looked eye to eye with his commanding officer.

"Must be hard. You look familiar to me, and that name is one I've run across before. Did you serve before?"

"No, sir."

"MacLayne...strange way to spell it too."

"My grandfather Patrick brought it to the colonies when he came from Scotland, just in time to fight in the War of 1812. We've kept it intact because he set great store in our highland heritage. He passed his love of military life down to my brother Sean."

"Sean MacLayne. That's why you look so familiar to me. You could be his twin. Your brother was my aide-de-camp in the Mexican War. We found out he was not eighteen so I tried to keep him off the battlefield as much as I could. He'd not have it, and he looked for every opportunity to fight. He died at Buena Vista—that bloody, senseless waste of fine men. He saved my life that day."

"We didn't learn much about what happened to Sean. He was a few years older than I am, but I remember a letter from Washington."

"A Mexican officer sliced at my head with a long saber, but Sean rode between us. Sean shot him, but the sword slashed into the throat of his horse. That handsome stallion stumbled and fell down the embankment where we fought. Sean's neck was broken in the fall."

"We didn't know. I hope I can share this with my pa soon. He'll be glad to know Sean died a hero."

"We buried Sean and two other young fellows under a grove of large trees just outside Buena Vista. Beautiful place with a small trickle of a creek. He was a fine soldier, Captain…a good man."

"Thank you, sir."

"I hope that when this Rebellion is over, I can meet your father. I'd like to share a few stories about your brother. Perhaps you can write a letter home to your family and tell 'em you're safe and back at the fort."

"I wish I could, but that's another long story."

As July approached, Mac kept his silence as he'd told Laurel he would. He ached to communicate with her. He had sent the one letter in care of his father in January, but he continued to believe it was a mistake. If he were able to write and get news back from her, tolerating the separation would have been easier. As it was the foraging and supply delivery trips kept him sane. The more he worked, the less time he brooded.

"Hey, Captain. Why's yer face so long this afternoon?" Reuben Massey spoke from across the campfire where they warmed beans and pork for their supper.

"Who said I was broodin' about anything, Ruben?"

"Maybe that scowl across that ugly Arkansas face of yours."

"Show a little respect for a superior," Mac said.

"You've been in the dumps since you had that meetin' with General Prentiss. Did he read ya the riot act?"

"No. Asked about the mission to Chalk Bluff and Stone gettin' shot.

"That didn't get ya down."

"Why don't you two leave it be? Talkin' about things won't fix 'em—not talkin' to you two Missouri hillbillies."

"We ain't hillbillies. We live in the delta."

"You know what I mean."

"You wanna talk but not to us. That's what you're sayin', ain't it?"

"I guess you two are smarter than I give you credit for."

"Don't take much smarts if a man's got eyes. How many times a day do you pull that silver case out of yer pocket and look at that picture of that girl? Is she your sweetheart, Captain?"

"She is the love of my life." Mac removed the picture from the case and handed it to Jonas and Reuben. "This is my wife, Laurel."

"Fine lookin' lady," Jonas said.

"And who are all these?"

"Those are our children."

"That can't be so. You said you got married in '57. That boy's gotta be twelve or thirteen years old. And two more of these kids are older than five."

"We've picked up a few along the way." Mac pointed to Mark Thomas and Leah Ann. "These belong to both of us, but all of 'em are ours. The Lord gave them to us to love. This tall one is my son, Andy. We also had an adopted son who was in the service."

"Which unit did he serve in, Captain?" Reuben asked.

"Arkansas 25th Infantry. He started with the militia in Greene County."

"Ain't that a Rebel troop?"

"Yes. We're just one of many families that has to deal with a difference of politics since secession."

"Does your wife blame ya?"

"Jonas, that ain't none of your business," Reuben interrupted.

"She blames the war. It's caused us to lose Roy. The war has caused me to leave her behind in Shiloh. I guess both those things helped to put the scowl across my ugly Arkansas face."

Major Lockwood walked up to the fire. The men stood to attention. "Sir."

"Captain, gather your team and prepare to leave at sun up. We want you to collect munitions, meat, and flour from Marianna. A boat is arriving on the L'Anguille in two days."

"Yes, sir."

"Scouts have reported a Rebel attack on Helena may be eminent. We know the Confederate troops across the river in Mississippi are asking for reinforcements to fight against Grant's campaign around Vicksburg. We need you to make a fast trip."

"Understood, Major. We'll leave at first light." Mac saluted and called his men together to plan the trip. A short foray to Marianna take would his mind away from missing his family. He wanted to work.

The river port on the L'Anguille was situated just a few miles above the town of Marianna. Mac felt sure this assignment was safe because Union forces currently held most of the area. True, on occasion, a small group of Rebels would raid, but they were bent more on vandalizing and harassing Union troops than starting a full-fledged battle.

By sundown the following day, Mac's unit had set up camp near the river to await the steamboat carrying the supplies. They'd not seen a Rebel uniform all day. As night fell, they watched brightly lit boats approach the piers, music pulsing through the quiet night. The decks were filled with bare-shouldered ladies dressed in white ballgowns on the arms of soldiers clad in Union blue.

"Land o' Goshen, Captain. Don't those folks know a war's goin' on?" Jonas asked.

"I guess they ain't much worried about it. Parties still go on. From the looks of the clothes, I'd say this one may be some wealthy young lady's birthday...maybe sixteenth. With no southern beaus to dance with on special occasions, they asked our boys to stand in tonight."

"I guess sometimes we're the enemy and sometimes we ain't."

"That's the way of war, Reuben. You have to make do with what you've got."

"I'd like to go to one of those fancy parties."

"Well, the next time we come to the L'Anguille, we'll just get us an invitation. The newspaper writes accounts of these shindigs all the time," Mac slapped the corporal on the back. "Better get some shut-eye. We'll head back to Fort Curtis tomorrow as soon as we load the wagons."

July 3rd dawned hot and humid. The men under Mac's command wore clothes wet through before the wagons were half loaded. Before the sun had been up two hours, the supply train headed back to the Mississippi. The well-trained mules moved at a steady pace until noon when a fierce thunderstorm broke the heat. In its place, Mother Nature served up a steady, fierce wind and jagged forks of cloud-to-ground lightning.

Mac sought refuge for his men and their animals. About halfway back to Helena, he ordered the wagon train to halt. He would refuge in the sheltered canyon at the southern end of Crowley's Ridge. The men took cover under the wagons to wait out the worst of the storm. By late afternoon, torrential rain and lightning moved across the Mississippi.

As Mac ordered the unit forward, he sensed something was wrong. The closer they got to Helena, the more the nagging concern bothered him. He rode a little further in front of his men to scout the area. The major had told him of the concern of an impending attack, but he sensed it was something more. The rain they'd ridden through had not come as far south as Helena. Perhaps the storm had not started here yet, he decided. They traveled on through the night to make up for the time they'd lost sheltering.

Just before daybreak, Mac's fear was confirmed. A couple of miles out from the first of the redoubts, what seemed to be thunder rolled across the land. But it seemed too frequent to be thunder. As the sun began to breach the horizon, Mac saw no storm clouds. Yet the constant crash silenced the birds and other wildlife.

Within another half-mile, Mac's small unit pulled up short of the last road that led to Fort Curtis. The mystery didn't exist anymore. The thunder proved to be the constant discharges from the twenty-four and thirty-two pounders positioned in the redoubts and perched on the high ground of Crowley's Ridge above the flat delta land that stretched from the foot of Crowley's Ridge south. Those huge weapons threw cannonballs the size of large cantaloupes well across the rooftops of any building in Helena and into approaching Confederate Cavalry. Each shell tore craters in the earth and dismembered any soldier unlucky enough to be within its reach.

Mac encountered a barricade meant to obstruct the enemy. Before the battle began, General Prentiss had acted on the scouting reports, and he sent the majority of his troops, both white and black, to barricade the trails and roads that led to Helena with trees. To prevent Cavalry invasion, the members of the Arkansas 25th Colored Brigade had built a seven-mile-long Trans de Loup—basically a long fence, another obstacle to the Rebels. The wisdom gained in previous battles, the last of which was Shiloh in Tennessee, had taught Prentiss that soldiers who came late to battles killed few of his men.

Mac was forced to detour time and again to reach the sally port of Fort Curtiss. The entry was heavily armed. "Halt. Who goes there?" He rode to the head of the wagon train.

"Captain MacLayne. We're bringing supplies to Major General Prentiss."

"Open the gates. Supplies comin' in." The private shouted over the chaos of the attack. "Captain, the Colonel asked you to report as soon as you arrived. He's on the rampart, front."

Mac dismounted and threw his reins to Jonas Massey. He walked to the rampart, looking out over the four redoubts below. Only two of them seemed to be in serious conflict.

"Sir, Captain MacLayne reporting."

"Did you get those munitions we need?"

"Yes, sir. Four wagons nearly filled."

"Good. I need you to take one of them over to Graveyard Hill. Those boys have been under heavy attack for some time. Repelled the Rebs twice already. They can't have much ammunition left."

"Yes, sir. One wagon west to redoubt C. How many men do you want me to take?"

"Use your judgment, but get those men their ordinance. Take your best teamster, though. Those mules won't like the noise. Take some men from the Arkansas 25th for security, if you need them."

Mac returned and ordered three of his wagon teams inside the fort to secure their loads in the armory. "Jonas and Reuben, you two bring your team, and let's take our boys some ammunition before they have to start throwing rocks at the Rebs."

Mac watched closely for attack by enemy troops. Six members of Arkansas 25th fanned out around the wagon, prepared to defend the supplies. Cannon shells whizzed over the trees and exploded into advancing men wearing Confederate gray. Closer to the river, the battleground became brutal and gory. Bloody sections of men's torsos lay across the raised breastwork. Mac felt nauseous seeing legs without bodies, arms torn from shoulders, and clothes so bloody that gray and blue were no different. He saw too many corpses of young men who died for the cause he rejected. The last thought that Mac had as they came to the crest of the fortified area called 'Graveyard Hill' was Roy's death at Corinth.

Finally, they found a sergeant at the center of the redoubt. "We've brought you ammunition. Where can I find your commanding officer?"

"He's hurt bad, Captain. We've lost a score of men here today. I'm in charge right now until a new officer can be sent."

"I guess that would be me." Mac shook his head. "Reuben and Jonas, get some men who can help and get those supplies out. Sergeant, try to regroup those who are able so we can continue to defend this area."

The sergeant's eyes rolled back and he fell. A bullet had struck him in the chest as Mac spoke to him.

"Reuben, get that wagon to a safe position and get yourself to cover. Jonas, when the men have ammunition, try to check on the wounded. When the wagon is empty, take those men who have a fightin' chance if we can get them to a doctor, back to the fort."

Mac began his rounds in the rifle pits, and under the protective ridge, he began to move the able-bodied soldiers into teams to repulse the invaders. "Men, fire at will. Push them back. Shoot straight and fast. We have to hold this redoubt."

In the hottest part of the afternoon, the third assault on their position was at its height. Mac managed to reorganize what was left of the troops into groups who focused their fire toward the approaching Rebel lines more effectively. The artillery from the bluffs showered shells, and the sharpshooters stationed higher on the ridge had an advantage over the Confederate troops approaching from below. Casualties continued to rise. Mac sent up a silent prayer when a Major from the Michigan Union battalion arrived to take command of Redoubt C.

Mac saluted his replacement and turned his mount toward the center of the fortification to find the men of his unit. He found Reuben Monroe with four of the black soldiers loading wounded soldiers into the empty supply wagon. "Thanks, Reuben. You're done. Great work helpin' these wounded men."

"Thank ya, Captain. Ready to roll? Those were the last words spoken by the fun-loving prankster from Missouri. A bullet removed the left side of his face.

"No! Reuben..." Mac screamed in disbelief. "Dear Lord, please don't let any more young men fall today. Please stop the bloodshed."

The bloody day finally ended on the bank of the Mississippi. During the last eight hours, Mac had experienced its worst of war since his enlistment. Mac tied his mount to the wagon and drove back to the field hospital with his cargo of wounded men—soldiers from both sides. In the short distance, he passed hundreds of men who were beyond the help he could give them. Blood-covered bodies were mangled and swarming with gnats and flies. The dead didn't seem to mind. Mac minded very much.

After delivering his wagon of wounded, Mac needed time to put the butchery of the day behind him. He climbed to the rampart and walked the perimeter. How long he didn't know. His thoughts were too heavy to brush aside. Looking across the earthen wall, he could see all four levels of the fortified mounds. What he saw was Arkansas dirt fortified with hundreds of felled trees, now pitted and broken by mortar fire and countless bullets. Instead of the rich soil he knew could grow anything for man's good, he saw Arkansas dirt defiled with the blood of hundreds of men who would never again live the life God had intended. Mac slumped against the wall of the rampart and shed tears for those lost lives.

As the twilight turned to dark, Mac shook off the gloom he'd let overtake him. Oddly, the night following the horror of the siege was calm and beautiful, as Arkansas spring nights tend to be. The darkness now hid the waste and destruction of the two previous days. Mac remembered Laurel's words from their last night together. He knelt on the rampart and prayed.

"Lord, please give me the will to help when I can. I hate this war, but I believe you have called me to serve. I miss Laurel and my kids. Please let this all be over so I can go home to Shiloh. Please, Father. I can't do it without you."

Mac ended his pleas. He had one more loathsome job to do. He had to find Jonas and tell him how his brother gave his life trying to help wounded soldiers. That was a job he dreaded. Then he thought of Laurel. He remembered her kisses on that last morning they were together. He saw in his mind's eye her smile in the afterglow of their lovemaking. *Yes, Lord, between the two of you, I can survive whatever it takes to get home. I forgot to thank You for all the wonder You've already given me. I need her. I need You. Please keep me going... 'til Shiloh come.*

# Chapter 21

*And the ransomed of the Lord shall return, and come to Zion with*
*songs and everlasting joy upon their heads: they shall obtain joy*
*and gladness, and sorrow and sighing shall flee away.*
*Isaiah 35:10*

"Did I do something bad, Mama?" Gracie looked up at
Laurel who was reaching for a jar of string beans on the shelf. She
turned and saw the tiny image of her best friend, Rachel, in the
face of the tearful seven-year-old.

"Whatever made you think I'm angry with you,
Sweetheart?"

Gracie clasped her arms around Laurel's waist and hid her
face in her mama's skirt. "You don't smile at me no more."

The words convicted Laurel. She knew too well how hard it
was just to get up and face each day. Mac had been gone from
Shiloh for more than seven months now. Except for two letters
he'd written to his father, and the brief message Laurel received
around their anniversary when he'd told her he wouldn't risk the
mail, she'd heard nothing. Since August when Mac sent a one-page
letter to his father saying he had not been injured in the battle at
Helena, no word had come. Fear and loneliness created a burden
Laurel struggled to overcome. The melancholia painted her world
in a hundred shades of gray.

The summer had been the hottest in memory for the folks at Shiloh. Besides the heat, little rain came. By the end of August, northeast Arkansas was a parched land. Laurel, Andy, and Cathy added irrigating the orchard and gardens to their already busy routines. The drudgery, heat, and isolation produced many sleepless nights. Laurel had told herself she had been coping well enough since Mac's clandestine visit in March. Gracie's tearful question destroyed her illusion. She missed her husband. Not knowing if he lived or where he was or if he was in danger ate at her confidence and her faith. Her prayers had shrunk to one short phrase, 'Lord, let me hear from Mac."

"Oh, Gracie. No, you are so dear. I'm sorry I made you think you had done something wrong. I'm so glad you asked me though. I needed to be reminded of all the wonderful gifts I have around me every day." Laurel pulled Gracie into a tight hug. "I love you. All of you are such a blessing to me." Laurel wiped Gracie's face. "You want to help me fix supper?"

A smile and a nod told Laurel that Gracie had been assured for the moment. She couldn't let her mood become a problem with her children. If she could, she'd keep the shadows away from Shiloh. Summer gave way to fall, but the heat didn't abate. September was nearly as hot and dry as August. Harvest time was miserable but short. The lack of rain produced low yields across the region. Even hay fields were stunted and brown. Thankfully, the MacLaynes had few animals to feed through the winter.

Then one morning early in October, Thomas MacLayne rode into the yard. He waved his hat in greeting. "Laurel, I got ya a letter."

"Is it from Mac, Pa?" Her smile faded. The name on the envelop read 'Samuel Campbell—Waco, Texas.' But the handwriting was familiar. She ripped open the envelop and read the closing words on the single sheet. Laurel laughed, spun around, pulled the letter to her lips. The children stared in disbelief.

"Mama, what are you doin'? I ain't never seen you act so silly," Andy said.

Cathy ran to her side. "Mama, are ya all right?"

242

"My prayers have been answered. Your papa has sent us word that he is well. I'm so happy I want to laugh and cry."

"Read it to us, please Mama." Andy plopped down on the top step of the porch ready to hear the news. "What's he say?"

Laurel skimmed the letter and read,

My darlin' wife and kids,

I couldn't stand not reaching out to y'all. I figured a letter from your brother in Texas wouldn't draw much attention from the postmaster. Surely, he'd only write to comfort his poor sister and nieces and nephews when he learned they'd been deserted by that low-life Yankee husband she threw out.

So much I want to tell y'all. I'm well. I didn't get a scrape in that attack at Fort Curtis in July. The Rebel forces tried with a mighty fight, lasting almost two days to take the port here at Helena. We managed to keep 'em out of the fort and away from the port on the Mississippi. What a price we paid though. More'n a thousand casualties from both sides. Bloody and savage waste. I lost two men from my unit. How I hate this damn war.

My main loss has been your company. I want to hold Leah Ann and toss Mark Thomas high in the air to hear him laugh and yell 'More, Papa, More.' What I wouldn't give to read the Bible with Cathy, Gracie, and Annie, if only for one evening. Andy, I wanna go hunting with that new rifle of yours as soon as I get home. I'll bet Roy has grown so big I won't know him. Laurel, I miss you. There's nothing I don't miss about Shiloh.

I can't tell you when I'll be able to sneak back home again. I've been re-assigned to the Arkansas Second Cavalry now that they've returned to the state. It'll be good to serve with Arkansas people again, but I have to admit I do like these Yankees from Missouri and Michigan. I'll still be doing Quartermaster work, but I'm leaving Fort Curtis. There are rumors about where we are going, but I can't say in a letter.

Mac wrote one last section in the letter, but Laurel didn't share it with her kids. Mac's declaration of love and his need for her were not for the eyes of others. "He ended the letter by sending his love and asking you to work hard at your schoolwork and chores. He says he'll come home as soon as the Lord allows."

"Well, Daughter, I'm relieved Patrick is safe for now. I'm glad he wrote."

"Thank you, Pa. I am at peace for now. I think I can sleep tonight."

φ

Laurel opened school the first week in November. The scant harvest was finished, and small yields from the garden limited the time she needed to can the vegetables. Strangely, the opening of the school seemed to coincide with the end of the drought. Several mornings in a row, a much-needed shower fell across the ridge. Temperatures also began to fall and within a couple of weeks, the leaves turned to a panorama of color so typical of Arkansas fall. The days were pleasant enough, but the nights became quite cold long before the official beginning of winter.

With the coming of fall, military travelers on the Old Military Road increased drastically. For some time after Chalk Bluff, units headed south had been almost non-existent. On some days, units as large as a hundred men marched southward. Rumors spread that their destination was the White River. Late, on Wednesday afternoon in the middle of the month, Andy ran through the back door. "Mama, come quick. Fifty Rebs are setting up tents behind the barn. Come on."

"Slow down, Andy. Did they tell you what they are doin'?"

"They didn't say nothin'. Didn't ask. They started puttin' up tents next to the fence down by the orchard. Some of 'em are clearin' spaces to build campfires. Go tell them Rebs to get off our land. Papa wouldn't want 'em here."

Laurel pulled her shawl from the peg by the door and walked to the porch. She called back for Andy to bring his rifle and cartridges. When she turned the corner of the barn, she saw Andy hadn't exaggerated. Tent after ten ran the length of the orchard fence.

Then she heard it, a dull thud sounded as an ax cut a gash into one of her apple trees. Laurel screamed. "Stop that! Don't put that ax into my tree again unless you want to feel lead in your backside."

The Rebel soldiers laughed. Three more gray-clad men joined the circle. Laurel moved between the tree and the private with the ax.

"Move aside. We need to make camp before nightfall. How do you expect us to cook our mess? We gotta have some heat. It's cold out here."

"You won't use my apple orchard for firewood." Andy handed her the rifle. Again the Rebel soldiers laughed at Laurel.

A sergeant, who joined the cluster around the damaged tree, spoke, "You think you can stop a whole unit with one rifle, Lady? Go back to your cabin before you get hurt."

"You'll have to hurt me before I let you use my apple trees for firewood." The private nearest Laurel grabbed her arm. "Stop it. These trees are valuable. I need them to help feed my family."

"Get outta my way. We're all cold. We gotta have campfires tonight." He jerked her, trying to get the rifle from her. Laurel kicked his shin. He swore at her.

"Leave my orchard. There are ample trees on this homestead." Another soldier pulled her by the waist. The gun discharged into the back of the barn. A second private pulled the rifle from Laurel, while the corporal who'd grabbed Laurel's waist trapped her arms against her body.

"You mangy Rebs. You let my Mama go." Andy jumped on the back of the corporal who held Laurel. He clawed the man's face. "You stop hurtin' her." The corporal pushed Laurel to the ground so he could remove the scrappy ten-year-old.

"Andy, stop. I don't want you hurt."

"What a little scrapper!" Again, the soldiers laughed, briefly.

"Stand down, troop." A tall, well-groomed major stood above Laurel. He bent down and offered his hand to help her up. "Sergeant, what's goin' on here?"

The troops snapped to attention. "Sir, nothin', sir. We were setting up camp. This woman used this gun to stop us from settin' up night camp."

"Who fired the shot?" The major continued to stare at the group in front of him.

"That woman shot at the private, but she missed."

"That's a lie." Andy defended his mother.

"Andy, let me deal with this." She hugged the red-faced boy. "Thank you for protecting me."

The major walked over and took the rifle from the private and returned it to Andy. Laurel brushed the dirt from her dress and pushed straggling tresses from her face.

"Major, your troops are trespassing on my homestead. I'd have no objection to y'all stayin' the night here, but you can't destroy my orchard. I have seven children and my daughter-in-law to feed. Next spring, these trees will bear fruit."

"But Major Cavenaugh, we gotta have fires for heat tonight," the corporal spoke in defense.

"The woods are full of trees, all kinds, and they don't grow apples. You can find enough fallen branches and limbs. You won't have to cut even one tree."

"Why should we have to carry wood so far, lady? It's our right to take supplies, food, and water. It's all right here. Why not use it?"

"Because I will shoot you if you harm my trees. I've tended these trees, carried water from the creek, and pruned these trees for six years. I'll not hesitate to shoot anyone who thinks they are are nothin' but firewood."

"Lady, I said…"

"Sergeant, leave this orchard be. She asked you reasonably. She offered you all the supplies you need. Go out and forage the woods to get your fuel. She said you're welcome to all you want."

"But Major…"

"Now, Sergeant. It'll be dark soon. In the mornin', I expect to see no damage to any tree in this orchard. Understand?"

"Yes, sir." The men moved away.

"And hear me plainly. We treat our southern women with respect at all times. This lady is a Southern lady, and I don't believe you paid her the respect she is due. She is sacrificing in the war effort, too. I'll deal with all of you later."

When Laurel and Andy stood alone with the major, she began to tremble. The major took her elbow to keep her from falling.

"Thank you, Major. This orchard means a great deal to me. My husband and I brought these seedlings across the state the year we were married. The trees were the first thing we planted on our homestead."

"Where is your husband, ma'am?"

"I'm not sure. He's not been a part of our household since February. We've had little word of him since that time."

"I apologize for the crude behavior of my men. Well, Mrs...I'm afraid I've not made introductions. Major Cortland Cavanaugh, M.D. I am servin' with the Arkansas 25th Infantry right now."

"Your drawl doesn't sound very Arkansan."

"Originally from Louisiana, but that's a long story. Please tell me your name and the others here on your homestead. I'll have to file a report."

"My name is Laurel MacLayne. This is Shiloh, my husband's homestead. This is my son, Andy. We live here with our large family. Only J.F. Clarke, our tenant farmer, lives on the land with us. He is our caretaker."

The attractive major bowed from the waist and kissed Laurel's hand. "Again, my apologies, Mrs. MacLayne. My men won't cut your orchard. I promise you."

"Thank you. Bless your kindness." Laurel pulled her shawl close around her neck to fend off the icy wind. With her hand on Andy's shoulder, they returned to the cabin.

The next morning, Laurel returned to the orchard. The tents were gone and had it not been for dozens of scorched spots where campfires had burned, no one would suspect an entire Rebel unit had spent the night so near her home. Major Cavanaugh's word proved to be solid. The orchard trees had only one scar.

*Φ*

Winter entered full force at the beginning of Advent. Bone-chilling cold lingered for days in a row, forcing local farmers around Crowley's Ridge to shelter whatever remaining stock they owned in barns and sheds. The children didn't even ask to play outside in the brutal cold, fed by icy northern winds that continuously swept down the ridge. Their restlessness and the cramped quarters fueled spats and larger arguments. Laurel's strained moods gave way too often, and her children heard harsh words and received mild punishments far too often in her attempts to keep a semblance of peace. She was exhausted.

"Give me back my book. Andy." Cathy yelled as she tried to jerk the worn copy of *Robinson Crusoe* from his hands. Andy refused to release the book, and several pages were ripped from the cover.

"Now, look what ya did. Mama, Cathy tore up *Robinson Crusoe* while I was readin'."

"I had it first. He ripped the book, not me."

"You told a lie, Cathy."

"Don't you call me a liar, Andy MacLayne."

"I didn't. I said you lied…"

"Stop it. Both of you, stop it. I've heard more than I want to hear. Give me that book. Andrew, go bring in firewood for the night. Cathy, go to the well and fetch three buckets of water before it freezes again."

"But Mama…"

"Andy, don't talk back to me. Do what I asked you to do, and do it now."

"Yes, ma'am."

Except for their nightly prayer time and scripture reading, that evening at the MacLayne's was subdued and uncomfortable. Even though Cathy and Andy began the spat, all the children felt the awkward tension. Laurel made an early night for them all. Without a word of disagreement, everyone was in bed before 8:30.

With Leah Ann tucked into her crib, Laurel fell into the four-poster, fully dressed except for her shoes. She rolled herself into the wedding ring quilt and fell into a troubled sleep.

At midnight, Laurel sat upright in the bed, shaking with fear. She'd awoken from a nightmare—one she'd had before. On the nights when she was pulled from sleep by this dream, Laurel struggled to remember what had fostered the fear. On those nights, she seldom slept again. The only image she could recall was the small wooden cross on a rawhide cord that had once hung above her father's bed. Why did such a dear object frighten her? She didn't know. She wrapped herself back into the warmth of the quilt and spent the rest of the night recalling the special memories of days spent with her husband at Shiloh. Sleep would not come.

Christmas was only two weeks away. Gifts that year would be few and, for the most part, homemade. Laurel did take some of the scant Confederate currency from the stash in hopes of finding apples, oranges, or some kind of fruit to give her children and those who attended her school. She also wanted to find some hard Christmas candy, perhaps peppermints, to have a special treat for her children's stockings on Christmas morning.

If the cold broke, she'd make a trip to Greensboro before Christmas Eve to look for the things that had become a tradition in their family. However, the closer the holiday came, the less Laurel wanted to deal with the trappings of Christmas. Her favorite parts had always been the church-related things, like the nativity pageant and the special music. The season just didn't seem the same without hearing those hymns. Since she had left the fellowship of Shiloh church, she missed those things. With her uncle Matthew continuing his chaplain's duties, even his singing at the family's Christmas Eve gathering would probably be missing this year.

By the sheer force of her will, Laurel set about making Christmas week as cheerful as she could. Her children deserved to be happy. She determined they would have gifts, a Christmas feast, and the company of as much family as was in her power to gather. She had no control over the absence of their father, but she would do the best she could in Mac's absence.

By the Monday of Christmas week, Laurel had finished the decorative touches on the girls' matching Christmas dresses. With fabric in short supply in Greensboro, Laurel had cut identical dresses from the expensive suit skirt she'd worn when she and Mac traveled to Little Rock aboard the luxurious paddleboat in '59. She had little use for the elegant dress suit at Shiloh. The beautiful blue sateen made up into fine new dresses for Cathy, Gracie, and Leah Ann. From the cloth of her Sunday Calico, she'd been able to fashion a new skirt for Annie, too. Andy and Mark Thomas had new shirts wrapped and ready for Christmas morning. Laurel had even sewn one for Mac because she always did. He'd get it when he was home again.

Toys were in very short supply this Christmas. Annie and Cathy made a small bunny from a scrap of an old blanket for Roy, Jr. Laurel had helped Annie embroider a face and whiskers. J.F. had whittled wooden animals and used his forge to turn out hoops for hoop rolling for the boys. Laurel supplied ribbons and bows for the girls. She and Annie had made homemade candy for the stockings when none could be found in Greensboro. At least, one piece of fruit finished the gifts that year. J.F. had found a half-bushel of pears at the home of a neighbor who was willing to trade for new horseshoes. Laurel was able to pull together a good Christmas for her family, and she spent less than five dollars of her Confederate money and not one piece of the gold or silver Mac had put away for the new start after the war.

On Wednesday of Christmas week, Thomas MacLayne, Paddy, and Sean came to Shiloh to get Andy. They would hunt that day for meat for the Christmas meals. They started early in the morning, and by noon, they returned with several large rabbits for the Christmas Eve stew and a very large goose to roast for Christmas dinner. That same day, Laurel and her daughters went into the woods to cut cedar boughs and holly bushes with red berries to decorate the cabin. When they decorated the mantle and window sills, the pungent scent of the evergreens filled every inch of their home. Annie found the red Christmas ribbons in the loft and laced them through the holly berries and greenery on the mantle. Laurel placed her mother's pewter candlesticks on either end of the table. In them, she put the last two beeswax candles she had made at the candling day in '61. Amid a circle of holly at the center of the table sat Ann MacLayne's remaining red crystal lamp. If only Mac were home to see the tribute to his mother, the holiday would be perfect.

The work was finished. Laurel felt not one iota of joy from her efforts. Her face hurt from pretending to smile for her children's sake. Her prayers were filled with petitions for strength to get through December 25th. If she could keep up her energy so her children's holiday would not be spoiled, the pretense would be worth the effort.

Christmas Eve about 1:00, her guests arrived. Her father-in-law brought gifts for his grandchildren to add to those Laurel had made. He attempted to fill the void he knew his grandchildren were feeling that afternoon. Peggy brought several special dishes to add to the holiday dinner, including an abundance of Christmas sweets. As they completed setting the table for dinner, Laurel received a surprise. Her Uncle Matthew arrived with her Aunt Ellie and Mary. All the family she was able to gather was at Shiloh.

By two o'clock, the feast began. The family gathered around the table, hugged the one next to him or her, held hands, and bowed their heads while Matthew blessed the feast.

"And Lord, please ease our loss. At this time of year, we sorely miss Roy and Martha. We are comforted to know they are with you. And we miss Mac and ask for his safety. Bless our banquet and comfort us all until we are together again. Amen."

The noise of the celebration filled every corner of the MaLayne cabin. In the confusion and chaos of the large family gathering, no one heard the knock at the back door. A man dressed in a blue captain's uniform stood in the open door and called out, "Do you have enough for one more?"

For a moment, the room turned silent. The bearded, unkempt soldier who interrupted the dinner stepped into the kitchen and shut the door.

Mark Thomas ran to the man. "Papa. Papa. You come home for Christmas." Laughter and tears filled the cabin. Mac's children surrounded him, each vying to be closer to him. Mac pulled them into his arms and hugged them until Mark Thomas cried out, "You're squeezing me too hard, Papa. Just a head rubbin' please." Again laughter erupted.

"Laurel, where are you, wife?"

"I am here, Patrick. Are you really here?" She walked through the throng around him into his waiting arms. His kiss told her that she was not dreaming. Mac had come home for Christmas.

"I'd love to share that feast. We get so little good eatin' since I left Fort Curtis. Even there, we had nothin' to compare to Laurel's cookin'." And they ate…and ate…and ate.

"Mac, I still can't believe you're home. How did you manage it?" Laurel asked.

"My dear family, I got me a Christmas pass." Mac pulled out a six-inch square of coarse yellowed paper written in pencil. Laurel saw his name scribble along with the dates of his leave. He didn't have to report back to Batesville until December 28th. He would be home until the morning of the 26th. They'd been given the gift of two whole days together.

Matthew held a poignant, if short, Christmas service for the MaLayne family. As was their tradition, they sang the familiar carols, ending with *Silent Night*. Christmas Eve couldn't have been more perfect.

At 5:00, the company left to return to the family celebrations in their homes. Laurel and the kids sat near to listen to Mac's accounts of the time he'd been away from them. He told them of his trips across Arkansas and Missouri as he foraged for supplies and delivered items to Union troops engaged in battles. He told them about outrunning a Rebel band who tried to capture his supply wagons near Mt. Petit Jean in the Ozarks. He mentioned a few of the skirmishes the Second Arkansas Cavalry had been engaged in, but he downplayed the violence he'd seen in Pocahontas, Helena, and at Benton's Barracks.

He told them he was rarely in danger. "The first duty of the Quartermaster Corps is to keep the supply wagons safe." Even as he spoke, Laurel was sure that he wasn't telling the whole story. Mac and his men were often targeted when they carried much-needed supplies. Some of the most dangerous times occurred when they attempted to help the wounded on the battlefields after their wagons were emptied of supplies.

"Come on now, kids. It's past nine-thirty. I'm beat. I haven't slept in a real bed since I left this house back in March. We got all day tomorrow to talk. Besides, we gotta get up early to see if Santa Claus could sneak through those Rebel lines." He hugged each one and kissed them good night. Tears wet his cheeks as he did. God had given him the most precious of gifts that Christmas Eve.

## φ

Laurel closed the door to their second pen bedroom. Mac threw logs on the fire which had warmed the room already. He couldn't find words to begin the conversation he'd spoken in his head a hundred times. He walked over to Laurel and sank his head into the cleft of her neck. He held her.

"Laurel, I'm so dirty. I'm not fit to hold you like this. I want to get cleaned up if you don't mind."

"Let me get you some hot water. You'll enjoy a hot bath in our copper tub." And he did. He sank into the steamy water and smelled the aroma of the lavender-scented soap. When Laurel knelt and washed his back, her touch was almost agony to his long-denied body. He handed him grooming scissors and a razor so he could return his beard to its usual neatly-trimmed style. He washed his hair, pulling the lather through the too-long strands of his chestnut-colored hair.

"Can I trim your hair, Mac?"

"You can if it will make me anymore presentable to you."

"You were the most handsome man alive when I recognized you standing in my kitchen. I didn't care what you looked like. You are well and you are home."

"Thank God. I wanted nothing more."

As Mac stepped from the copper tub and dried himself with the soft, clean towel, Laurel changed into her winter nightdress with its long sleeves and high collar. Before she'd removed all the pins from her hair, Mac walked behind her and wrapped his arms around her. He pulled her hair away from the nape of her neck and kissed her repeatedly.

"You needn't have bothered with that nightdress, Laurel. This night I intend to feed myself on what I've missed most—you." He captured her lips and picked her up. He carried her to their carved four-poster bed and slipped her nightdress from her shoulders. He lay beside her, just to feel her skin touching his. Once again tears wetted his cheeks.

"Mac, darlin', what's wrong?"

"For one night, not one a thing in this universe. You don't know how many nights I've prayed for this time. The chance to touch you...to feel the warmth of you as you lay next to me. Sometimes when I faced battle, I feared I'd never know this joy again. Thank you, Father."

No more words passed between Mac and Laurel. They made love until their need was met. Then they fell asleep, entwined in each other's arms. This night brought them true rest.

# Chapter 22

*Beloved, I wish above all things*
*that those mayest prosper...I have no greater joy*
*than to hear that my children walk in truth.*
*III John 1:2,4*

The scent of cinnamon, evergreen, and hot coffee spread the MacLayne's home that Christmas morning of 1863. The chatter was full of life and laughter, and the word 'Papa' was heard again and again. Tousled hair and unexpected hugs happened all day. A captain dressed in Union blue didn't sit at the head of the table at breakfast. Their papa was there now—rested, at ease, and happy as he basked in the attention of his family.

After the filling meal, the family gathered around the fireplace and opened the gifts left on the hearth. The children squealed to find so many gifts, some from Santa, some from their mama, and even some from their papa. They enjoyed the time until the last package had been unwrapped. Then Mac asked, "Where is my shirt, Laurel? I always get a new shirt."

Laurel handed him the package she'd forgotten to put out and placed a cup of steaming coffee in front of him. "It's been forever since I've done that. I'm afraid it's the last I have in the stash. The next time you come home, I'm afraid you'll get chickory." Mac smiled. For that time, everything felt right. All the

255

MacLaynes were at Shiloh and nothing outside the walls of their cabin held sway with them that day.

Mac planned to spend some time with each of his children alone. He wanted to assure each of them how much he loved and valued them. When he was forced to return to the Second Arkansas Cavalry at Batesville, he needed them to know their place in the family. He wanted to assure them their father had not deserted them, regardless of the rumors spread through Greensboro and Shiloh.

With Andy and Cathy, this task was not a difficult one. When Mac explained why he'd felt compelled to join the Union army, they were mature enough to understand. Mac found he was truly enjoying the conversation with his grown-up kids. Mac and Andy shared an early hour hunting trip. Andy showed his prowess by taking down two ducks that would become dinner. Mac saw the pride in his son's eyes when he simply clapped his shoulder and said, "Well done, Son. I don't have to worry about your mama and the kids goin' hungry."

Mac spent a pleasant half-hour with Cathy in front of the fireplace talking about plans for her upcoming birthday. He told her about the celebration he'd witnessed on the steamboat on the L'Anguille River and promised after the war they would have an elaborate celebration like that at Shiloh. The most important part of the conversation happened when Cathy talked about losing her brother.

"Papa, I don't know if I could have stood losin' Roy if I didn't have Mama and my family. Thank God, we have little Roy, too. Without him, Annie would have mourned herself to despair."

"Cathy, we all feel that way. Only Roy bein' gone keeps this day from bein' perfect. We all love him."

"I love you, Papa. Please take special care. We need ya to come home to us."

Mac spent a long time talking with Annie when she went to put Roy, Jr. down for his mid-morning nap. She spoke with pride that her son learned to walk early and at his attempts at talking. She told Mac about recent contact she'd had with her pa. She said there were a lot of things still hard to accept in the way he'd rejected her marriage to Roy, but she believed her father wanted to mend the broken ties.

"Mr. Mac, I'd like to have my pa know my little boy, but you'll always be his true grandpa. I know you and Mrs. Mac are kinda young to be grandparents, but you've always been here for us. You didn't put rules on Roy and me. You just loved us and supported us. I won't never forget that."

Dealing with his younger kids couldn't be done with words. Time spent in play and lots of hugs proved to be a better approach. Mac enjoyed the ride with Mark Thomas, as Midnight carried them both around to check the fences. Mac spent a happy half-hour with Gracie cutting out the paper dolls he'd brought her as a Christmas gift. With Leah Ann, he simply held her as she slept in his arms. He occasionally wrapped one of her tawny curls around his finger.

At evening worship time, Mac read the story of the prodigal son to his family. In his prayer, he mentioned each family member by name, asking for God's protection. "Thank you, Holy Father. This has been a blessed day at Shiloh, a day filled with love. Amen."

Then Mac said his good-byes. "Kids, I'll be gone before ya get up in the mornin'. This pass I have in my pocket only allows me a six-day leave. I have to be back in Batesville on the 27th. Thank you for this wonderful Christmas celebration. Being with y'all has been a gift more than I deserve. Take care of each other and your mama for me until I can get back home. I love you. God will be with each of you."

"Papa, please stay home with us." Mark Thomas clasped onto his arm.

"I wish to all that's holy I could, Son. I'm prayin' this war will be over soon."

"Don't you worry none about us here at Shiloh, Papa. I'll watch over things until you get back. You just take care to get back. Come on, Mark Thomas, it's bedtime. Goodnight Mama, Papa." Andy took his brother's hand and went to the loft.

The girls hugged Mac's neck. Gracie held on the longest. "I love you, Papa."

And then the MacLayne homestead was quiet. Mac and Laurel sat before the blazing fire near the hearth holding hands. The snapping of the pine knots was all that broke the silence. Mac turned and stared at Laurel, filling his thoughts with all the things that he loved about her. She smiled at him.

"It's been a fine day, Laurel Grace. I want to soak up every remaining minute to carry back with me."

"I'm happy. You seem at ease and truly with us these couple of days."

"It's been more than just a good time. Being here with our family has given me back my strength. I even have enough will to go back. I had gotten so empty by what I've seen and done since I last saw you. I didn't know if I could make myself go back or not. When Major Livingston handed me that scrap of paper and it said 'Christmas Pass,' I thought to myself—that pass will get me home. If I have good sense, it will keep me there."

"Because you have good sense, you know you have to go back."

"Laurel, I think this stupid conflict will be over soon. I am comin' home to you. When the Lord brings me home, I'll never have the urge to leave again."

"Mac, don't make promises you can't keep."

Mac pulled Laurel from her rocking chair into his lap. "Please look at me, Laurel." He turned her to face him. He gazed into her gray-green eyes that haunted his sleep almost every night. "Laurel, I am coming home as soon as this war is over. For the rest of our lives, we'll be together here at Shiloh. Believe me and pray for me every night. Pray that I can be home soon."

"I do that now, Mac. I make this request each night. Keep Mac safe. Bring him home."

"Let's go to bed, Laurel. Dawn is only a breath away."

At sun up, Laurel awoke to the sound of horse hooves on the road. The memories of two very short days and nights did little to quell the ache in her chest. Loss is such a loathsome emotion after the joy and passion she'd lived that Christmas. Despite her promise to Mac, she couldn't contain her grief. She wept.

Before the household roused, she laid her grief aside and returned to the routine of life without Mac. There were fires to stoke, bread to bake, children to feed, and a household to maintain. The holiday had passed and real life called. Day to day existence was a harsh reality at the dawn of Mac's return to the army. After all, it was winter in Arkansas.

φ

New Year's Day of 1864 came and went. The community celebration was almost non-existent. Laurel heard a sole gunshot break the still of the night about the time she imagined to be midnight. Shiloh families need to celebrate was great, but their will to do so had been lost to three years of conflict, scarcity, and uncertainty. Shortages in staples brought hardship to many families, and the small harvest in the last growing season added to parents' fear of not being able to feed their children.

Shiloh suffered human loss, as had nearly every household in the community. Fathers, brothers, and sons would not return home due to the three years of on-going conflict. Laurel couldn't name one family that did not deal with grief, loneliness, hunger, or despair. Shiloh was now populated by women, children, and men over the age of fifty-five. The few younger men were those who returned from the war with injuries that would be life-long reminders of their days fighting for the Confederate cause.

To compensate for Mac's absence, Laurel began to read old newspapers he'd left behind, books he'd told her about, and even old notes he'd scribbled and left behind in his desk—anything to bring back a memory. One afternoon she found a small leather journal tied with a rawhide cord shoved in the bottom drawer. She'd seen him write in the book a few times in their life together but rarely given thought to what he'd written. She let the book fall open in her hand. The entry there was dated August 12, 1861. In Mac's clear, bold hand she found these words,

*A peoples' contest...we are all in this war; those who fight and those who stay at home.' A. Lincoln*

*—St. Louis Dispatch, July 4, 1861.*

*The president is right. As much as I want to protect my family, I don't know how I can keep the tragedy of war away from us. I'll stay here and try to push the ugliness away as long as I can, but I know the time will come when I will be forced to leave them in God's hands. I pray Laurel is strong enough to go on in my stead. I pray she will forgive me when I have to go.*

Laurel reread the words. Mac had known from the beginning of the war that he would have to serve. He had tried--very hard--to stay, but he'd always known what the war would bring. She understood now his extreme efforts before he left them. Blessedly, she and her family had been spared the worst of the hardships. Due to Mac's foresight and reliance on God's guidance, the stash beneath Cathy's bed had prevented the hunger too many homesteaders faced. Even now when so many were dealing with low crop yields and the added burden of the war tax, Laurel knew her family would not be hungry. In the stash, the MacLaynes still had salt, which couldn't be bought at any price, bags of cornmeal, some flour, and jars of canned goods to feed them throughout this winter. They would not have great variety and little meat remained, but they wouldn't miss a meal.

Mac had also left ample money. He joked with Laurel he would never again leave her penniless as he'd done the first year of their marriage when he traveled to Maryland to see his mother. He had even brought her more than five hundred dollars in greenbacks and gold he'd saved from this army pay. Of course, that money was of little value around northeast Arkansas. Supplies were becoming scarcer each month. Few freighters brought supplies to towns like Greensboro, Gainesville, or even larger towns like Batesville. Many of them had been conscripted into the army. Even when supplies were shipped, they often wound up in larger, besieged cities like Little Rock. With most of the river ports under the control of the Union army, crucial goods, like medicine and manufactured goods never arrived.

Mac's note read like prophecy. Those who remained behind were victims of the conflict. The women, children, and the elderly suffered greatly. Their greatest needs were often not material. Loneliness, anxiety, uncertainty, and grief proved the worst enemies of the ones who stayed behind. Laurel buried her distress pretty well most days, but when her children needed their papa, she felt chinks in her armor.

Just before Cathy's birthday, Laurel took her children across Big Creek to visit their grandfather. Thomas made a weekly trip to Shiloh but seldom did the two families spend a day together. This day proved to be a special occasion, especially for Andy and Cathy. They missed the company of their peers. Getting to spend the day with Sean and Maureen was a treat for them. Mark Thomas wanted to tag along with his older brother, but Andy and Sean ignored him for the most part. They were too busy talking about 'man stuff', like guns, hunting dogs, and horses. They read an account of the battles taking place in the east--who won and lost the battles. Andy read some of the horrendous numbers of dead and wounded reported in the paper aloud.

"Can you believe those Rebs killed more'n 1600 Union soldiers at Chickamauga?" Sean asked Andy.

"I think it was worse than that at Gettysburg. The paper said it was the bloodiest battle yet."

"I don't know about that one, Andy."

"Mark Thomas, go sit over there and don't bother us. Sean, Papa told me some stuff he heard in his camp. That Chickamauga battle was in a big swampy woods over in Georgia. He said it was the bloodiest battle that happened in the whole war."

"Who won?"

"Papa says no one wins battles like that. The paper said the Rebs won, but that General Bragg was stupid for not chasin' after them and finishin' them off. Who knows?"

"Sounds pretty bad. A whole lot of soldiers died, didn't they?"

"Yeah. Papa said it was partly because the troops from Longstreet's Northern Virginia Rebel unit got some repeatin' rifles. They can shoot lots faster. Lots of blue uniforms got bloody that day."

Mark Thomas sat nearby taking in every word. About midnight, the entire household awoke to the screams of a frightened four-year-old. When Laurel had climbed to the loft, she found Andy trying to shake Mark Thomas into consciousness.

"Andy, enough. I'll take him."

She sat on his bunk and cradled him in her arms much the way she had when he was an infant. She sang softly. *Sleep, my child and peace attend thee, All through the night. Guardian Angels, God will send them, All through the night....* As she gently swayed to an old lullaby, images of her mother came to her. Shortly Mark Thomas rested and drew himself closer to her. Laurel continued to hold him as he slept.

"Andy, go on back to bed after you go down and check on your sisters. Tell them Mark Thomas is all right." Laurel pulled her winter wrapper closer around her and leaned against the wall. An hour later, the boy awakened. He sniffled, as he'd done at times during his sleep.

"Mark Thomas, what terrible thing brought you such a scare?"

"Mama…" He began to cry again and buried his head in her neck. "I saw Papa—him and a lot of soldiers in blue in a bloody pile. When did Papa go to Chickenmago?"

"Son, you had a nightmare. Papa is in Batesville, just two short days from here. God is watching over him for us."

"No, Mama. Terrible battle happened. A million soldiers was fightin'."

"No, Son. It's not so. Papa is safe here in Arkansas. Where did you hear about a terrible battle?"

"The papers. Sean and Andy read about it. Andy said Papa told him about the battles."

"Mark Thomas, I'm tellin' you the truth. Your papa is not in a battle anywhere. He carries supplies to soldiers here in Arkansas."

"You promise?" Laurel nodded and kissed his cheek. "Hold me some more, Mama. I don't wanna see that bad dream no more."

The following morning, Laurel confronted Andy with Mark Thomas's story.

"It's true, Mama. Sean and me was readin' a newspaper that Papa brought home. There was a story about a battle in Chickamauga. I guess we got carried away."

"Andy, there will be no more war talk from this family. Your papa hates this war. He never wanted to be a part of it. There is nothing glorious, proud, or good about men dying out there. Please do as I say. Your brother and younger sisters are too little to understand."

"Yes, ma'am. I didn't think how Mark Thomas would take what we were sayin'. I'm sorry. I'll try to make it up to him. I promised Papa I'd watch after things here at Shiloh."

Laurel hugged the young man who daily grew more into the image of his father. "Thank you, Son. I know you will."

Cathy's fifteenth birthday in the middle of January would be the next extra item on Laurel's 'to do' list. Mac had told her after his long talk with Cathy on Christmas Day that the young woman needed something special on her birthday that year. He said that Cathy missed her brother more than she'd ever revealed to either of them. He wanted her to have a party that year. He'd said, "If you can manage it, Darlin', make her the best birthday celebration she's ever had." Laurel had promised Mac.

That became her plan. Laurel didn't know how many young people would come to a party at the MacLayne homestead, but she would try. Although some people held grudges against Mac, over time a few in the community had shown sympathy for Laurel. Some believed that perhaps she was the victim of a man who'd deserted his family and his heritage to fight for the wrong side. Laurel would invite the community and pray they would respond.

Laurel preferred to avoid social events. She felt uncomfortable because at times someone would make a comment that would call for her to defend her husband. It took all her will to hold her tongue. She would simply walk away or change the subject because she knew her children needed and wanted to be with their friends. Growing up in isolation made for a sad lonely time for young people who were approaching young adulthood.

Laurel knew this all too well. Perhaps she would still be in that situation had Mac not married her, removing the stigma of being the 'Spinster of Hawthorn.' Laurel wanted her children to be accepted and valued by everyone in their community.

Laurel planned a barn dance to celebrate. She found a banjo picker, two old gentlemen who played guitars, and a lady who played the violin. The lady often used her old instrument to pluck a lively fiddle. Laurel also planned a menu using some of her precious stores from the stash. The main item would be a large chocolate cake, Cathy's favorite. The gifts would not be extravagant, but Laurel was able to find green ribbons for Cathy's hair and a copy of Hawthorn's *The Scarlet Letter.* Of course, the book was a hand-me-down, the copy that William Woodruff had sent her when she had written four articles about her Arkansas travels for the Gazette during Mac's service to the General Assembly in 1860.

The week before the party, Laurel learned that her Uncle Matthew had returned early from his last chaplain circuit. He had taken a bullet in a raid of a Union camp he'd been visiting. Matthew Campbell had sent a young Confederate private to his niece, asking her to come to his homestead. The private had no other information to share with her, so she went immediately.

"Uncle, are you seriously injured?" Laurel blurted out her question the minute she saw him lying in his bed, covered with three quilts.

"Don't be a frettin', Laurel. I got a minor wound in my leg, but I caught a bad case of the grip comin' home from Jacksonport. Can't seem to get warm."

"Thank goodness the wound is minor. The messenger scared me because he wouldn't tell anything except you'd taken a bullet."

"Flesh wound in my thigh. I was tryin' to see to some wounded soldiers when we got raided near Jacksonport. I was at the wrong place at the wrong time."

"I thought medics and chaplains were not supposed to be attacked. Both sides are supposed to honor those who give aid to the fallen," Laurel said.

"That's the general rule, but in the heat of the moment, some people forget to pay attention to the rules. Anyway, that's not the reason I asked you to come over here on such a wet, cold day. Laurel, I got to spend several hours with Mac the day before this bullet found me."

"How is he? He wasn't in the hospital, was he?"

"No, darlin'…I stopped at an encampment near the convergence of the Black and White Rivers. Mac's unit was there pickin' up supplies to return to Batesville. We talked most of the night."

"How did he look? What did he say? Is he well?"

"Hold on, Laurel. He said that he runs a regular route to the river ports from camps in Batesville to Pocahontas. He asked me to give you the name of his commanding officer in case you need to contact him for any reason. The commander at the camp is Colonel Phelps."

"Is that all he said?" Laurel asked.

"Laurel Grace, you know what he said. He wants to come home. He misses you and the kids. He sent you a letter. I'm sure it says things he wouldn't tell me, even if he is my best friend."

"Can I have it please?"

"Ellie, will you fetch my saddlebags? I know I put that letter in my Bible for safekeeping."

"Uncle Matt, you've been there. Is the area dangerous?"

"Not bad. Once in a while, a Confederate troop will raid one of the riverports, but it usually don't amount to much. They call 'em skirmishes. The Union troops have that area locked down pretty tight. Anyway, Mac's on the move all the time. His unit is patrolling the river like most of the Second Arkansas Cavalry."

"I know you're probably telling me part of the truth. I'm so happy to hear about Mac. I'll take what I can get. Thank the Lord, Mac is safe."

Ellie returned and handed Laurel the letter. "I hope it's good news, Laurel Grace."

"Thank you, Aunt Ellie. Uncle Matthew, are you going back to the circuit?"

"Not for a while. I'm staying here at Shiloh until I heal. I think I'd like to go back to the Shiloh congregation. I'll have to wait and see. The church committee may not want me back."

"Laurel Grace, you may want to head home. The snow has begun to fall much harder in the last few minutes." Ellie said.

"Ride careful, Niece. We'll visit soon. We plan to come to Cathy's barn dance."

Laurel wanted to tear open the envelope bearing Mac's bold clear script, but when she saw the heavy snow and the nearly covered roads, she tucked the letter in her coat and headed for home. A two-mile ride in this weather could be treacherous, and her responsibility was at home.

The January blizzard was among the worst since Laurel had moved to Shiloh. Intermittent periods of ice and snow in temperatures ten degrees below freezing locked down the area for more than two weeks. Cathy's birthday dance was postponed, as was every other activity not vital to people's survival. J.F. Clarke came from his cabin in the forest area of the MacLayne property, bringing Mac's bull to be sheltered in the barn.

He explained to Laurel, "Mrs. Mac, I know this is risky, but if I left old Starface in the woods alone, he'd likely freeze. I just hope the Rebel troops and the bushwhackers don't like the cold any more than we do."

"I appreciate your concern, J.F. I know Mac wants to use this bull to rebuild his herd after the war."

"I'll try to keep him safe, ma'am."

In February, life at Shiloh returned to some normalcy. The roads cleared, and Laurel once again planned Cathy's birthday celebration. Her daughter would have her barn dance, even though it was nearly a month late. Invitations went out, musicians were contacted once again, a feast was prepared, and the barn was cleaned and decorated. Saturday, February 6, would be a day of delayed celebration.

To the surprise of both Laurel and Cathy, the MacLayne barn was filled with Shiloh residents, both young and old, all the family, and four young Confederate soldiers who were now posted at a medical camp not far from Herndon. Matthew Campbell had

invited the young men he had known during his circuit ministry.
The privates were between seventeen to twenty years old. They
supplied an element that would have been missing from the barn
dance—the presence of young men to dance with the young ladies
in attendance. Cathy received more than a fair share of attention.
She loved every minute of her special celebration.

Her most special gift was a note written to her from Mac.
He had sent it in the letter Laurel received from her uncle before
the mid-January blizzard.

My darling daughter,

I am so happy with the beautiful young woman you are becoming. I hope
your celebration is happy and fun. Remember, when young men begin to
pay attention to you—and they will—your best beau is your papa. I love
you, Cathy. God bless you on your birthday,

Papa

And like the letter Laurel received, this precious note would be
read scores of times until the paper began to break in the folds.

One gift--not so welcome--also came to Cathy the night of
her birthday dance. One of the privates brought it…measles. Cathy
was the first exposed, and the dangerous disease quickly spread to
Andy, who was also at the party. Then the disease worked its way
to Mark Thomas, Gracie, Leah Ann, and Little Roy. Only Annie
and Laurel avoided the illness that spread through the household.

Cathy's first symptoms were coughing and a runny nose.
Laurel thought little of it because young people frequently caught
colds during the winter. The next day, though, Andy hacked and
coughed all day. Both complained of feeling bad. Before the end of
the third day, both felt warm to the touch. Cathy showed Laurel
several itchy bumps on her forehead and complained that her eyes
hurt.

Laurel knew her children had been exposed to something
bad, even though she didn't know what illness they'd caught. On
the fourth day, Andy's fever spiked. Laurel soaked his fever-
racked body in wet cloths, but within a couple of minutes, the cool
cloths had taken on the heat and had to be replaced.

Before Laurel could ease Andy's pain, Gracie too developed a fever. Then Mark Thomas and Leah Ann needed cool baths too. Annie worked alongside Laurel nursing the MacLayne children until Little Roy broke out with the rash across his tiny head and down his back. Five very sick children demanded the constant attention of Laurel and Annie.

Laurel set up beds, pallets, and a cot in the second pen. She covered the windows with quilts to darken the room. This seemed to ease the pain from the children's inflamed eyes, but the spiking fever among them demanded constant care. Laurel and Annie continued to carry in cold water to soak rags and wash down the feverish bodies. The two babies began to cry constantly after the second day of the rash. Laurel held Leah Ann even while she nursed another child.

For almost a week, this rotation of bathing, urging children to drink water, dipping spoons of chicken broth into little mouths, and singing cranky kids to sleep took a toll on both caregivers. By the twenty-second of February, the worst was over. Laurel felt an eternity had passed. Fevers receded and little by little the red splotches faded. The children slept more easily and longer. None of the MacLayne's nor Roy Jr. had succumbed to the deadly disease that was killing so many soldiers on both sides of the conflict.

Laurel sent word to her father-in-law that the threat to the children seemed to be over. She asked him to visit now that he would not take the illness back to his wife and the Flannagan children. He sent back word that each of them had also contracted the red rash about the same time. Laurel later learned that several other families in the community who had attended the birthday dance had also contracted the measles.

The community had been blessed, though. None of the people died as so many had in the field. Laurel wondered at the difference. She would ask Dr. Gibson the next time she went to Greensboro if she ever got to town again.

Then the evening Laurel declared her family to be 'spot-free,' she collapsed. Annie, Andy, and Cathy worked to get her into bed. She was dead weight.

"I gotta go get help for Mama. Annie, please look after the kids. Can you and Cathy get them some soup and make'em drink some more water? Mama said to keep the water comin'. I'm ridin' to Greensboro." Andy headed out to saddle Sparky.

In the late afternoon, Andy arrived with the doctor. Laurel had roused, but she didn't have the strength to get up.

"Clear this room. Let me see what's goin' on with this lady."

"Dr. Gibson, I'm all right now. I'm just tired. Annie and I have been nursing sick kids with the measles non-stop for nearly two weeks."

"I see how that could wear ya down, Laurel, but I want to check ya over anyway. Have ya been eatin' and drinkin' enough water? Had any rest at all?"

"No. We've been caring for six kids who've had the measles."

"Before that, since harvest time, say."

"Off and on."

"Uhh…" Dr. Gibson completed his examination. "Well, Laurel, now you're gonna have to take care of yourself. You will add another MacLayne to your family…I'm thinkin' sometime in September. I didn't know Mac had a Christmas pass, but it's either that or we have another case of an immaculate conception."

Laurel blushed at Dr. Gibson's attempt at humor. "Dr. Gibson, you can't tell anyone about this right now. I have to think about how I can explain this to the community. Our neighbors in Shiloh believe Mac deserted us to join the Union army. Only our family knows Mac left to protect our home and family."

"I wondered about that. The man I know would go to hell and back before he'd desert his family. He must have been pushed hard."

"Bushwhackers, Rebel conscription, and the Sequestration Act. Mac believed he had no recourse. He refused to see our property forfeited and his family destitute."

"Well, Laurel, I'll keep this to myself, but before long, you'll tell everyone yourself. Babies grow pretty fast before and after they're born."

"I want a boy," Laurel said.

"I just want a healthy child." The doctor responded. "Get some help next time. Neighbors at Shiloh would've come if you'd asked for help. You can't work for weeks on end without rest and food. Be good to yourself and the new MacLayne."

"I'll try.

"Try hard...and write a letter to Mac. He'll be glad to hear the good news."

# Chapter 23

*Greater love hath no man than this, that a man lay down his life*
*for his friends.*
*These things I command you, that ye love one another.*
*John 15:13,17*

By the middle of February, the members of Mac's
Quartermaster's unit had made five supply runs from Batesville.
Trips to Jacksonport, Powhatan, and Pocahontas were common
since these port towns were key to providing medicine, food, and
ammunition to
Union troops. Longer trips to posts on the Mississippi, like Helena
and Esperanza, were less frequent but not unheard of. The wagon
trains were crucial because Rebel forces were more likely to strike
supplies coming by rail, probably because scheduling was more
regular. The occasional skirmish was not usually much of a
hindrance as Mac's men were better armed than the Confederate
troops sent to attack them.

The frequent supply runs left Mac's men worn and longing
for a day or two when they could sit beside a warm fire at camp or
bundle themselves in warm, woolen blankets to sleep a night
through—on a cot in a tent. To assure supplies were delivered as
scheduled, nights were usually short with makeshift camps along
the trail. Sleeping on the cold, frozen ground happened more often
than not.

Valentine's Day, 1864, found Mac and his men in such a camp. The temperature hovered around the freezing mark and drizzling rain continued to fall well into the evening hours. On such a night, Mac could think of nothing but home and Laurel. He ordered his drivers to pull the wagons close together so they could stretch oilcloths between them. This would allow them to create make-shift tents to keep the rain off the pallets they'd sleep on that night. Near the edge, they built small fires so beans and coffee could be heated for a meager supper.

Mac settled near one of the fires and ate, speaking little to his companions. When he dumped the last of his coffee outside the enclosure, he took his Bible and the silver picture case from his saddlebag. He lifted the cover of the case and stared down at the likeness of his family and Laurel.

"Captain, you've sure been mighty quiet tonight. Whatcha stewin' about?"

"Missin' my sweetheart, Josiah. Today is Valentine's Day. I'd sure like to be home with her tonight. We always made this day a special time just for us."

"What's so special about today? Rotten time of year, cold and wet."

"Don't you know what Valentine's Day is? This day is a time set aside to show the person you love how much they mean to you. It's a perfect time of year for spoonin' and holdin' your sweetheart. I sent Laurel a valentine I made her—folded up this fancy paper into a little pouch and cut off a twig of my hair to put in it. I put it in the post a couple of weeks ago at Batesville. Wonder if she got it?"

"Did she send you a letter?"

"If she did, I didn't get it yet. I hope so. I haven't heard from her since I was home at Christmas. Six weeks is a long time not to hear from home."

"Maybe there'll be a letter waitin' for ya when we get back on Tuesday."

"I can hope."

"You gotta a big family, don't ya, Captain?"

"I do, Tom. Laurel and I have two kids of our own. I have a son that Laurel adopted, and we have two daughters we both adopted. We had an adopted son who was killed at the Battle of Corinth almost two years ago. Except for losin' Roy, the Lord's kept most of the grief and want of this war away from us."

"How in tarnation do you handle all those young'uns? I'd run away to the war, too!" Another teamster joked.

"I'd not left them at all if I'd not been forced away by those damned laws passed by the Confederate legislature. I stayed at Shiloh until I feared my bein' home put my family in too much danger. The Conscription Act was bad enough—forcing people into military service or threatenin' them with death as a traitor. But, when they passed that Sequestration Act that made the forfeit of all possessions, land, and goods to the Confederate government for anyone considered an enemy alien, I had no option. I couldn't let my family starve to death."

"But you ain't no foreigner, Captain."

"Jedidiah, I am a transplant from Maryland to Arkansas. If I refused to join the Confederate army, my family could have been left with nothing and no means to support themselves."

"I didn't know that was why you joined up. Didn't the Rebs take your homestead when they found out you joined up with us?"

"No, the Southrons are a gentlemanly lot. They'd never take a Southern lady's property when her husband deserted her."

"She's all alone now with your kids?"

"Not exactly, Josiah. My pa lives just a piece down from my place, and I have a tenant farmer who lives on our place. He works out his rent. Laurel's uncle lives a couple of miles north of us. Most important, the Lord is takin' care of my family. I ask him to see over them every day."

"Do you believe in that religion stuff, Mac?" The other captain asked. "I've been watchin' you read that Bible all the time."

"I know the Lord is takin' care of them. I don't have a doubt. I couldn't have left them if I didn't know it."

"How do you know this stuff?" The private who joked about Mac's kids asked him.

"The promise is made time and again in the Bible, Son. I've seen it worked out in my life more times than I can recall. I'd be a fool to reject what I know to be true."

One of the teamsters got up and walked away from the fire, but Jedidiah and Tom sat down next to the private, Garvin Parnell. Jedidiah then asked, "Where does it say our loved ones will be safe?"

Mac opened the Bible he held and began to read passage after passage that promised believers all were in God's care. "The verse I say to myself every day—sometimes many times a day is Romans 8:28. It says 'And we know all things work together for good to them that love God, to them who are called to his purpose'."

"I don't believe it, Captain," Parnell said. "I know lots of folks who've been hurt in this war. Some of 'em died, and some lost everything they owned."

"That may be. Sometimes bad things happen to good people. My son Roy found the Lord only a short time before that Union bullet took his life in Mississippi, but if people believe in the promise, they aren't lost. In the end, all believers will be blest. I know this to the core of who I am."

"You seem mighty sure."

"Read this book, Parnell, and you will know I'm tellin' you the truth." The conversation ebbed at that point. Mac opened his Bible and turned to Solomon's Song of Songs to read the verses he'd read so often to Laurel. Then he offered a prayer of thanksgiving for her love and the blessings of their family.

"Goodnight, Men. Get some sleep. We're westbound when the sun comes up over the horizon. I may have a valentine waitin' for me."

But he didn't. Mac did receive a brief letter from his father, dated the third week in January. Thomas MacLayne told his son of the harsh winter and about the measles outbreak at Shiloh. The major portion of the letter reported that Mac's family was now well, and Laurel and the children lacked for nothing—medicine, food, or heat. Thomas conveyed his concern for Mac's welfare and pleaded for him to write soon.

Mac wrote and waited…. He wrote again and waited some more. Still, no word came from Craighead County. Finally, on the first of March, Mac sent a letter he hoped Laurel would receive before their anniversary on March 17.

Dearest Wife,

Pa told me you are nursing our kids through the measles. He said they seem to be getting better, but you seem pretty worn out. I want to hear from you, Laurel. I need to know from you that all is well at home. Why have you not written to me? Have you not been able to forgive my leaving you? Three months are nearly gone without a word from you. I need to hear from you. A single line will put my mind at ease. Please write to me.

Even if you can't forgive my broken promise, Laurel, I want you to know how grateful I am for the six years of your love I've had. I am a better man because in the time you have been my wife, you have believed in me. I know I've hurt you often when I've broken my promise to you—too often I have left you alone and for too long. Truly, Laurel Grace, you've never been away from me. I carry you in my mind and heart every minute. Since we've been apart because of this war, I've learned I am not whole without you. We are meant to be together. I hope you feel the same. Since I've no more paper, I'll close tonight. I love you. I can't wait to hold you again.

May the Lord keep you until I can,

Mac

At daybreak, the commanding officer sent Mac's unit back out again. This time the trip took them west to the Ozarks. The occasion to 'sneak' home for a brief visit didn't arise.

φ

On the evening of March 21st, Col. Phelps sent for Mac as he was about to turn in for the night. That afternoon, he and his unit returned from the Buffalo River with a shipment of medicine and uniforms to be sent to soldiers further south. Mac's men were exhausted, wanting only to sleep for a few days. He felt the same way.

"Sir, you called for me?"

"Yes, MacLayne, have a chair. First, I'd like to commend you and your men. You've carried out mission after mission, always on time, and with few injuries. Your concern for your men is well-known around camp. You've not lost one member of your unit since you came to the Second Arkansas from Fort Curtis."

"Thank you, Sir. We've been lucky that we've not run into many Rebel forces, and those we have encountered were small groups."

"You're being modest, Captain. I've heard the stories bantered around the campfires. Men talk. I wish I could reward such merit—a few days off."

"That would be an answer to a prayer, Colonel Livingston. I'd love to ride back to Shiloh to see my family, just to know they are well and have all they need."

"I'll grant that leave, MacLayne, when you get back from this next mission. This one is crucial so I need to assign the best unit I have."

"Again, I thank you for your faith in my men."

"We've had some scouting reports that a troop of Confederates is planning to raid this shipment we are bringing up the White River. A steamboat is offloading about two dozen crates of repeating rifles along with the munitions they use. We can't let these weapons fall into Rebel hands."

"I understand," Mac responded.

"I want you to lead your team and one other over to the White River to retrieve these supplies at Jacksonport and bring them back to Batesville. From here, we'll send them north with the Second Arkansas when they return to Pilot Knob in Missouri."

"Yes, sir."

"MacLayne, I can't impress on you how important it is to get that shipment to Missouri. You may encounter skirmishes up and down White River, but your focus is those firearms. I'll send other troops out to deal with the Rebels."

"We'll be ready to leave at sunrise. One other thing, sir. Will you see that this letter gets in the camp's mail? I just finished a note to my wife."

"Of course. It's a short trip, MacLayne. I'm thinking you can procure that shipment at Jacksonport and be back here within three days. You could be headed home on leave by Sunday."

"Yes, sir. Thank you." Mac stood, saluted his commander, left the make-shift office in the dining room of a now-deserted Garrott house on Main Street. He shook his head and stretched his taut shoulders. *No rest for the weary…Get it done, man. Before the end of the week, you'll be in Laurel's arms.*

Before returning to his tent, Mac walked the short distance to the livery stable in Batesville where he boarded Midnight. Mac disliked the rule that all cavalrymen had to ride the stock provided by the army. He missed the fine black stallion that had served him since the days of his trip to Washington County. Mac knew the horse to be steady, loyal, and obedient. The military rule that banned personal mounts was just wrong.

"Hey, Midnight. How's my good friend tonight? You want some attention?" Mac placed a handful of oats into the trough. Then he picked up the brush and stroked the flank of the beautiful black horse he cherished. "Midnight, we're goin' home at the end of the week. Won't it be fine to be back with Sassy Lady and Sparky again? You'll get to sleep in your stall for a few days. We'll have a chance to get rested up, boy. We're gonna make a fast trip back to Shiloh. Our family's there."

Midnight whinnied and pranced. Mac continued to brush his prized animal. "I'll see ya on Saturday. Maybe I can find you a carrot. An early garden somewhere may have one to spare. Goodnight, fella."

As the sun turned the eastern horizon golden, Mac led his troop of nine men and another unit of ten men southward toward

Jacksonport. The second wagon unit was under the command of
Lt. Hudson because his captain had been granted leave.
Mac didn't see a problem with supervising the younger officer.
They were making such a short, routine trip.

The trip to Jacksonport was quick. The four empty wagons
pulled by four sturdy Army mules covered the distance in a day
and a half. Mack knew the trip back would not be quite as fast with
each wagon loaded, but the mules were well-trained healthy
animals. Mac also knew his troops to be the best around. By noon
on March 23$^{rd}$, the loading of the rifles and ammunition was near
completion. Mac called his men together with the second crew.

"Men, I see no need wastin' the afternoon here in river
gnats and mosquitos. Let's take advantage of a river port town and
go scout out a decent meal. At 1:30, I want to head north toward
our camp. I believe we can get near Oil Trough where we will
spend the night. By mid-afternoon tomorrow, we should be able to
deliver our load."

"Captain, where are we gonna find any decent food?"

"Jedidiah, you've been to riverports dozens of times.
Wander around the docks, and you'll find fresh fruit and new-
baked bread…who knows what else. I'm dependin' on you to get
us somethin' good to eat."

Within a few minutes, the troop sat on the back of the
wagons and stuffed themselves with fried chicken, yams, and slabs
of cornbread. "That widow lady sellin' grub on the dock cooks
better than my ma," Tom said. "I just wish I had some cold cider to
wash it down."

Mac wiped his lips with his handkerchief. "I'm just grateful
for what we got. Now you men, get a move on. I wanna head
back." Mac rose and wrapped a wedge of cornbread and stowed it
in his pocket.

Within a quarter-hour, the wagon train of four army
wagons, sixteen mules, and four soldiers on horseback left
Jacksonport. They lost no time heading toward the setting sun.
Mac and the other armed guards stood vigilance over their cargo.
Gossip on the docks had confirmed what Col. Phelps had warned
Mac about. The Rebel forces frequently raided in the area. They

were notorious for bushwhacking small Union units, especially those with supplies. Even in their heightened state of alert, neither Mac nor any of the other men saw any hint of a Confederate band.

They traveled on until Mac found a place not far from White River just outside of Oil Trough, where a small grove of trees offered them some protection. The small clearing provided ample water and pasture for the mules and horses. Mac ordered the men to set up camp. Four armed guards would walk sentry all night.

"Men, I know you're all tired, but I don't have to remind you that we have one task. We get our supplies back to Batesville. We don't need scouting reports to tell us that what we're carrying would draw an attack if the Rebs knew we are in the region. I'll set a relief for ya in two hours. Keep a close watch."

They passed the night without incident, yet Mac felt the hair on his neck bristle. He scanned the area constantly as they prepared to set out on the last leg of their trip. Just before he called the men to move out, he took the silver case from his pocket and stared down at his family. He spoke his morning prayer over them and returned the precious case to his inside pocket. He put his bedroll behind his saddle and patted the gelding's rump. "Boy, let's make this a quick trip today. It's less than twenty miles."

He checked his saddlebags. He saw the cross Laurel gave him, the morning she told him for the first time that she loved him. *Laurel, Darlin', I can hardly wait to hold you again.* He threw his saddlebags across the hind part of his sorrel. But before he mounted, he took his Bible out. He unbuttoned his coat and tucked it next to his heart and then rebuttoned his coat.

"Men, head'em out—northwest along the White River. Let's make it a fast trip." The first mile was fine indeed. The weather was warm but not hot. The river sang as the current pushed its way downstream. Mac saw two frisky otters playing in the swift, clean water. "Hey, Jedidiah, have you ever seen two happier critters than those otters out there?"

A gunshot shattered the silence, but it was out in the distance. Mac didn't feel any immediate danger, but the shot was close enough to end the pleasant thoughts of otters and sun dancing on the caps of the current on White River. "Arm yourselves and protect our goods. Move on toward Batesville, while I go back a piece and see if I can find out where that shootin' is comin' from."

Mac returned within half an hour. "Men, there is a skirmish over in those bottoms. I wasn't close enough to see much. I did see twenty or thirty of our soldiers and maybe a group of forty or so Rebs...Looks like our troops caught 'em by surprise. The whole thing is chaos...men trying to put on their boots, others loadin' guns. Get those wagons out of sight until I can find a way around this mess."

"Let's go help 'em out, Captain," Tom yelled.

"Private, I said to remove those wagons from plain view. We have one order. Get those supplies back to Batesville."

"Yes, sir." The men bolted into action and moved the wagons and mules some distance off the road into a thicket of trees. Then they waited. Before an hour had passed, the gunfire became very sporadic, and the sound became more distant.

Lt. Hudson asked," Do you think it's over now, Captain MacLayne?"

"I don't know. We can't take a chance of goin' into a pocket of Confederate soldiers, especially if they routed our boys. We'll wait a while longer." They sat for about another hour. When no more gunfire was heard, Mac called to the corporal. "Josiah, take my horse and ride down to the bend in the river. That's where I saw the skirmish when I went out. Bring me back a report."

When the corporal returned, he reported that the battle had ended. "Captain, ain't no soldiers, either us or them down there right now. No live ones anyway."

"What did ya see?"

"I didn't take time to count'em, but I saw bodies. More in gray than blue, but some of both, I guess."

"Do you think we can move through there now?"

"I didn't see no reserves guardin' the place. I saw lots of tracks down by the river crossin'—like maybe one unit chasin' after the other. Course I couldn't tell who's chasing who."

"Men, let's make good time. We need to get out of this area. Double time."

The men pushed the mules harder than they normally did. In a short time, Mac saw where the battle had happened. Several bodies lay along the road. Mac motioned for the teamster to keep up the faster pace. Then he heard moaning. He waved the teamsters on. Only the last wagon, he motioned to stop. He dismounted and went to the wounded boy. He knelt and found a pulse.

"Sergeant, put this man in your wagon. He's been wounded but doesn't look too bad. Try to stop the bleeding and bandage it. Let your partner drive on. Y'all catch up with the other wagons and keep movin'."

"Yes, but Captain..."

"Go on. I'm gonna check these other men. I don't think any of them are alive, but I'll see. Go. I'll catch up with ya." The wagon moved out at a quick pace. Mac moved among the men, mostly Confederate boys, searching for a pulse. He found only one man still breathing, but he was very weak. The wounded man wore captain's bars.

"Captain, can you hear me?" Mac asked.

The dying man opened his eyes. "Thirsty."

Mac went to his horse and brought his canteen. He lifted the captain's head and helped him drink.

"My men...how many down?"

"I only see three privates..."

"So young." The captain's breath became raspy, and blood gurgled to his lips. Mac could see a fatal chest wound.

"Where are you from, Captain?" The man didn't answer. "You got a family in these parts?" Again, Mac got no reply from the wounded Confederate soldier. He continued to sit next to him until his final breath. Mac closed the eyes of the enemy captain. Mac returned to his horse, mounted, and pulled the reins to direct the big gelding west again. He rode away from the river.

Before he reached the road, a Rebel cry broke the silence. Mac kicked his horse into a run. Four men dressed in butternut-colored uniforms followed close behind. A shot rang out. Mac's horse dropped, penning his leg beneath it. He was dazed by the

281

fall, but he tried to push free with his other leg. Before he could dislodge himself, he was surrounded by the small band of Rebels.

"Lookee here, fellas…we done got us a real live Yankee captain. He done got his leg trapped under a dead horse."

"Well, let's just shoot'em and put'em out of misery, Yancey. Whatcha think?"

"Let's take a vote…all in favor of a bullet…What only one?"

"Nah…let's take that devil back to camp. We got a couple of other fine Yanks goin' to Andersonville. He can keep those other blue bellies company on a fine vacation in Georgia."

*ф*

Two days later, a small group of Second Arkansas Cavalry returned to Oil Trough and to a second skirmish site called Crossroads to search for Mac and two other men who had not returned. Union casualties had been very light. The wounded private that the Quartermasters unit had brought back with the supply train had been sent to a field hospital. He would lose part of his leg, but he would survive. Being part of the Eleventh Missouri Cavalry, he'd earned a permanent trip back home to Springfield.

Sgt. Jedidiah Mason headed up the search party, and Corporal Josiah Parchman scouted the area since he was the last of Mac's unit to leave the area. He found Mac's sorrel not far from where he'd last seen him. There were no longer bodies of soldiers along the river at Oil Trough, but the carcasses of three dead horses lay in the bend of the river where the heaviest fighting had occurred.

"Hey, Sarge, ain't this that little wooden cross that Captain MacLayne always rubbed his thumb across when he read us the Bible at night?" Cor. Josiah Parachman held up the carved wooden cross, tied to the rawhide cord that once belonged to Laurel's pa.

"Yeah. He always pulled that cross out of his pocket every night. Do you see anything else that he'd brought in his saddlebag" Is his Bible around here anywhere?"

"Nothing else is here but a couple of soggy pieces of paper. Do ya think this name is Laura? Maybe they're letters, but the rain ruined 'em last night. Even his saddlebags and the reins from his horse are missin'. You reckon they took his body away when they moved those Rebs soldiers?"

"If they did, no way we can find him to take him home. Damn shame—U.S. Quartermasters are supposed to bring home our fallen. There is something in our creed about bring 'em home and lay them down in fields of honor."

"Mac deserved that. He was a fine man—a good officer. He shouldn't be gone." Jedidiah wiped his cheek. "Let's go on back. We can't help Captain MacLayne now."

# Chapter 24

*Keep thy tongue from evil, and thy lips from speaking guile.*
*Depart from evil and do good; seek peace and pursue it.*
*Psalm 34: 13-14*

Another night, one of many, an image of a small carved cross laced onto a rawhide cord pulled Laurel from sleep. That dream plagued her, though she didn't understand why since that cross so cherished by her father had always meant hope and comfort before. She never put much stock in dreams, but this one came too often and too clearly to be meaningless. Laurel had not seen the cross but once since Mac had left her to join the Union army. She knew he never left Shiloh without it in his pocket or saddlebag. The one time she had seen it, he'd ridden more than half the distance back from Big Creek to get it the day he had left from his short visit after Chalk Bluff.

Laurel shook off the dread and rose to start her day, even though no hint of sunrise yet lit Crowley's Ridge. She knew she wouldn't sleep so she decided to tackle the day's work that lay ahead. She pulled her skirt around her growing torso and found it uncomfortably tight. Soon, her wrappers would be the only clothes she would be able to wear. They wouldn't stand up to the rigors of the outdoor work that had to be done this time of year. The limitations of her wardrobe would certainly keep her at home. She could no longer postpone business in Greensboro. September was still many months away, but evidence of her expected child was becoming more obvious every day.

A long hard day wiped the dread from Laurel's mind. Andy, J.F., Cathy, and she spent the entire day planting the last of the feed crops for the animals. The oat field was crucial as their livestock numbers continued to grow. Mac had deliberately depleted the herds before the war because he knew much of it would be confiscated by the armies. To date, though, Shiloh had only been raided for their beef once. Their heifers had delivered healthy calves, and now the herd was twice the size Mac had left. The sows also produced healthy litters. This blessing meant extra feed would be necessary. If they didn't fall victim to another scavenging raid, the MacLayne's would be well-fed in the coming year.

With the seeding complete, spring planting came to an end. Maintaining gardens and fields demanded less effort, so Laurel felt she could take a day to go into Greensboro to do some delayed business. Andy hitched Sassy Lady to the buggy, and he drove his mother into town on a sunny Wednesday morning the third week in April.

"Andy, I want to go see Dr. Gibson first. Please meet me at the mercantile in about an hour."

"All right, Mama. Is there somethin' ya need me to do while I'm waitin' for ya?"

"Yes, Son. Why don't you go over to the barbershop and get that mane trimmed?" You're not a tow-headed little boy anymore. A young man needs to have a grownup haircut." Laurel took a couple of Confederate bills from her reticule and handed them to Andy.

She stepped down to the wooden sidewalk in front of the doctor's office. "See ya in about an hour." She knocked on the door and entered. Ed Gibson sat at his desk. A tall man with his back to the door sat across from him. "I'm sorry, Doctor. I didn't mean to intrude. I'll wait outside until you are finished."

"Come on in, Laurel. We're just passin' time. Do you know Dr. Cavanaugh?"

Laurel looked at the well-dressed man who seemed vaguely familiar, but she didn't recognize him.

"I don't think I do, Ed."

"We've met only once before, Mrs. MacLayne. An incident with an ax and an apple tree if memory serves me."

The scene flashed before her. This man was the major who'd saved her orchard from the Rebel unit who camped at her homestead in the early fall. He sat before her, dressed in an expensive, tailored civilian suit. Dr. Gibson had introduced him as Dr. Cavanaugh, not Major Cavanaugh. The man stood and took two halting steps toward her. A slight grimace on his face told her some degree of pain was associated with the limp.

"Yes, I remember. You are the officer who ordered his men to spare my orchard. If you could see it now, you'd be so glad you did. Today, those trees are filled with hundreds of pink and white blossoms. The scent coming from that orchard is almost like paradise. Come summer's end, my kids will be eating apples for the first time in two years. Thank you again."

"My pleasure, I assure you. I'd love to see those trees in bloom. Would you mind if I ride by one afternoon?"

Laurel hadn't meant to offer an invitation to a Confederate officer, but what could she say?

"You'd be welcome, sir."

"Laurel, did you need to see me about something today?" Dr. Gibson returned to business.

"I can come back later when you aren't busy."

"No, no. I'm just on my way out. It's been my pleasure to see you again, Mrs. MacLayne. Time permitting, I'll come to see those apple blossoms." The stately, attractive man picked up his hat and a cane. He limped to the door before he turned to speak to Dr. Gibson. "Ed, I'll be back in touch. I appreciate the offer to work with you. Let me look around the area and consider all you've said. Perhaps we can have supper tonight."

"I look forward to hearing about your decision, Cort." The door closed behind him. "Well, now will you tell me why you came to see me, Laurel?"

After a quick examination and a stern scolding about excessive workloads, Laurel joined Andy at McCollough's store. She was relieved that the cramping in her lower back was not a sign of distress on her baby. When she entered the busy store, she saw Andy talking with a friend, but she also saw three boys who once frequently visited the homestead turn their backs to him. She decided to approach them. "Good mornin' to you boys. I haven't see y'all around lately. How are your folks?" The boys sputtered, blushed, and shuffled trying to make some kind of reply. "I don't think I know your friend. Did he come to the house with y'all when you came to hunt or swim in the creek with Andy?"

"No, ma'am. He's just moved here."

"Oh. Well, nice to see ya. Hope y'all come to visit soon." The boys made a bee-line to the front door. Laurel giggled with guilty pleasure at their discomfort for the ridiculous shunning of Andy. Andy and his friend Rafe had witnessed the entire conversation. Andy was grinning from ear to ear.

"Ya got some real gumption, Mama."

"Never mind that." Laurel looked at Andy with his newly cut hair. The barber had tied it back with a rawhide cord, just as he did Mac's. Andy looked more like his father every day. "Come on, young man, let's see if we can pick up a few things we need at home." Laurel and Andy looked around the depleted shelves of McCollough's store. Of all the things on her list, Laurel found a tin of baking powder and a five-pound bag of brown beans.

"John, do you have salt, a bag of flour, or any kind of fruit?"

"No, Mrs. Mac. Not much chance we'll get any before fall. Salt is so costly people can't afford it when I can get it. I think Wiley's got cornmeal down at his gristmill if that'll do."

"I think I got plenty of cornmeal. I just wanted some variety. Biscuits once in a while instead of pone would be nice. What about canned peaches? Or maybe a bag of sugar or even sorghum?" Laurel asked.

I think I may have a couple of cans of peaches, but sweetening's been gone for months."

"All right, please give me those peaches. I also need yard goods. My little ones are outgrowing everything they have."

"I don't have one bolt of yard goods in the store. Since the Yanks blockaded all the ports around the Mississippi, we don't get nothin' from the north. All the textile mills are up there, ya know."

"I hope this war ends soon. My kids will be wearing their bedsheets."

"Well at least, they got bedsheets." A woman behind Laurel spoke. When Laurel turned to see who had spoken, she saw Willa Ferguson, Mac's former sweetheart, standing just beyond the counter.

"Hello, Willa. How are you?"

"Pretty much sheetless, Mrs. MacLayne. We patriots have given most of our linens to the cause. Takes lots of bandages to bind wounds caused by traitorous Yankees, like your husband."

Laurel did not miss the venom in her voice, but to avoid a scene, she turned to pay for the few items she'd found in the store.

Willa jerked her around by her arm. "He did desert you to run off to that Yankee army, didn't he?"

"Excuse me, Willa. My son is waiting for me. We need to return home."

"Your son? Ain't likely…you ain't known Mac long enough to have a kid that old. I guess he's that brat your father-in-law dragged up from Tennessee. Is that right?"

"Andy, please take these packages to our buggy. I'll join you."

"Let him stay. He oughta know what a low-life deserter his father is. He deserted that kid's ma, and now he's deserted you with a passel of kids. Thank the Lord, I had the sense to refuse him when he asked for my hand."

"Andy, please go now." Laurel stood her ground. When she saw her son was beyond earshot, she spoke, "Miss Ferguson, your petty attack on my eleven-year-old son is unforgivable. Your anger should be directed at Mac. He is the person who rejected you. As far as his decision to join the Union army, that is between him and his Maker. I'll not defend nor blame him. He left us well-cared for. I want my children to have a chance for a happy normal life. My children can't make decisions for Mac or me. Please step aside and leave us be."

Laurel stepped around Willa Ferguson and walked to the door. There stood Cortland Cavanaugh, hat in hand. He held the door open for her. "Good afternoon, Mrs. MacLayne. I hope our paths cross again very soon." He bowed to her as she stepped into her buggy.

Laurel flushed. The confrontation with Willa was unexpected. They'd never been friends, but until that day, the other woman had never been openly hostile to her. Laurel was more than able to defend herself, but Willa's insult to Andy was mean-spirited. She could not let it go unchallenged. Then to have a man she hardly knew treat her with such respect and dignity caught her off guard. His kindness defused the anger she'd felt when she left the store.

"Son, I'm sorry Miss Ferguson said those things in public."

"It don't matter, Mama. Papa told me about my mother and him a year or so ago. I know what happened. I know Papa loves me and that you do, too. I'm fine. Lots of kids don't have it near as good as me."

"You've certainly grown into a fine man very quickly, Andrew MacLayne. Your papa is proud of you."

"I know."

"Let's go see if we can find a newspaper--if there is one to be had in this town. Then I wanna go home."

They drove down the main street of Greensboro to Davis's General Store. Davis had won the Confederate mail contract that year, and the post office was set up in the back corner of his large clapboard building at the end of the street. Andy flung the reins across the hitching rail and went in to ask for the mail. Laurel stepped into the store and searched for any copies of newspapers that were left behind. She found a month-old copy of a True Democrat from Little Rock and an even older copy of the St. Louis Dispatch.

"Mr. Davis, can I buy these papers, please?"

"No, you can have 'em if you want 'em." Both old as the hills, just takin' up space."

"Still good for wrapping things."

"Suppose that's so."

Andy returned with a letter for his grandfather and a broadside addressed to Patrick MacLayne, reminding county residents to pay taxes before the deadline. Laurel stuck them into her reticule along with the folded newspapers. They would keep until evening when the family gathered after supper.

Laurel found little of interest in the St. Louis paper. The general news of the war was mostly political. A man named Grant had been named commander of the Union armies, and he'd pledged to wipe out the Confederate resistance to end the war. Of course, the three previous commanding generals had vowed the same thing, but the war still wore on. Laurel did find a bit of news in the Little Rock paper that caused some concern. The True Democrat reported on a battle in Independence County near the White River. The article stated that sporadic fighting lasted for two days. While the Union losses were slight, the article did report that the Second Arkansas Cavalry had skirmished both days. Laurel knew Mac was a part of the Second Arkansas Union Cavalary.

The other matter that caught her attention was the broadside they'd found about the taxes due. Laurel had followed Mac's directions and used her Confederate currency sparingly, but she doubted if enough remained to cover the taxes with the ten percent increase levied by the legislature in Richmond to pay for the war. She would have to take some of the gold reserves Mac left to cover the tax. She dreaded the trip to Jonesboro where she had to go to pay the taxes. She also dreaded explaining how she'd come by the gold. So far, no one in authority had questioned her status as a deserted woman. She didn't want to have to explain her situation. Laurel certainly didn't want to put her husband in the bad light, even if it were necessary to save their homestead. The Sequestration Act was still in full force, and if the military officials didn't believe her story, they had the authority to confiscate all Mac's property. Shiloh could be forfeited, and Mac's enlistment in the Union army would all have been for nothing.

Laurel planned to ask Thomas MacLayne to drive her to the courthouse on the first Monday in May. She took enough silver and a few gold coins from the stash to cover the amount she believed would cover the taxes. She also pulled together all the Confederate currency she had. Perhaps she could use some of the paper money and finish with the silver. If she didn't have to show too much gold, the tax collectors wouldn't ask questions or bring the collection to the attention of the military authorities. Laurel whispered a prayer that things would go smoothly and quickly. She planned for this to be her last trip to the county seat. Within another month, her condition would be impossible to hide so she preferred to stay at home.

When Thomas and Laurel reached the Craighead County courthouse, Laurel took his hand and stepped from the buggy. "You can stay here if you want, Daughter. I'll pay the taxes for you."

"Thank you, Pa. I'll do it. If questions come up, I'll have to answer them. Maybe just as well to get it over with."

As she went to the counter in the tax collector's office, she introduced herself and asked about the amount of the taxes on Shiloh.

"Mrs. MacLayne...let me look at the tax ledger. Uhhh...your property taxes and war tax together come to $200.00."

"Are you certain? I'm sure we didn't pay half that much last year."

"Yes, ma'am. We assessed 450 acres with your double-pen cabin, a barn, smokehouse, toolshed, and chicken coops. In stock, we have sixty head of prime cattle, twelve hogs, two dozen chickens, and thirty chicks. The tax is accurate. Plus, you owe another ten percent for war support."

"Where did you come up with this list of livestock?" Laurel asked.

"Your deeds show your acreage. You paid taxes on the same number of buildings for the last five years."

"Yes, I know that, but we paid about $100.00. Since the war, we have nowhere that number of animals you have listed."

"Do you wish to contest the assessment?"

"Yes, we do," Thomas MacLayne answered.

"Fine. You will meet with the county judge and military commissioner—let me see when they meet again—two weeks from tomorrow."

Laurel had been dismissed. The thing she feared most had come to pass.

"Pa, perhaps we should just pay the taxes and not make a fuss."

"Laurel, the collector is cheatin' ya. We'll fight this thing and win."

"I hope you're right."

Two days later around dinner time, an unexpected visitor came to Shiloh. Dr. Gibson arrived with Dr. Cavanaugh just as Laurel was about to call her family to the table.

"Well, Dr. Gibson, come on in and have a seat. You're welcome to join us for dinner. We're not havin' much, but it'll be fillin' if you care to share our meal."

"Thank you, Laurel, but no. Maybe we'll have a glass of cool water."

"Dr. Cavanaugh, can I get you something?" Laurel asked.

"No. I'll have a glass of cool water from, Andy."

"Laurel, don't let us keep you from feedin' your family. We'll not take much time."

"All right. Give me a minute to get the kids settled in and then I'll be with ya."

Laurel called her family to sit around the table and asked the blessing for their meal. As she said stood up, Mark Thomas said, "Mama you didn't ask God to look after Papa."

"You're right, Son. Go ahead and eat. We'll ask a special blessing for Papa tonight. Annie, please see that everyone eats before they get up from here."

Laurel led the visitors to the front porch and offered them chairs. She handed each a cup of the cool water Andy had drawn from the well. She leaned against the porch rail. "Well, gentlemen, what can I do for you in the middle of this lovely spring day?"

"As far as you know, Laurel, is the Widow Parker's cabin empty now?"

"Yes. Since my father-in-law married Peggy Flannagan, they've not rented her section that I'm aware of."

"Will you consider renting it to Dr. Cavanaugh for a spell?"

"It's a bit far out of Greensboro to be convenient, don't ya think?"

"Not at all. It's perfect for what I've got in mind. We want to move Dr. Cavanaugh over in this area to make it easier for people to get to a doctor when help's needed. I spend quite a bit of time in Jonesboro now and my place is closer to Buck Snort. This would let the northern section of the county be closer to a doctor and give me more time to work on the county government over in the county seat."

"I see, but I thought you were in the army, Dr. Cavanaugh," Laurel remarked.

"I was until I caught this bullet in my leg at the Battle in Helena last summer. Crushed my knee cap and I can't walk without a cane. I got put out on medical leave until I heal some. Frankly, I think the commander in the medical corp thinks I'm more trouble than I'm worth. Anyway, I decided to settle here for the time bein'. Just don't have the heart to go home right now."

"We can use doctors in this area, but I can't rent you the widow's place. Ed, that property belongs to Peggy now. I guess it legally belongs to Thomas. You'll have to talk to them."

"Mrs. MacLayne, would you object to havin' me as a neighbor if they'll agree to my rentin' the cabin?"

"Dr. Cavanaugh, I owe you a debt already. You saved my orchard. I'm truly grateful. You'd be a welcome neighbor."

"Well, now that we have your permission, will you do me the honor of walkin' me through that beautiful orchard while the blossoms are still coverin' the branches of those trees?"

"Speak for yourself, Cort. I've seen an apple tree in bloom before. I'll sit here on the porch and wait." Dr. Gibson propped his feet on the porch rail.

Laurel's cheeks showed a faint blush, but she allowed Cortland Cavanaugh to help her down the steps, and they spent some time strolling through the orchard together.

Within a week, Laurel had a new neighbor. When her father-in-law came to tell her he'd rented the Widow Parker's place, he was relieved to have put another person so near who would help to look after his family.

"Laurel, I'm glad you are all right with havin' the doctor so close. Peggy and I didn't want the place sittin' idle, but we decided not to sell it. Paddy's gettin' close to an age where he'll be lookin' to have his place in a couple of years."

"Pa, it's your property. If you think it's the right thing to rent it, it's not my place to object."

"I know but to have a doctor near will be a good thing—especially with…" Thomas stopped mid-sentence. "Well, with the kids, someone's always getting' hurt or sick."

"And a daughter-in-law who's going to have a baby. Is that what you were thinking?"

Thomas grinned and nodded.

The next afternoon, Laurel, Annie, and the two youngest members of the household drove the short distance to the tiny homestead where Dr. Cavanaugh had taken up residence. In the two short days he'd been there, he'd already made some changes in the small cabin. He converted the living area into a space to see patients. He left the small kitchen area intact. He'd converted the loft into his personal living space. As cramped as it was, he managed to fit an armchair, a small writing table, a bookcase, and a narrow one-person bed into the small space.

"Doctor, I see you're ready to see patients already," Annie said.

"Well, nearly. I've got some unpacking to do…my instruments and medicine. I need some personal items to make it more my space."

Laurel handed him a basket they'd brought as a welcome gift. "Dr. Cavanaugh, we wanted to welcome you to Shiloh. We always try to bring a house-warming gift for new neighbors. We didn't have everything we usually share because of war shortages, but I guess it's the thought that counts."

"That's a generous gift from my neighbors."

"Well, the basket has fresh bread, a small container of salt, and a canning jar of apple cider. I'm sorry we didn't have any candles or a bottle of wine. They are part of the tradition, but we do bring wishes for good times and blessings for you in this home," Laurel said.

"Thank you, ladies, for your hospitality." The former Confederate major bowed to his neighbors. "I'm not sure I've ever felt so warmly welcomed in my life."

"Well, we'll head back home so you can get on with your work."

"A moment, Mrs. Mac Layne. On Saturday when I went to inquire about this homestead from your father-in-law, he told me you were going to have to go before the military commissioner about your taxes."

"How did he come to talk about that with you?"

"Please don't be offended. It came up when I told him about my service with the Confederate medical corp. I'm not sure how the topic came up exactly. I told him I'd be glad to go with you before the authorities. I still have some connections with our local officers. Maybe I can be of some help."

"Dr. Cavanaugh, I couldn't impose…"

"It will be my pleasure to help a neighbor if I can be of any service."

"Thank you—if you think I'll need your support I'd welcome it. I can pay the taxes if that is the issue," Laurel said.

"From what Mr. MacLayne told me, the larger concern may be the circumstances of your husband's enlistment in the Union army."

"Oh. I suppose that could be a worse problem than some money. Thank you for your offer of help."

*ф*

The following Wednesday, Laurel traveled to Jonesboro again. This time she was accompanied by both her father-in-law and the doctor, dressed in his full officer's uniform, complete with his saber and plumed hat. He looked every bit the army major whom she'd met that cold October evening in her apple orchard.

When they entered the office of the tax-collector, he wasted no time escorting them down the hall to a large courtroom where three military officials sat behind a long-raised table. The Craighead County judge sat at a small table alone toward the side. It was clear that his role there was ceremonial and he would have little influence in what would happen.

"Please be seated with your party there, Mrs. MacLayne. We were told you wanted to contest your taxes. What is the basis for your complaint?" A major sitting in the center of the panel spoke.

"Major, I didn't complain. I asked why the taxes had been appraised on property we don't have."

"You don't own a homestead at Shiloh?" he asked.

"Yes. I own the land and the buildings on our homestead. It's the livestock I questioned."

"You don't have any livestock?" A jeer on the major's face unnerved Laurel.

"Yes, we have some, but not the numbers recorded by the tax office."

The major rose and walked before Thomas MacLayne. "Why are you here contesting these taxes? Isn't this property owned by a man named Patrick MacLayne?"

"Yes. The land belonged to my son until he left his family at Shiloh in January of 1863," replied Thomas.

Laurel intervened, "Major, I'd like to talk about the livestock count, please. I am head of my household now."

"Mrs. MacLayne, speak your mind."

"At Shiloh, we have six heifers, four calves, one milk cow, three hogs, and six laying hens. We had more but a Confederate troop came over a year ago and confiscated more than half of all I had."

"Is it true your husband left you to join the Union army?" A second member of the panel snapped back at Laurel.

"Yes."

"What does this have to do with the increase in taxes at Shiloh?" Thomas came to Laurel's defense a second time.

"And sir, who are you?"

"My name is Thomas MacLayne. I am here on behalf of my daughter-in-law and grandchildren."

"We've been told by neighbors that your son had a large herd of quality beef. Did he take that herd to the enemy when he left?"

"No, sir. When Patrick left Laurel and my grandchildren at Shiloh in '63, he took his horse, clothing, and one firearm."

"What happened to the herd?"

"I don't have a herd. You are welcome to come and count the animals." Laurel replied. "I have nothing to hide."

"Madam, we have been charged to determine whether your property should be forfeited due to your husband's treason against the Confederacy."

Laurel stood silent before the panel for what seemed an eternity. All Mac had feared seemed about to happen. She reached out to clutch the chair back to steady herself. "Major, I have seven mouths to feed at Shiloh. Besides my four children, my daughter-in-law and her son depend on the livelihood we earn from our homestead. I have paid my taxes, including the extra war tax every year. I gave up more than half of my livestock to a Confederate troop last March—after I had paid all my taxes that year. My daughter-in-law is a widow of a Confederate soldier killed at Corinth more than two years ago. How am I to support my family without my land?"

"Your husband should have realized the harm he'd put you in. The homestead is his property, is it not?"

"We worked the land together when he was here. I have worked it with my children since he left."

Cortland Cavanaugh rose. He helped Laurel to a chair. "Major, permission to speak?" He then went before the raised table where the three men sat.

"Major, what concern is this to you?"

"Sir, I am Major Cortland Cavanaugh, on medical leave currently from the Trans-Mississippi Army under the command of General Sterling Price. I was wounded at Graveyard Hill at Helena. Since takin' the bullet at Helena, I've been furloughed until I can return to active duty. I've been under the care of a doctor in

Greensboro, near Mrs. MacLayne's home. I've had several opportunities to deal with this lady and her father-in-law. I can not speak for Mr. MacLayne's son, but I've found no evidence of treason in either Thomas or Laurel MacLayne."

"Can you support your claim, sir?"

"First, in early spring of '63, Mrs. MacLayne offered the hospitality of her homestead to a troop of fifty Confederate troops, allowing them to camp in her pasture. She offered them firewood and water for themselves and their horses. She also provided hot cornbread for an evening meal."

"Seems little enough to do for men who are defending her home from northern invaders," the angry captain said.

"She also made it possible for me to find shelter while I am recuperating from this wound I got in battle."

"Major, the law says..."

"Captain, our Southern code of honor demands we protect our women and families. Mrs. MacLayne cannot be held responsible for what her husband chose to do. She has remained loyal to her duty. She pays her taxes to support the war. She is caring for the widow and son of a fallen Confederate soldier. She is raising her children, not asking for aid from anyone. All she is wants is to keep her land so she can continue to raise her family." Cortland turned toward the major. "Major, surely you don't see this woman as a threat to the Confederacy."

"Mrs. MacLayne, can you pay your taxes?"

"Yes, Major, if a fair tax is levied on the stock I have."

"Will you report your husband if he returns to the area?"

"No, sir. I will pay what is required, but Patrick MacLayne is the father of my children. You cannot ask me to betray my family. I don't know if he is alive or not, but I know he will not return until the war ends."

The panel of men discussed the matter for several minutes. One of them shook his fist at the major. Another covered his eyes for a moment. The angry captain became very red-cheeked just before the major rose to speak.

"Mrs. MacLayne, this panel has not reached a unanimous decision. We may reconvene this discussion next year. But for today, we are not going to confiscate your homestead. Because Major Cavanaugh has vouched for your loyalty to the southern cause, we will allow you to remain on your land until we have more proof that your family has failed to maintain the loyalty demanded. Be warned, though, that you will be watched. If we learn that you are aiding the Union cause, you will forfeit all property belonging to Patrick MacLayne."

"I understand, Major." Laurel returned to Thomas MacLayne who took her in his arms.

"Go down to the tax collector's office and pay the property tax on the adjusted livestock count and pay the additional war tax. I hope I have no further occasion to deal with you."

"Yes, sir. Pa, let's go take care of this and go home."

When they left the courthouse, Thomas offered his hand to Cortland Cavanaugh. "Thank you, Major. Without your support, I doubt that Laurel and I could have persuaded those men."

"Let's forget the major, all right? You may call me Dr. Cavanaugh, but I'd prefer Cort. It's been my pleasure. Mrs. MacLayne is a fine lady. She deserves to be treated as one." He smiled and helped her to the wagon seat.

# Chapter 25

*Such as sit in darkness and in the shadow of death, being bound in*
*affliction and iron. Then they cried out unto the Lord with their*
*troubles and He saved them out of their distresses.*
*Psalms 107:10,13*

Mac spent his first night as a captive tethered to a huge
evergreen tree in a thicket a few miles from the White River. He
and three other Union soldiers were given a cup of hot chicory and
a half a cup of cornmeal mush with a touch of sweetness. The
soldiers had probably taken some sorghum in a recent foraging
raid. The tin utensils were dented and none too clean, but
serviceable. Mac noticed the Rebel soldiers ate no better. The
choice of shelter sites proved to be a blessing. The thick low
branches of the trees acted almost like a thatched roof and kept the
intermittent rain off them.

Just before dark, Mac took his Bible and his silver picture
case from his coat. He would take what comfort he could from
them. They were the only possessions he'd been able to salvage.
The Confederate troops swept the battlefield after the Union troops
left the area, and they confiscated any items they considered of use
to them. He'd watched two men fight over his saddlebags and the
reins they took from his dead mount. The soldiers also tossed aside
Gracie's hand-drawn picture of their family, the one letter he'd
received from Laurel, and the copy of the book he'd been reading

into a fire. His blanket, extra ammunition, a bit of hardtack, and his extra shirt all found a way into the backpacks of young soldiers. Thank the Lord, he'd put his most valuable items inside his coat that morning…the only day he'd ever done that.

He opened his Bible and started to read the book of Job.

"What'cha readin', Captain?" asked the private tied up next to him.

"The story of Job. He's a man who faced great loss but refused to let go of his faith. I need to have that kind of encouragement right now."

"You think that's gonna help?" Another prisoner smirked.

"Sure ain't gonna hurt." Mac turned his back on the rude corporal. "What's your name, Private? Where ya from?"

"I'm Travis Fancher. I'm from Boone County. Joined up with the Second Arkansas Cavalary last year."

"Ya hardly seem old enough to be in the cavalry. Fancher, you say? You have any kin that was part of that wagon train that was massacred back in '59 out in Utah?"

"Sure did. My uncle's family was in that group. How do you know about that?"

"My daughter, Gracie Wilson was rescued with about fifteen other young'uns from that group."

"Your daughter?"

"My wife's goddaughter…we adopted her."

"Captain, what's gonna happen to us?"

"Unless we get a chance to escape, I guess we'll wind up in a Confederate prison somewhere."

"Where would that be, I wonder?" The corporal seemed more interested.

"Across the Mississippi, I'd guess. The Rebels have a better hold on the territory over there. I heard one of the officers say the word 'Andersonville'. I don't know where that is, but he laughed after he said it."

"That can't be good." The private dropped his head to his knees.

"Hey, you blue bellies over there, shut yer traps. We're tired and want some sleep." The Rebel captain in charge bellowed.

Mac went back to his reading, barely able to make out the words in the twilight. *In the land of Ur, there was a man whose name was Job. This man was blameless and upright; he feared God.* When he could no longer see to read, he opened the picture case and ran his thumb over the pictures he could barely make out.

"Laurel, I miss you, Darlin'. I miss the kids. I have to put y'all in God's care. I don't know what the future holds for me, but I know He is in control. Lord, thank you for my wife. I do love you so, Laurel." Mac tucked his Bible and picture case back into his coat and crouched against the tree and fell asleep.

As the sun rose, three members of the Rebel troop roused the four Union prisoners. They'd been ordered to an encampment near Cotton Plant, a two-and-a-half-day journey on foot. The small detachment had no extra horses for their captives. The route may not be a direct one either. Their captain had ordered them to keep the captives away from Union troops. "Men, we got us a real trophy here…a Yank Captain," the Rebel captain said. So, Mac and the three other Union prisoners set out southeast, headed to an uncertain fate. With each step, he knew he was moving farther from the only place he wanted to be.

By the time they reached Cotton Plant, Mac learned his fellow captives were the boy from Boone County whose name was Fancher, a sarcastic corporal from Michigan, named Swenson, and another member from a Quartermaster team, Sergeant Golden. Fancher and Swenson had been part of the scouting team who'd discovered the plan to take the river crossing at Oil Trough. They had been captured the night after they'd sent the message back to the commander at Batesville. They'd been captive for more than a week before the battle took place. Golden had been captured trying to remove wounded men from the Oil Trough skirmish, much as Mac had.

They learned their stay at Cotton Plant would be a short one. The group of Confederate troops already had several other prisoners in the compound. That night they planned to move all the prisoners to a plantation midway between Helena and Arkansas Post. Union control in south Arkansas was spotty, and the Rebels still had a fair hold on the area in the southern delta. The

Confederates used a landing at the Snow Plantation to transport supplies and troops across the Mississippi River. When they had a sizeable group of prisoners, they moved them across the river the same way, like so much cargo to the strongholds in Mississippi.

Four days of continual walking left Mac footsore and worn beyond belief. When supper came that day, he wanted nothing but sleep. He was disgusted with his own filth—he longed for enough water to wash his face and hands, but they'd been given only small amounts of drinking water. The heat and the persistently glaring sun added to the misery, especially since he'd lost his hat when he fell from his horse. Mac needed every iota of self-determination bolstered by his faith to force himself to put one foot in front of the other. Without his daily reading of the trials of Job and the time he spent talking to Laurel and his family, he would not have the will to go on the next day.

That night when he took his family out for his nightly visit, one of the guards took notice. "What'cha got there, Yank?"

"Just pictures of my family."

"Let me see that. Looks like somethin' that shoulda been confiscated."

"It's just a case with two pictures. Please, let me keep them."

"Here. Give it to me. I need to look at what ya got."

"Please, I need those pictures." The guard pushed the stock of his gun into Mac's neck, pinning him against a tree.

"I told ya to give me that case, Yank. Do it or git your head bashed in."

Mac released the silver case. The guard turned it over in his hand a time or two.

"I think this here is real silver. We gotta confiscate this. You got anything else you been holdin' back from us?"

"I got nothin' else except my Bible."

"Let me see that." Mac handed it to the man.

"Well, that ain't no prize. Looks pretty worn-out." He tossed it aside.

"Corporal, please, let me keep the pictures of my wife and children. Those don't mean anything to your army. They are only valuable to me. You can take the case."

"Why should I give ya anything?" He snapped back.

"Corporal."

The man snapped to attention when his captain approached. "Yes, sir."

"Give this man the photographs. You are right to confiscate the case for the cause, but we have no use for those pictures. Return them."

"Yes, sir."

"Thank you, Captain. Bless you."

"We've no call to be cruel. Our Confederate leaders ordered us to treat our prisoners with civility. You are captive only to prevent you from harming our cause—nothin' more."

"I thank you anyway. Those photographs mean a great deal to me.

"I have a family, too. Wish I had a picture to look at."

After the captain left the stockade where the prisoners were held in Cotton Plant, Travis Fancher said, "Captain, I'm surprised that Rebs was so nice. Ain't you surprised he let you keep your photographs?"

"Not really. What did they mean to him?" Mac stretched the length of his body to retrieve his Bible that had been tossed aside. "He didn't want these things. I guess he didn't know they're the most valuable things in the world."

"I guess I don't get it either. That Bible's nothin' to look at, for sure."

"That's because in the past thirteen years, it's gone everywhere I've gone. With few exceptions, not one day's gone by that I've not used it to keep me connected to my Father in Heaven and my Brother Jesus Christ."

"Means that much to you?"

"It's kept me alive—in every way. It'll keep me alive through the end of this war."

"How can you believe that when they're takin' us to prison?"

"I know it. I've not got a single doubt, Travis."

"Will you tell me more about that fellow Job you've been readin' about?"

"That would be my pleasure, Son."

"Why did you call me son?"

"Just something I learned in this book."

The next several days, Mac, along with a group of twenty-three other Union prisoners were shackled together and pushed even further into Confederate-held territory. The enlarged guard made a wide circle around Helena, knowing a strong contingency of Union troops still held the river port there. The detour kept them away from a skirmish with enemy troops and added at least a day's walk to their destination. A group of loyal Confederate planters who lived inside the Laconia Circle Levees had access to piers on the river where they could ferry prisoners over to Mississippi. The goal was to deliver the detainees to Laconia Landing by the end of the month. A small riverboat had been scheduled to board the Yankees and deliver them to Clarksdale, Mississippi, securely in Confederate control.

Two more days should have seen the trek across Arkansas come to an end. Fate had other plans. Just outside Lawrenceville, the Confederate troop was alerted that a unit of Union soldiers was headed west. The commander of the troop wanted to avoid confrontation. He ordered his men to take the prisoners into the thick pine forest and shackle them so they couldn't run. He also ordered gags.

"If you Yanks want to see the sunset tonight, don't make a sound. If those blue bellies find us, we'll shoot you first and then fight our way out. You understand?" He rode away to check the preparations his men were making.

"Captain, ya think we can escape?"

"No, Travis. We can't run with these shackles on. We've got no weapons. All we can do is try to do what the commander tells us to do. I'd like to escape, but we've got no chance today."

The corporal from Missouri said, "We could make a ruckus and let that unit of our men know we're here."

"And get a bullet for it? I'd rather not." Mac shook his head. "We'll have a better chance later. This ain't the time."

"Quiet. The Yanks are just over the rise." The Rebel commander hissed at them.

Time stood still. Then the rhythmic pounding of a dozen military mounts filled the air. The thunderous thudding shook the ground, the troops were so nearby.

"Yeah, Yanks…Help us. We're prisoners." The deep guttural call came from somewhere behind Mac. He turned around but didn't see anyone.

Then another, more youthful voice yelled out, "Over in the pine thicket. We're federal troops." Again, Mac looked, seeking the man who tried to call for help. Then there was a third and a fourth and then too many to count…all cries for rescue.

Shots rang out. The Confederate unit began targeting the unsuspecting cavalry that had ridden into the ambush. Gunfire continued for at least twenty minutes before the Union leader called a retreat. Several of his men had been wounded by the well-hidden and larger force of Confederates who had the upper hand. The Union suffered no fatalities, but too many were wounded to continue the skirmish. They had not rescued even one of the prisoners who had called for help.

"Now do you see why I told you to stand down? That was foolish, a sheer waste. How many of our men are wounded now because you didn't take orders?" Mac was furious.

The commander returned. "Scout the area and make sure that detail is gone. Secure those prisoners and see if anyone is wounded. If they are, shoot 'em. We don't have time to carry dead weight." After seeing no one was so badly wounded he couldn't march, the commander ordered them to move out. "Pull those men to their feet and double-time it out of here."

The Confederate troop pushed the prisoners as fast and as long as they could go until they began to fall out. Only then did he order a halt to inspect his charges. Two of the prisoners had received minor wounds in the skirmish, and one had lost considerable blood. The commander showed little empathy.

"Which one of you idiots caused these men to get wounded? If you'd kept your mouths shut, no one woulda got hurt. You wouldn't have spent the last three hours running across this swampland. And ya would'na lost your supper. 'Cos you acted like fools, now you'll walk the rest of the night to get out of the area before they send more blue-bellies back to try to save your worthless hides. You Yanks ain't got the sense to know when yer well off." The captain of the guard shook his head and walked away. "I outta kill the lot of ya and report that the Yankee patrol did it."

"Major, some of these men are wounded. They need medical care." Mac tried to speak up for the men who'd not taken his orders earlier.

The Confederate captain turned and faced him. He slapped him across the face with his gloves. "I don't need no advice from you. You're lucky none of my men need a doctor. If I'd lost even one man, the pack of you would be floatin' face down in that river right now. I don't know why we have to keep you in prison, anyway. You disobey again and you won't see Andersonville. I'd rather be killin' Yanks than herdin' them to prison any day."

Twenty-three Union prisoners walked into the moon-bright night. The able-bodied troops supported the wounded and those whose strength was gone. Before they reached Deshea County, the sergeant from Missouri with the most severe wound died from blood loss. The commander allowed a break just long enough for the prisoners to dig a grave and to bury their comrade who was now free from the captivity of the Rebel forces.

After another day and a half, the tired, dirty troops arrived in Laconia Circle Levee district where the guard could transfer their prisoners to the unit on the boat that would take them across the Mississippi River. They had to wait for another riverboat to make shore at Laconia Landing since they had missed the one because of the skirmish. The family at White Pine Plantation was a staunchly loyal Confederate household. They often provided space in their barn to house prisoners as they waited for transportation. Of course, they always asked for compensation in the form of labor from those they kept. The Tradwells had no shortage of workers on

307

their land, but the Yankees deserved no better treatment, according to the overseer. Because of this demand for labor from Union soldiers, their barn was the cleanest, best organized one in the state.

Mac and the other twenty-one remaining prisoners spent two long days at hard labor to pay for their keep. The pay for work well-done was a small portion of pork with the grits on the second night of confinement. They also received a small wedge of pone for supper and a cup of fresh milk. Mac hadn't had a cup of milk since he'd left Batesville in the middle of March. He whispered, "Thank you, Lord."

At midnight on the second day at Laconia, the guard roused the prisoners. "On your feet, Yanks. Time to take a little boat ride across the river." He marched them out into the pitch black and led them to a sturdy wooden dock that was partially hidden in thick foliage at the bend in the river. At the end of the dock, a small sternwheeler sat, belching thick smoke from its single stack. A few windows showed faint lights, but for the most part, the boat was a black, ominous shadow against the night sky.

The guard in charge ushered them across the wooden pier onto the deck of the *Southern Cross*, a supply ship of the Confederate navy. He saluted the ship captain.

"They're all yours, Captain. Orders are to take them to Greenville. You'll meet a new guard troop that will march them to Grenada to the train. Once you load' em on those cattle cars, head 'em on to Andersonville."

"Yes, sir. How many are we transportin'?"

"I only got twenty-two left. One got hisself killed in a little skirmish with some Yanks. They don't seem to have no leader, but MacLayne, that captain with the Quartermaster insignia, seems to have some good sense."

"Thanks, Captain. My men will take charge now. Safe return to your camp." They saluted and within minutes the antiquated steamboat moved away from the west bank down the river.

The newly posted guards took no chance their new charges would attempt escape. They herded the men below into one of the holds and barred the door. Once inside, Mac realized the group from Cotton Plant was not alone on this journey to Andersonville, Georgia. At least seventy other captives sat around the dark, dank holding pen. He found an empty crate and sat down, leaning against the hull of the boat. The room was stifling without any source of fresh air, and the odor was putrid.

"Hey, Captain, how long ya think they're gonna keep us down here?" One of the privates had attached himself to Mac.

"Your guess is as good as mine. I suppose they have some plan to keep us away from Union troops."

A prisoner who'd been locked up on the *Southern Cross* when Mac came down said, "Where'd y'all come from?

"We are part of a Union troop out of central Arkansas. We got caught up in a surprise skirmish. How long have you been on board?"

"We got picked up below a town called Blytheville at a landin' called Tomato. Ain't that a hoot? Some of us got captured in Northern Tennessee and marched over to the river, ferried across to get on this boat. The Rebs are avoidin' all the major ports because our boys got 'em blockaded. The boat crews have been traveling by those places late at night."

"We walked a big circle around Helena for the same reason," Mac replied. "At least, we ain't walkin' anymore... I think my boots are worn through."

"Be glad you got some boots. The Rebs have taken a lot of boots from our boys. Captain, you don't sound much like a Yankee. Your drawl sounds mighty Southern."

"Might say that. Maryland born—Arkansas blessed. Name's MacLayne, Second Arkansas Union Cavalry."

"O'Neal, Sergeant, First Illinois Infantry. Nice to know ya."

"O'Neal, do you know anything about this Andersonville camp they keep talking' about?"

"Just some rumors. They say it's a death camp. The prison staff is the worst kind of brutes ever rode herd over a prison camp.

Our best hope is to find a chance to run. I done lived through three years of this danged war. I ain't gonna die in no Rebel hell-hole."

"Captain, do you think we can escape once we get off this boat?" The private's voice reflected the fear Mac couldn't see."

"Travis, don't worry tonight. Stretch out and rest. Let's thank the Lord we're ridin' and not walkin'. Enjoy tonight for what it is and leave tomorrow's problems for tomorrow. It's in God's hands. He'll take care of us."

The river ran slow that night. The heavily loaded steamer made about five miles an hour. By late afternoon, the *Southern Cross* tied up at a plantation landing about two miles north of Greenville. The captain had avoided the busy ports in the town. Two dozen guards pointed weapons at the ninety-plus prisoners as they disembarked and marched across the wooden dock to a partially burned barn standing behind the burned-out ruins of what had been an enormous pillared plantation house.

"You Yanks, we're gonna stay here 'til nightfall. We've been told they's been some blue-bellies lurkin' around. We gotta a little hikin' to do for a few days. Settle yerselves in this fine barn, and we'll get a bit of supper for ya in a while."

"Do you think we could get some water? We're pretty close to the river. Could we have some water to wash with?" Mac asked.

"We ain't got enough manpower to let y'all loose. We ain't fools." The lieutenant laughed at the request. "Maybe it'll rain tomorrow while we march ya toward the rail line. It's only about seventy-five miles to Grenada. When we get there, y'all can ride to Georgia—one-way trip." The Rebel guards laughed at the comment as they barred the doors from the outside.

Five days of hot, arduous marching brought the body of ninety-two prisoners and twenty guards to the rail line at Grenada, Mississippi. Again, the prisoners were passed to another unit of soldiers and loaded onto cattle cars linked to the Confederate train line. This railroad had been built to connect critical parts of the Confederacy. The prisoners were locked into two cars. The walls were slatted, allowing fresh air and light to enter. The openness also let in flies, gnats, and a wide array of stinging insects. The floor was strewn with matted, filthy straw that smelled of weeks or perhaps months of use. Each car was supplied with one large barrel to serve as a toilet and a second smaller keg with drinking water. Cars of this sort had transported thousands of Union prisoners to the prison camps in the deep south.

At 9:00 in the morning, the train pulled away from the platform at Grenada, moving at the speed of twenty miles per hour, headed due south. Six hours later, the men were forced into other boxcars on a train in Jackson. Conditions on the new train were not one iota better. Only the direction changed. From Jackson, the train rolled due east. The constant clacking of the low-cheaply made tracks created a racket so loud that talking was all but impossible. As the heat increased in the afternoon, the stench from the straw and the sanitation barrels became unbearable. The men in the slatted cattle cars moved against the outside walls to get fresh air to breathe. This act proved to be God's providence at work.

As the train reached the Alabama state line, sometime after midnight, the incessant clacking was interrupted by a horrendous ripping sound as a section of the strap rail tore a seven-foot gash in the floor of the car in which Mac and forty-eight other Union prisoners rode. A man from the Illinois Infantry screamed as a portion of the metal that was once strapped to cheap wooden rails tore into his thigh. A second man, a corporal from Michigan moaned in agony as his left shoulder was ripped open by a six-foot section of metal that had ripped through the floor and knocked him against the back wall. The screech of the train's brakes added to the din. The yelling, swearing, crying, and confusion among those trapped in the destruction continued until the commander of the guard fired three rounds into the air. The gunshots restored order.

"Is anyone badly injured here?" A Confederate commander yelled. Mac tried to move around, looking for wounded men, but the dim light hampered the search. He heard the Illinois soldier cry out. Another officer from the rear of the car brought the Michigan man forward.

"Major, it looks like we have two who are hurt pretty bad."

"Bring 'em out to me." The men were lifted down from the car. "Now I need a dozen men. We gotta fix this rail before we can go any further. Any of you want to get out and stretch a bit? I need some men who can handle a sledgehammer."

"I'll help." Mac jumped down, followed by the three men who'd been with him since Oil Trough. A few others joined the work crew before the guards slammed the door back into place.

A man who remained on the train called out, "What about all this metal in here and this hole in the floor? What do you want us to do?"

The commander yelled back. "That's not my problem. Keep it or get rid of it—all the same to me."

Mac and the rest of the work crew worked about three hours to make a patch in the rail. They hammered huge iron spikes into the ironclad wooden rails to scotch them back into place. Finally, the train was able to get beyond the tear. The men were pushed back into the cattle car at the end of the train. Before noon, the train pulled into a fueling station near Cahaba, Alabama. A talkative Confederate guard said this town was the original capital city of Alabama. "Didn't last though…too many floods here, but she's still a pretty nice town. I oughta know. I'm a Cahaba boy myself. Great fishin' in our two rivers. 'Course you won't be goin' fishin'," he laughed.

The commander of the Confederate unit was met at the fueling station by a messenger from the Confederate prison warden. "Sir, Colonel Henderson sends his regards. He's had a dispatch from Andersonville. They can't take all the prisoners you got on board. Col. Henderson has ordered you to unhitch your last car of prisoners on the sideline there. When we can get a large enough force, we'll transport that group to Castle Morgan."

"Just as well. That car was damaged pretty bad when a rail curled last night just west of the state line. Glad to get 'em off my hands. That'll be fifty fewer men to handle these last two hundred miles. Fewer mouths to feed. They're all yours. Tell Colonel Henderson, he's welcome to the lot of 'em."

# Chapter 26

*Charity beareth all things, believeth all things, hopeth all things,
endureth all things.
Charity never faileth.
1 Corinthians 13:7-8*

No news came. May passed and June was near its midpoint.
Laurel had no word from Mac. The routine of homesteading filled
her days. Teaching and nurturing her children helped ease the
emptiness left by Mac's absence. Attempts at prayer and reading
the Word kept a small ember of hope alive, but Laurel felt her
strength, connection with her faith, and her will to continue the
struggle alone ebbing.

She was grateful for Annie. Too many days Leah Ann or
Mark Thomas demanded more attention than Laurel had the will to
give. Even as she felt guilty for passing so much responsibility off
to Annie, she knew she failed to tell her how much her presence
meant to her. Annie knew the loneliness she felt. Annie also knew
that Roy would not be returning.

Her pregnancy hadn't been particularly difficult. Except for the lower back pains brought on by the strenuous work during planting season, Laurel felt well since her days with morning sickness ended. Work in the fields and gardens was much easier now in the growing season. Frequent rainfall had also kept the orchard well-watered, eliminating the need to irrigate this spring. Laurel's burdens were not physical day-to-day tasks. She was plagued with constant fear, the need to be held, and the dread she would never find comfort in Mac's arms again.

On Sunday, Laurel roused her children and dressed them for church. Her uncle Matthew was holding services near Eden for a few people who had left the Shiloh congregation when their preacher answered his call to the chaplaincy. Laurel missed going to church, but she'd not felt comfortable at Shiloh since Mac had enlisted. Truthfully, she hesitated to go into public at all. Only her wrapper fit now, but she promised her uncle she would come. Perhaps an outdoor service in the shady glade near the creek would be a blessing.

By the time service was to start, a small group of about twenty-five people sat on quilts, logs, wagons, or leaned against the ancient trees at Eden. Brother Mathew started the service, singing the Lord's Prayer. The beauty of the day, the gentle breeze, the gurgling water dancing across the rocks in the creek, the rustle of the leaves, and the spirit of praise in Matthew Campbell's voice moved the people to a true sense of worship. Before he began his sermon, he read a single verse of scripture, I Corinthians 13:7.

Tears streamed down Laurel's face. Throughout his sermon, she couldn't stop her grief. She was convicted again and again by her uncle's words. When the people stood to sing *Just As I Am,* Laurel knelt before her uncle and poured out her guilt and hurt.

"Laurel Grace, what has brought you so low, Girl?"

"Uncle Matthew, I've given up on Mac. He's been my strength. He was the person I placed my faith with. He made me know I was worthy…now he's gone."

"Laurel Grace. You don't know that. We've had no report on him. But did you hear what you just said?"

314

"I can't go on without him."

"Yes, you can. If you have to, Laurel, you will. Mac's not your Savior. He may have helped you see his Lord, but he'd never want you to put him in Jesus's place. You haven't lost your strength. The Lord is still right here. Your faith has to be in Him, not in your husband. You're not worthy because Mac loves you. You are worthy because you are God's child. That is what Mac knows—what he wants you to know."

"You're right. Please pray for me."

While she prayed, a calmness came to her that she'd not felt in many weeks. Her aunt, who had come to kneel by her, pulled Laurel into her arms. "Darlin' girl, don't lose hope. Mac is in God's hands. Regardless, all will be well." A slight smile touched Laurel's lips.

"Please keep praying for me, Aunt Ellie. Mac is alive…he has to be. The Lord will take care of the MacLaynes. He always has."

Matthew Campbell had promised afternoon singing to begin the new church. Ellie and Annie pulled several women together and began to spread the Sunday meal on two quilts under the oak tree. Andy brought a pail of cool water from the creek. Just as they were about to say grace, Dr. Cavanaugh walked up to the MacLayne family.

"Good afternoon, Mrs. MacLayne, family. I wanted to stop and say hello before I head back to the office."

"Dr. Cavanaugh, I didn't know you were here."

"I was standin' at the back of the glade. I got here a bit late. Didn't want to disturb anyone. Your preacher stopped by my place in the middle of the week and invited me."

"You don't wanna go now, Doctor," Annie said. "The best part is the afternoon singin' that Brother Matthew leads."

"I didn't know about the afternoon singing."

"We have plenty of food. Join us for dinner," Andy said. "It's all right, ain't it, Mama?"

"Of course. We have plenty to share."

"Thank you, I'd enjoy the company and gettin' to know my neighbors." Dr. Cavanaugh sat on a fallen tree at the foot of the

315

MacLayne wagon. After a pleasant dinner, the children made their way to visit with friends, and the babies took afternoon naps. Laurel and Cort sat on the old fallen log near the MacLayne gravesite under the beautiful old tree.

"Are these your people, Mrs. MacLayne?"

"Yes. Our first child was stillborn. We named him Campbell, my family name. That marker is for Roy, Annie's husband. He died at a battle in Corinth in '62."

"Campbell...are you related to the preacher?"

"Yes. Matthew Campbell is my uncle. He and Mac, my husband, are best friends. Uncle Matthew was the one who played matchmaker. He's the reason I live in Shiloh now."

"I see. You lived in my place at one time, I've been told."

"We did. The Widow Parker let us rent her cabin while Mac built our place."

"He must be quite a man. He built your cabin by himself. Your father-in-law told me his son served in the Arkansas General Assembly before secession."

"Patrick MacLayne has a servant's nature. He thought he could make a difference for our part of the state. He voted against secession in both of the conventions, besides serving two terms in the legislature."

"He has been away from home a great deal, hasn't he?"

"Only when he was called to do so. Mac is a wonderful husband, and there is no finer father. Our kids adore their papa."

Cortland Cavanaugh didn't respond to Laurel's lavish praise. Their silence was broken only by birds chirping and talk from others around the area.

Finally, Laurel asked, "Did I say something you take issue with, Dr. Cavanaugh?"

"No. Of course not. I don't know your husband so I don't know what kind of response I should make here. So I didn't say anything."

"I should return to check on my children. It will be time for afternoon singing soon."

"Let me explain, Mrs. MacLayne. I didn't mean to offend you."

" Good afternoon, sir." Laurel walked back to the wagon.

Midweek, Laurel rode to Greensboro with J.F. Clark. She planned for this to be her last trip to town until the new baby made his entrance into the world. At nearly six months, Laurel's girth had already become uncomfortable. The heat of early summer added to the burden of making the long trip. She planned to stock up on all supplies she could find and talk with Al Stuart about the legal status of the homestead. As her time grew nearer, she worried more about that with Mac's being gone so long.

At McCollough's, Laurel found she'd come on a good day. A freighter had brought some supplies the day before and the shelves were not bare. Laurel bought flour and a pound of sugar. She still could find no salt. She also looked for yard goods, hoping to make a new dress for Leah Ann and herself, but again, she found nothing at McCollough's.

She and J.F. walked down the boardwalk to Davis's General Store to see if he'd had better luck with supplies. Mr. Davis showed Laurel his order. He'd gotten about a quarter of what he'd asked for. Laurel bought a second bag of flour, a small box of cinnamon and cocoa. On the shelf next to the post office in the back corner, Laurel found one bolt of pink calico. She grabbed it and hugged it to her.

"Mr. Davis, tell me how much yardage is on this bolt. I want it all."

"Mrs. MacLayne, that calico ain't sold because it's too expensive. Are you sure you want it?"

"I do unless it cost me my life. My girls haven't had anything new in more than two years." Laurel took a twenty-dollar gold piece and paid for her purchases. Mr. Davis began to bundle things when Willa Ferguson approached with two other women from Greensboro that Laurel had met but didn't know well. Willa tapped Laurel on the shoulder.

"I thought that was you."

"Good afternoon, Willa. Is there something more you want after our last meeting? I know you don't consider me your friend."

"No. We won't ever be friends, but I am a concerned neighbor. My friends and I were wonderin' about this new baby you seem to be expectin'. I didn't know you'd found a new husband…Oh wait, is the old one even dead? Or maybe you've just got a new friend. No, not this saintly niece of the good pastor Campbell. I suppose this is another immaculate conception."

"Willa, keep quiet," Laurel said.

"Why? Surely you want the world to know about this miracle. You've not seen your husband in more than a year and a half, and now you're havin' another baby. A miracle or adultery? Wonder which one it is?" Laurel turned to walk away, and Willa grabbed her arm.

Cortland Cavanaugh removed her hand from Laurel's arm and dropped it. "Miss, I think you've made quite a scene here. Are you finished? I'd recommend you leave."

"Who do you think you are?"

"I know who I am. I'm the person askin' you to leave this lady be."

Willa stomped by him and headed toward the door. Before she reached to shove the door open, a crowd had gathered. She stopped and yelled back, "Mac put you on a pedestal when he brought you to Shiloh. It's gonna be quite a fall now that your community knows about this new baby. They'll be wondering who's the father of this newest bastard in that questionable family of yours."

Laurel wanted to scream at the vicious slanderer. She wanted to protect her family and her husband. Instead, she turned and ran from the building. J.F. followed immediately, lifted Laurel into the buggy, and urged the horse toward Shiloh.

Before noon the following day, Cortland Cavanaugh stood at the front door of the MacLayne cabin. He drew a couple of deep breaths and rapped sharply. Laurel pulled the door open. He saw her red swollen eyes and disheveled hair. She wore the same green wrapper she'd had on the day before.

"What do you want?"

"First, to know that you are all right."

"I'm fine." Laurel started to push the door closed.

Cortland put his shoulder at the jamb. "And I brought your things from Davis's General Store. You didn't pick them up yesterday when you left so quickly. Mr. Davis said you already paid for them. He also sent this letter."

Laurel grabbed the letter and looked at it. The momentary hope Cort had seen on her face faded as quickly as it had come.

"The letter wasn't from your husband, was it?"

"No. Do you need anything else?"

"I'd like to explain about Sunday. I would like to be friends."

"Dr. Cavanaugh, you don't have to explain anything to me. I had no business going to the service on Sunday. I certainly shouldn't have gone to Greensboro yesterday."

"Please drop the doctor. My name is Cortland. My friends call me Cort. There is no reason you shouldn't go where you want to go."

"You heard what Willa Ferguson said about me. The entire town of Greensboro is gossiping today."

"No doubt they are. Did you do anything wrong to cause that gossip?"

"Why should I talk to you about this? Surely you have misgivings about our 'questionable family' just like the rest of the community."

"I don't. I don't know if Mr. MacLayne is a fool or a saint, a hero or a villain, or a man or something less. I know you are a lady. That's all I need to know. I've no reason to judge."

Laurel walked out to her rocking chair on the porch. She sat down, not speaking for some time. Cort remained. He didn't sit next to her, as he assumed the second chair to be Mac's. He perched instead on the porch railing and waited for Laurel to speak.

"Well, Doctor, what do you want me to say? You came here. I didn't ask you to come."

"When I made the trip across the meadow today, I just wanted to ease the tension between us from Sunday. I didn't mean to intrude or make you angry with me. I'd like to be friends, or at least neighborly.

"You already said that. I don't intend to be rude or inhospitable to you or anyone. I am going to stay here at my homestead. I am pretty self-sufficient when people will leave me alone. I don't need outsiders."

"Doesn't sound like you've forgiven my slight to your husband. Won't you at least tell me what I did so I don't repeat the blunder in the future?"

"Nothing I can talk about. I appreciate your going to the military commissioner with me. You helped me keep my property. You were trying to help when you intervened at the general store. I don't talk about my husband with outsiders. My children don't talk about their father outside the family. That's all I am going to say."

"I suppose that is the reason I couldn't respond to your remark on Sunday. Truthfully, I can't understand how anyone could abandon an exceptional lady and a fine family as MacLayne has. Yet you said he's a good man and an outstanding father."

"Dr. Cavanaugh, I think you've said enough. I'll accept your apology because I know you meant no insult. Let's leave it at that."

"I'll agree if we part as good neighbors today. We can't change the past so let's just go on from here, putting the misunderstandings behind us."

"Fine. Now if you'll excuse me, I have small children who need my attention. Good-day to you."

Cort swung his leg atop his dappled gray, one of the few things he'd brought from his military service, and spurred the horse toward his cabin. As he reached the road, he turned to look over his shoulder one last time. He smiled. He'd look forward to Sunday when another opportunity to encounter the plain-spoken, intriguing lady would present itself.

Φ

Laurel didn't take her family back to the new church gathering her uncle started. She refused to expose her children to the stares and gossip she felt they would encounter. She would continue to conduct Sunday worship as she had so often since Mac had gone to join the Union cavalry. After lunch, Thomas came to spend some time with Andy and Mark Thomas.

"Laurel…I'm gonna take the boys out for a ride this afternoon. I'm thinkin' they may be needin' some 'man time' this afternoon. Is it all right with you?"

"I'd appreciate it, Pa. I know the boys miss their papa. I'm not sure Mark Thomas can even remember him."

"Don't lose heart, Laurel. Christmas hasn't been that long ago. We had a wonderful family time that day."

"Six months seems like an eternity. If we'd had a word …."

"We won't ride far. We'll be back before supper."

Thomas ushered his two grandsons out to saddle Sparky. As they were about to leave the corral, two Union soldiers rode up to the front porch, leading an extra horse.

"Hold up there, Boys. Take our horses back into the barn. Those soldiers may be out confiscatin' mounts. Hurry on." Thomas dismounted and walked briskly to meet the blue-clad visitors who had just climbed the stairs to the porch.

"Can I help you, Major?" Thomas greeted the soldiers.

"You can if this is the MacLayne homestead."

"Grandpapa, that horse is Midnight. Papa's home!" Andy cried out. "Is my papa inside? Papa!" Andy ran toward the porch.

The younger of the two men spoke, "You gotta be Andy. Captain MacLayne talked about you all the time. You're taller than he said."

"Stand down, Corporal. Sir, is this the MacLayne place?" The major shuffled from foot to foot and smacked his hat against his leg.

"I think that must be pretty evident if my grandson said that black stallion is his papa's horse. I'm Thomas MacLayne. Patrick is my son."

The major took a couple of steps toward the older man and offered his hand. "I'm Major Livingston, second in command of the Second Arkansas Cavalry. We've come from Batesville. This is Corporal Josiah Parchman, one of the members of the Quartermaster unit led by your son."

"Gentlemen," Thomas nodded his understanding. "Have you brought us news about Patrick?"

"I have brought a commendation to the captain's wife. Is she inside?"

"Yes. This is Shiloh, Patrick's homestead. Laurel is here."

"May I speak with her?" The major spoke in a professional, calm tone, but he didn't make eye contact with Thomas MacLayne. Andy opened the door and walked to the chair where his mother sat rocking Leah Ann.

"Laurel, these two men are members of Mac's company. They have come from Batesville," Thomas MacLayne said.

"Mrs. MacLayne, I'm Major Livingston. I regret I come with unwelcome news. On March 24, Captain MacLayne was lost in an attack near White River near a community called Oil Trough. He was helping wounded men and loading wounded on supply wagons after a Rebel ambush of our troops as they crossed the river…"

Laurel looked at the major, her eyes blank and wide. "Lost him? What does that mean?"

"Mrs. MacLayne," the corporal spoke up, "Captain MacLayne stayed behind to help more wounded. Some were Rebels and some were our boys. He wouldn't leave until he knew he couldn't save anymore. I was drivin' that last wagon. He yelled for me to go on to save the ones I had. I saw the captain's horse shot down with him. We found the captain's horse the next mornin'."

"Are you telling me that my husband was injured or killed?" Laurel cried out.

"The next mornin' we were told that all the fallen had been buried by the Rebel troops. No one remained on the battlefield. We know three Union soldiers and a dozen or so Rebel troops were killed during the exchange. A few from both sides are unaccounted for. The bodies were removed before we could identify them. I am sorry to say Captain MacLayne is among the latter." The major handed Laurel the letter of commendation he had brought.

"Ma'am, I am sorry. Mac, I mean Captain MacLayne, was a great friend to me and all our unit. I am sick that we couldn't bring him home. He loved this place. When we found his mount, none of his things were there except this." The young soldier handed Laurel the carved cross laced with rawhide that once belonged to her father. "I know this belonged to him because he used it every day. I've seen it often…this cross, a silver picture case, and his raggedy old Bible."

Cathy and Annie began to cry. "I know that's Papa's cross. He was never without it." Cathy dropped to her knees to hug Laurel.

"Ain't nothin' to prove they killed my papa," Andy shouted. "And where did you get Midnight? Papa always took the best care of his horse. You said he got shot out from under my papa."

Thomas pulled Andy to him. "Calm down, Andy. We'll hear 'em out."

"Mrs. MacLayne, your husband died helping other soldiers. He saved the lives of at least four men before his mount was struck down. The Commander of the Army of the West has issued a commendation for his service with the Second Arkansas Union Cavalry. I offer the United States Army's greatest condolences for your great loss." Major Livingston stood and handed Laurel the parchment document from the Department of War.

Laurel did not respond. She sat dangling the cross by the rawhide cord. Leah reached for it, causing it to swing. When the baby could not reach the cross, she began to cry, adding to the confusion in the room. Mark Thomas began to whimper. Laurel made no move to comfort the children.

Thomas walked with Andy to pick up Mark Thomas. "Annie, please take Leah Ann and put her down for a nap."

"Grandpapa, what's wrong with Mama?" Gracie whimpered.

"Darlin', she'll be all right. Laurel, let's go outside and get some fresh air."

She'd showed no indication she had even heard her father-in-law speak to he

"Come with me, Laurel. Let me take you out to the porch." He walked to her and took her arm. He pulled her to her feet, and she crumpled into a heap at his feet. All her children called out to her at once. "Andy, go get Sparky and ride to get Dr. Cavanaugh as fast as you can ride."

Thomas lifted his daughter-in-law and carried her to the second pen. At the foot of the chair where Laurel had been sitting lay the wooden cross.

# Chapter 27

*Let brotherly love continue. Be not forgetful to entertain strangers;*
*for thereby some have entertained angels unawares*
Hebrews 13:1-2

About fifty exhausted, dirty men stood behind an austere, brick building on the bank of the Alabama River. After one last miserable night locked in the stinking, slatted boxcar on the siding at the fueling station, the prisoners being allowed to stand outside in the fresh air beside a river was a gift from God. Mac hardly noticed the barbed wire fences and the armed guards that walked the sentry posts above.

"Attention. The commander will be here anytime now. When he comes, pay close attention to what he says," a Rebel sergeant said.

Then, an ordinary-looking, dark-haired man climbed the steps to the platform. Dressed in a clean, grey officer's uniform, the colonel looked more like a schoolteacher than a prison warden, especially as the sun obscured his eyes behind his round eyeglasses. Any doubt as to his authority disappeared the moment he raised his hand. The Confederates standing guard snapped to attention and all talking ceased.

"I am H.A.M. Henderson, commandant of Castle Morgan. I am charged with the responsibility of overseeing this camp where you will remain until you are exchanged or until this conflict comes to an end. You will not be mistreated as long as you do as you are told and respect your place. Remember, you are prisoners of war of the Confederate States of America. Any escape attempt will be futile. Be respectful and allow us to treat you the same. Follow the sergeant around to the front of the building, and he'll assign your sleeping areas."

The commander stood and watched as the new prisoners made their way inside. Mac noticed before he turned the corner that Colonel Henderson had bowed his head and appeared to be praying.

Once inside, Mac's assessment of Castle Morgan plummeted. A huge gap in the roof allowed plenty of light to show that this building had once been a warehouse of some sort and had never been finished. Along the sides of the room were tiers of bunks, in some places as many as five levels high. Mac didn't try to count them, but anyone could see that the number of men far outnumbered the beds provided for them. The sergeant took four men from the group and led them to a section under the roof in front of a set of bunks. "You make your sleepin' area here. We'll try to find you a mat or a blanket to sleep on.

He continued until he'd spaced all the new arrivals around the room. When he showed Mac and another officer their places near the fireplace, he said, "When we ship another group out for exchange, we'll assign ya bunks. For now, it's the best we can do."

Mac sat down next to the fireplace and leaned back. He pulled out his Bible and opened it to find the pictures of his family. He stared at the photographs for a long time.

*Laurel, how long will we be separated? I'm starved for the sight of you and ours. Five minutes holdin' you would quench this thirst in my...*

"Whatcha got there, Captain? A brash young lieutenant broke Mac's private musings with his wife.

"Only the most precious things on God's earth."

"Can I see?" Mac turned the photographs toward the curious young man dressed in a tattered uniform of the infantry. "That's your family, ain't it?"

"It is. You got one waiting for you back home?"

"Had me a sweetheart, but I hadn't heard from her in more'n a year, but then I been here at Castle Morgan for nearly nine months. We don't get no mail here."

"Where are ya from, Lieutenant?" Mac asked.

"Indiana before I enrolled at West Point. I was nearly finished there when Carolina put us into this war. I wanted to be an engineer. I never planned to be shootin' at other Americans."

"I tried to stay out of this conflict for more than two years."

"You got a strange accent for a Yankee officer. Are you a spy?"

"Son, they don't need spies in prison. My name is Patrick MacLayne. Captain, Second Arkansas Cavalry…Union Cavalry."

"Dang. I thought Arkies were all Rebs."

"I thought all Indiana boys were corn farmers." They laughed and a new friendship began on the floor of Cahaba prison.

"My name is Andrew Mayfield. My friends back home call me Drew on account my pa is Andy."

"Drew, my friends call me Mac. I gotta son back at Shiloh whose name is Andy. Thank God, he's too young to be caught up in this useless war."

"My church is named Shiloh."

"So is mine…and the name of the community where we live. My wife Laurel--this is her picture--and I named our homestead Shiloh, too."

"That word must mean something special to you."

"It does…comes from the book of Genesis. Talks about a place of belonging and acceptance for all who live with the Lawgiver."

A loud voice interrupted the conversation between Mac and Drew. "Any officer over the rank of captain who came in here yesterday, listen up." Not one prisoner responded to the call. "All captains and lieutenants from yesterday's prisoners stand up." Mac and three others rose. "You four, out to the green." They gathered in the area where they had been inducted that morning.

"Commander Henderson wants to talk to y'all. I'll take ya across to his headquarters directly. Before we go, go take a dip in that river and see if you can get some of that Yankee stench off ya."

One of the lieutenants responded, "I can't swim, Sergeant."

"Then don't get too far from the bank. And don't get no stupid idea about trying to swim to the other side of the Alabama. The river is deep in spots, and the current is swift. If you get to the other side, it's still Alabama over there. Our guards are the best marksmen in the South."

All the men stripped to the skin and jumped into the almost blue cool water. Mac hardly listened to the warning. He felt he'd been given a blessing from Heaven. How long had it been since he'd been clean? Even without soap, the time to wash the grime and smell from his body seemed to strip away part of the gloom he'd felt during the long trip to Cahaba. Mac dove beneath the water and felt it pull his too-long hair behind him. When he surfaced, he shook his head and cried out, "God is good." Even locked in a Confederate prison, this was the best day he'd had in many weeks.

Before he left the river, he washed his clothes—every stitch. He knew that meant he'd be in wet clothes all day, but he didn't care. At least they would be somewhat clean. One of the lieutenants saw what Mac was doing and decided to follow suit, but the other two officers balked at the idea of wearing a wet uniform for the rest of the day.

"Did that guard go through your belongings, Captain?"

"I didn't notice. Nothin' was missin'. Why?" Mac asked.

"I can't find my harmonica nor a letter I had from my ma. I was sure I had 'em in my pocket."

"Let's ask the commander about searches. By the way, I'm Mac. Second Arkansas Cavalry."

"Weston. New York Artillery. I got trapped over near Memphis about a year ago. These Rebs prisons fill up so fast they're always shufflin' us. I sure wish they'd catch a few Rebs captains so I could get exchanged."

"You prisoners get yer clothes on and your boots. I'll take ya across the road."

Just outside the stockade, a two-story square building with a copper-clad dome stood in strange contrast to the unfinished warehouse across the road. With the four columns adorning the porch, it was clear the building had been built for something more than a prison office. The sergeant led the four prisoners into the foyer and pointed to a long bench just beyond the door. "You Yanks make yourself at home in the past capitol building of the state of Alabama. Ain't she a fine old palace? Just sit down and wait until the Reverend wants ya."

"I thought you said Commander Henderson called for us," Mac said.

"That's what I said. Commander Henderson is the reverend, a fully-ordained Methodist preacher."

Another well-spring of hope arose for Mac. A man of God who had the task of overseeing the prison. He spoke a silent prayer as the sergeant opened the commander's office door.

Behind an orderly desk, Commander Henderson sat, bent over a list of names that continued for pages. On one of the corners of his desk lay a well-worn bible opened to the Psalms. He looked up when the sergeant saluted, and he returned the salute. He removed his glasses and rubbed his nose. "Please sit down, Captains. I've called you here to ask for your help."

Mac looked up at the man behind the desk who certainly surprised him.

Henderson continued what seemed to be a well-rehearsed speech. "Since this morning, Cahaba Prison has a population of 660 men. Two years ago, the construction of this camp was started to serve about five hundred, but that work was not completed. I suppose you realized that when you were assigned sleeping areas in the barracks."

"Yes, sir, I noticed the shortage of bunks and the limited space. Seems we are even missing a fair size section of the roof," Mac replied.

"What's your name, Captain?" Henderson asked.

"MacLayne, Second Arkansas Cavalry.

"And you?"

"Captain Jameson Weston, New York Artillery." His terse, growl seemed out of place to Mac but didn't seem to phase the colonel.

"Well, MacLayne and Weston, I need your help. I expect three things to be observed at this camp. I can't do it alone. I demand it of my guards and expect it of our charges. I demand compassionate treatment, discipline without abuse, and good order. To do this, I use officers from among our population to oversee smaller units.

"I won't spy on my fellow prisoners," Weston barked back.

"Captain, I didn't ask you to report on those under your charge. Keep an eye on them. If they are sick, let us know so we can get them help. Protect them from the bullies inside, and there are some. Try to draw them into a community so they don't feel isolated."

"You want me to mollycoddle grown men?" Weston spat back.

Mac rolled his eyes at the belligerence he felt from his fellow captain. "Weston, he's askin' you to be the leader those bars on your shoulders suggest you are."

"That's the gist of it. I will assign each of you an assistant, probably a lieutenant, and then I'll divide the roster of new prisoners between y'all. That is my system. To date, it's workin' pretty well. Do you have any questions?"

"Yes, I have one. While we were in the river, one of the guards went through our clothes, One of the men lost a harmonica and a letter from his mother. Are we not allowed to keep personal items?"

"MacLayne, I confiscate valuables from the men as soon as they come in. That's the only way to keep them safe. Jewelry, money, and mementos are looted by muggers in the prison. It keeps down problems if I keep them here. I return those items when the prisoners are released from Cahaba. Do you have anything you want me to keep for you?"

"I've got nothing left except these three things." Mac pulled his Bible and the two pictures from his coat. "I was looted by Confederate troops the day they shot my horse out from under me. They even took my saddlebags, saddle, and reins from my dead mount."

"If you'll get me the name of the man who lost his harmonica and letter, I'll get it back to him. The things you have aren't in big demand by our muggers. You can keep them. I must say, though, your Bible is about as tattered and worn as mine."

"It's seen a lot of miles with me. I'm proud to have it. I don't know how I'd make it through a day without it. Never been much good at memorizing."

"What about you, Weston? Do you have valuables you want to keep safe?"

"I ain't got nothing. I've been robbed by Rebs more'n once since I joined up in '62."

"I've finished what I called you here to discuss. I'm not happy to have to retain people here in these conditions, but I have a job to do. I will carry out my orders. I ask you to do the same. You are dismissed."

When the two lieutenants who had been called out at the same time had seen the reverend, the sergeant walked them all four men back to the stockade. They arrive just in time to have their first Castle Morgan supper, the one meal of the day. Mac looked down at his bowl of cornmeal mush, which may have been about the size of a large cup and three fatty, not very fresh slices of hog belly. The cup of water he was given, he couldn't drink. Nevertheless, he made himself eat. A man couldn't survive if he didn't eat. Mac intended to survive. Laurel waited for him at Shiloh, and he promised he would not leave her there alone.

## φ

Mac didn't have long to wait to get his 'unit' assigned to him. One of the lieutenants who met with Commander Henderson the same day was assigned as Mac's assistant. The very next morning, Melvin Grigsby, a member of the infantry from Wisconsin, was a pleasant young man and pleased to move from the group he'd been given when he came in. Drew Mayfield also found a way into Mac's group, along with a mixed lot from Arkansas, Michigan, Missouri, and Nebraska. There was also one giant of a man from Tennessee. In total, the "Arky's Troop" numbered thirty-four men. The Confederate guards allowed some shifting inside the building so the units could share a common area. Since none of them had the luxury of a bunk, the more established residents didn't care. One parcel of dirt floor was as good as another as long as there was a roof overhead. For now, all the prisoners were able to sleep in the dry.

As spring pushed into summer, the heat made life inside the converted warehouse unbearable. Mac found every opportunity possible to take his men outside. The green behind Castle Morgan was not a large space, but it was near the river and partially shaded. On afternoons when even a small breeze moved the leaves, the area made a good place to play a new game the northern soldiers brought with them. Within a few days, most of Mac's group became avid baseball players. They fashioned a ball with pieces of a worn-out boot stuffed with bits of clothing torn from uniforms. Bats were sturdy branches from trees inside the stockade. Scraps of lumber made up the bases. Some of the friendly guards who had taken an interest often played the role of umpire or coach. Many afternoons were filled with competitive but not always peaceful matches.

Other days, the men would occupy themselves playing a game of skill, like throwing rock-filled bags into a wooden box some distance away. This game took the place of horseshoe tossing they played back home. Of course, they had no real horseshoes, so the three-inch squares filled with gravel seemed to work as well. In these friendly competitions, the men came to know each other and the tedium of prison life eased. In Mac's group, only two men decided they didn't want to be a part of the team.

Mac didn't force the ones who chose to remain loners to get involved. Instead, he made attempts to get acquainted with them one to one. Some evenings after supper, he gathered his men around their sleeping area to talk. As they grew to know each other, the men began to share their life stories and vent their frustrations. On many occasions, they sought him out to ask his advice for problems they were dealing with. One night, he learned two of his men developed dysentery, but they'd not gone to sick call.

"Baxter, why didn't you go see Dr. Whitefield? That stuff can get serious."

"Thought it'd get better. I had it when I was a kid."

"Tomorrow, you go see the doctor. I don't want y'all sick."

"Yes, sir."

"Anyone else got somethin' that needs fixin'?" Mac asked his crew.

The tall giant of a man from Tennessee who rarely opened his mouth stood up. "Captain, I'm so parched I can't make spit. The water we got is plain ole nasty. Do you think they'd let us go to the river to get a drink of water?"

"You're Pierce, aren't ya?"

"Yeah, I am. I ain't no problem maker, but we've been here more'n two months. I ain't complainin' about the food. We get the same stuff as the Rebs who work here. But dag nab it, we oughta be able to get a cup of decent water. I ain't done nothin' but sip enough to keep me alive."

You're right, Pierce. I am thirsty, too."

General grumbling increased in their corner near the fireplace. "Quiet men. We don't want the guards thinkin' we're riotin' over here. I'll bring it up with Dr. Whitefield tomorrow."

"That may be all we can do, considerin' we're stuck in Castle Morgan." The six- foot-ten-inch tall Tennessean returned to his coat that he used as a pallet.

"Look at the bright side, men. It's been a good day. We had a fine time playin' baseball this afternoon. We got us some cornbread for supper instead of mush. That was a real treat. I've got time to read some scripture if any of you want to join me. Keepin' my Bible has kept me sane since I joined this army. I still have two photographs of my family. I got a lot to be thankful for. Tomorrow we're gonna ask for clean water. Y'all come over and join me while I read some more of Job."

Five or six men moved nearer to where Mc had settled, but also several men from other groups moved closer so they could hear. Mac read Job's words of anger and confusion toward God. A corporal from Missouri questioned him. "Captain MacLayne, ain't those pretty harsh words to speak against God?"

"They are. Do ya think it's okay to speak your heart when things go wrong?"

The young man and most of his companions sat silently. They were not comfortable answering the questions, even though most had come to like and respect Mac in the time they'd been together. One man said, "I don't know."

Another replied, "I never done it."

Drew Mayfield responded, "I just haven't felt as low as Job. He said he came to the end of his hope and he loathed his life."

"Some pretty awful things happened to Job. I've been in his place a time or two in my life. In '58, I went up into Missouri to buy a herd to start my cattle ranch at Shiloh. My wife asked me not to go. Laurel was expectin' our first baby. I went. While I was gone, she lost our little boy. When I found out, I was angry with God—and myself. I cried out against God."

"Don't make no sense to me," a sergeant from Michigan spoke out. "You're always readin' the good book and prayin'. God should never be an enemy to you."

"It's because he's my closest friend, I can speak my mind, fellas. No matter how bad things are today—and since Oil Trough, I've felt pretty low at times—I won't quit hopin'. I have one scripture that guides me through every day—no matter how good or bad that day may be." Mac turned to Romans 8:28 and read the words to his listeners. *And we know that all things work together for good to them that love God, to them who are called to his purpose.*

"You believe that don't you, Captain?"

"Like I believe the sun will rise in the east in the mornin'."

A shout came from the rampart near the front of the room. "It's Taps. Get to your places." Mac's men shuffled to their pallets.

"Goodnight. Remember Baxter and Pierce, y'all get to the doctor first thing in the mornin'." Mac balled up his jacket for a pillow and fell asleep.

The following morning, Mac accompanied Baxter and Pierce to sick call. The men were perfectly capable of handling the visit to the doctor alone, but Mac wanted the opportunity to ask a few questions. Because the doctor had only one colleague, the town doctor, who wasn't always available, Dr. Whitefield had little time for non-medical appointments.

Inside the town hotel that had been set up as the prison hospital, Dr. Whitefield lined his patients up and examined, diagnosed, and treated them as quickly as he could. When Baxter showed up in the Captain's care, the doctor glared at Mac. "Is this man seriously ill? Does he require someone to bring him to me?"

"Not particularly. Baxter and Pierce are part of my unit, and these men both have an on-going bout with dysentery."

"No surprise there. Half the men I see have the same complaint."

"Usually caused by bad water, ain't it?" Mac asked.

"That's what they think."

"Why can't we get some better water, then? There's a river not twenty feet from the back wall of the stockade." Pierce said.

"I know the water ain't fit to drink. Half the people in Cahaba use the same artisan well to wash their feet, clothes, and chamber pots. The saloons empty spittoons there, and the livery rinses the slop buckets there. The farmers water hogs, dogs, and cows in that same water. The filth off the street just flows down the hill to Castle Morgan."

"Dr. Whitefield, don't ya think we could do somethin' about that? Some of my men complain of thirst every day, but drinkin' that swill is impossible. I'll volunteer my team as a work crew if you need some manpower. I'll guarantee they'll not try to escape."

"I don't know if I can get permission, but I'll talk to Reverend Henderson. Now get your other man up here. I've got scores of men with worse problems than these two."

The doctor did as he promised and within the month, the commander had found some piping to connect the well underground to the prison. The clean water not only helped improve the health of many soldiers, but the morale of the prisoners rose, too. Hope returned to some who'd felt their plight in the Alabama prison would be death.

Toward the end of September, Reverend Henderson sought out Mac one afternoon in the green. The Arky's Unit had invited another unit that slept near them to join in an afternoon throwing tournament. The prize would be a 'trophy' that Mac's men had fashion from a couple of pieces of scrap lumber. One of the men from Michigan was an excellent whittler and he had carved an intricate laurel wreath from the wood. A couple of other units came over to watch the games.

Each team could have fifteen men per round. Every man got to throw three bags at the box which was seven paces from the throw line. Each bag that landed in the box earned a point. The game consisted of three rounds, which allowed every man to play. In the end, whichever unit had the most 'ins' got to keep the trophy until the next tournament.

Through the afternoon, the score was close and the lead changed frequently. The crowds cheered and clapped. Men lounged on the ground and made seats on wooden crates and barrels. Laughter and smiles spread across the campus that afternoon.

"Captain…It's MacLayne, isn't it?"

"Yes, sir." Mac rose to attention when he recognized the commander.

"Will you walk with me?"

"Of course."

"I wanted to commend you for the change you've brought about with your unit. I'm sorry to say I've not been around enough to know exactly what you're doin', but your men have had fewer doctor visits, no disciplinary reports, and seem to deal with confinement better than other groups here at Castle Morgan."

"Thank you, sir, but I don't deserve any credit for that. They're fine men. I only did what you asked us to do…build a community. We talk about things, we play together when we can get out, we work when we get the chance so time passes. We read the Bible together about every night and talk about the scripture if there's time before Taps."

"I can see the difference. They have a leader who cares about them, MacLayne. The reason I'm gone so often is that I'm the regional commissioner of the prisoner exchange. Right now, Grant's bein' mighty stingy with those exchanges. He says he's tryin' to end the war."

"I see. I know we just get more crowded and never seem to lose anyone."

"I believe a large exchange is comin' in December. I'm gonna recommend your exchange with the other men who are helpin' to lead your unit. You're helpin' me do what I set out to do. We are keepin' men alive. We have different politics, Captain, but I believe we serve the same Lord."

"Thank you, Reverend Henderson. If you can see me as a servant like yourself, I must be doin' somethin' the way He' like."

That very night, Mac's team had another chance to improve living conditions in their section of the prison. After the Arky's Unit presented their opponent with the whittled laurel wreath for winning the tournament with a score of 74-72, the men turned in early. The excitement and enjoyment of the day had worn them to a frazzle. About midnight, a mob of six or seven muggers descended on Mac's team and the two groups nearest them. They chloroformed several men with rags soaked in the noxious substance and hit a few in the head with clubs. Then they rifled through the meager belongings, taking anything of value they wanted. Some of the men had hidden personal keepsakes instead of surrendering them to Reverend Henderson.

While the muggers worked their way near Mac, one of the men stumbled over someone's leg. When he bent over to club Richard Pierce, the mugger slipped and hit the gentle giant's shoulder instead of his skull. Pierce rose to his almost seven-foot height and picked the man up by his shirt front and spoke, "What the devil you doin' at midnight, creepin' in our space?"

His words woke others who hadn't yet fallen victim to the chloroform or the clubs.

The man cowered at the sheer size of the giant who held him, feet dangling off the floor. Several items he'd stolen fell to the dirt floor. His fellow thieves tried to run but were tripped, tackled, or knocked out before they could escape.

"Please let me down."

"Why should I? You low life. Ain't we all in here tryin' to survive together? And what are you doin'? You got no right to take the little bit we got left of home and family."

"Here. You can have it all back. Just let us go."

Mac inched his way over across the fallen men. "Where'd y'all get this chloroform? No one in here's got any medicine. Y'all been stealin' from the doctors when they got little enough to help our sick and wounded?"

"No, Captain. I swear we ain't took nothin' from the hospital. We never did."

"Where did it come from then?" None of the muggers spoke. "Well, you'll tell Reverend Henderson. And if you ever try to take things from our area again, I'll let my Tennessee friend here do what he's dying to do right now. Pierce, you and Lt. Mayfield and Lt. Grigsby see these thieves get to the commander directly. Make sure he knows the whole story. Tell him we'll help with the investigation if he needs us."

Within a week, Reverend Henderson had used the Arky's Unit to help him answer the questions the muggers didn't want to answer that night. After intense questioning, a day or two without rations, and more than one glimpse of Sergeant Richard Pierce, the truth came to light. The gang of muggers had routinely made rounds among new prisoners at Cahaba with the help of the three guards who supplied them with clubs and chloroform. The muggers who took whatever objects the men hid when they checked in divided the spoils with the guards. In return, the guards gave them additional food and special privileges. Their criminal activity ended after they met the gentle giant from Tennessee and a good reverend who did his job.

# Chapter 28

*For unto us, a child is born, unto to us, a son is given.*
*Isaiah 9: 6*

Dr. Cavanaugh arrived to attend Laurel within the hour. After a brief time with her, he assured Thomas and her children that she had collapsed from the shock of the news and that neither she nor the baby she carried was in any danger. His advice was simple. "Let her sleep. When she wakes, feed her a light meal and get her to drink as much water as she will. Then make her stay in bed for the next two days."

"I thank you, Dr. Cavanaugh. I'm so happy I let ya move to the Widow's cabin so near here," Thomas MacLayne said.

"Mr. MacLayne, please accept my condolences on the loss of your son. Tell Mrs. MacLayne, I'll be back tomorrow. We'll make sure that she delivers a healthy child in honor of your son."

"You don't believe those rumors, do you?"

"Even in the short time I've known Mrs. MacLayne, I could never believe her to be an unfaithful wife. She's never talked to me about her husband, nor have her children, but I know she loves him. I know he's spent some time here—say around Christmas last year if I am guessin' right."

They returned to the main pen where the visitors from Batesville sat at the table. Thomas smiled and patted the doctor on the back. "You're a good man, Cavanaugh. You and Patrick may have chosen different sides, but I have to believe he'd think that, too."

Colonel Livingston looked up at the man who stood next to him. "Sir, do I understand Mr. MacLayne right? You're a Confederate soldier?"

"I was a major in the medical corps until I took a couple of Union Minie Balls to my knee and thigh at the Battle of Helena in '63. I mustered out after Christmas. I can't walk or stand for long periods so I'm not much use to the cavalry. Now I'm just a country doctor."

The major asked, "Sir, where do your loyalties lie?"

"At the start of the war, I thought I was fightin' for my home, Louisiana, and my family. Now I don't want to fight at all. My wife and daughter died of Yellow Fever in the summer of '62 because I wasn't there to take care of them. They had no medicine. Three months later my family home was burned to the ground. Right now, I'm lookin' for peace and a place to start over. Dr. Gibson in Greensboro gave me the chance to do that here."

"If you will take the loyalty oath, I'm sure the Union will leave you be."

"I'll consider it. Right now, I'm just gonna try to get myself established as a member of this community." He turned to face Thomas again. "Mr. MacLayne, make her rest. I'll see you soon."

Major Livingston and Mac's friend Josiah Parchman stayed another hour, answering questions and filling in the details concerning Mac's disappearance and Midnight's return. When Laurel didn't awaken, they left after telling Thomas to contact the camp if the unit could help in any way. Corporal Parchman promised to return on leave later to pay his respects to the wife of his friend and captain.

In the darkest part of the night, Laurel awoke. She pushed herself up and slumped against the carved headboard of the walnut four-poster. She ran her hand across the cool pillow next to her—Mac's pillow. How many nights had his place beside her been empty? She tried to count the days since she'd last shared the beautiful old bed with him. Six months. No, it had been more.

Independence Day had passed. July was more than half over. Now Mac would never return to share their place again.

But she couldn't believe it was true. She loved Mac beyond life itself, and she felt no grief. She'd shed no tears. Mac wasn't dead. She would know if her soulmate no longer breathed in this world. That loss would have to leave a void. A person can't lose her heart and feel nothing. Yet, she knew the visit from the two Union soldiers hadn't been a nightmare. One of them said he'd seen the horse shot out from under Mac, but neither of them had seen his lifeless body. They hadn't brought Mac home to lie next to Campbell.

The whole thing had to be a mistake. War was confusion. Those in charge seldom really knew the details. Laurel pushed it all away...the not knowing...the fear of never seeing Mac again...the agony her children would face...it was too much. She wouldn't deal with it now. Her family needed her.

She got up, dressed, pulled her hair into two long braids, and wrapped them around her head. She couldn't deal with her wild mane in her present mood. *Why did I ever give up my braids? They served me so well because they were the best way to tame the mess.* She went to the kitchen to begin her work for the day well before the sun broke Crowley's Ridge.

When he awoke, Thomas found Laurel in the henhouse gathering eggs. "Laurel, are you all right this mornin'? You gave us quite a scare last night."

"I'm sorry, Pa. I didn't mean to cause a scene. That report from Mac's superior caught me off guard, I guess."

"What are you sayin', Laurel?"

"I don't believe it. Their report has to be a mistake. No one saw him die, did they?"

"Laurel, I wish it was a mistake, too. They got the report that the enemy troops buried all the fallen soldiers. Mac's own man, Corporal Parchman, found his horse and his cross. Mac wouldn't leave that cross behind."

"I can't accept it."

"What about the kids? Mark Thomas, Leah Ann, and Roy are too young to deal with this, but Annie, Cathy, and Andy understood those words. What are you gonna say to them?"

"Pa, I don't believe Mac is not coming home. Right now, I'm gonna say he's missing. Mac is missing and that is all we know."

"You have to think about what is best for those kids, Laurel. Cathy's cried most of the night. Andy sat in Mac's armchair all night. He didn't sleep a wink and didn't shed one tear. He built a wall around himself. He wouldn't speak to me this mornin'." Thomas walked over and took the basket from her and pulled her into his arms. A long silence flowed. "We need to go to the kids, Laurel."

"I don't know what to say to them. I know Mac will come home. He promised me he'd not leave me alone."

"Laurel, I'm not sure this is the best way to deal with the news we've been given. Ain't it like keepin' an open wound? Is it realistic to hope he'll return?"

"Isn't all hope unrealistic?" Laurel's tone of voice told Thomas too much. Laurel was not ready to let Mac go. "Pa, it's all I can do right now."

Laurel called Andy, Cathy, Gracie, and Annie into her bedroom where she waited with her father-in-law. She returned to her bed as the doctor had ordered. "We had some hard news yesterday, and I'm sorry I fell out. I should have been there to talk with y'all about what the major told us." Annie walked over to lay her arm across Cathy's shoulder.

Andy walked to the side of the bed and sat next to Laurel. "Mama, we ain't upset with you. You just scared us a little."

"Thank you, Andy. I need to be here for all of you, and I need you here with me. I won't fall out again."

"Mama, do you think Papa is dead? Him and Roy?" Cathy's words broke with her grief. Laurel pulled her hand so she sat next to her on the opposite side of the bed. She kissed the wet cheek nearest her.

"The major didn't say that. He said your papa was lost in a skirmish. They didn't find him yet."

"The corporal who knew Papa said he saw the horse fall on him," Andy said.

"He said he saw your papa fall from his horse that was killed. We don't know anymore."

Andy withdrew. He didn't say anymore. His face was blank, and his storm blue eyes were red and swollen. He turned his head from Laurel. "Andy, do you want to say something?"

"No."

"Gracie?"

"So, Mama, do you think Papa is all right and comin' home now?"

"Right now, we just don't know. We don't know anything different than we did before those two soldiers came here yesterday. We just have to wait and see what happens. We'll keep praying for Papa and let the Lord take care of him because we can't."

"I want my papa to come home. He's been gone too long." Gracie began to cry. Cathy and Annie also had tears streaming down their faces.

"Are we done yet? I wanna go out and brush down Midnight." Andy stood and waited for permission to leave the room.

"Yes, Andy. We're finished after we say a prayer for your papa."

"I don't wanna say no prayer. I got work to do." He ran out the door with his grandfather following him.

## ⌀

Dr. Cavanaugh arrived shortly before sunset. "I apologize for being so late. A patient near Herndon had a difficult delivery."

"We're all well here. You could have saved yourself a trip." Laurel's voice was flat.

"I left orders for you to rest a day or two. You didn't listen very well."

"No reason for me to stay in bed. I was caught off guard by the news yesterday. Now, I'm in control again. I've got a family to care for, in case you haven't noticed."

"I've noticed. That's why I said you should rest. You have a new baby on the way. I am here to check you over and make sure you and that new one are still all right."

"Fine. If you'll leave me be, then, go ahead.

"A bit of privacy, perhaps?"

Laurel went back into her room with the doctor following.

"Cathy, will you come with us, please?" Dr. Cavanaugh asked.

"Why do you want her?" Laurel questioned.

"I just thought you'd be more comfortable with your daughter here."

After the brief examination, the doctor put his instruments in his bag. "Most things appear quite normal. You're a bit edgy, but I guess you've got a right to be stressed today. Besides, I know you're still put off with me. You've never quite forgiven me since that Sunday I didn't praise your husband. I think you need more rest, but I know you won't listen."

"I can't believe you have the audacity to mention Mac to me the day after…"

"Whoa. Yesterday, I promised his father we would deliver a healthy baby to honor your husband. I want us to be friends so we can work together for that goal. Great stress can cause complications with pregnancies."

"I got no…"

"I heard it the first time. You have a family to care for. Well, you also have an unborn child here that needs a healthy mother for at least two more months."

"I will have a healthy son."

"If you take care of yourself, you can have a healthy baby. You can caudle your kids and hug them and dry their tears without the physical labor you do every day. You have people in this house who love you and are capable of sharing the load."

"I'll rest more."

"And what did you do to your hair? I've never seen you look so …so…stern and matronly."

"If you'll excuse me now, I need to get supper ready for my family."

"I thought you said you'd let others help."

"At least, I can get them started so we can eat. Good day, Dr. Cavanaugh."

Laurel stumbled through the days that followed doing whatever was required to maintain her homestead. J.F. Clarke and Andy managed the livestock and began preparing for the coming winter. Annie and Cathy took over most of the childcare and cooking. When harvest season came, Laurel worked with her girls to can the bounty of her garden, but she did little of the outside work as she had in past years. Annie and Laurel spent many hours preserving the bounty that year and were happy to do so. Reports from Greensboro told of empty shelves at both general stores in town. The demands from the war were greater than what could be supplied. The public suffered as the trickle of goods from the cities had stopped. Shiloh would have to feed the MacLaynes in the winter of 1864.

A continuous flow of visitors came to Shiloh through the fall. Matthew Campbell and Laurel's Aunt Ellie made a weekly visit. Peggy and Thomas MacLayne spent the night nearly every Saturday night. Dr. Cavanaugh found his way to check on the family every other day or so. All saw that the basic needs of the family for food, shelter, and any necessity was met without delay. Laurel made sure the routines established by Mac remained intact. They ate meals together, too often in silence, read scripture before bedtime, and prayed for their father nightly. Thomas made sure they kept to their weekly worship time. Nothing changed, except the house was devoid of laughter and any sense of pleasure. The MacLayne children grieved, even the little ones who didn't know the reason for the gloom. Life at Shiloh was bleak. Laurel didn't notice.

The last Sunday in August, Dr. Cavanaugh stopped Matthew Campbell as the members of the church in the arbor began to leave for their homes.

"Afternoon, Brother Matthew. Good sermon today."

"Hello, Doctor. Thanks. I always love to preach on the gospel of John. How's our flock at Shiloh?"

"Mostly healthy, I am glad to say. A broken bone or two. One new baby. Some gout. One terrible case of melancholia—infectin' a whole family."

"I know. My niece, Laurel. She's runnin' away again."

"Again?"

Matthew told the doctor of Laurel's past reaction to loss. "I'd hoped her faith was strong enough now to deal with Mac's death."

"You believe Mr. MacLayne was lost at Oil Trough, don't you?"

"I hate it. He's my—he was my best friend. No reasonable person can think anything else. He adored Laurel. Those kids were the center of his world. He'd move heaven and hell to get home to her if he was alive."

"I can't understand why he left them to join the Union army."

"Cort, Mac was a man of principle. Once an oath was made he'd die to keep it. He tried for two years to avoid leavin' home. Even after Roy died at Corinth, Mac looked for an out. Then at the end of '62 when the Confederacy passed those three bills, I don't remember the names of 'em, he was eligible for conscription. His home was in jeopardy if he refused. He thought if he deserted Laurel, the Southern code of honor would support her since she was a woman trying to raise her children alone. That was the story they spread…that Mac deserted her. So far it's worked."

"I know a little about that. I went with Laurel to the military commissioner back in April."

"Most of the Shiloh community didn't buy the story because they knew Mac too well, but the folks in Jonesboro and Gainesville that were in charge of the militia didn't know. The people around here have had a hard time forgivin' Mac for choosin' what they see as the wrong side."

"That's why she won't come to service very often."

"That and because of the rumors about the baby's father."

"What fools they are. "

"Mac made a vow to Laurel's father that he'd provide a home for her and that she'd always be safe and taken care of.

346

Mac's grandfather was a decorated patriot in the War of 1812. I guess Mac's pretty much a patriot, too. He was…He couldn't support secession."

"What do you think we can do to help this family? I don't have any medicine to cure melancholia."

"We'll just have to pray and visit. Laurel has lost her anchor. If the people of the community hadn't rejected Mac for his politics, it would have helped Laurel. She rejected them because they turned on Mac. She'll defend him to her grave."

I wish she'd told me this. I know why she's miffed with me now. When I didn't react to her praise of him, she saw my silence as a rejection, too."

"What are you talkin' about, Doc?"

"Nothing. Thanks for helping me understand."

"We'll all see her through. Laurel is family, and she will find her way back to grace if we lift her up to the Lord."

For the next three weeks, the heat in northeast Arkansas was unbearable. During that time, Laurel was almost impossible to live with. She had come to the last month of her pregnancy. The stress of finishing the harvest, preserving the last of the fall harvest, and the depth of her grief made her short-tempered and sharp-tongued. She became a drill sergeant to her older children, pushing them to get their chores done and constantly reminding them of the hunger they'd endure if they wasted any of the garden produce. Cathy and Andy worked hard to please her, but even their efforts didn't seem to ease the tension they felt. The younger children stayed away from her as much as possible. Gracie, Mark Thomas, and even Leah Ann found attention and comfort in Annie.

The worst part of everyday was after supper. Before the war, this had been the best part. The family continued to walk through their routine before bedtime, but the spirit was gone. The rote activity brought little comfort to anyone. One night during evening worship time, Mark Thomas picked up a wooden horse his grandfather carved for him. He pretended the horse was Midnight, prancing across the meadow at Shiloh. He clicked the hooves on the floor a couple of times, interrupting the scripture reading.

Laurel snatched the toy and slapped his hand sharply. "Mark Thomas, you know better than to play during evening Bible reading. What's gotten into you. That is so disrespectful."

Andy interrupted the scolding. "Stop it, Mama."

"Andrew, don't tell me how to deal..."

"Mama, calm down. He's only a little boy and he's tired."

Laurel turned her anger toward Andy. "Now you're sassin' me. How dare you talk to...."

"I didn't mean no sass, Mama. Let's finish our prayer time and go to bed. We'll talk this out later after we've had a while to think about it."

Laurel sank into her rocking chair and her stoic façade returned. "Annie, please say the evening prayer and put the children to bed." After the amens, the children hurried from the room. Only Andy and Laurel remained.

"Mama, I don't think this can wait. We gotta clear the air. Will you go out on the porch with me?"

"Boy, what do you think we need to talk about?"

"I ain't no boy, Mama. I'm nearly thirteen years old. Papa told me to watch over this house. I aim to do what he asked me to do. Can we talk about this outside?"

"Yes, I suppose."

"I'm sorry I sassed ya, but I had to help Mark Thomas. He misses Papa real bad. That horse is a way he remembers Papa from when he was home."

"He knows how to behave during our prayer time. That was your papa's rules, not mine."

"He's five years old. He lost his papa and his mother, too. You got no time for him. Not for any of us. When was the last time you hugged him? We work, eat, sleep, and nothin' else much. This ain't the home we had three years ago. You used to love us and talk to us and touch us."

"That's not true. I love all of you. I always will love you."

"How are we supposed to know it?"

Stunned at his words, Laurel choked out her frustration. "Andrew, I love you! You know I love you, don't you?"

"I used to, but you and Papa taught us actions speak louder than words. When was the last time you brushed Gracie's hair? Do you know she lost two teeth last week? She told Annie about her teeth. What about Leah? You used to rock her and sing lullabies. Now, Annie does it."

"That's enough, Andy."

"Last week, Leah called Annie 'mama'. Did ya know that?"

"I said enough. I'm sorry. I'll try to do better. I never meant to…" Laurel tried to rise but she couldn't stand. An agonizing cramp doubled her over. The pain increased as she tried to sit upright. She felt the water from her womb spread down her legs.

"Mama, are you all right? I didn't mean to hurt ya."

Through her clenched teeth, she spoke, "Andy, tell Annie to come and help me. Then ride Midnight to get Aunt Ellie. Tell her it's the baby. Please hurry."

Annie hurried to Laurel's side. After the initial cramping ebbed, she was able to help her remove her soiled dress and change into a cool, summer nightdress. "Do you want to lie down, Mrs. Mac?"

"No, Annie. I'll sit here in this chair for a while. You know this chair once belonged to my grandmother Wilson. Now, why did I tell you that?"

"Are you hurtin' now?"

"Not so much. Annie, have I been expecting too much of you lately? I've left all the childcare for you. Have my children decided you're their mother?"

"Of course not. They know, well maybe not Leah Ann, but the rest. They all know how sad you are. I know you're tired. It's hard to carry a baby in this summer heat and put up harvest at the same time."

"Annie, you don't have to protect my feelings. I haven't been a good mother this summer. I know it. Please don't let me hurt my children. I need you to tell me when I'm pushing them away."

"Mrs. Mac, you're doin' the best ya can. You've just forgotten to ask the Lord to help you. Andy, Cathy, and Gracie—

me, too, I guess—we're all broken right now. We've all lost people we love. They lost Mr. Mac, but think of how many others they cared about have gone on, too. They're kinda afraid they are losin' you, too. Mark Thomas and Leah Ann are like Roy. They are so young they just need to be held a lot. They need their mama, the one they knew."

"When did you get so wise, Annie? And so smart? Thank you for taking over for me when I can't. Ohhh…" Laurel cringed at another pain deep in her back. "Maybe you should help me to bed. Perhaps I can sleep awhile before my aunt gets here to help me."

Before ten o'clock, Matthew and Ellie Campbell arrived with their daughter Mary. Ellie promptly bedded her daughter down with Gracie and Cathy. She and Matthew went in to see about Laurel and found her asleep. Matthew sat by his niece, laid his hand on her head, and prayed. Then he and Ellie sat watch until Laurel awoke, hurting once again.

By eleven-thirty, Laurel's labor pains became more pronounced and closer together. Ellie helped her turn to her side and propped her up with pillows to ease the pain. Laurel began to sweat profusely. Ellie washed her with cool water again and again. Mathew swished a fan across her face. Little seemed to help. Laurel's labor grew harder as the hours crept toward sun-up, yet there seemed to be little progress toward bringing the baby. By seven o'clock, Laurel began to cry out with the severity of the pain. Ellie had delivered scores of babies, including two of Laurel's, and rarely had she seen a woman who had given birth to three children already have such deep, agonizing contractions without some evidence of the baby's movement toward delivery.

She called for Annie. "Sweetheart, please sit with Laurel for a few minutes while I go talk to my husband." She ran to the barn where Matthew and the boys were finishing morning chores. "Matthew, I need to talk with you." She nodded toward Andy and Mark Thomas. "Send them to the house."

"Andy, will you carry the milk in and gather the eggs on the way? Annie may need 'em to have enough for breakfast."

"Is Mama okay, Aunt Ellie?"

"She'll be fine, Andy."

"We were havin' a spat when all this started."

"Now don't be thinkin' you did anything wrong. This baby is right on time. Now get this food in so we can feed everyone this mornin'."

After the door closed, Ellie clasped Matthew's arm. "Darlin', something's not right. Laurel's been in labor twelve hours, and I can't see this baby is one bit closer to getting' born. Her pains are too hard, and they get longer each time."

"You want me to find the doctor?"

"I think that's best. I've brought lots of babies into the world, but I don't know how to help her."

Matthew flung a saddle on Midnight and galloped off toward Widow Parker's cabin where he hoped to find Dr. Cavanaugh. When he got there, he found a note saying the doctor had been called to Lorado. Matthew scribbled a message and urged Midnight into a strong pace toward Greensboro. It was a long shot, but perhaps Dr. Gibson could be found.

At noon, Laurel's pains were continuous and traces of blood seeped onto the sheets. Ellie sent Andy across to Big Creek to bring Peggy and Thomas MacLayne. Even when Matthew returned, Ellie felt no less anxious, for he'd found another note saying Dr. Gibson was in Jonesboro and wouldn't return until suppertime. All she could do was soothe her niece with the cool baths and try to scotch the bleeding. She had nothing to stop the pain.

At one o'clock, Dr. Cavanaugh galloped up to Shiloh. He entered the house without knocking and rushed to examine Laurel. When he saw her extreme pain, his concern doubled. He never gave laudanum during childbirth because no one knew how it affected an unborn infant. But Laurel's deep moans and the occasional cry unnerved him. He could barely stand to see this woman, his friend, suffer as she was. He poured the milky liquid into her mouth to ease the pain.

"Mrs. Campbell, how long has this been happenin'?"

"Annie said that Laurel had a very hard cramp about eight o'clock last night and that Laurel felt her water break in the middle of that cramp.

"Did the pain continue.?"

"I don't know. Matthew and I got here at about ten. Laurel has had some bad pains, but they didn't last too long. By sun-up, she was hurtin' all the time, but I've seen no sign of the baby. When I noticed the bleedin', I told Mac to get you. That was early this mornin'."

"I wish I'd gotten here sooner. Come help me turn her on her back. I need to check the baby's heart."

Together they repositioned Laurel, causing her to cry out. Cathy and Andy rushed to the door. "Is my mama gonna die because of what I said to her?" Andy cried out. Matthew came to pull the children back.

Ellie Campbell took charge. "No, Andy. We just moved her. Matthew, please take the kids down to the creek to swim. Annie, can help you watch them?"

After several minutes of listening to the baby's heartbeat and examining Laurel's abdomen, Dr. Cavanaugh knew where the problem lay.

"This baby's in the wrong position. The head hasn't turned toward the birth canal. That's the cause of this long labor and why the pain is so intense."

"What can you do?"

"I'm not sure. The safest thing for Laurel…what the medical texts say is to save the mother. I could do that and if she doesn't bleed too much or get childbed fever she could survive."

"You mean to sacrifice the baby?"

"The stress of prolonged labor causes stillbirths or the brutal method of removing the baby …"

Laurel lifted her head. "You have to save my baby. Cortland, please don't let me lose this part of Mac. Please." Laurel screamed in pain once again.

"I wish I had some chloroform. I don't know how much more she can take."

"Doctor, please talk to my husband and Mr. MacLayne. They're still in the yard. Make the decision that is best for Laurel."

Thomas, Matthew, and Cortland considered the decision they were called to make. "She's in terrible pain, and now she's beginning to lose too much blood. There is the traditional way I can remove the baby and save her life. The child will not live. I will have to surgically dismember the child to remove it."

"Cortland, surely there is some way. As low as Laurel's been, losin' this baby will kill her. Don't ya know some way to save them both?" Matthew pleaded with him.

"I've been reading in some medical journals about an operation where a baby was delivered through an incision. I've never done it or even seen it done it. The medical texts say it's an old procedure used in Asia and Europe. Queen Victoria had her last two children using this procedure, but I've only read about it..."

"Do you think it'll work?" Thomas asked.

"I've not had the trainin' to do this."

"Do you think there is any hope without it?"

"Lord if I only knew." Cortland closed his eyes and under his breath, he whispered, "I wish I knew more. Lord God, be the great Healer for Laurel tonight." He turned and ran to the porch. "We'll have to hurry. She's lost too much blood already."

Cortland Cavanaugh returned to the cabin and asked Ellie to leave the room. Matthew took her place. He sterilized his scalpel and handed Matthew his medical book. "Keep this opened right here." He made Laurel swallow a spoonful of laudanum to sedate her more deeply.

"Matthew, please pray for me. She wants this child, but I can't do this alone."

Cortland began to work, step by step as his medical manual directed. Because of his need to check and recheck each direction, the surgery went very slowly. Laurel continued to bleed much more than he wanted. Finally, he was able to remove the baby boy, alive and well. When he patted the backside, the little one cried out. Cortland handed the baby off quickly to Matthew and went to work, stemming the blood flow that was now the threat to Laurel's life. To stop the excessive blood loss, he was forced to take steps he didn't want to take, but Laurel's life hung in the balance. He knew she would never have another child.

Laurel awoke briefly the next morning. Her aunt called the children in and laid the newest MacLayne in her arms.

The doctor smiled at Laurel and said, "You've given your husband a handsome, healthy son. Now you have to get well so you can raise him to be the man his father was."

"Laurel Grace, what are we gonna call this newest MacLayne?" Thomas asked.

"His name is Patrick Matthew. We'll call him Macky until he decides what he wants to be called." Laurel brushed a kiss across Macky's forehead and promptly fell asleep.

# Chapter 29

*Servants, be subject to your masters with all fear,*
*not only to the good and gentle but also to the forward.*
*In this is thankworthy, if a man for conscience toward God*
*endure grief, suffering wrongfully*
*I Peter 2:18-19*

    Summer at Cahaba prison was not the nightmare Mac believed it would be. Not to say it was so good he'd have chosen it, but after the piping was completed from the artisan well in the town, the men had adequate drinking water and were able to wash regularly. Mac had forgotten what a blessing it was to have his hair washed and his face and hands clean. While the weather was good, Mac and his unit spent much of their time outdoors. Without a doubt, Alabama was hot in the summer, but the green around the prison was shaded by trees, and most days a breeze blew across the Alabama River. Inside the warehouse-turned prison, the temperatures were unbearable, and with only four windows to ventilate the entire building, the air was sweltering during the daytime.

    Outdoors, time passed more quickly than when they were confined inside the warehouse-turned-prison. Mac used most of his free time to get better acquainted with the men he'd been assigned to look after. A few had become good friends. Drew Mayfield and the giant from Tennessee, Richard Pierce, and Mac had become an almost inseparable trio. Together, they kept their unit healthy, as content as possible in Castle Morgan, and most importantly, out of spats with other units. Personally, the men built a comradery, leading them to share details of their lives before they became Union prisoners. Often in the evenings after he read scripture to those who chose to listen, Mac and his two pals would find themselves sitting near the stone fireplace talking about home.

Drew asked one night, "Mac, do ya think we're ever gonna get out of this place?"

"Wish I knew the answer to that question. Ya know, in all the frettin' I did about goin' to war or not goin' to war, I never even considered I'd be sittin' in a Reb prison. I thought I might die. I even talked to my pa about that. My son Roy got killed at Corinth two years ago, but to waste away like this. I never imagined."

"Seems so senseless," Tennessee said. "Neither side can afford to take care of all the men they lock up. I'm so sick of cornmeal mush. If I ever get home, I'll never eat corn again."

"If I ever get home, I won't leave again. I promised Laurel so many times. I miss my wife. Without her, a part of me is just gone."

"Mac, you got it bad. I hope it's not catchin'."

"Tennessee, it'd be the best sickness you ever got. I wished I'd packed up my family and gone west. We talked about it, but we love our homestead. After what's happened though, I believe we coulda built a new life in Colorado or Nebraska. What scares me most is not knowin'. Lord, I hope they have what they need."

"She must be truly beautiful for you to miss her that much."

"You've seen her picture, Drew."

"Well, those photographs don't do justice to most people."

"Hey, Drew, you sayin' the captain's missus ain't so much to look at?" Tennessee teased.

"I didn't say that." Drew threw a tin cup he'd been holding.

"You two knotheads! Ain't no picture that can show how beautiful Laurel is. She is a good woman. Her worth comes from inside. This woman adopted my son. She loves him like he's her own. She adopted two of her students when their grandmother was killed in an ice storm. She adopted her goddaughter when her parents were killed in the Mt. Meadow Massacre. Laurel was alone when she miscarried our first child. I didn't make it back from a trip when I promised, but she forgave me. Laurel Grace MacLayne is the most beautiful woman on this earth."

"She sure has a big heart, Captain." Drew smiled at his friend.

"I hope ya built her a big house! All those kids!" Tennessee punched Mac on the shoulder and smiled.

Toward the middle of October, Mother Nature stepped in to change the routine for Castle Morgan's residents. The days were still mild, but the rain became more frequent and nights became too cool for comfort. On rainy days, the men cursed the 1,600 foot hole in the roof for good reason. Men whose sleeping areas were under that hole scrambled to find a place in the dry. Since the prison population had risen to more than a thousand, space not already assigned was non-existent. The push away from the open roof crowded men into spaces that would not allow them to lie down anymore. Those on the floor could claim less than five feet and the tight quarters set tempers on edge. Fights broke out nearly every day, especially among the units that had made no effort to develop bonds among the men. Mac and other unit leaders were in the middle of more brawls than Mac wanted to remember.

Halloween day was miserable. The entire population had been cooped up all day, as the rain began before sun up and didn't stop until well after taps sounded. Many of the bunks around the walls held two men, and those who were pushed into smaller places on the floor found it almost impossible to get out of the water and mud. Temperatures fell into the thirties. The fire roared in the one fireplace at the end of the cavernous hall, but the heat hardly touched anyone. Many of the scattered campfires inside the building were soaked by the rain.

Mac and his men in their assigned area to the right of the fireplace felt no warmth, but they were a good distance from the open roof. Using teamwork, they arranged a camp around a central

357

fire, which did allow them some comfort. They also rotated places so all in their unit could have the benefit of the heat. Unfortunately, not all groups had learned the teamwork as Reverend Henderson asked.

A couple of hours after taps, a private from Ohio who'd been crammed into an area out of the wet zone jumped up and yelled. He jerked up a corporal who lay at his head and slammed his fist into his face. "Dang it, man. I've asked ya to stop kickin' me in the head five times. Well, you've kicked me for the last time. It's bad enough I'm soaked to the bone and freezin' to death. You tryin' to kick my brains in is too much."

The corporal fought back. Together they stumbled over other men lying nearby. Within seconds, ten or twelve men had joined the brawl. Other men crouched back to get out of the fray. Chaos broke out across the barracks, and men far from the original fight began to throw punches and scream.

Three shots rang out from the scaffolds about the prison floor. Then three more. Silence followed. Guards lit lanterns. Two men lay dead on the dirt floor. Others were wounded.

A Confederate guard yelled down, "You prisoners, get back to your places, and don't ya get up again. If another escape attempt happens, more of you Yanks will meet yer maker this night. Now move it and get back to where you belong."

No attempt was made to aid the wounded until the guards called in more help. They carried four men out and removed the bodies of the two who died. The following morning, Reverend Henderson called the unit leaders to his office to inquire about the fight and the escape attempt from the previous night. The twenty-seven unit leaders had been brought in after the prison guards had already told their side of the story. Of course, they felt ill at ease, not sure of what was expected of them. The leader of the unit where the fight started denied any knowledge of an escape attempt. He reported the man who started the brawl was not in his unit at all. Two others who were assigned nearby also hem-hawed around the issue.

"MacLayne, you're square with me. Can you tell me what happened last night?" Colonel Henderson asked.

"Reverend Henderson, I was at the far end of the room, but I did hear someone yell out that he'd been kicked in the head several times. I didn't hear or see anything that looked to be an escape attempt."

"But the guard said before he shot, men were runnin' toward him. He said the fight was a ploy to distract them.

"Sir, it was pitch black in there. With the rain and clouds, there wasn't even moonlight or stars out. The guard didn't light the area until after the shots. That much I know is true."

Henderson looked over the group of leaders. "Do you agree with what MacLayne just told me?" Several nodded and a couple said that was what happened. "All right. I'll deal with this. Is there anything else since I've got y'all here?"

One leader spoke up, "Commander, this fight and others that happen nearly every day are caused by overcrowding. When it rains, men are packed in like cordwood in a rick."

Another said, "That gaping hole in the roof makes things worse. With winter comin'—well, most of the men are wet and freezin' now."

"Men, I'm aware of the supply shortage." Henderson's somber face reflected his understanding of the complaints.

"Reverend, one of the worst problems is nothing to do. Time is a huge enemy. If we had books, cards, or scraps of paper to write letters home. Anything that could help pass the time would ease the tension in the barracks," Mac said.

"I know it all too well. Dismissed. Try to keep your units under control." Henderson turned his back and slumped into the chair at his desk.

Later that same afternoon while Mac and his unit were walking the perimeter of the green, Reverend Henderson came around the corner of the building. He motioned to Mac.

"Drew, why not hold some races to kill some time. I'll be back shortly." He walked the short distance to meet with the commandant. "Yes, sir."

"MacLayne, again I'm in your debt. We found out that the shooting last night was a mistake. Raw recruit, his first night on the scaffold. Nerves got to him when the fight broke out. He shot into the air and screamed out. A couple of other guards thought he'd been attacked, and they began shooting. All because of the dark…We'll not have a repeat of that. As long as we have kerosene, we'll keep a light burning. Senseless loss."

"Yes, sir. Thanks for the update. I'll share it. The men will feel better."

"One other thing. I've gotta be away for a while. I don't like to go off and leave Lt. Col. Jones in charge. We don't see eye-to-eye on the treatment of prisoners."

"What can I do?"

"Try to keep the peace. Jones doesn't need much reason to punish a man for any infraction of rules. Appears to me, he looks for chances to beat men or take away rations, meager as they are."

"I can do that with my unit, but others aren't so easy to handle."

"Maybe you could plan a tournament of some kind like you did back in the summer. Anything to help with morale and order. I don't want a repeat of last night."

"I'll do what I can. Good travel, Reverend."

"You know, Captain, if we weren't on opposite sides of this infernal conflict, I believe we'd be friends."

"I believe we are, Reverend Henderson. Thank you for the fair treatment you've given me. You've offered grace here to all who will accept it."

"I know you're a believer, MacLayne…"

"Mac is enough."

"Mac, how long have you walked with our Lord?"

"I wish I could say all my life. My mother tried to show me, but I had my rebellious years. In '52, my best friend, an old Methodist circuit rider, and the Lord brought me to my knees. I've tried to walk in grace since then. I failed more'n a few times, but He always helps me back up."

"I knew you had a Wesleyan strain. Well, I've got things to attend to, but Mac, try to keep the men alive while I'm gone. I'm still working on that Christmas exchange. Keep the faith—Maybe you'll be home for the New Year."

As fall temperatures edged downward, more and more prisoners fell ill with coughs, chills, and pneumonia. Most had no cover to provide any semblance of warmth at night. Some men lacked jackets or coats because those things had been lost on battlefields or during transport to this prison. Some had fallen victim to thieves. As the population of Castle Morgan grew by a hundred men or so every week, the need for winter clothes and blankets grew to a crisis level.

Reverend Henderson had no luck getting supplies from the Confederate military. His pleas to Richmond had been largely ignored by the legislature there, too. He felt no recourse but to ask the local citizens of Cahaba to provide what aid they could. He visited the local churches, asking the congregations to consider the plight of the men who were dying for the lack of a coat or a blanket. He was blessed. Many people responded, and little by little, an old quilt found in an attic, a coat too worn out for a well-dressed citizen, or a frayed floor mat found its way to Cahaba prison. Some local sewing and knitting groups made new scarfs and mittens. Enemy soldiers locked up in the small Alabama town began to have some of their needs met. Of course, the entire population of the town was little more than the number of men locked in the stockade so they weren't able to meet all the needs; however, the gifts were welcomed and gave many men hope that had all but disappeared.

Just outside the stockade of the prison sat an average-sized family home made of white clapboard siding. Its back porch faced the prison. In the backyard was a well-kept garden plot, a chicken pen, and a covered well. Mac had seen a woman sitting on the porch with a young girl who looked to be about Gracie's age. Neither reminded him of those he loved back home, both being quite fair and blonde, but he enjoyed watching the scenes of home life he saw there. Those were the things that brought him the images from Shiloh.

One afternoon, Mac saw Reverend Henderson walking inside the stockade with the blonde girl from the porch. He could hardly believe his eyes. Surely, allowing a child inside a prison camp was not a standard practice in Confederate prisons. When they got a bit closer, he saw both the girl and Henderson carried several books.

"Afternoon, MacLayne. How's the Arky's Unit?"

"We're doin' all right. Tryin' to survive the cold. Some of the men are sharin' what they have."

"Good to hear. Have you met Belle Gardner?"

"No. How do you do Miss Gardner?"

"Very well, thank you. Would you like a book to read?" she said.

"Yes, I'd love one. That's so thoughtful for you to share your books with us, Miss."

"The books belong to my mama. We live right there." The girl pointed toward the house just beyond the stockade. "See my mama on the porch? Her name's Amanda Gardner."

"Will you thank her for me? I'll return the book soon."

"MacLayne, how many of your men are sleeping on the ground?" Henderson asked.

"All of us. They offered me a bunk a few weeks back when one came open but it was too far from my men. Most of my men sleep on the dirt now because they need their coats and jackets to cover themselves."

"Conditions are deplorable and getting worse with each new man that comes in. I've asked for supplies but haven't gotten any yet. I'll go again and demand some relief. I promise I will."

"We've had some help when a few coats came in and a quilt or two. Even those scarves have been nice. The men know you got those things for us."

"The people of this town helped some, but they can't give us all we need. Mrs. Gardner and Belle have been real angels. I wish I had a dozen like them."

"I'll ask mama to see if we can find some more pallets. Her friends might be able to help some, too," Belle told Mac.

"Bless you, Darlin'. You and your mama are God's way of answerin' our prayers. Please remember to tell your mother thank you for all she does."

"MacLayne, enjoy the story. *Robinson Crusoe* is a good read-aloud book. I'll bet your men will enjoy it." Henderson took Belle's hand and continued his rounds to deliver the books.

The next afternoon Mac and seven other unit leaders were taken across the street. Reverend Henderson and a blonde woman greeted them in the foyer of the office building. Behind them lay a stack of woolen carpet pieces cut into pallet sizes. Each leader was given two of the sections to use in their units.

"I'm sorry I didn't have more to use, but I have a warm, tight house. I don't need these rugs to keep me and mine warm. I only had enough to make eighteen pallets, I'm afraid. I believe some of my friends will come up with some old rugs they can spare. Maybe it will help some."

"Mrs. Gardner, you cut up all your floor coverings to give to us?" Mac asked.

"Not all. My mother-in-law gave me a woolen Persian rug as a weddin' present. I didn't have the heart to cut that one up, but the others can be replaced someday."

"God bless you, Ma'am," Reverend Henderson bowed over her hand and kissed it.

"I'm doin' no more than the Lord has charged us to do. How can I not look to those in prison with Castle Morgan bein' in my back yard?"

The mercy Mac saw in Mrs. Gardner took his prayers in a new direction. After the conversations with Belle and Amanda Gardner, he felt a wellspring of hope. He knew there were some he needed to forgive as well. Mac began to talk with the Lord about when he got home instead of if he got home. He took to heart Reverend Henderson's promise of exchange, so his vision of homecoming became almost a reality in his mind. Mac made his resolution for 1865 before December even started.

## φ

Mac's optimism lasted about four days after the second in command at Cahaba took the reins. Lt. Colonel Samuel Jones had arrived at Cahaba in late June of 1864. Jones was the opposite of Henderson in about every way possible. He had chafed under Henderson's compassionate leadership style and disagreed with nearly every policy the kind minister had put in place at Castle Morgan. Jones's cruelty to the prisoners and his absolute dictatorship over his staff made life at the prison brutal. Reverend Henderson had not been gone two weeks when the first fatal incident occurred.

At the end of November, the temperatures moderated in South Alabama, and the rain held off for more than a week. Mac and two other unit leaders asked permission to take their units outside for exercise. The barrack guards, happy to reduce the huge numbers inside, granted their request for a baseball game.

The Arky's Unit took the field against a team from Illinois and Indiana. All the men were excited to be outside and playing the game they'd come to love. To be outside in the fresh air and with space to stretch and run was a blessing after being cramped inside for more than two weeks. The teams were evenly matched and quite competitive to boot. Near the end of the game, the Double I team sent their best batter to the plate. Mac motioned his men who were playing the field to move farther back. A youngster from Missouri named Private David Varner moved three steps back, putting him within ten feet or so of the stockade fence. Drew Mayfield, Mac's best pitcher slung a fastpitch across the wood plank serving as the plate. The burly sergeant from Illinois smacked the ball with the branch, sending it arching into the cloudless sky. A shot rang out and a second one. All the prisoners fell to the ground across the green. Lt. Col. Jones strutted across the scaffold above the playing area. Another shot rant out.

"Cease firing. The escape attempt is over," Jones yelled. "Prisoners, fall into rank. Now."

The prisoners began to merge into their units, but as Mac's unit started to move toward the front, Private Varner didn't get up from where he'd fallen. Mac and Mel Grigsby ran toward the field.

"Halt. Take another step, and I'll order the guards to fire. I said fall into ranks."

"Colonel, I have a man down. I wanted…" A shot flew over Mac's head. Both Mac and Grigsby fell to the ground.

"Damn, Mac. That Reb is insane." Grigsby whispered.

"No. He's just playin' war. Power-hungry like the rest."

"What are we gonna do about Varner? Damn, he's just a kid."

"Pray is about all we can do." They inched their way back to the unit and stood at attention for the next half hour while the commander spouted his new rules for Castle Morgan. When he dismissed the prisoners, Mac and Grigsby returned with several members of their unit to carry Private Varner to the gate to ask for the doctor. He didn't need a doctor. Varner had been shot through the heart with a single bullet. Mac knew he'd died instantly.

That afternoon, Mac was called to the commandant's office. "You the unit leader of that dead prisoner?"

"Yes, sir."

"Who planned the escape attempt this mornin'?"

"That wasn't an escape attempt. We were playin' baseball."

"Don't call me a liar, Captain. You'll find yourself in solitary." Mac stood in silence. "Now, answer my question."

"I can't tell you what I don't know. The boy who died was a part of a team made up of men in my unit. He was playin' baseball."

"What's yer name, Yank?" Jones barked.

"Captain Patrick MacLayne, Second Arkansas Cavalry."

"Arkansas? Traitor to the Confederacy. Worse than I thought. Got a traitor in charge of a unit of Yanks. No wonder they're out of control, tryin' to escape." Mac made no response. "Ain't ya got enough gumption to defend yerself, MacLayne?" Again, he was silent. "I'm gonna give ya one more chance to defend yerself before I throw ya in the box. Speak up."

"That boy, Private David Varner, a recruit this year from St. Louis, had been at Castle Morgan about a month when you had the guards murder him. He was trying to catch a flyball hit by a sergeant from Illinois. Private Varner won the game for us. He had the ball in his hand when we carried him to the doctor. That is my report. Now you can do with it what you will." Mac moved from attention to rest with his arms behind him.

Jones's face turned blood red. He sputtered in an attempt to respond. "Ya done yerself no favor here today You think Cahaba is a hell hole. Let's see how much you like Andersonville. It'll take me a few days to get you transferred, but a couple of days in isolation may take part of the starch outta the stiff Yankee backbone."

Jones called for the guard. He ordered Mac to be moved to the isolation box beside the latrines. The box was about the size of an outhouse, made of four plank walls and a tin roof. There was one small hole about the size of a gallon jug near the roof for air and illumination. The three-foot-square building was big enough for a man to sit or stand, but not to lie down. Colonel Henderson had not allowed the use of the vertical coffin during his time at Cahaba. Unfortunately, Lt. Col. Jones felt no need to observe the directives of his superior.

Mac slept through the first night curled into a ball on the dirt floor. The day was much worse as time seemed to stand still. The confined space denied any movement beyond turning around or squatting. When a prisoner had to relieve himself, he had to choose a place that he may be able to avoid later. Mac tried to pray and he did thank God it was winter. Time spent in the box in the summer would have been more than a human could bear—heat, sweat, odors from the latrine, insects—Yes, winter was a blessing. At sundown each day, a cup of water and a wedge of pone was shoved through the slot in the door, his sole rations for the day.

Mac survived through day two and day three. By the fourth day, he lost all sense of time and place. About noon, the guard jerked the door open. Mac nearly fell as he'd been leaning against it. He squinted at the brilliance of the sun after spending nearly a hundred hours in the dark. After his eyes adjusted to the light, he recognized Reverend Henderson, who seemed to be speaking to him. Mac swayed, unable to stand after being cramped for so long. His eyes darted from place to place around the prison yard.

"MacLayne, can you hear me, Son?" Reverend Henderson yelled.

"Water, please."

"Get this man some water. Then carry him over to the hospital. Quick." Henderson ordered the guards.

Dr. Whitefield's touch to Mac's forehead told him immediately that Mac had a high fever. He listened to his chest and back. "Reverend, it's a good thing you got him out of that box. Another day and he'd probably have died. I'm guessin' a touch of pneumonia has set in. I'll see what I can do."

"Keep him with us, Ray. He's a good man. He's been a big help to me."

When Mac had recuperated enough to hold a coherent conversation, Rev. Henderson came to the hospital to ask about what had landed him in solitary.

"MacLayne, what did you do to get sideways with Jones so fast? I wasn't gone two weeks."

"Tried to do what you asked. Keep the men occupied. We were playin' baseball."

"Jones's report was more than vague. Something about you aidin' an escape attempt and insubordination."

"You didn't see my report, I take it," Mac said.

"Jones wrote you refused to explain."

"Not true. I refused to confirm his lies."

"Tell me your side of the story." Mac began to cough and continued until he was breathless. Henderson helped him sit up to relieve the congestion. Dr. Ray Whitefield brought a cup of tea made from berries, tree bark, and honey, a natural remedy he used for croup. When Mac was able, he explained how Private Varner had been murdered during the ballgame.

"I knew it was something like that. Jones is so bitter. He takes his grief out on anyone who wears Union blue. His son died at Gettysburg, so he gets revenge any place he can. That's three men who've died in senseless shootings since he got here in July. I wish I could get rid of him, but Ray, no one even seems to know how he came to be here."

Henderson paced the floor in the make-shift hospital. "Ray, will MacLayne get well?"

"I think so. He'll need a few more days of rest and a lot of that awful tea to clear out that congestion in his lungs, but you got him here in time."

At the end of that week, Rev. Henderson came to escort Mac back to his place with the Arky's Unit. He began to talk to Mac as soon as they left the earshot of any in the hospital.

"Mac, I went to find you as soon as I returned from the exchange meeting. I am glad I did. I wouldn't have seen the punishment roster until the next day."

"Thank you for intervening. You probably saved my life. And I do want to go home."

"That's what I need to tell you. Grant has refused to exchange any more prisoners. He says that putting those Confederate officers back into the battlefield is lengthening the war. I tried to explain about our extreme overcrowding and lack of supplies. He said he knew, but war is hell. We have men to spare, but the Confederacy doesn't."

"I understand. I wish I didn't, but if I was Grant and could stop this insanity, I'd keep some of my men in prison, too. Let's pray it'll be over soon for all of us."

"I've got one other piece of bad news—maybe not so bad for me—I'm being reassigned. Next week, I'm bein' sent to Richmond to co-ordinate all prison supplies and prisoner exchanges, whenever they can be negotiated. I may get to come back briefly, but I'm afraid some think I'm too lenient."

"Who will be in charge here, sir?"

"Temporarily, Lt. Col. Jones. I will try to remedy that as soon as I am able. Once I reach Richmond, I'll try to get him replaced."

"Oh, dear Lord. Please don't leave us in his hands, Rev. Henderson."

"Mac, you know as well as I do, since this conflict started, we've all been in His hands. You hang on to your faith, take care of your men, and He will take care of you."

# Chapter 30

*Out of the depths have I cried unto thee,*
*O Lord. Lord, hear my voice;*
*let thine ears be attentive to the voice of my supplication.*
*Psalms 130: 1-2*

Macky was a beautiful child. His birth blessed everyone in the MacLayne household—everyone except Laurel. After the brief kiss she brushed across his pink forehead, she fell into the drugged sleep produced by the laudanum. Dr. Cavanaugh administered it as soon as he'd assured himself the baby could be safely delivered. The surgery and the complications of Macky's breeched position caused tremendous blood loss and extensive sutures to stop the bleeding. Laurel would have no more children.

The pain from the impromptu surgery and Laurel's already deep melancholy provided the ideal climate for her to withdraw. Sleep, even the unnatural kind rendered by the opium shut out her grief, her worry, and the demands of life at Shiloh. For a while, others carried her burdens, and she retreated from the life she didn't want to face.

Cortland Cavanaugh made a daily visit to the cabin, first to assure himself that infection and childbed fever had no opportunity to take Laurel. He also knew the dangers of too much laudanum too often. During the time he'd treated men with severe injury from battle, he'd witnessed too many of them become dependent on the drug long after their wounds had healed. The second disease was worse than the first.

His worst concern was that Laurel had little interest in returning to her role as mother and head of her household. Her father-in-law, her uncle, and her two oldest children had taken every responsibility out of her hands. Annie had taken charge of the new baby. The first two weeks when he'd used the pain medicine, Laurel could not feed Macky. After a quick search for a wet-nurse, Annie remembered a strange porcelain vessel her grandmother had given her. It resembled a small teapot with a long narrow spout. The tip of the spout had three small holes in it that allowed diluted cow's milk to be suckled by a baby. Macky didn't take to it well, but he would nurse from the pot for a few minutes at a time when he was hungry. The doctor also brought an implement he called a pap spoon. Aunt Ellie tried to pour milk into Macky's mouth with the small silver spoon but soaked both of them in a very short time. Between the two substitutes, the baby got some nourishment, but he was never satisfied. He cried a great deal.

The doctor decided Laurel must take over the role of feeding her new son, so he weaned her off the pain medicine. Cortland believed the maternal act could be the key to bringing Laurel back to her family. He decided to call a family meeting.

"Folks, Macky is now more'n two weeks old. Laurel will recover. She has no sign of childbed fever, and her surgery is healin'. She's still weak because she lost a lot of blood, but her strength will return in time. Right now, she's gotta want to get back to her routine. She don't have to because y'all do everything that she normally does. It's time for you to get back to your lives so she has to come back to hers."

"But, Dr. Cavanaugh, can Laurel take over runnin' this homestead now?"

"Mr. MacLayne, the first time I ever saw your daughter-in-law, she was holding off a troop of twelve men with one gun to prevent them from cuttin' down her apple orchard. She can do what she has to do."

Peggy MacLayne spoke up, "But Doctor Cavenaugh, Laurel has lost so much. She has not been the same since we found out that we lost Mac. The family is worried about her."

"Bless ya, dear Peggy. I know ya are, but right now we've gotta give her a reason to get out of that bed and come back to her family. The baby needs to be fed, but even more, they need to build a bond."

"What do you want us to do?" Matthew Campbell asked.

"Go home. Go about your own business. Visit a couple of times a week, but force Laurel to get back into her routine."

"Sounds kinda heartless."

"Reverend Campbell, makin' a cripple of your best friend's wife is heartless. We ain't desertin' her. We're bein' the neighbors we're called to be, but sometimes good neighbors gotta remember where the fence lines are." They put The first step of the plan into motion that afternoon.

Laurel sat in the four-poster, her hair wound into its coronet. She stitched a piece of lace onto the collar of a dress she was making for Leah Ann. Cortland entered the second pen with Macky in his arms. The baby squirmed and wailed. He was hungry.

"Good afternoon, Laurel. Time to feed this boy. He's surely got some healthy lungs to scream so loud."

"What about the laudanum?"

"You've not had any for a few days. It's safe. The cow's milk we've been usin' has been all right, but not what the boy needs. I think you can feed him."

"I'm not sure…"

"Laurel, your son needs his stomach filled. And you need to get to know him. I seem to remember about two weeks ago, you begged me to give you a healthy baby. Are you gonna let him starve?"

Laurel undid her lawn nightdress and began to feed the beautiful baby for the first time. He pulled hungrily at her breast and laid his tiny hand on her face. Without thought, she cradled him and tilted her head to nuzzle his cheek. She smelled his clean baby scent. Precious memories of the births of Leah Ann and Mark

371

Thomas came flooding back. How she'd loved those earliest days of new life. Tears flowed down her cheeks. This child was a precious gift, Mac's son.

"I'll see you tomorrow, Laurel. Call Cathy when you're finished. You can get up tomorrow, but only to sit in the rocking chair. Understand?"

She nodded and returned her attention to her son.

Cortland Cavanaugh visited the next day and nearly every afternoon the next couple of weeks. Laurel followed his instructions. She dressed every day and fed Macky and sat in her rocking chair. Yet the melancholy she continued to live with since she'd been told of Mac's death remained a very real part of the life at Shiloh. Andy and Cathy continued to maintain the homestead. Annie mothered the smaller children, only taking Macky to Laurel when he had to be fed. Even then, she hated to ask her to feed the little boy because Laurel cried whenever she held him for any length of time. The doctor saw little improvement in the family situation by the time Macky was a month old, except that the baby had gained the expected amount of weight because he was being fed regularly. Cortland had to intervene if Laurel was going to get past the depth of her grief.

He went to talk with Matthew Campbell once again.

"Brother Matthew, you are Laurel's uncle and have known her most of her life. Why has she moved into this depth of melancholy? I was sure that taking over Macky's care would help snap her out of it."

"I don't know except she has lost a great many people she has loved in this lifetime. Her mother, a sister, a brother, her father, Roy, her first child, and now Mac are all members of her immediate family. She has always been dependent on family love and support. Since she's been in Shiloh, I've seen her faith grow. I thought she'd developed a strong enough connection to lean on the Lord, but I guess losin' Mac was just too much. I don't know what to tell ya."

"I don't want to cause her any more hurt, but I've seen what can happen if melancholia gets too deep and lasts too long. Some people withdraw from the world. During the time I worked in an asylum back in medical school, I saw many people who turned their backs on life."

"You don't think that is gonna happen to Laurel, do ya?"

"Didn't you tell me she did something like that when she was a girl after an attack by some boys from her school?"

"Well, she didn't withdraw exactly. She just stayed home with her father...."

"For more than twelve years, did ya say?"

"Yes, but she went out to church and took care of her father's house."

"And hid away her entire young adulthood. No, I think we have to intervene in some way. She's been blockin' all this out too long. If she needs to grieve, let it be. If she needs to have a tantrum, that's better than burying herself to prevent admittin' the truth."

"What are ya gonna do?"

"I don't know for sure, yet. I will need to talk with Mr. MacLayne first. I may seem to be pretty heartless for a while."

"What do you mean?" Matthew Campbell scowled.

"I think the Bible speaks somewhere about the truth will set us free. Sometimes, the truth appears pretty harsh."

"John 8:32. What truth do you need to share to set you free, Cort?"

"What are you talkin' about, Matthew?"

"Why all this effort and concern for my niece?"

"She's my patient. I'd do as much for anyone who's hurtin' like Laurel is."

"Coulda swore that concern in your voice and the look on your face meant somethin' more. Maybe I'm just a pryin' ole preacher."

"Matthew, I have admired Laurel since the first time I laid eyes on her. She's courageous, spirited, and as determined as any person I've ever met. She's a great lady and a faithful, loving person. Good people like her are in short supply. We gotta keep 'em around."

"And?"

"And what?" Cortland picked up his hat and headed to the door. "I've grown attached to those kids. I just want to see things go well for Laurel's family."

"Uh, huh."

"Good afternoon. Just remember when I seem cruel and in her face, I warned ya. I'll need ya to let me do my job."

℔

Laurel sat on the front porch one late October afternoon. She had just finished nursing Macky and was rocking him to sleep. She motioned for Cathy to take him to the cradle inside. Gracie walked over with a hairbrush and started to crawl into Laurel's lap.

"Gracie, what are you doing?"

"Mama, make my hair like yours, please."

"Your hair looks fine the way it is. Didn't Cathy fix your ponytails this morning?"

"Yes, 'em, but I wanna be like you. I love your braids, Mama. They look like a crown. If I had some, I could be a princess."

"Gracie, I'm too tired. Don't be so silly. Braids don't make you a princess." Laurel snapped at the little girl and put her down from her lap.

Gracie began to cry. Through her tears, she said, "I'm sorry, Mama. I didn't mean to bother you when you are tired. Don't be mad at me." She vanished around the side of the cabin.

Laurel rose to go after her, and she saw Cortland standing at the other end of the porch.

"What did that sweet girl do to deserve that scoldin', Laurel?"

"What are you talking about?"

"I heard you growl at her... 'Don't be so silly.' What did she want from you? Did she ask you to show her a bit of attention?" Cortland stepped toward Laurel.

"Excuse me, I need to go find her and talk with her."

"You did enough talkin' to her for now. She understood you just fine. What you said to her is you don't mean enough to me for me to spend my time on you. You need to take a walk instead."

"Why should I do that?" Laurel squared her shoulders and crossed her arms in front of her.

"Because I am your doctor, and you need some exercise. You've been sittin' around quite a bit since your baby came." Cortland took her arm and led her down the steps and out toward the apple orchard. "You know the first time I saw you in this orchard, I thought you had a lot of gumption. I'd never seen a lady stand up to protect anything the way you stood up for those trees."

"What are you getting at?"

"Gracie is worth a million of these trees. You have all the strength in the world if you feel something you care about is in danger. Can't you spare concern for your children?"

"I still don't know what you're getting at. Anyway, I'm tired. I'm gonna go take a nap."

"I don't think so. You need a walk more than more sleep." The doctor took her arm and pulled her along with him as he walked through the trees, which were nearly leafless now.

"What are you trying to do?"

"Help an uncooperative patient get a bit of exercise."

"Let me go. You are a great bully sometimes."

"Like you were to that darlin' little girl who said she wanted to be just like her mama? Like you did when you ignored the comment that if she was like her mama she'd be just like a princess?"

"What?"

"Laurel, do you have any concept of what you did to that sweet child?"

"I just told her that I was tired and her hair looked fine."

"Are you so lost in your grief that you can't see the same loss in your children? Take a few minutes to look at them. See the fear in their faces. They lost their papa. Mac is dead. Those children aren't. They feel they've lost you, too. They mourn too."

"You can't talk to me like this. I love my children."

"Then love their father a little less. Let him go. Give them back their mother."

Laurel drew back and slapped Cortland with all the strength of her being. She turned and ran toward the corral fence. Just before she reached the fence, she tripped at the corner of the trough, falling face-first in the dirt.

Cortland picked her up and set her back on her feet. "I guess I've lost my first name privileges now. Mrs. MacLayne, think about what I've said. I'll see you tomorrow." He handed her back the shawl he'd retrieved and walked back toward his horse.

Laurel was quiet all through supper and hurriedly finished worship time that night. She wanted only to get back to her place of solitude, away from the eyes of her children. With every glance, she felt those beautiful eyes accusing her of the sins laid bare by Cortland Cavanaugh. If she could just retreat to the four-poster and remember the beautiful times she'd spent there with Mac, perhaps those memories would erase the pain she lived with at that moment. If she could make the past real enough, maybe she wouldn't have to think about the present or the future.

But she couldn't sleep. Laurel tossed and turned for hours. She finally got up, lit the lantern on the bureau, and searched through the drawer for the bottle of laudanum. She found the blue vial empty. She returned to bed, frustrated and exhausted.

In the wee hours of the night, she fell into a restless sleep. She tossed and turned, fought with the quilt, and knocked her pillow to the floor. Then the dreams started.

*She rocked in Grandma Wilson's chair back in her father's cabin. The light sifted through the greased-paper windows. The yellowish light from the kerosene lamp produced a gloom across the room. Laurel stood at her father's bed, his carved wooden cross hanging from the bedpost. His cough jerked his emaciated frame. He struggled to breathe. The man who lay in the bed by the fireplace was withered and gray, his face wrinkled beyond recognition. He was so much older than her papa had been. When Laurel looked into her pa's small shaving mirror, she saw the middle-aged, graying image of herself.*

*"Laurel, Darlin', I'm goin' to be with your mama soon. I'm sorry I couldn't take care of ya. Never meant to leave ya behind as a spinster with no one to take care of ya."*

*"Papa, don't worry about me. Daniel's gonna take me in to live with him. I can teach his children."*
*"I shoulda found ya a husband..."*
*"No, Papa. Remember, I'm plain. I'm plain."*

Laurel awoke, trembling at the hurtful dream. Macky began to cry. Laurel realized it was near two o'clock in the morning, the time that the tiny replica of her husband expected to be fed. She lit the lantern and went to pick him up from his cradle. His storm-blue eyes captured hers. Almost as if audible, Laurel felt the words Mac had spoken to her the last time they'd shared the bed. 'Laurel, I love you beyond my tellin'. Please take care of our kids, and take care of yourself. I love you. So very much wife, I do love you."

"No, Papa. You gave me that life. I have had a husband, and he loved me. I know what it is to be cherished and worthy. Why did you bring me such a painful memory when I am already so sad?" Laurel began to cry, sobbing as if her heart had been torn apart with grief. She poured out her anger, her fear, her loneliness, all the negative emotions she'd carried since July were laid open. She admitted to herself what she'd not been able to accept. Mac was gone. She rose and laid Macky back into his cradle. "Your papa charged me to take care of y'all. He loved his children. I'll find my way back somehow." She went to her grandmother Wilson's rocking chair and slumped into it. Humming the tune to *'Jesus, Lover of my Soul'*, she drifted into a dreamless sleep.

The rising sun gilded the hills of Crowley's Ridge. The cock's shrill call echoed across the hillsides and over the dewy valley beneath. Laurel still sat in her grandmother Wilson's rocking chair—not moving. Her blank eyes were unaware of the dying embers in the fireplace at her feet. Clinched in her fingers so tightly that her knuckles had taken on the pallor of death was the old whittled cross that had hung above her father's bed, the one Mac had carried with him the first time and every time they'd been separated. Through her swollen, tear-blurred eyes, she looked at the discolored wood and the dirty rawhide cord. She didn't remember taking it from the bureau drawer last night. As if a weight too heavy to bear rested on her shoulders, Laurel pushed herself from the rocking chair. She stood there, unsure why she'd arisen from the seat. Her shoulders drooped, and her head fell into her hands. Tears again flowed unchecked down her cheeks, yet not one sound came from her mourning.

"Stop it, Laurel Grace...You've got to pull yourself together. You have a family to care for." Although the admonition was not spoken, she heard it. The message was as clear as any she'd ever been given. She pulled the sleeve of her dress across her face to wipe away her tears, yet the weight of her grief pulled her back into the chair she barely managed to push herself from minutes before. *I won't go on without Patrick. I can't do it. It's too much to bear. God help me. Please...*

Light poured through the windows of their bedroom. Laurel once again pushed herself from the chair and stumbled toward the window, planning to draw the curtains to close out the morning light. As she took two steps forward, she stopped. She gasped at the reflection in the beautiful carved walnut-framed mirror, the last Christmas present Mac had given her. She froze in her tracks. What she saw was not Mrs. Patrick MacLayne, the grieving widow of a man who had cherished and loved her so well. What she saw was the childish, selfish, faithless Spinster of Hawthorn. The image of that silly girl Mac had worked so long and hard to erase with his love, his patience, and his faith in God stared back at her. That awful sight mocked her tears, her love for Mac, and the very foundation of her faith. Had their nearly seven years together been for nothing?

She pulled the mirror from the wall and slammed it against the bureau. The glass shattered into hundreds of pieces and spread across the walnut plank floor of the bedroom. Light danced on the shards of broken glass, laughing at her grief. "No! Mac, you made me a better person. This is not who I am." She dropped to her knees. "Father in Heaven, help me. You promised never to allow more than I could bear to be my portion. Without Your strength, Holy God, I can't live without Patrick. Give me the courage to be the capable, worthy woman he loved. Please."

# Chapter 31

*We glory in tribulations also: knowing that tribulation worketh*
*patience; And patience, experience, and experience, hope.*
*Romans 5:3-4*

"Why, Lord? Why did you let me dream I was goin' home and then dash all hope?" Mac cried out his pain. Not since the day he'd mourned the loss of his first son on the creekbank at Shiloh had he been so angry with God. Two pieces of bad news like those Reverend Henderson brought had been a blow Mac was ill-prepared to hear. Coming only a few days after he'd returned from the Bell Tavern hospital, the disappointment had taken an emotional toll on him as devastating as the four days in the box had taken on his physical strength.

Yet his role as the unit leader did not stop. He felt an obligation to watch over the thirty-four men, keep them active, boost their morale, and protect them from any danger. How could he do that when he felt he'd lost the last of his strength, energy, and hope? His temper was short and the attentive, compassionate nature he'd tried to present to Arky's unit all but disappeared.

One particularly cold December night after Mac had read a passage from Romans, Tennessee asked, "Captain, do ya think that passage of scripture is talkin' about us?"

"What are you talkin' about?"

379

"I've been tryin' to figure out why we didn't get exchanged as Reverend Henderson said."

"I still don't know what you're gittin' at, Tennessee."

"Didn't ya hear what ya just read to us? I thought all this Bible stuff meant somethin' to you."

Mac couldn't have been more stunned if his friend had socked him in the mouth. He knew the gentle giant was right. He'd read the words without one thought to the message—all because of his disappointment. He turned back to the passage in his Bible and re-read the words. This time he searched for the message Tennessee, a novice to the Word, had understood. Then he spoke, "Please forgive me, Tennessee. You're right. These words are too special to be read as noise. I confess, I've not been much of a leader since I came back from Bell Tower hospital. I know better, but I just haven't been actin' better."

"It's been hard on all of us, Mac. Disappointment hurts almost as bad as this dagnab cold," Drew replied.

"Fellas, we gotta keep it together. If we lose our faith, we'll lose our determination to get out of here. I want to go home."

"Mac, I wouldn't have faith to lose if you hadn't been here for us. I hate this place, but I'll thank the Lord for the one good thing that came out of it. I don't know if I'd have ever met the Lord without these hard times and you."

"Thanks, Tennessee. You don't know how much I needed to hear that." Mac's prayer that night was one of repentance but also of gratitude. He saw some purpose for the time he'd spent at Cahaba, and he'd grown from his friendship with the men he'd served. His time had not been spent in vain.

Mac redoubled his efforts to see to the welfare of the Arky's unit. He scheduled exercise times outside when the weather allowed, and he and his men always scouted for broken limbs, scrap lumber, or any other source of fuel for their fire. He continued to read from whatever book Belle Gardner loaned him that week. The unit tried to find ways to alter their fare by putting their portions together and baking johnnycakes in a scavenged piece of a broken skillet. These things helped a little, but the cold was a difficult obstacle to overcome.

Then Lt. Col. Jones became the lord and master of Castle Morgan. Reverend Henderson had probably not even reached the Alabama state line when Jones began to overhaul the rules. One of the first things he ordered was a change in the barracks guards. Anyone that seemed to be too soft on inmate discipline was moved to stockade duty or perimeter guard posts. The barrack guards were men who, like Jones, held bitter opinions of Yankees and kept little reserve in exacting discipline through brutality and vengeance.

That first week, three different Union officers found themselves as residents in solitary confinement—the horizontal coffin Mac had known and two new ones built practically overnight. Entire units were denied rations because one or two men in the troop stepped across Jones's acceptable line of conduct. Mac, Drew, and Tennessee kept a special watch on Arky's unit to keep them away from Jones and his squad of punishers.

Fear became as thick in the Cahaba barracks as the flies and gnats around the cook yard. Jones strutted the stockades daily, smirking as he scanned the room looking for someone to use as an example. When guards beat men for seemingly no reason, the commandant turned a blind eye. This kind of brutal treatment had never happened when Reverend Henderson controlled the prison. To the men at Cahaba, it seemed Jones made the most of every opportunity to exact his revenge on any Union soldier, although few had been at Gettysburg where his son died. Mac and the other unit leaders didn't intervene, not until the incident on December 15th.

The day was a nice one for mid-December. Many prisoners took advantage of the nice weather and went out to walk the yard. Of course, with the number of prisoners as high as it had ever been—about 2,500—the yard was crowded and boisterous. A sergeant named Hawkins, who was a particular favorite of Jones, had pulled stockade duty that afternoon. He'd tried to get a couple of men to swap duty assignments with him, but no one agreed. He'd not been on the twelve-foot scaffold ten minutes when he shot into a crowd of men and killed a Union lieutenant from Pennsylvania. Three days later, Hawkins again killed another prisoner while the man carried a large kettle back to the cook yard

for the Confederate sergeant who'd called him out of his unit to
help. The very next day a third man, this time a major from
Maryland was shot in the back. Fortunately, his aim was off and
the major was carried to the hospital.

Mac met with a few of the other unit leaders after the third
shooting. He knew the men were ready to revolt and attack the
guards, which would only lead to more deaths and injuries. He
promised his unit he would try to find a solution to the senseless
killing.

"This man's gotta be stopped. He's crazy." A colonel in
charge of a group of men from Missouri said.

Mac held up his hands to stop the clamoring. "Men…men.
We gotta be sensible. Jones ain't gonna listen to one of us. We
have to go as a group.

"How many do you think it will take, MacLayne?"

"Must be about seventy units in here now. I'd say at least
half. He can't throw thirty men in the box at the same time.

"All right, who'll go?" a captain from Michigan asked.

"I will," Mac replied. Four others from the group
volunteered. "That makes five. Well, we've got our work cut out
then. We'll have to convince twenty-five more men to go with us
before they shoot that many more innocent men." He started to
walk away, quite disgusted with the lack of gumption shown by the
other leaders.

"Hey, MacLayne, you gonna do the talkin', right?" the
Missouri major said.

"Let's worry about that when we get the other men to back
us up."

Before they could build a group to approach Jones, another
nightmare struck Castle Morgan. One evening while a group of
men was preparing night rations, a teenage guard, who looked to
be about fifteen, walked up and shot two of the cooks at close
range and bayonetted a third man who was stoking the cook fire.
He smiled broadly and walked away.

The unit leaders formed within the hour. They knew the
time to speak out was now or risk more of their men dying in riots.

The committee approached Lt. Col. Jones in the cook yard the next day. Mac had been elected to speak.

"Sir, please give us a minute to talk with you."

Jones glared at the thirty-two men who confronted him. For the briefest moment, fear showed in his eyes. "What the devil do you want?"

"We need to talk about the shootin' and violence that's happened in the past three weeks. The men are mighty edgy and angry."

"I'm lookin' into it." He turned his back and took two steps away.

"Lt. Col. Jones. I'm not sure you understand. There are nearly 2,500 men in that barracks. You have fewer than two hundred guards. I don't want any of my men hurt, but all this random, purposeless killin' is gonna cause a riot. When it starts, lots of men are gonna die. Not all of them will be Union soldiers."

"Captain, are you threatenin' me?" Jones bellowed at Mac.

"No. I'm givin' you the facts. If I were you, I'd get rid of those two who murdered innocent men. They ain't helpin' your cause."

"You stupid Yank. You can't tell me how to run this camp."

"I can tell you this. You are outnumbered twenty to one. That's a mighty uneven battle that will happen if we can't convince our men you are tryin' to take care of this problem."

Jones walked away in a huff. His face was the color of the flag flying over Castle Morgan. The committee had done its job. Hawkins was transferred to Selma within two days, As for the boy assassin, Tennessee learned from one of the friendly Confederate guards the seventeen-year-old had been given a furlough.

"Ya mean they gave him a reward because he killed all those prisoners?"

The guard drawled, "That's what we've heard." Regardless, the violence also took a furlough. Maybe it was just that Christmas was approaching.

The week of Christmas brought blessings for the Cahaba prisoners. Reverend Henderson returned from Richmond. This time he didn't come empty-handed. When he'd made his report to the legislature about the conditions at Cahaba, the legislators permitted him to seek aid from the Federal government for the relief of Union captives at Cahaba. The legislature in Washington honored Henderson's request.

When he arrived at Castle Morgan, a Union steamboat, flying a flag of truce, was sitting at Cahaba port. The steamer was loaded with crate after crate of supplies designated for Cahaba prison. Henderson had obtained more than 2,000 complete uniforms, 4,000 pairs of socks, 1,500 blankets, 100 tin mess kits, and some paper and envelopes. This was an extraordinary Christmas present for the prisoners who were wise enough to appreciate what they had been given.

Unfortunately, too many of the soldiers didn't consider the long-term value of the gifts. The new clothes, blankets, and socks were often bartered to the Confederate guards for extra food. After the meal or two was gone, the promise of the warmth was gone also. Colonel Henderson, although saddened by the lack of foresight, still arranged for the prisoners to have some semblance of a Christmas dinner. There was no turkey, but he'd found plenty of beans cooked with ham chunks to share. He couldn't supply pumpkin pie or cake made with sugar, honey, or molasses as no Confederate soldier had those either. Instead, the citizens of Cahaba supplied sweet potatoes the men roasted in their campfires and then slathered with butter. A good portion of the men had a cup of milk, the first they'd drunk since they'd been confined in Castle Morgan. The day was a blessing.

Mac was doubly blessed. The majority of his men had kept their uniforms, socks, and blankets. This would help them survive the winter yet to come. The best part of his day was the opportunity to write a letter home. For the first time since March when he'd been captured, he had hope that he'd be able to communicate with Laurel and his father. The paper, a single sheet, would let him reassure his family he was alive and would be home soon.

In January 1865, Reverend Henderson left Cahaba prison for the final time as commandant. He carried Mac's letter, which

he'd promised to mail the first time he came to a town with a
postal system that was still carrying mail north. The three weeks
the reverend had been back allowed a return to the livable
conditions he'd fostered. Yet Mac and the other leaders knew that
nothing short of a miracle would keep it that way when Lt. Col.
Jones became the permanent commandant of Castle Morgan. They
began to pray for a miracle.

Mac and his men didn't know that their prayers would be
answered by Mother Nature's intervention. By mid-January, rain
became a daily event along the Alabama and Cahaba rivers. The
water and the winter temperatures made life miserable for both
sides. The overcrowding, mixed with the confinement of the entire
prison population provided the exact conditions for frayed nerves
and short tempers. Brawls broke out constantly among the men
confined in such misery. Instead of looking for men to punish,
Jones had his hands full dealing with the unrest among the
prisoners.

Then in early February, Cahaba's historically greatest
drawback worked its way into the equation for the already
overwhelmed commandant.

"Lt. Col. Jones, we just been told by the local constable that
the Cahaba River's out of her banks." A frightened private ran up
from the town square. "The flood water's gettin' mighty close to
the artisan wells. Some of the buildings to the north are in danger
of floodin' already."

"Be calm, Private. The Cahaba overflows her banks all the
time. Castle Morgan's a good way from that river."

"But we ain't more'n twenty feet from the Alabama, sir."

"You said the Cahaba was a floodin'. That don't mean the
Alabama will flood, too. Besides, the barracks won't flood. Get
back to your post." Jones left his office and pulled his greatcoat
around his neck and ears as he walked the short distance to the
center of town. The private hadn't exaggerated his report. The river
ran the streets at the depth of two and three inches at the lower end
of town, and the rain continued to fall. He saw the merchants along
the streets moving their goods to higher shelves and second floors
of buildings.

Jones hurried back to his office and called in his staff. "Men, I'm afraid we're in for the worst thing that can happen in winter. This flood ain't near over, but I swear we ain't gonna lose one man on our watch. Go order your men to be on full alert. We're gonna have to contain all these Yanks in the barracks. If we let the prisoners out, some will sure try to escape."

"Lt. Col. Jones, do you think the water will get up here?"

"Cahaba is no stranger to floods. I know it's comin'. Just don't know when or how much. We'll have a riot on our hands if we don't show our full force."

"We only got 178 men here to guard all these Yanks."

"Sergeant, I know exactly how many guards I command. I want every last one of them armed and on those scaffolds, now!"

By mid-afternoon, the Cahaba River had made its way to the south side of town. The Alabama River had risen to the tree line, not twenty feet from the prison stockade. And the rain did not stop. The prisoners shuffled around restlessly, and the noise level increased. The head cook was ordered to prepare the evening meal two hours early. Before taps, the men whose spaces were nearest the side of the building facing the Alabama River saw water seep around the doors and the foundation of the barracks.

"Captain, the Alabama must be floodin' too. The water from the Cahaba would come from the north." Drew called over to Mac.

"Drew, I don't think it's gonna make a difference which river gets to us first. With all this rain, the flood is far from over."

"What are we gonna do, Mac?" Tennessee asked.

"We need to get our stuff up someplace. We'll be mighty grateful for a dry shirt or blanket if this rain keeps on."

"Men, get yer stuff up off the floor. Hang clothes on a nail or ask someone with a bunk to let you put your pallet and blankets up," Mel Grigsby called out to the Arky's Unit.

Mac ordered, "Help the men around you get their stuff out of the floor. Higher up the better." Mac's unit, which had become a cohesive team, worked quickly to secure their meager belongings and then the blankets and mats of the men around them.

A New York major cried out, "Dang it all. The water is covering the floor here near the latrine. Already there are two inches of water on the floor." Mac and some of the other unit leaders began to move some of the sick and weaker soldiers to sit two men to a bunk along the east and west walls. Of course, with only 473 bunks attached along those walls, less than a quarter of the men could get out of the rising water.

And rise it did. By taps, water stood three inches deep across the entire dirt floor. Men who could not share a bunk were forced to stand in the ankle-deep water. If there was a blessing to be had that day, it was that the temperatures were not at or below freezing. At dawn the next day, the water was knee-deep in Castle Morgan. More than half the population of Union prisoners spent the past twenty-four hours standing in the cold, knee-deep, fetid water. As the floodwaters rose, the sludge from the latrines had been added to the dirt and debris washing in from the rivers. Mac and three other unit leaders asked to speak to the commandant.

"Well, MacLayne, what the devil do you want now? I can't do nothin' to stop this flood."

"Sir, please move the troops who are standing in the risin' water to higher ground."

"What kind of fool are you, MacLayne? I ain't lettin' y'all loose in this town. I got no way to keep ya from escapin'."

"Where could we possibly go, Colonel Jones? The whole area is flooded, and we're so far from Union lines, ain't no way we'd run. We gotta get men out of this cold, nasty water."

"You heard my answer. No one's leavin' the stockade. Guard, get these troublemakin' Yanks outta my sight, especially this Arky traitor."

That night there were no rations and only a tin cup of water brought from an unpolluted well above the town. Flood water continued to creep up another inch or so. Men who had been assigned bottom bunks on the north wall found their ticking soaked and blankets wet. They began vacating their bunks. Several tried to climb to upper levels, but the extra weight of a third man broke at least five bunks away from the wall, causing the bedding and clothes of even more soldiers to become soaked in the stinking water filling Cahaba prison.

On the third day, again Union leaders asked for the Confederate commandant to move the prisoners to higher ground. Even sixty of the Confederate guards signed a petition asking Jones to relent. Again, the answer was no. Not until the morning of the fourth day did the demands for more humane treatment seem to register with the commandant. He still refused to let them outside the stockade, affirming his position that not one Cahaba prisoner would escape, but he did allow them to build platforms of scrap lumber high enough to get many of them out of the water. The wooden islands in the flooded barracks were one of two blessings that day. The rain also stopped.

That evening Jones loaded several wagons with prisoners and took them to Selma to the prison camp there to lessen the crowding. Between the six hundred men taken away, the wooden islands scattered through the barracks, and doubling men on the bunks along the covered walls, no Cahaba prisoner had to stand in the cold flood water the rest of the time the prison floor remained underwater.

The new problem was now the grippe, pneumonia, and lung fevers brought on by the terrible conditions left by the flooding. Once again a blessing had been put in place. The Bell Tavern Hospital had been restocked with medicine in the Christmas shipments arranged by Reverend Henderson. The sickest men were moved when the water receded from the town and the good doctors Whitefield and Profile were able to treat them with life-saving medicines. Mac was one of them. After his stint in the box, he was left with a severe cough, but the grippe, which could have been fatal due to his weakened condition since his time in the box, had not developed into pneumonia.

One other miracle bolstered morale as the men worked to clean Castle Morgan after the floodwaters receded. The third week of March, Lt. Col. Jones ordered the prisoners to form ranks on the green. He stood above them on the stockade, scowling down as if he hated what he was looking at. He slammed one gloved hand into the other, paced a few steps, and shouted, "Cahaba prisoners are to be exchanged. I have been ordered to parole the lot of ya." A shout of joy that shook the ground rose from the yard.

"Silence, you ignorant Yankees. You ain't free yet. You'll continue to follow my rules until transport can be arranged to take y'all to Camp Fisk on the Mississippi near Vicksburg. The entire group that is paroled will go north to Cairo, Illinois, to be mustered out. Until trains, ships, or wagons come to take you west to the Mississippi, you'll continue to follow orders."

Mac threw his arms around the shoulders of Drew and Tennessee. "Thank the Lord, we're goin' home."

"You're right, Mac. We kept our faith, and He kept the promise. Hallelujah! Tennessee, here I come." The gentle giant did a gig as his friends laughed at his antics.

"It's a bit further to Indiana, but I believe the Lord's gonna see me home, too."

"Yeah, and when you get there, you'll still have time to get that corn crop in the ground." The three friends laughed with real joy—the first they'd felt in a long time.

# Chapter 32

*Now I rejoice, not that ye were made sorry, but ye sorrowed to
repentance...For Godly sorrow worketh repentance to salvation
not to be repented of.*
*II Corinthians 7:9,10*

Laurel continued to pour out her private time with God,
which she'd neglected for some time, since that hot, horrible
afternoon in July. A murmur of words not meant for human ears
poured out as she knelt beside the beloved four-poster. As the sun
began to warm the room and cast a single stream of light through
the curtain, Laurel could almost feel an embrace. The despair that
had led her to destroy Mac's last gift was swept away by the
realization that so many precious gifts remained.

Macky, who stretched in the cradle across the room, and
Mac's other two sons would grow to be constant reminders of the
love she'd known. Mac had also brought Gracie back to her.
Because Gracie lived in her house, her best friend Rachel would
never be far from her thoughts. What a blessing Cathy had been!
Laurel remembered the night Mac asked her if they had room in
the cabin for two orphans. Cathy had not been quite eight that
winter of '58. She and Mac had been married less than a year, but
his servant heart even then laid out a plan for their lives together.
Even the tragedy of the war had added so much love to their family

390

when Annie and Roy Jr. came to complete their family. Laurel could not have survived the depths of the melancholy the past two months without Annie to care for her children.

Mac had gifted her with a purpose to go on, and he had provided the means to make it possible. He left her with all his worldly goods so they could survive. She began pulling the pins from her coronet of braids. She pulled her fingers through the tawny strands of her mane and shook the locks into a free-falling cascade of waves and curls. She turned to the bureau, picked up her brush, and pulled it through the long tresses, beginning to return her hair to the glory that Mac reveled in when he made love to her. Mac hated those braids. She would not dishonor him nor his constant hope for her. No part of the Spinster of Hawthorn would return to her world.

Laurel looked around at the light dancing across the floor from the shards of her mirror. How much brighter her world looked that morning. She began to remove the remnants of the glass. She carefully wrapped the four pieces of the carved frame, vowing to replace the looking glass after the war. She would need a looking glass since Mac would not be there to reflect the worth he'd helped her find. She wouldn't lose sight of it again.

Laurel spent a busy day, working and playing with her children. Simple things put a smile on her face. Leah Ann even ran her fingers across Laurel's lips and said, "Pretty, Mama." Gracie asked for help with her hair, and Laurel pulled her into her lap and brushed her raven locks into two long ponytails. Gracie clapped her hands when she saw the blue ribbons Laurel placed on them. Leah Ann got to try on her new dress that Laurel had used as an excuse to hide away the past few weeks. She threw arms around her mother and danced around the room to be admired by her brothers and sisters.

"Pretty, Mama. I look pretty."

"Of course, you do, Sweetheart. You're mama's pretty girl."

Before she knew, the day had gone and suppertime was approaching. A knock on the door ended the hubbub in the main room where the family had been playing a noisy game of 'I Spy.'

"Good afternoon, Dr. Cavanaugh. What brings you by today?"

"Well, Mrs. MacLayne, I'm sure it's not slipped your attention that I've called on you frequently since young Macky made his way to us."

"That is true but I'm quite well."

"I can see that." He continued to look at her. You seem much livelier today. Have ya been up and busy like this all day?"

"Only since sun-up. We've had a full day, wouldn't ya say, young'uns?" The rowdy, noisy response followed and Leah Ann pulled on Cort's coat tail.

"Look at my dress! Mama made me so pretty."

He smiled at the little girl and then at Laurel. "It's heartening to see you up and about in such a fine mood. If it's all the same to you, though, I'd like to check for myself that you've made a full recovery."

"Do you think that's necessary, Doctor?"

"Just humor me, please." Laurel nodded and led him to the second pen, where he listened to her heart, counted her pulse, and looked into the pupils of her eyes. He also tested for tenderness at the incision site.

"I'm satisfied that you have made a full recovery of your physical ills, Laurel. Tell me about the change I see in your mood. Melancholia doesn't usually vanish overnight."

"I'm sure it's not gone, but for now I've decided I'm gonna pretend that I'm in control. My family needs me, and I need them."

"That's not changed. Macky was born more than a month ago. I expected you to be bedridden for two weeks while your surgery healed, but five weeks have gone by already."

"Cortland, if the truth be told, I could return to that bed and never get up again. Part of my heart is missing. Yet, if I do, I'd be denying the blessings Mac brought into my life. I can't dishonor him by turning my back on all he gave me. He taught me that God is in control. He has a plan for me. This is Mac's—that was Mac's guiding principle in life...Romans 8:28."

"What does Romans 8:28 say?"

"Look it up. It wouldn't hurt you to get to know the Lord a little better."

"I'm aware of my shortcomings, Laurel."

"Anyway, I gotta go finish supper for my young'uns. It's getting late. Care to join us? I'm afraid it'll be simple fare, beans and ham, pone, and boiled potatoes, but we do have some oatmeal cookies. Andy found some honey back in the summer so we have sweets once in a while."

Φ

Cortland rode back to his office across the meadow after spending the evening with the MacLaynes. He had come to treasure these stolen evenings with the family, not only a supper around a table, but the antics of the young people during their family time. He sensed this was the routine their father had established. He'd not experienced this kind of pleasure since the spring of '61, the last time he'd eaten at the grand mahogany table with Eugenia and Gracelyn at Beau Coeur. The images of the cut-glass chandelier, the polished silver, and gleaming wood in that elegant room still impacted his senses. He could almost hear Gracelyn's gentle voice as she blessed the food. His daughter had spoken grace at the Cavanaugh table since she was old enough to recite the words. He felt the brush of Genie's hand across his as she offered him the napkin he often forgot to lay across his lap. The soft 'tsk-tsk', as a reminder that children learn best by example, followed.

All the beauty of that life lay in a smoldering heap the last time he'd seen it. Beau Coeur lay too near the river. Her docks and warehouses were too great a prize to be ignored by the Yankee forces. On their way to blockade New Orleans, Cort's ancestral home built by his grandfather Etienne Cavanaugh was occupied for a time, and when it was needed no longer, burned to the ground.

Cortland was grateful that his wife and daughter had not lived through that horror. Because the Federal forces surrounded the area, they had remained at Beau Coeur during the fever season in '61. Both Genie and Gracelyn contracted Yellow Fever and died before Cortland could reach them that hot September, nearly four years ago.

When he arrived at his practice, he cared for his horse and closed the barn. He entered the small cabin, and without lighting a lantern, climbed to the loft where he made his personal space. He kicked off his boots, lit a sole lamp, and reached for a Bible from the desk. He turned to Romans 8:28 and read the words Laurel had challenged him to find.

Cortland was not very familiar with scripture. Genie insisted they say grace at the table, and she, being a devoted Catholic, held vespers at their home. She also taught Gracelyn all the expected rituals and catechisms. For Cortland, most of this had been a formality of family life, but he'd never really attended to much of its meaning. Since coming to Shiloh, he began to attend church because Matthew Campbell invited him. It seemed the expected thing to do in Shiloh. He had no idea of the importance of faith to the MacLaynes or the Campbells. He sensed the scripture meant more to them than to most of the people he knew.

He read the words a second time and shook his head. *'For those that love the Lord?'* It wasn't that he didn't love the Lord. He realized how little he knew about the Lord and the scripture, especially compared to Laurel. The meaning of the scripture escaped him. He lay the book aside, and as he did, he realized how little use he'd given that book. Perhaps that was the reason he didn't grasp the meaning of the simple words he found inside. He knew he would have to make an effort to get familiar with the Word.

Cortland also vowed to make a sincere effort to win the affection of Laurel MacLayne. Since their meeting in the orchard nearly two years past, he found himself thinking of her. He wasn't sure why. That day they'd exchanged only a few words. Perhaps the courage she showed defending her property drew him to her or the spirit she showed against the males who tried to intimidate her. Whatever it was, he was more than pleased to find her a friend and patient of Dr. Gibson.

He counted it in his favor that Laurel had decided to accept her husband's death and deal with the dark depression she'd lived with since July. The hope he felt that afternoon only cemented his resolve to someday build a family with her and her children. She would need help rearing such a large group of children, and he wanted that role. He didn't care that Laurel could have no more children. Macky, Leah Ann, and Mark Thomas were all very young. He would raise them as his own.

The idea of having the companionship of Laurel MacLayne was exhilarating. In the time they'd spent together, even though she was sad much of it, he'd found her to be intelligent, well-read, informed about current issues, and quite witty. He even liked that her wit leaned mostly toward sarcasm. Those who knew her before her loss spoke of Laurel as being kind, generous, hard-working, and a bit headstrong. He knew her values lay in faith and family. Physically, she looked nothing at all like his delicate Eugenia, but Laurel was a strikingly desirable woman. She was all he wanted in a wife. Perhaps with some gentle wooing when the time was right, she would be Laurel Cavanaugh.

φ

The weather had forced an end to the church in the glade. Matthew Campbell announced he would hold services for any who wished to attend in the MacLayne homestead until spring. The present congregation of about twenty-five people would fit comfortably at Shiloh. The first meeting there was a bit of a surprise. About forty people arrived by 9:00 to hear Brother Matthew speak. The steady flow of people set Laurel and Matthew scampering to find space to seat everyone. Putting the children along the loft rail freed up several spaces for adults. Thankfully, the benches Laurel used for school seated more than one. When she brought in the chairs from the second pen and the rocking chairs from the front porch, everyone found a seat. Of course, those sitting on the hearth and the table weren't quite so comfortable with no back to lean on, but then the wooden pews at Shiloh church were backless, too. The service was spirit-filled and the music lifted everyone's spirits. Having more people than places for them to sit was a wonderful problem to have. Some of the people from the Shiloh community were beginning to lay aside their political agendas to return to worship, even in the house built by a Yankee traitor.

After the final hymn, Laurel rushed to the kitchen to finish the Sunday dinner for her family. Dr. Cavanaugh followed her as she went to the porch to draw water. "May I help with that, Laurel?"

"Yes. I appreciate your help. Did you need something?"

"I just wanted to thank you for opening your home to the church today. The crowd was larger than I thought, but the service was fine."

"You're welcome. My uncle Matthew asked if we could use my house. It's more central than his place and I've got more room."

"I'll put this pail on the counter and take my leave. I just wanted to tell ya I appreciate your hospitality."

"You're welcome anytime, Dr. Cavanaugh."

"Do you think I could persuade you to call me Cort? My friends do."

"Yes. I will try to remember."

"Have a good afternoon, Laurel. I'll head across the way."

"You're welcome to share Sunday dinner with my family if you have no other plans. My father-in-law and his family are going to be with us."

"Thank you. I'd be pleased to stay. Goin' home to leftover biscuits and perhaps a piece of cold bacon doesn't tempt me much."

"Friends are always welcome at our table, Cort."

Two weeks later, Cort stopped by in the middle of the week. He found Laurel, Andy, and Cathy in the barn laying in hay for winter feed. "That's pretty heavy work for you, Laurel. I don't remember tellin' you that you're ready for this kind of labor yet. Where is Mr. Clarke?"

"J.F. and my uncle are laying in extra firewood. My mother-in-law tells us the Farmer's Almanac is predicting a very cold, snowy winter. They want to be well-prepared. That is why we decided to put up extra hay. Our oat crop was low this year, and we have a few more cows than we did last year."

"I wouldn't say that too loud. Some rovin' army band will be havin' itself a beef dinner if they find out you have extra cows here."

"Since the Partisan Raiders group lost their leader, we've not lost many cattle from our herd." Laurel moved another bale with Cathy.

"Here, let me do that." Cortland worked with Andy until the extra bales had been stacked in the loft.

"Thanks, Dr. Cavanaugh. I don't like for Mama to have to help with the outside chores."

"Andy, you've taken on a man's job here at the homestead. You've taken great care of your mother and your brothers and sisters."

"That's what I promised my papa."

"Well, Cort, did you come over here to scold me for working?" Laurel asked.

"No. I actually rode over to ask if the MacLayne family would go with me to a harvest festival in Herndon. Some people I take care of over there insisted I come, and I don't wanna go alone."

"Well, I don't know…" Laurel's hesitation caused a frown on several faces.

"It's a family celebration. There'll be things for all ages to do. You know I got no family, so I hoped maybe I could borrow yours for the day. It's this Saturday."

Cathy's eyes pleaded the case. "Mama, it could be fun. We've hardly been anywhere in forever. Do you think we could go?"

"Could be good for the kids to get out," Laurel said.

"The younger kids could enter the contests and races. I heard there's to be a dance after supper. Won't y'all go with me so I don't have to go alone?"

"I'm not sure it's right. Mac's…"

Cortland interrupted, "Laurel, I'm not askin' ya to go courtin'. We're neighbors riding to a festival together. I expect ya to wear your widow's weeds, and I will treat you with the respect a widow deserves. I think, speaking as your doctor, that you and your family need a little fun."

Laurel looked at Andy. "Son, do you want us to go?"

"Mama, Papa would want us to have fun. He knows we love him. If he's in Heaven lookin' down on us, he'd expect us to go on with life and enjoy the good times as they come."

"Cortland, the MacLayne family will accept your invitation to Saturday's festival."

The Herndon Community Harvest Festival was fun for the MacLayne family. Cort kept his word that his behavior would not lead to gossip. As they arrived, he led Laurel to the area of the church where the new mothers sat with their infants. Another young woman, like Laurel, wore black. She held a tiny girl who must have been ten or eleven months old. Four other new mothers sat together in a niche. Cort made introductions, and Laurel was drawn into conversations quickly. Two of the new mothers were women from the Shiloh community, but all of them reached out to include her as the day went on.

From that point, Cortland took special pains to make sure each member of the family became involved in some activity during the afternoon. He and Andy competed in a horseshoe tossing contest and won. The prize was a pumpkin pie that became dessert at the family supper. Mark Thomas wore him out with the races, but Cort smiled through them all, even when he tore his trousers during a fall in a three-legged race.

As the dancing began, Cortland led Annie onto the dance floor. At the age of twenty, Annie was a beautiful young woman. Cortland knew the young men of the area wouldn't hesitate to ask the pretty newcomer to dance once they saw her dancing with him. He was right. He didn't get another dance with Annie all evening. He also introduced Andy and Cathy to dancing at the festival. The parson of a local congregation called for a reel. Cort lined the two young people up and told them to watch him. Soon they were in the line of young folks having a wonderful time. They danced, clapped, and laughed as if they'd been doing the reel since they could walk. Andy got up the nerve to ask a girl with copper-colored curls to dance. She blushed and nodded. He only stepped on her toe once.

Laurel sat with the mothers, watching the laughter and joy radiate from the faces of Annie, Cathy, and Andy. Her younger children had settled on pallets nearly exhausted from a long day of fun, food, and friends. She too had enjoyed this day. Just time to talk with other women who shared some of her same concerns had been a blessing. She hadn't been aware of how much she missed that kind of fellowship. Watching her older children told her how much they needed to be in the company of people their ages, too. The day had been a wonderful gift, and she owed a debt of gratitude to Dr. Cavanaugh for bringing them to this festival.

"Mrs. MacLayne, are you ready for me to drive you all back to Shiloh?"

"If the others are ready, and you, of course."

"I've arranged for a friend to bring Annie, Andy, and Cathy back when the dance is over if you approve. He and his wife live between you and your father-in-law."

"They do seem to be having a lot of fun. More than they've had in a long time."

"But you've been sittin' here with the babies all day. They're all tuckered out. You must be too."

"I've had a wonderful day. Thank you for bringing us. My kids needed this outing."

"Let me bring the wagon. We'll bed the little ones down in some hay. They can sleep while we drive."

Laurel enjoyed the drive home with Cortland, too. The hay-filled wagon rocked her sleeping children as they traveled back to Shiloh. They hardly stirred, warm in the hay and quilts that Cortland had thought to bring. As much as she'd enjoyed talking with the women at the festival, she found herself drawn into conversation with the good doctor. He'd asked her about her orchard, her teaching, and the books she loved to read. He wanted to know about her life in Washington County and how different she found the world in the northeast part of the state. He even asked her how she felt about Abraham Lincoln as a leader of the country. She enjoyed having him listen to her. How she'd missed that since Mac had been gone.

Cortland told her some about his life in Louisiana and what it was like to grow up on a plantation. He spoke of the grief caused by the death of his only daughter and wife so early in the war. "I carried a lot of guilt for a while. I was not home when the fever broke out, and my family didn't have the medicine they needed."

"I'm sorry for your loss, Cort. It's hard to lose people you love."

"You've been very strong, Laurel. I'm happy you came with me tonight. I didn't think you'd do it."

"Cortland, you've made this entire day very special for all of us. I was thinking how long it'd been since I'd seen my children so happy. I enjoyed the conversation with the other women today and your company tonight. I don't know how to thank you."

"It's been my pleasure. At times today, I felt I had a family. When Mark Thomas and I fell during that silly race, we both laughed so hard. Then I saw I tore my pant leg. We laughed even harder."

"If you'll bring those over to me, I'll fix them for you."

"I'd appreciate that. I did enjoy your family today. I am enjoying this private time with you tonight. Laurel, you are a beautiful lady. I'm so pleased you've allowed me to become a friend."

She became very quiet.

"Did I say something wrong, Laurel?"

"No...I..."

"Forgive me. I forget your time of mourning is so new. I don't expect anything more than your friendship."

"I appreciate that. Today you have been a true friend to my entire family. I'll not forget that."

Their friendship continued to grow. Throughout November and December, Dr. Cavanaugh found many occasions to spend time with the MacLayne family. He came to the school one day a week to teach science to the students. Because of his schooling, he could explain the concepts of biology and chemistry to the older students. Cathy loved the biology lessons and told the doctor she wanted to study to be a nurse.

Cort also became a Sunday driver for the MacLayne family. The congregation grew too large to fit in Laurel's cabin, so Matthew moved the services to the home of Thomas MacLayne. His place was not quite so centrally located, but he and Peggy had an adjoining living and dining room which made seating much easier when the number of people reached fifty. Each Sunday morning at 7:30, Cort arrived at Shiloh to take Laurel and her family to church. That meant, of course, they spent the largest part of every Sunday together.

On the Sunday afternoon before Christmas, Cathy approached Laurel. "Mama, can we start decoratin' for Christmas now?"

Laurel stopped in her tracks. She'd given no thought to decorating for the holiday. She gave little thought to the fact there was a holiday approaching. Her uncle had been preaching his advent sermons for weeks, and she'd taken comfort in the message but had not connected the Sunday sermon to the reality of the day her children always looked so forward to.

At school, they'd been involved in science activities, spelling tests, and history essays, but they'd not made any Christmas decorations or prepared any kind of program for Christmas Eve. When she thought back over the past two weeks, she recalled several times when she'd called a group down for whispering or scolded a child for doodling on their slate with a picture of a snowman or snowflakes. They whispered about what they'd been afraid to speak out loud. She was more than angry with herself.

Laurel knew she'd shut out the idea because she didn't want a Christmas without Mac. For the first time in several weeks, she burst into tears. She quickly turned her back to Cathy and went over to stoke the fire.

"Mama, I'm sorry. We don't need to do it. I just thought with the little ones...I didn't want to make you sad."

"No, Sweetheart. You are right. We have to have Christmas. I've been so thoughtless. Please forgive me."

"Mama, we know how much you miss Papa. We do too."

"He'd be very upset if we don't have our family celebration. Your papa loved Christmas time. Yes. Yes. Go ahead and let's get the cedar boughs for the mantle and some holly, too. You know where the ribbons are packed away."

"Do we have any beeswax candles for the table?"

"Yes, Cathy, but we can't burn them until Christmas Eve. I only have two partly burned candles left. I didn't do any candling this fall. And Cathy, take the younger ones to help you so they can begin to feel like it's Christmas time."

Laurel knew she'd have to put some serious effort into finding Christmas gifts now. She had about a week to do what she'd normally spend months planning with Mac before the war. As much as she hated the prospect, she would have to make a trip to Greensboro to see what she could find at the mercantile stores. She would also have to use some of her stored gold pieces. The Confederate script was all but worthless now. She didn't care about the cost. She just wanted something to please her children. Again, Cortland came to her rescue and volunteered to drive her into town the next day. He told her that he'd not get in her way as he had business with Dr. Edwards and would be busy much of the morning.

Pickings were sparse and expensive in the stores and shops. Like in all small towns in Arkansas in December of 1864, the merchants rarely got the things they ordered. The freight routes were nearly non-existent because of heavy Union blockades on all the river ports. Some local craftsmen had items to offer, but Laurel's late start at shopping left limited choices. After several hours of browsing through every store in Greensboro, Laurel had found one gift for each of her children, Annie, and J.F. Clarke. By 1:30, she was exhausted. She found a straight-back chair near the stove at McCollough's store, and she sat down to wait for Cort to complete his meeting.

"Hello, Mrs. MacLayne. I haven't seen you in town for a while." The overly sweet voice of Willa Ferguson was not one Laurel wanted to hear. "How is that little family of yours doin' over at Shiloh?"

"Good afternoon, Miss Ferguson."

"I heard you have a new son."

"Yes, I do."

"How does his pa like the new addition to your family?"

"You know we received a report that Patrick was killed in action. We've not seen him since Christmas last year."

"Not the story I heard. Seems people in our community say that Mac left ya back in July, about a year and a half ago. That would make your son…"

"Miss Ferguson, my son is none of your business. This is the last time I intend to speak to you about him. You've never had a kind word to say to me since the day we met when Mac brought me to Shiloh church the year we married. You have tried to spread lies about my fidelity as long as I have known you. If my husband had wanted you, he'd not have made a trip across the entire state to find a suitable wife. He knew you for nearly five years before he knew I existed. Obviously, you didn't meet his standards."

"How dare you speak to me like that?"

"I don't believe I've ever called you the names you've bandied about me around this community. Perhaps I should fight fire with fire. Let me see…Willa Ferguson—gossip—liar—an old maid—a troublemaker…. I suppose that's a fair start." Several people standing around the store applauded Laurel's defense of herself. Willa threw down the bag of potatoes she carried and stormed from the store.

"Bravo, Laurel. I was about to interrupt the scene when I heard her suggest you were lying, but your standin' up to her was so much better. I bet she'll never attack you in public again. I'm certainly proud of you."

"Thank you, Cort. I hate conflict, but I do feel good about standing up for myself."

"Finished your shoppin'?"

"Yes. Thank you for bringing me to town."

"You didn't need me today."

"It's still nice to have a friend around for support. Speaking of friends, what are your plans for Christmas Eve and Christmas Day?"

"I have none. You know I have no family. I plan to enjoy a new book and a good fire."

"We'd enjoy your company at Shiloh. Please come to spend the holiday with us."

"I wouldn't miss it."

φ

Christmas in '64 was different, not sad or mournful, but different. When the MacLaynes sang *Silent Night,* the fine baritone harmony of Mac's voice was missing. Andy did a good job of reading the nativity story from the book of Luke. Thomas praised the boy for his fine recitation. Andy said, "I'll never do it as good as my papa." The love they shared comforted them, but Mac's absence left a huge emptiness that could not be filled with friends or family. On Christmas Eve, there were no tears, but the laughter rang a bit hollow.

Laurel spent Christmas day at home with her children, Annie, and Roy. They'd invited J.F. and Cort to share their holiday dinner. The day was more relaxed as the children were home and excited about the gifts Santa had left on the hearth. Cort added to their Christmas haul by bringing each member of the household a small gift. Laurel was relieved she'd thought at the last moment to gift one of her books to him as she'd not thought to buy a present in town. The MacLaynes feasted on their traditional Christmas dinner, a goose that Andy had provided, hot yeast rolls, and pumpkin pie. Only the fruit and cocoa were missing.

After a fine meal, they'd shared stories, sang hymns together, and enjoyed each other's company, just in a quieter way than they had in years past. By the end of the day, the members of the household were ready to fall into bed.

"Thank you, Dr. Cort. I like havin' a slingshot for my own."

"You're very welcome, Mark Thomas. Shoot at all the rocks you want, but be kind to the birds, okay?" Cort laughed with him.

"Yes, sir. I won't kill no mockingbirds."

Echoes of goodnight followed. Cort made no move to leave although J.F. Clarke had returned to his cabin much before

404

sundown. Laurel scurried around, seeing that all her children said their prayers and were tucked in warmly.

When she returned to the main room, Cort sat cradling Macky, his feet resting on the hearth. Both were asleep. Laurel continued to pick up around the room, getting ready to close up the house for the night. She blew out the stubs of the beeswax candles on the table, turned off all but one lantern, lay two large logs on the fire, and set the screen. Cort awoke.

"Here, I'll take the baby. I'm sure you must be tired. You fell asleep while I was tucking in the kids. You've played with them all day."

"No. I'm not the least bit tired. I've not had a better day in the last four years. I'm not sure I've ever had a better Christmas. Thank you for lettin' me be a part of your family this holiday."

"You're welcome. My young'uns enjoyed your attention."

"Did you?" Cort looked into Laurel's eyes. She didn't answer. She raised her eyes to meet his for a moment to get some sense of what to say. "I'm sorry, Laurel. That was out of line. I know you are mournin' a husband that you love."

"Yes. I do love Mac. I wish I had some hope he was coming home to us. I have to live with the truth. I have to build a life for my family."

"That's what I hope for, too. When you are ready, I want to be a part of that life. I want to be a father to Macky, Mark Thomas, and Leah Ann. They are so young, I'm afraid they'll have no memory of your husband. I'll never try to replace him in the eyes of your older children, but I'll be proud to support them and look after them like an uncle would, if they'd let me."

"Cortland, I'm not ready to...."

"I know that, Laurel. I couldn't wait any longer to make my feelings known to you. Once I know there is a possibility of a future, I'll be satisfied to wait until you are ready to move forward."

"What if..."

"No what if's. Laurel, I've admired you since the afternoon I watched you fend off a troop of soldiers to protect those apple trees. I've learned to care more as our friendship has grown. I've never seen the depth of strength and courage it took to let me deliver Macky as you did. You would have had it so much easier to let me take him the usual way."

"I couldn't lose Mac's last child. Look how precious he is sleeping there in your arms."

"I almost feel that he's mine, too. I've watched him grow from the first minute he took a breath."

"I am so grateful you could give him to me."

"I know what you had to give to bring him here. Laurel, I could have lost you that night."

"It was all in God's will. He took care of me. He made sure you had the skill to save Macky."

"That's another thing—that bedrock faith you live by. You can teach me so much about that. I understand so little now."

"Cortland, such wonderful compliments. Thank you."

"Laurel, I'll say this and then I'll say no more. I have fallen in love with you. I want you to be my wife. When the time comes, when you believe you have honored Mac long enough, I will propose to you. I want us to build a life together—here or back on my land in Louisiana. All I want from you now is the promise that you will think about it."

Cortland picked up Laurel's hand, brought it to his lips, and reverently kissed it. "You are a beautiful, strong woman, Laurel. I love you." He laid Macky in her arms. "Good night. I'll see you soon."

# Chapter 33

*Oh Lord, how long shall I cry, and Thou will not hear! Even cry*
*out unto Thee of violence, and Thou wilt not save*
*Habakkuk 1:2*

Mac and the Arky's Unit were ecstatic the first few days after Jones's parole announcement. Added to the fact that the floodwaters receded, the men took on the demeanor of younger, hopeful men once again. Commander Jones's wooden islands remained, keeping scores of men from sleeping on the dirt floors. The most humane improvement came in the department of Jones's handpicked guards. They curtailed the beatings and ignored the misdemeanors of the prisoners. Not one man was locked in the isolation boxes after the paroles were announced.

After a few days, the spirits of the men began to falter when rations, which had never filled the stomachs of the prisoners, were cut further. Amanda Gardner and a few of her neighbors tried to ease the want, but the people of the town were also finding it nearly impossible to find staples for their families. The flooding had devastated the civilian population, too. Flour, oats, and meat were confiscated, and the Union army had control of nearly every port on the Mississippi and rivers to the north. Grant, who commanded all military action for the Union, ordered no supplies were to fall into Confederate hands. Starving soldiers didn't make for fierce enemies. When Richmond couldn't feed its armies, they had little concern with Union prisoners.

As the week passed, more and more complaints came from the stockade. A common rumor spread like wildfire—*It's a lie—Jones lied to us—Why did the Rebs lie to us?—There's no parole.*—Murmurs like these were heard everywhere. Mac and some of the unit leaders tried to bolster spirits. They reinstated the competition days and baseball games and races between units. When those things didn't help, they began drills to keep everyone's mind off what they considered to be the broken promise. The task was hard with everyone's stomach grumbling from hunger. Mac sensed that open rebellion was about to happen, and he feared more men would die needlessly.

Most of the Confederate guards, those trained by Reverend Henderson anyway, were sympathetic to the plight of the prisoners at Castle Morgan. They wouldn't want to, but they would use gunfire to prevent a prison break. They knew Jones would pour out his wrath on them if they failed to keep order. Everyone at Cahaba knew the warden's motto: "My job is to make them damn Yankees suffer."

Grace intervened once again. March 6, 1865, Mac and his unit were among the first group of prisoners marched to the landing on the Alabama River and boarded onto a Union steamboat. The first leg of the long trip home would be a pleasure, a steamboat ride for the entire fifteen miles up the Alabama River to Selma. For the ten longest months of his life, Mac had been outside those walls only four times. Sitting on the deck of the *River Queen*, he soaked up the early spring breeze, the beauty from the earth coming to life in the warmth of springtime, and a sense of freedom that came from being outside the stockade of Cahaba prison. He realized he was on the way back to Laurel.

After a pleasant two and a half hours, Mac and the other three hundred men aboard found themselves in another make-shift camp to await a train to carry them to the Mississippi River. What awaited them, they had no idea, but by the end of the week, most of the Cahaba prisoners were loaded into grimy boxcars, much like the one Mac rode when he was brought to Alabama. Too many men were pushed into the filthy covered boxcars that smelled as bad as they looked. When the almost two thousand prisoners had been crammed into seven cars, the train pulled away from the Selma depot headed to Meridian, a distance of about a hundred miles. The trip could have been completed in four uncomfortable hours, except a problem with the old engine forced a delay. The two-day delay forced a campout for the homeward-bound soldiers in the sleepy Mississippi town.

When the trip resumed, conditions were a bit more tolerable as another boxcar was added. The new car was no cleaner. Neither did it smell any better, but the extra space allowed the men to move around a step or two as they completed the trip into Jackson, the end of the rail line. At Jackson, the Union soldiers were corralled into a fenced camp guarded by Confederate troops. A rumor buzzed through the men and stirred excitement among them. Union troops were entrenched at Big Black River less than forty miles from their holding pen.

Tennessee let out a yell that could have been mistaken for the infernal Rebel yell. "Praise be! For the first time, I know I'm goin' home! This blamed war is over." He spoke words that every man in the camp felt.

"Shut it up, you Yanks. Better get some rest," an armed Rebel sergeant yelled. "Tomorrow, y'all start earnin' yer ticket home. You get to walk the rest of the way to Vicksburg. You Yanks done tore up all the rails between here and the river. I'm thinkin' tomorrow night ya won't be quite so chipper. It's only forty miles or so."

So, the march began with the sunrise. More than two long grueling days westward until on March 16, they reached the Big Black and on its opposite shore, Old Glory flew above a camp of federal troops. The Union soldiers shouted and cheered. For some, the sight of the flag brought tears.

"Praise be, I feel like dancin', Tennessee. May need to get ya to pinch me to make me know I ain't dreamin'," Mac said.

"Captain, You're the one that got us through. Lots of men didn't fare near as good as us. You melded us into a team and kept us goin' on hope."

"That wasn't me. The Lord was the reason we had that hope."

"Some of us didn't know about that until you showed us," Melvin Grigsby spoke up.

"Yeah, you and all that Bible readin'. Sure am glad ya managed to hang on to that raggedy ole book," Tennessee teased.

"Had to have someplace to keep my family safe." Mac took out his Bible and opened it to the middle where the photographs of Laurel and the family always stayed. "Darlin', I'm on my way back to Shiloh."

"You sure do love that lady, don't ya, Captain?"

"Mel, I sure do. Next to knowin' the Lord, Laurel is the best gift this old sinner never deserved. If you're smart, you'll go find you a good God-fearin' woman like her."

"I'm not sure I want me a wife that will give me quite so many kids."

"Come on, Tennessee! Are you afraid of the challenge?"

"No. I'm afraid I wouldn't be able to feed 'em." Laughter exploded around them.

Arrival at Camp Fisk was an early day of independence for Mac and his friends. The Confederate guards turned them over to the custody of General Dana's Union soldiers. They were no longer prisoners of war. Mac's unit of thirty-seven men disappeared among a mass of more than forty-seven hundred Union troops waiting for a ship—any northbound steamboat to carry them home. Groups of men found shelter in tents in the quickly thrown together camp, but they didn't seem to mind. Thanks to the pleasant spring weather, they found life on the riverbank more than bearable. They approached each day with the hope that it would be their turn to board a steamboat home.

A week into the stay at Camp Fisk, Mac ran into an old friend from Cahaba. Reverend Henderson arrived to make a tour of the work being done to return the prisoners to health. Mac learned that the reverend had worked in league with the Union General Dana to end the imprisonment of the Cahaba and Andersonville prisoners. The South continued to lose troops, many from starvation and disease. The depletion of men at home to work the land did little to suggest fortunes at home would improve any time soon. With these political pressures in Richmond, lawmakers were glad to get rid of the burden of feeding the Union prisoners held in the Confederate prisons.

"Reverend Henderson, I am mighty grateful to you. I'm not sure if I'd have lived to see Shiloh again without your intervention."

"Captain MacLayne, I don't deserve any gratitude. I need to make an apology to every man who walked through that prison. I live with sorrow and shame for the horrors of that shameful place."

"But under the circumstances, Rev. Henderson, your protection of us kept the worst away. When we got here a couple of weeks ago, the camp surgeon said that of the 2,200 men who arrived since the end of March that more'n 1,100 were sick, some to the point of death. More than 1000 of those came from Andersonville."

"I tried, Mac. But before I left, I know that at least 147 men died under my watch."

"And in the three months since you've been gone that many and more died or were maimed by Jones and his hand-picked guards. Had it not been for those men you trained, many more of us would have died during the flood. Did ya know that sixty of your Confederate guards signed a petition asking Jones to take us out of the stockade when the water was knee-high? He refused."

"I'm glad it's near over. Brothers should never turn against brothers. That's how I feel about you and other officers who helped me keep order and build morale with the men. You and those like you are the reason so few died at Cahaba. It wasn't me."

"What are you gonna do now, Reverend?"

"Well, I'd say the war's all but over. General Lee surrendered the Army of Virginia to Grant a couple of days ago. I think it was on the ninth of April. Lee was the glue that held our troops together. Johnston still has a fair-sized army in Tennessee, but I expect he'll follow suit soon."

"But what about you?"

"I think I'll go back home and hope my bishop will give me a little church somewhere. That is my callin'. Where are you goin' after you get mustered out in Cairo?"

"I've got only one plan. I'm goin' home to Shiloh as fast as these legs will carry me. I've got a wife and four wonderful young'uns, a fine daughter-in-law, and a grandson waitin' for me."

"You've got a grandson?"

"Laurel and I adopted two of her students the first year we were married. Roy was a fine young man. Chose to serve the Confederate side and died in Corinth in '62. His wife and son are part of my family now."

"God bless ya, Mac. I'm happy we had a chance to meet again so we can part as brothers and not enemies."

"Good-bye, Reverend. I hated every minute in your prison, but the Lord blessed me with your friendship."

Mac and his friends from the unit spent their days resting, playing baseball, strolling the green meadows surrounding Camp Fish, and eating better than they had in months. Cahaba prisoners fared so much better than those from Anderson who spent most of their time healing, gaining strength, adding much-needed weight, and sleeping.

In the evenings, Mac and his best friends spent much of their leisure talking of the comradery they'd developed and the memories they would carry home with them to Arkansas, Tennessee, Indiana, and Missouri. One night about an hour before taps, they began to talk of the first meeting when Mac had gathered them in their spot near the fireplace in the prison.

Drew said, "Ya know, Captain, you didn't make a very good first impression."

"What is that supposed to mean, Lieutenant?"

"Well, when you called all your guys to meet that first time, you stood up on that crate. Your uniform was a rag, and you had a huge lump right above your belt—looked like ya was smugglin' a cantaloupe. Your hair was pretty shaggy and that beard…"

"You think you looked a heap better?" Mac asked.

"Drew's right. You looked kinda sickly with that big bulge under your coat," Tennessee grinned.

"I don't care how I looked. Without that bulge, I'd have died a long time ago. When my mount got shot out from under me, all I saved was my Bible and my family. I had to have'em both."

"I've been curious about that. Why wasn't that in your saddlebags?" Mel asked.

"Almost always was. I'd already packed up my bags before I picked up my Bible that mornin' we left to pass around Oil Trough. I stuck my Bible in my coat for the day. I always carried my photograph case in my breast pocket. That was all I got to take with me when the Rebs captured me."

"Sure lucky."

"Not luck at all, Mel. God knew I couldn't make it without those things. He took care of my needs."

"Ya know Captain, I never believed all that 'til I met up with you. That raggedy old Bible of yours has been a blessin' to the lot of us."

"That's true, Tennessee. Romans 8:28."

Drew interrupted, "Yeah, we know it by heart. You preached it to us often enough."

Mac smiled and patted his giant friend on the back. "Let's call it a night. Tomorrow may be our day to head up the Mississippi."

That was not to be the case. Mac and his friends saw men come and go for several weeks. Every few days, two or three hundred men would board whatever steamboat that had space to carry them north. Troops from Michigan and Illinois, others from Iowa, Indiana, and Pennsylvania, and even a few from Missouri and Kansas were called. Drew Mayfield, who had served Mac so loyally since his first day at Cahaba, was boarded on March 28 with a group of twenty other soldiers who were bound for Indiana. Yet troops from the Southern states rarely made the daily roster. Some began to question if they'd been overlooked on purpose. The good thing was that all the remaining prisoners were being well-treated and the food was filling and healthy.

They would wait. If Mac weren't so anxious to be back at Shiloh, he may have enjoyed the time with Tennessee and Mel. They did miss Drew but certainly didn't wish him back. The guards at Camp Fisk didn't consider the men prisoners, and they often wrote day passes for them to visit Vicksburg and the surrounding area. One day, the trio visited the site of the Battle of Vicksburg where more than 19,000 men, both Union and Confederate, were killed or wounded when Grant crossed the Mississippi into the heart of the Southern homeland.

"Mercy me, Captain. How on earth did Grant ever manage to beat the Rebs at this place? Look at the earthen works they pulled up here."

"Just another reminder of the loss and death this war has cost, Mel. Lord, I pray it's over soon."

Another week passed and not one of the remaining 3,500 men at Camp Fisk headed for home. Reverend Henderson called a meeting of the unit leaders from Castle Morgan that remained. He explained that Grant had once again halted exchanges because of the delays in the return of Confederate prisoners being held in the North.

"Men, don't lose hope. General Dana is still working on the release. We don't want to have to return anyone to Cahaba or Andersonville. Be patient a few more days."

That night in his tent, Mac fell to his knees. He spoke in anger. "Lord, please. You promised to deliver us if we are faithful. I've tried to serve while I've lived in conditions not fit for an animal. I've waited, hoped, asked to go home—nothin' more. Please God, don't send me back to hell. Please, Lord."

A couple of days later, Reverend Henderson and the ranking Confederate soldiers who were overseeing the prisoner exchange were ushered across the Big Black River to the Confederate lines under cover of night. When the Union soldiers asked why, they were told the move was for the safety of the reverend and his aides. They had no other explanation.

The reason came to light very quickly. Rumors spread across Camp Fisk. Abraham Lincoln had been assassinated in Washington by a Confederate sympathizer. A riot broke out at the camp, and the Union soldiers demanded the arrest of all Confederate guards and Rebel soldiers there. Of course, by that time most of them had fled. Loud chants and choruses of 'Let's hang Jeff Davis from a Sour Apple Tree' rang across the area. The next day many in the camp sat in sorrow. Lincoln was dead, the war was not officially over, and so many men were still so far from home.

Special Order #35 brought back hope. In mid-April, a directive from Washington ordered the commander at Camp Fisk to send all men from Missouri and Louisiana to St. Louis to be processed out of the army. General Dana decided the mandate included all the remaining prisoners at Fisk. He chose to send men northward in whatever size groups a steamboat could manage—a thousand at a time if it was necessary to empty the exchange camp.

On April 22nd, 1,500 men made the short trip from Camp Fisk to the landing at Vicksburg. A large impressive riverboat with the name Henry Ames painted across the bow dropped anchor. She was a good-sized boat, but certainly not large enough to carry 3,500 soldiers. By noon, the group of 1,100 filled every inch of the decks. They shouted and waved to the last group of prisoners who stood on the dock. Mac arrived with his men just in time to see the Ames reach the midpoint in the river.

Again, the men returned to wait. How long they didn't know. Surely another steamboat large enough to carry them would soon reach Vicksburg. At long last on April 24, the final group of 2,200 prisoners, some on cots that had to be carried, were delivered by train were shipped the short distance from Camp Fisk to the riverfront. The largest steamboat Mac had ever seen was approaching the dock. Great bold red letters across the side of the boat spelled out SULTANA. The three impressive levels reminded Mac of a wedding cake he'd seen at the wedding of Marsha and Lewis Rawlings, where all the elite of Baltimore had witnessed his best friend Louis marry the woman Mac had been betrothed to. The irony was that two tall stacks vented black smoke into the blue sky and over the dazzling white paint of the new boat. This was the Sultana's first trip up the Mississippi, just having finished its maiden voyage down to St. Louis in record time.

"Goodness, Tennessee, have you ever seen such a boat?" Mac asked.

"No. It's big all right, but do you think there's another one? Still, a lot of men to fit on one boat."

"Surely is. I see one over there called the *Pauline Carroll*. I heard the skipper say they'd take any overflow. General Dana emptied Camp Fisk today."

About 1:00, the officers began boarding the *Sultana*. At first, it was very systematic, sending officers into the Grand Salon and enlisted men on to the open deck. Checking on the names and rosters was too slow, so finally, they simply tried to count heads and allow the men to go where they would.

As the decks filled, the aides of the Quartermaster moved men into tighter and tighter spaces. By the time they reached the last five hundred men, of which Mac and his men were a part, they stopped and refused to board.

A major from Tennessee spoke out, "That boat is past full now. That boat is not safe. We'll go on the *Pauline Carrol*, yonder."

"No, Major. There's ample room. Your men can use the roof of the Texas deck. Of course, you are welcome inside with the other officers."

"Why the overcrowding? Get permission for us to board the *Carroll*."

"Major, we've been told they have smallpox over there." The discussion went on for a while, but no one asked to go to the *Carroll*. Finally, a Colonel who seemed to be in charge of the process came down and ordered the remaining men to board the *Sultana*. Those in charge of loading, hefted men to the roof of the hurricane deck, under every stairwell, and next to the paddlewheels where water constantly splashed up from the river. Mac, Tennessee, and Mel were pushed under a stairwell that led to the passenger cabins. None of them could stand up straight, but being near the walls did provide some protection from the elements.

Just before dark, the *Sultana* was loaded. More than a thousand men from Castle Morgan and nearly twelve hundred men from Andersonville were wedged into every inch of the monstrous steamboat, which now seemed quite small. A small engraved plaque on the wall next to the hallway to the cabins said *Sultana*: Occupancy limit 367.

Tennessee pointed this out to his friends. "Somebody didn't count very well."

About 9:00 p.m. the captain of the *Sultana*, J. Cass Mason, steered his overloaded boat into the swollen Mississippi River, headed north. He'd broken a speed record on his trip south to New Orleans, but that wouldn't be the case on the way north. His vastly overloaded boat would bring a profit to make the slower trip well-worth the extra time.

When the *Sultana* pulled away from the landing and made its way to the middle of the river the boat seemed steady, even though the river was running fast and was well out of its banks. Within a few minutes, the engines brought the boat up to speed and the *Sultana* zig-zagged its way against the strong current at a good clip. The hoard of soldiers settled in for the night, nearly all sitting with knees pulled into their chests. That was all the space would allow for most on the crowded decks. The lack of space seemed almost a blessing as the night was cold. Men shared blankets, two or three to each because provision had been made for less than a quarter of the number that had been pushed aboard the *Sultana*.

Some thirty-four hours later on the morning of April 26th, the grand steamer reached Helena. Some of the cargo would be unloaded at the dock and a few civilian passengers would board to make the trip to Memphis. A photographer on the dock was almost the undoing of the trip, though. As he began to set up to photograph the vastly overloaded ship returning Union soldiers home, many of them pushed to the port side to see the spectacle. The great boat tilted in the water to the point that the boiler on the starboard side was emptied of water. The boat nearly capsized before the men could be returned to the places they'd come from. The momentary chaos made for a quick awakening for those who had not been up already.

"Golly, Captain. I thought we's gonna have to swim for a minute," Mel said.

"What are you talkin' about. You know you can't swim." Tennessee reminded him.

"Sometimes soldiers act like a bunch of sheep! One spook and the whole lot runs with 'em. Dang fools. They oughta know this boat's top-heavy."

"Oh, laugh about it, Captain. They're just curious. Let 'em have a little fun."

"Mel, swimmin' in the Big Muddy ain't much fun, especially this time of year. That current is so swift you'd get pulled under in a heart's beat," Mac scolded.

"I'm so hungry, I could eat me a raw catfish right about now. Do ya think we'll get rations tonight?" Tennessee asked.

"Yeah. If you can sneak into that fancy dining room up these stairs and swipe us some of their vittles," Mel teased.

"I don't care. Fellas, a few more hours on this floatin' city, and I'm sayin' good-bye. When we get to Memphis, I'm leavin' to start home. Shiloh is only about seventy miles west."

"Mac, you can't do that. You'll be a deserter if you don't muster out at Cairo," Mel told him.

"I've been a deserter since December 27, 1863. That was the day I kissed my wife good-bye and hugged my ten-year-old son and told him he was the man in the family until I got home. My daughter hadn't reached her first birthday the last time I saw her. Nothin' in Cairo is worth any more time away from them."

"What about your pay, a horse, a set of decent clothes...you gonna walk the whole seventy miles to Greensboro?" Mel asked.

"I hope it won't come to that, but if I do, at least I still have my boots."

"Excuse me, Captain." A well-dressed man in civilian clothes accompanied by an attractive lady stood above them on the steps.

Mac and his men looked up through the slatted stairway over their heads. "Yes, sir. Can I help you?"

"No, but my wife and I thought we may help you. We heard that lieutenant say he was hungry. We brought you some left-overs from our breakfast. It's not much, only a few biscuits, but we did manage to sneak a pot of jam." The man bent down and handed Mac two napkins filled with fresh biscuits. The man must have gathered food from several tables as there was enough for at least a half-dozen men.

"Thank you, Mr…'

"My name's Seth Hardin and this is my bride Claire. We're headed back to St. Louis from our wedding trip to New Orleans. This trip has been an experience we'll tell our grandchildren about one day."

"Oh, Seth." The new Mrs. Hardin blushed. "Such a thing to say."

"I understand, Mrs. Hardin. My Laurel would have scolded me too. This is a treat, Mr. Hardin. We didn't get much last night by the time the Quartermaster got to us. God bless ya for bringin' us bread. I hope the rest of your journey is a good one," Mac said.

As the day warmed, many of the soldiers relaxed and began to sing old tunes, tell stories of good times before the war, and share hopes of their first hours back home. Somewhere from the keel of the boat, a hound dog began to howl. Mac never figured out how anyone managed to sneak a pet aboard the crowded boat. At one time, he heard a baby cry—such a strange collection of life was aboard the *Sultana*.

As the sun was sinking on the Arkansas side of the river, the *Sultana* began to edge her way into the landing at Memphis. This would be an extended stop because freight would be unloaded on the dock. Mac planned to volunteer to help unload the cargo.

"Men before I go, I wanna say thank you for your friendship and standin' with me all these months at Castle Morgan. I'll never forget ya. We've been true brothers. I hope we meet again."

"Captain, ya sure you won't go on to Cairo with us? It's only one more day."

"No, Mel. Ain't nothin' I need any further north. And there's a lady I need just seventy miles west. Write to me in Greensboro when you get home."

"You've been mighty good to us, Mac. You're a great friend. Thank you for showin' us about life with the Lord."

"Tennessee, that was my greatest pleasure. We got through this together. Will ya let me pray with y'all one more time?"

The remaining members of the Arky's unit hugged each other one last time. Mac asked God's blessing on them. He shook Mel's hand and reached for Tennessee's. The gentle giant pushed him away.

"I don't like good-byes. Anyway, I'm goin' with ya. Cairo ain't on the way to Jackson either."

The two men walked together to volunteer with unloading the huge hogshead of sugar the *Sultana* had brought from New Orleans. At first, the clerk in charge refused to let them help, saying none of the soldiers were supposed to leave the ship. However, the drizzle turned to a downpour. The clerk decided the offer of help would get him in out of the cold and wet sooner.

"When the whistle blasts, you get back on board. The captain ain't waitin' for stragglers."

"Yes, sir. We understand," Mac replied.

Mac and Tennessee rolled the huge containers down the gangplank. Once on land, they left their cargo and walked down the landing. Mac turned one last time, hoping for a last glimpse of Mel, but he knew that would be unlikely.

"Well, Tennessee, we need some shelter. This thunderstorm ain't lettin' up none."

"Well, Mac. This nice empty crate might do. At least, we can be dry for the night."

The two friends settled in for the night in an empty crate in the Bluff City. Within minutes, both men were sound asleep.

# Chapter 34

*Open rebuke is better than secret love. Faithful are the wounds of
a friend, but the kisses of an enemy are deceitful.*
*Proverbs 27:6-7*

Cortland Cavanaugh had brought Laurel a mixed bag of
emotions that Christmas. His declaration of love had certainly
taken her by surprise. Of course, she was aware they'd become
close friends. She enjoyed the time they spent together. Cort talked
with her about things she cared about--things like books, places
he'd visited, and social and political issues of the day. They had
serious, personal discussions, much the way she had with Rachel
when they grew up together in the Ozarks.

More than that, he was open and not afraid to talk about his
dreams, hurts, and regrets. In some ways, Laurel felt she knew him
better than she'd ever known Mac. Cortland always answered
questions she asked him, never evading things that were personal
or awkward. Mac had often done that, mostly to protect her, she
knew, but still, they proved to be barriers that never seemed to
come between her and Cort. Laurel felt there was much about Mac
that she'd never know or understand because he was a more
private person than the doctor.

Laurel enjoyed the intimate talks they shared during the cold winter evenings in front of the fire. In February, after a pleasant family meal of rabbit stew and boiled potatoes, the kids turned the conversation to families.

"Ya know, Dr. Cort, my mama is a Campbell. Her papa brought her and her brothers all the way to Arkansas from North Carolina."

"Is that so, Andy?"

"Yes, sir."

"How is it you know so much about your family, young man?"

Cathy didn't let him answer. "We all know. It's in our family Bible. Important stuff about our family's all written in there. Can we show him, Mama?"

"If he wants to see it. It's just an old scripture book that's come down through my Campbell family, not so much to look at."

"Andy seems to think it's pretty special," Cortland said.

"We all do, Dr. Cort. I'm in there and Andy, too. Cathy and Roy...that's how we got to be MacLaynes." Gracie went to the table under the window where the old book lay.

"I'd sure like to see how a book can be so important as to make a family."

Gracie handed the Bible to Laurel. "Here, Mama. Show Dr. Cort our family history."

Laurel spent some time going over the entries, showing the adoption dates and birthdays of the MacLayne children. She pointed to the slightly smudged entry noting the date of the Battle of Corinth when the family lost Roy. The smeared date came about as Annie's tears fell on the page when Mac had shown it to her.

"You haven't written in Macky's birth yet," Cort said.

"We're waitin' for Papa to get back. Our family book only gets written in by the head of our family," Andy explained to the doctor.

Cort looked at Laurel. "Does that mean Macky isn't part of the family yet?"

All the kids responded with a negative reply. "Macky's our brother!" Mark Thomas snapped.

"Dr. Cavanaugh is right. Macky needs to be in our family record. Andy, you are the man of our household now. You need to put him on the family list."

"I can't do that, Mama. Papa will do it when he gets home." A hush fell over the room.

"We don't know when that will be, Andy. Macky needs to be in our family record. You write it in for him."

"Are ya sure I should be doin' this?" Andy hesitated. Laurel nodded to him. He took the pen and inkpot from his father's desk and brought it to the table. "Tell me how to put it down, Mama."

"Just make it the way your father wrote the entry for Mark Thomas and Leah Ann."

Patrick Matthew MacLayne was born to Patrick and Laurel MacLayne on September 23, 1864, at Shiloh, Craighead County, Arkansas.

"This is a wonderful family, Laurel. I know you are proud of them all."

"Yes, Cort. I am. Now it's time for me to get them bedded down for the night."

"Will you let me hold Macky while you help the other little ones?" Cortland asked.

"If that's what you want." She spent the next fifteen minutes listening to prayers and tucking in quilts. When she returned to retrieve the baby, she found Macky asleep on Cort's shoulder. "You seem to have a way with my little one. He never goes to sleep that easily for me."

"We're good friends. I do love holdin' that young fella."

"You miss your family, don't you?"

"I miss the fact that I didn't have the family I wanted. My wife, Eugenia, lacked the strength to bear children. We had a daughter about two years after we married, but there were no more children. I am afraid my wife was a bit like a china doll…a joy to look at but very fragile. Genie didn't care much for her wifely role in our bedroom." Cort rubbed his hand across his eyes. "I apologize for that remark, Laurel. I shouldn't have said that to you.

I'd never want to offend you. I sometimes forget. You're always so easy to talk with."

"I'm not offended, Cort."

"I loved Genie. My wife was a beautiful woman, a perfect mistress in our home. Beau Coeur was a gracious, welcoming place for all who came."

"I've heard you speak of a daughter."

"Gracelyn was the apple of her daddy's eye. The little pixie wrapped me around her finger the day she was laid in my arms. When the fever took her, well, a part of me died that day. I hadn't felt that pull from a child until the day Macky came."

"I know what it is to lose a child. My first son was stillborn. His name was Campbell."

"You've been a strong woman through all your grief, Laurel. Your strength is one of your most endearing qualities. Where does it come from?"

"It's not me, I tell you truly. I couldn't deal with any of the hardships without the promises of grace. Mac helped me learn that. The Lord sustains me, even when I want to give up."

"Where did you find the will to believe after so much bad happened?"

"Mac made me promise."

"Do you believe he's still alive, Laurel?"

"I don't know. The colonel from his unit told me Mac died at Oil Trough, but no one saw him. I've had no word that he's alive, but I believed I'd feel his loss if he were gone." Laurel's words were barely a whisper.

"My dearest friend, how can you hold on to hope when you've not seen nor heard a word in fourteen months? Are you holdin' out false hopes for yourself and your children? Even Andy said he wanted his father to write in the family Bible. Laurel, you know Mac will probably never return to Shiloh."

"I realize that, but until I say it, I don't think it will be real. I'm not able to make that step yet."

He squeezed her hand. "I won't push you to make a decision, Laurel. You are dear to me. When you are ready, I'll still

424

be here. My greatest hope is that one day you will let me become a part of this family."

"Cortland, I can't promise…"

"I'm not askin' for a promise. I just want ya to know that helpin' you raise your babies would be a joy. I'd always help support your older children. I will treasure the opportunity to be your husband."

"Thank you for caring. You have become my best friend. Right now, I can't offer more than friendship, but know I don't offer it lightly."

"I understand, Laurel. You'll find I'm a patient man."

"You are a kind man and a good one."

Macky woke and cried out as a five-month-old is likely to do at feeding time. "I think this one is hungry and ready for bed."

"I'll let myself out. Sweet dreams, Laurel, dear."

Toward the end of February, Gracie asked Laurel for a biscuit. There was plenty of cornmeal, and her family didn't lack for vegetables or salt pork. They were blessed to still have more than half a barrel of salt, which was unheard of in her community. They had not gone hungry because Mac had stocked the stash so well. Laurel had even been able to share some basic supplies with her family since Mac had been away. They'd seldom done without anything because of his good planning. But flour and yeast were luxuries in Craighead County in the last few months. Fresh fruit, except for their home-grown grapes was almost non-existent. Laurel felt Gracie's sweet request for bread warranted a trip to town to seek out flour and yeast.

To her surprise, Laurel found a small bag of flour at the Davis general store, and McCollough had a box of yeast. The fact these items cost five times more than they had before the war didn't make a difference. Laurel would bake fresh bread for her children that week.

"Mrs. MacLayne, we have a letter addressed to you back in the mail pouch." Mr. McCollough said.

"May I have it please?" For the briefest moment, Laurel's breath caught in her throat. After all this time, could it be from Mac? "Is it from the army?"

"Don't look official. It's not from Richmond," he answered.

"Mr. McCollough, you know my husband didn't join the Confederate army."

"Ma'am, we don't get mail from the Union mail here. Once in a rare moon, we get mail brought by the Confederate mail service but not very often. Here's the letter. Looks like it came from Washington County."

Laurel hadn't received a letter from Washington County since the spring of '61. She knew much of that area had been under Union control, especially after the battles of Pea Ridge and Prairie Grove. She looked at the envelope and knew immediately the letter hadn't come from Elizabeth Wilson, her dear friend who helped her regain Gracie. The handwriting was masculine but not recognizable. She tucked the tattered post into her reticule, picked up her parcel of yeast, and headed home. She was barely out of town when she pulled Sassy to the side of the road and ripped open the letter.

December 20, 1864

My dear sister,

I'm writing to tell ya that Maggie, me, and our kids have come home to Arkansas· Texas ain't no place for a farmer· The war's been bad there, and the outlaws and bushwhackers even worse·

We bought back our farm from the Tomlins· They run on hard times after the war started· They decided to go west· California they said· I gave them our wagon and mules and fifty dollars· I told 'em I'd take over the last year of payments to you· Then they told me they didn't make the last two years' mortgage to you either· I agreed to pay that, too· Will this work for you? I

*can't make a payment now, but I will send the first year's*
*mortgage payment at harvest.*

*My family is well. So far I ain't had to go to the war.*
*Things are winding down around here so I pray I can stay home.*
*Hope your family is well and safe. Elizabeth sends her love and*
*prayers to you. Write and tell me how you are faring.*

*Affectionately,*
*Your brother Samuel*

Laurel laughed and cried with the news she'd received. Thankfully, her brother and his family were safe and back at the Campbell homeplace. She'd hoped he would come to Shiloh to make his home near her, but she knew he'd be happy in the old family cabin in the Boston Mountains. What a nice surprise the letter had been. Only one thing could have made it better. The letter could have come from Mac.

Perhaps Cort was right. Mac couldn't send her a letter because he lost his life on the Arkansas River near a little town she'd never heard of before. She'd received no word because the dead do not communicate. The man she loved would not go so long without letting her know where he was. She'd not allowed herself to feel his loss because she kept Mac alive in her dreams and hopes. Was her delusion fair to her children?

On the trip home, Laurel decided that between the last day of February and her birthday in April, she would do some heavy soul-searching. She would decide whether she would go on hoping Mac would return or if she would face the horrible possibility that the colonel from Batesville had told her the truth. She knew she couldn't make the decision alone. She needed to talk with her father-in-law, her uncle, Andy, and Cathy. Only then would she know she was making the decision God would have her to make.

That next Sunday, Laurel asked Thomas to talk with her privately. He led her into his office and pulled two chairs in front of the fire.

"Well, Daughter, what's weighin' so heavy on your mind?"

"I guess I'm not doing a very good job of putting up a brave front, am I?"

"Why would ya try to hide your feelin's from your family, Laurel? We all miss Patrick, just like you do. Ya know, the last conversation I had with my son, he was sittin' right here in front of this hearth. He made me promise to watch out for you."

"I miss him so much, Papa." The crackling of the logs in the fireplace filled a time of silence. "Do you believe what the colonel told us—that Mac died at Oil Trough last March?"

"Laurel, I pray every day that Patrick will return, but truthfully, each day that hope gets a bit dimmer. I know how much he loved you and his family. It's been almost a year since that battle happened. My son would move heaven and hell to get word to us if he could."

"Do you think it's hurtful to my children to carry on the dream their father will come back? Do I need to tell them he won't return to us?"

"I can see you are overwhelmed with all the things you're trying to deal with alone."

"I guess I am. Some days I get up and I'm not sure I can make one more decision, solve one more problem, or figure out any way to stretch our supplies. I manage. But how can I reassure my children when I have no answers myself?"

"Bless your heart, Laurel. I don't know what to say to make things any easier. I can't say it myself—Patrick died at Oil Trough. It's too final. A part of me has to keep the ember alive. I don't guess I was much help to ya, Daughter."

"You've always been here for me, Pa. Thank you for listening. I'll pray about it some more. God will tell me the right way to handle this when the time comes. I can't be the only woman in the South who is trying to decide whether to tell her children their father isn't coming home from the war."

Another week passed. Laurel spent more than one restless night that week. Two nights she didn't sleep at all. On Saturday afternoon, she loaded her two youngest children into her buggy and drove to her uncle's place. Between him and her aunt, surely she could get some advice that would ease her mind and let her make the decision that wouldn't let her rest.

Putting the little ones down to play, Laurel sat with Matthew and Ellie Campbell at their table. They sipped a cup of hot cider—weak cider as the supply was so scarce it was watered like every other luxury in the area—but hot.

"Niece, I'm glad ya came. Seems like a long time since we've had a real talk. How are you dealin' with things?" Matthew asked.

"We're making do."

"No doubt. That's why you're all smiles and got those lovely dark circles under your eyes." Laurel's Aunt Ellie's gift for sarcasm rang through.

"All right. I've not been sleeping well, for a while."

"You wanna tell your preacher what's botherin' ya?"

"Uncle Matthew, do you believe Mac is dead?"

"Why are you askin' me this now, Laurel? You were notified more'n six months ago that Mac disappeared in that skirmish over by the White River."

"Disappeared, but not found. I don't know what I should believe. I don't know what I should tell my children."

"Has somethin' brought all this to a head right now?" her aunt asked.

"Just daily living. A few weeks ago the kids were showing Dr. Cavanaugh our family Bible, and Cort mentioned Macky's birthday wasn't recorded there."

"So did ya record it?" Matthew asked her.

"You know it's a family tradition that only head of household writes in that book. Andy said we'd wait until Mac got home."

"Oh, I see."

"What if he never comes home? He never knew I was expecting Macky. Now that sweet boy is nearly six months old, and his name wasn't even listed as a part of our family. I asked Andy to write about Macky's birth in the family record." Laurel stood up and paced.

"Darlin', are you considerin' a courtship with Dr. Cavanaugh?"

"Oh, Aunt Ellie, I don't know. I haven't been acting too brazen, have I."

"No, of course, you haven't. But I've seen the way he looks at you. I know you've done nothin' to dishonor Mac's memory."

"Cort is a good friend. He saved my life and Macky's. I enjoy his company. We like many of the same things, and he's easy to talk with. Truthfully, there have been times he's kept me sane when I missed Mac so badly I didn't want to go on."

"Laurel Grace, I don't know if Mac will come home. I'm glad you've found a friend you can rely on. Take your lead from the Lord. If the time comes that you are ready to move on, you'll get the sign you need." Ellie hugged her niece.

"Be patient, Laurel Grace. The Lord will be with you every day. When Mac was home, three made up your marriage. Well, two are still in your marriage. Don't forget to share the load. You don't have to do anything alone unless you decide to." Matthew took Laurel's hand asked a blessing for his grieving niece and himself that he might be a balm for her.

With the return of warmer weather in April, one of Laurel's spring projects took her outside. She wanted to clear away the winter clutter from the orchard. Already, tiny nodules clustered on some branches. Laurel knew these small brown knots would open into glorious pink and white apple blossoms within a couple of weeks if the temperatures stayed warm. With the seven years of love and tending, these precious trees should deliver on their promise this year. What a blessing for Shiloh!

That afternoon Laurel decided she needed to have that final conversation. Andy and Cathy weren't children anymore. The roles they accepted and successfully filled since Mac had been away led them to maturity much earlier than would have happened otherwise. They needed the opportunity to be heard before Laurel made any decision that would impact the family. After planning with Annie to care for the four younger children, she asked Cathy and Andy to ride with her to Eden.

"Mama, why'd we come out here today?" Andy asked.

430

"This place has always been a very special place to me and your papa. The first day he brought me here, we named this place Eden—too perfect to change. We decided to build our house where it is now and keep this place as it was when the Lord made it."

"You love it here, don't ya, Mama?"

"Yes, Cathy. When I'm here and in the orchard, I always feel Mac is with me. He is so much a part of these places."

"So, Mama. Why'd you bring us here today?" Andy repeated.

"I wanted to know how you feel about..." Laurel faltered. "I need to ask..."

"You wanna ask us about Papa, don't you?" Cathy reached out and took her mother's hand.

"Yes. I probably should have asked you two about this a while ago. I didn't, and I still don't rightly know what to say."

"Mama, we both miss Papa. Except for those three days at Christmas more'n a year ago and that one day when he rode through from Chalk Bluff, we ain't seen him—that's been two years. 'Course we miss him, Cathy said."

Laurel squeezed Andy's shoulders. "Son, I know you and Cathy can remember having you papa at home. Gracie can remember some things, but the little ones. I don't think they have any memory of their father. The army commander thinks he was killed in a skirmish over by White River. You know that, don't you?"

"I know." Andy refused to look at his mother.

"I have been trying to decide if I need to help the other children understand that perhaps their papa is not coming back to Shiloh."

Andy stood up and walked away. The three remained silent for some time. When he returned to the fallen log where they'd been sitting, he said, "Mama, you've done a good job takin' care of all of us since Papa's gone away. I'm glad you let me be your son."

"Andy, you've been one of my greatest strengths. I couldn't have survived without you."

"What I'm sayin' is you've been carryin' a heavy load to keep us together and fed and safe. Whatever ya decide, I'm on your side. I know you'll do what's best for us."

"Mama, I know Dr. Cort likes you. If Papa's not comin' home to us, do you think he might want to be a part of our family?"

"Cathy, whatever made you ask such a question?"

"It's easy to see y'all are good friends. He's here all the time. He loves the babies. I've watched him hold'em and play with 'em."

"Daughter, I've not thought beyond what I've asked you two. I don't want to cause any more confusion in our family right now. If I need to help my children move beyond our loss, I will try to do it."

"Mama, we love Papa. We love you. We know you care about our papa. We trust you to do what is right for our family," Andy said

Laurel struggled with the question still. Even after a frank conversation with her father-in-law, her uncle and aunt, and her children, she was no closer to an answer. She took comfort in their praise of her ability to make the right choice, but in all their words, she'd found not one hint of what they'd do in her place. Eight days would bring her to the deadline she'd set for herself. Laurel would turn thirty-five.

As she sat in her bed reading the sixteenth chapter of Proverbs, Laurel ran across verse after verse repeating things her family had said to her recently. She laid her Bible aside and went to her knees. "Lord, I need to know your will. If I am truly a widow, do you want me to help my children grieve and move on? Is it your will for me to marry Cortland and allow him to help me raise my children? Please give me the insight to do what you want me to do. Amen."

She fell into a deep dreamless sleep almost immediately and didn't rouse until Macky cried out to be fed about 2:30 in the morning. She rose and sat in her rocker to feed the boy, again asking the same questions of God. When the baby was satisfied, dry, and burped, Laurel returned him to his crib. When she returned to sleep, her night was filled with dreams—memories of all the happiest days she'd spent in her Shiloh home with Mac and a passionate dream of their first night as man and wife which left her in tears. Laurel relived Mac's homecoming from the second legislative sessions when he'd been away from home more than two months and how they'd lain spooned together the entire night, not making love but simply absorbed with the presence of the other. The memory of their beautiful weekend honeymoon spent in Eden camping out under the stars left Laurel calling out Mac's name and craving his touch.

"Enough!" Laurel got up and dressed even though it was two hours before sunrise. She wanted no more dreams that made her loss deeper. After a few minutes of frustrated pacing, she sat down. "Thank you, Lord, for the past. I was a woman blessed above all reason. Help me move beyond the hurt."

She pulled out the mending to take her mind off the dreams. This would be a good way to spend the time until she could begin her day without waking her family.

The next night, Laurel chose another part of scripture to read. She wanted a peaceful night's sleep. Her bible fell open to the small chapter of II John. Laurel hadn't read the tiny book in a long time. When she read the thirteen verses, the peace she'd sought came to her. *Live a life of love…Jesus Christ will be with us in truth and love.*

The dreams Laurel remembered from that night were sweet, happy pictures of family life at Shiloh. She recalled the birth of Leah Ann with Mac at her side, and the day he'd brought Gracie home from Little Rock in her new buggy. Laurel remembered the day Mac had awakened from the terrible gunshot, and the day they'd entered Andy's adoption date in the family tree at Mac's bedside. Then she recalled the last Christmas the MacLayne's had spent together, standing around the hearth and singing *Silent Night* together. She could almost hear Mac's warm baritone as the family ended with *Sleep in Heavenly Peace.*

She knew exactly what she would do—what God was telling her to do. When she awoke at first light, she uttered, "Thank you, Lord."

φ

After supper that night, Laurel called her family around the table. She'd included J.F. and Annie and Roy. All those present were stakeholders in what she had to say. She held Macky on her shoulder, even though he was far too young to understand what she was about to say.

"Family and J.F., all of you know I've been a bit short-tempered and mighty distracted for a while, I guess since Christmas."

"You could say that, Mama." Andy's quip made everyone laugh.

"Thank you, Andy. I figured you'd agree with me."

"You taught us to tell the truth."

"I try. Well, that's what I wanna talk to ya about tonight. I know you've had questions, but you didn't ask me because you were afraid to upset me. Time to get it out in the open."

"Mrs. Mac. We don't have to be here if you just want to talk to your kids."

"Annie, sweetheart, you are as much a part of this family as any person here. I want you and Roy with us." Laurel stood up at the head of the table. "Kids and J.F., you know the commander from Mac's company in Batesville came here in the late spring last year and told me that your papa was missing after the skirmish at Oil Trough. He said that when the men who had died in that battle were removed from the battlefield, the Confederate troops buried them. No one saw your father after he fell. One of the men who knew Mac saw his horse shot out from under him. He also found your papa's cross near the dead horse the next morning. That is all we know."

"Mama, is Papa not comin' home ever?" Gracie asked.

"Precious, I honestly don't know. I know Patrick MacLayne loved you all and me. He loved us so much that he would do whatever he had to do to get home or send us word that he's all right. But Gracie, I can't tell you that Papa is coming home."

"But what are we gonna do about it, Mama?" Mark Thomas asked.

"We aren't doing anything different, Son. We're gonna keep our homestead going, and we'll raise beef. J.F.'s been doing a good job already. You young'uns will keep growing up and going to school. We'll pray for your papa and wait to see what happens."

"Mama, we can help you with the work," Cathy said.

"You all have already done that. You, Andy, and Annie have carried more'n your share. We are going to be fine."

"I'm really sad about Papa," Gracie said.

"Kids, it's all right to be sad. When people we love are not with us, we are sad. If your papa can't come back to us, though, I want you to remember he's with Jesus. Your papa believed in the Gospel. That is one of the reasons I love him. We can miss him, but not grieve too much because he's living in joy."

Laurel had one thing left to do. She'd promised herself she'd clear up all the complications before she got another year older. She had three days to finish. She drove to the doctor's office at the Widow Parker's place so she could avoid the distractions at her home. She pulled up to the front porch and tied Sassy Lady to the rail. She knocked at the front door.

"Good morning, Laurel. What a nice surprise."

"Are you busy this morning, Cort?"

"No. I've just finished with the only two patients I knew about. You have a problem at your place?"

"Things are fine. If you've time, I thought we might take a drive. I've got a couple of things I'd like to talk about with you."

"Alright, let me get my hat and put out a sign. It's a pretty day for a drive along the ridge."

They set off down the old military road, enjoying the new spring along Crowley's Ridge. A gentle breeze danced through the burgeoning leaves, distorting the sunbeams from bright to dark to bright again. For a while, only Sassy's hoofbeats and an occasional bird's call broke the silence.

"You're awful quiet for a lady who wanted to talk, Laurel. What's on your mind this mornin', my dearest friend?"

"Cort, I've been thinking and praying about us a lot lately. I mean seriously, not just a random thought now and again."

"Am I glad you've been doin' that?" He looked at her, trying to catch a glimpse of her eyes.

"I hope you will be." She smiled briefly. "I talked with my children, and I told them I didn't know if their father would return from the war. I told them what the colonel told me and that Mac may be in Heaven now. I think the older ones already knew but for Gracie and Mark Thomas, well, they took it a bit harder than I thought. Of course, the little ones can't even remember who Mac is. All of them were worried about how we'd be able to keep our farm going."

"How are you doin' after sharin' the news?"

"I don't feel much different. After I got a hold on my depression this spring, it's been a gradual return to my routine. I have to keep my promise to Mac. I told him I'd live in faith, knowing my value, and depending on God to take care of my needs and help me protect my family. You have helped me put that low time behind me, Cort."

"You are strong in your faith, Laurel. No one can deny that. Does that leave any place for me?"

"Yes, Cort, there is a place, but I'm not sure it's one you want. In my adult life, I've never had a better friend than you have been to me. I've never had a person I could speak my thoughts to the way I've talked with you this past year. I love that."

"I feel that way, too. We are fine companions. We share so many interests."

"And Cort, I will be eternally grateful for the care you have given Leah Ann and Macky. They thrive under the kind, fatherly sort of love you give them. They need your attention."

"You know how much pleasure it's brought me. I love those young'uns. I feel Macky's mine—the way we labored together to bring him into the world."

"I can never repay that debt. If you'd not been here, Macky would be resting next to Campbell, and I probably would too. You were God's gift to us that night."

"Laurel, where is all this talk goin'? You know I want you to marry me. I know you're not ready to say good-bye to Mac's memory yet. I told you I'll wait."

436

"I can't marry you, Cortland. I'm sure that I'll never marry again. Mac is probably buried in an unmarked grave over by the White River, but I still love him. My soul craves his presence. I'll never lose the need to be Mrs. Patrick MacLayne."

"Laurel, please, you're bein' rash. You're still grievin'."

"No. Let me explain. Last night, I read II John. Have you read that tiny letter in the back of the Bible?"

"Not in ages, I'm sure."

"The words spoke to me. I know how I feel now. Cortland, I love you. I'll always want the best life can give you to be your portion. I can't give you the things you want and need. I can't give you children to carry on your family. You know that."

"Laurel, you've got a beautiful family already."

"Yes, I do, but you're still a young, virile man. There is a woman out there who will give you children. They will be Cavanaughs—not MacLaynes. She will love you passionately, not with the friendship that I feel for you. You deserve to know that passion. I want that for you, my dear friend. And Cort, I want us to remain friends. I never want to lose the connection we've built. Do you understand what I am trying to tell you?"

"I wish I didn't."

"Cortland Cavanaugh, you are a good man, my best friend. You deserve a real marriage. God will provide your soulmate if you ask him."

"Give me some time, Laurel. Right now, I don't know how to reply to you. For now, I should go back to work. Let me drive us back."

# Chapter 35

*Thou hast ravished my heart, my sister, my spouse; Thou hast*
*ravished my heart with one of thine eyes…*
*How fair is thy love, my sister, my spouse!*
*How much better is thy love than wine!*
*Song of Songs 4:9-10*

A cold drizzle continued through the night. Mac and
Tennessee shivered in the crate near the warehouse, but both were
grateful for the protection it offered. Fatigue and hunger were best
forgotten in deep sleep, which Mac found almost the minute he
curled up inside. His escape lasted less than two hours. The men
awoke to the sound of deep rumbling from a distance.

"Mac, ya think Memphis is bein' shelled?"

"No. It's probably thunder. The storm's just gettin'…."
Before Mac finished his comment about a storm, a second, sharper
blast echoed down the river. "Now that sounded like mortar fire."

"What do we need to do? We'd be in trouble whatever
army found us. Deserters from one or a spy to the other." Then a
third explosion, so strong and loud the wharf shook. Mac and
Tennessee crawled from their crate to witness scores of men
running toward the docks and even further north down the banks of
the Mississippi. Noise, confusion, and rampant speculation built to

a roar outside. A man who appeared to work on the docks yelled, "Look yonder. Fire upriver. Can't tell what it is, but it's big. Those flames are shootin' up twenty or thirty feet."

An old riverboat hand answered, "That there's a riverboat done exploded. Seen more'n one in my day. Nothin' else on the river makes a light like that."

Within minutes a flotilla of steamboats, tugs, fishing scowls, and even rowboats set off upriver. Word began to spread through Memphis, and people from the city made their way toward the riverfront. Many were spectators, but most were people who came to volunteer whatever help they could give.

In no time, debris and survivors floated down past the docks, some yelling for help. Others were beyond the point of asking. Mac and Tennessee joined teams of men, pulling the wounded and half-frozen victims out of the bitterly cold, muddy waters. People grasped any floating object they could find. Six men and one woman were pulled to land, hanging on to a single cabin door. Cotton bales saved three and four people at a time, sometimes with one or two more holding onto the heavy twine that bound it together.

Tennessee was nearly dragged under the water when he tried to disentangle a man with a broken arm who feared losing his grip. One badly burned man, obviously a civilian passenger from the looks of his fine shirt, the only clothing he had left, had somehow remained alert. Mac and Tennessee lifted him out of the water. "*Sultana* done burned down to the waterline," he said.

An hour or so before dawn, the *Bostana II*, a steamboat headed downriver, moored at the Memphis wharf. On her decks, she carried 150 men, a few women, and a couple of children the crew had pulled from the cold water. Many of the survivors were more burned or injured than those who'd floated down themselves. Some of these people were missing limbs. Others had deep cuts where they'd been struck by flying debris from the blasts. The worst were the people who had been scalded by the steam from the boilers or those caught by the horrendous flames.

"Tennessee, grab a blanket from the nuns on the dock. We'll make a litter and help carry some of these people down to the doctors."

"Sure thing, Mac." In a few minutes, they concocted a litter and spent the next several hours transporting scores of the worst wounded down to the triage area where doctors made hasty exams to decide which one of the hospitals to send the injured person to. Blessedly, some of the lesser injured Union soldiers found a place to rest in the Old Veteran's Home in the city. Far more were lined up on the riverbank and covered. No mercy could help them now.

By noon, the *Bostana II* had all her rescued passengers released to the medical professionals in Memphis. The United States Sanitary commission stationed in the city during the war pulled from their stores to provide a meal of hot soup and meat sandwiches for the volunteers who had worked through the night. Mac and Tennessee sat under the tent the commission provided and devoured the meal. When offered a second bowl of soup, both men eagerly accepted the gift. This was the first food they had since they'd left the *Sultana* at 6:00 p.m. the day before. They took full advantage of a time to rest.

Neither Mac nor his friend had spoken of that night's tragedy. Mac was at a loss to even believe what had happened. By this time, enough reports had come back to confirm the words of the burned civilian were true. The *Sultana* had exploded. Both Tennessee and he should have been on that steamboat the previous night. "I can't believe this happened, Mac. This night just couldn't happen. We musta carried fifty people off that boat. Faces burned away, clothes all but gone, one man lost both his legs. Maybe it wasn't the *Sultana*."

"I'm pretty sure it was. Timin' was right. That boat eased outta here about midnight. They crossed over to Arkansas to load up with wood and coal…at Hopefield. A lousy name for the last stop, wasn't it."

"Do ya think we toted any of our men tonight?"

"Dear Lord, I hope not, Tennessee. I'd hope we could recognize our boys. I pray Mel is all right."

"I don't understand how God let this happen, Mac. We lived through the worst of all times at Castle Morgan. Some of those fellas were in hell at Andersonville. They're all so close to home. I don't get it. Didn't ya tell us God is a lovin' Father?"

"We've seen some horrible sights tonight. I don't know how to answer ya, Tennessee, except to say I believe He is."

"It's so hard to keep yer faith when ya know your friends died like this."

"War is horrible. We've seen all kinds of evil, like this accident tonight, cruel men like Jones, diseases, and senseless murders."

"We've seen too dang much of that. Don't it make you question the stuff you taught us at Castle Morgan?"

"Ain't bad to question, but then we gotta look at the good too. Remember Amanda Gardner and her daughter Belle who shared her books and garden vegetables with us? That lady cut up her carpets so some men didn't have to sleep on a dirt floor."

"Yeah, I think a lot of that good lady."

"We had Reverend Henderson for our warden, not that demon from Andersonville. We had doctors, and we became brothers-in-arms."

"You always did choose the bright side, Mac."

"Somewhere in the book of Jeremiah, I don't know where exactly, there's a scripture that tells us to do that. It says something like, 'I don't want a sorrowful day, but it may come even when I do right.' It goes on to finish like 'the Lord is my hope on my worst days.'

"Is that the gospel according to the Arky Yank?"

"Maybe, but it's a good one to remember on days like today. Maybe we need to go back to see if they need more help with the wounded."

They continued to work until near nightfall. Both men were near exhaustion. One last boat docked carrying a few more soldiers they'd removed from the river. Not many had to be carried to the medical tent. One of the last bodies Mac and Tennessee moved wore the partial uniform of a Union private. He had received some heavy wounds to his chest and lower torso, but his face was recognizable. This boy, just eighteen years old, had been one of the last men added to the Arky's Unit. His name was Isaac Bright. Drew had taken a special interest in the young soldier because they lived in neighboring counties in Indiana. As they carried him to the line of deceased, Tennessee asked, "Wonder if Mel made it to safety?"

"I hope he did, but it's in God's hands now. I'm so happy that Drew got a chance to go upriver earlier and didn't come up with us. I've got no more in me tonight. Let's go get some sleep."

Taking a couple of blankets from the stack in front of the tent set up by the Sanitary Commission, they returned to their empty crate. They stripped out of their partially dry, filthy, bloody clothes, wrapped in the blankets, and promptly fell asleep. Mac's final prayer was that they'd seen the worst of the *Sultana* disaster.

Well after sun-up the next day, Mac and Tennessee returned to the docks to find swarms of people removing debris from the tragic accident. Most were dealing with the dead who lay in long lines down the river bank. Mac and Tennessee decided to walk the lines to search for their friend, Mel Grigsby. Although many could not be recognized, of those whose features were still partly intact, they did not find anyone whom they believed was Mel. "Tennessee, I take this as a good omen. Mel was a good swimmer. I'm gonna believe he swam to the Arkansas shore and is now on his way back home to Missouri."

"I hope you're right, Captain."

Mac decided it was time to go home. He knew there was nothing more he could do for his comrade from the *Sultana*. "Tennessee, I'm gonna find me away across the river. I don't have the price of a ferry, but maybe I can work a day or two or find me a place on a boat that's gonna fuel up across stream. I'm goin' home."

"That's what I'm thinkin' too. After finding Isaac last night, I don't think I wanna stay here anymore. It's less than a hundred miles to Jackson. If I have to walk every step, I can be home before a week is gone."

"Well, I've not got the strength to swim Ole Muddy there, but once I get on that west bank, I can make my way back to

442

Shiloh. So long, Tennessee. If you get home and don't like what the war's left ya there, we got some mighty good land and some pretty girls in Arkansas. I'd gladly share it with you. God bless you. It's been a joy to call you brother."

"I hate good-byes, Mac. Let's just say 'til we meet down the road. Thank you for your friendship." The two men parted with a strong pat on the back and Tennessee's final salute to his well-respected captain.

φ

Mac worked three days loading freight onto riverboats to earn the fare to ride a ferry across the river to Hopefield. When he stepped on Arkansas soil just before noon on May 2, 1865, he had the clothes on his back, a pair of worn boots, one blanket from the U.S. Sanitary Commission, and four-bits in his pocket. He also had seventy-five miles between him and Shiloh. He counted himself among the most blessed men. If he had to walk every step of the way, he believed he would be home before five days passed.

The sun shone brightly, and a gentle breeze from the river kept the temperature comfortable. Mac began the long trek down the old military road west. He'd walked less than a mile when he realized he'd be forced to follow the road and not go directly home across the fields and forests because the spring rains and floods that had spelled doom for the *Sultana* on its trip up the Mississippi had also turned Arkansas's northern delta into a massive swampland. The route through the northern regions was out of the question. Mac headed out of Hopefield toward Bolivar.

The first day Mac met a few freight wagons and a rider or two along the road. The freighters were headed toward the river so Mac didn't ask for a ride. One of the sole riders wore Confederate gray. Mac's only clothing clearly showed he'd fought for the opposing side, so he kept his head diverted and continued north and west. Before the sunset, Mac had walked what seemed to be five hundred miles. He was foot weary and hungry. He continued until he found a small grove of trees at the edge of a healthy-looking cotton field where he kicked off his boots, tucked them under his arm, rolled up in his blanket, and promptly fell asleep.

On the second day of his walk, he set out at dawn. Mac searched at every bend of the road for a homestead or settlement, hoping to be able to find something to eat. Finding water was no problem. Creeks and streams were out of their bank with spring rain, but Mac had no means to fish or hunt. He would have to rely on other compassionate souls to provide him with something to eat.

About noon, his needs were supplied. Mac ran across a family in a covered wagon headed toward the Mississippi River. They'd stopped along the side of the road to eat a noon meal.

"Friend, do you have a bite to share? I'm afraid I didn't prepare well for my trip home, and I've gone two days without much to eat," Mack said.

"I guess we can spare some," the man standing by the wagon bed said. "How'd ya come to be out here on foot, Yank?"

"I'm no Yank anymore. I'm an Arkansas homesteader who's tryin' to get back home."

"Now that the war's over, we're goin' back to our place in Tennessee. Been on the road for near a week, comin' out of Springfield. The floods have made travel slow."

Mac devoured a plate of lukewarm beans and a slab of cornbread that the homesteader's wife offered him. "Where did y'all start out this mornin'?"

"We left a church ground where we camped last night. The last town we passed through about noon yesterday was called Bolivar."

"I thank you for the food and the information. I'm headed to Bolivar now. On foot, I guess I got another day and a half of travel to get there. I've got a friend in Bolivar."

"Safe travel, Soldier."

"Thanks again for the vittles. A full stomach makes a long walk possible. Bless ya." Mac picked up his blanket and walked again until dark.

By sundown of the third day, Mac stood at Lizzie Lee's door, knocking to rouse his old friend. After several minutes, the fragile old woman opened her door to him.

"Lizzie, can I stay with ya tonight? I'll tell ya on the front end, I got only four bits."

"Mac! How fine to see ya, again." She ushered him to her kitchen. "How long has it been?"

"I went to Fort Curtis in March of '63. Then I spent the next year fightin' with the Second Arkansas Union Cavalry. Then I went to Cahaba Prison until March of this year. Now I'm almost home."

"Praise the Lord. Too many of our young men can't ever say those words. Let me look at ya!" Lizzie stared at the walking skeleton in front of her. The Mac she saw last had been a well-built, healthy man of about 180 pounds. This person would have been doing good to tilt a scale at 135 pounds. She saw the outlines of his bones under his skin. "Goodness, Mac, have ya been sick?"

"No, Lizzie, but the Rebs didn't have supplies to feed their prisoners very well. Since I left Memphis three days ago, I've not had but one meal."

"I know I can fix that."

"Lizzie, remember I told ya I only have four bits."

"So, when I charge ya for room and board, and maybe even hot water for a bath, I'll expect ya to visit me someday and bring me what ya owe. Besides, I'll expect to meet all those beautiful MacLayne babies."

"It's a promise, Lizzie."

Lizzie fed Mac on her plain, filling fare until he could eat no more. She then set up a hot bath for him in the corner room he'd shared with Laurel the night he'd found her in Bolivar in September of 1857, the night he'd first admitted his love for her. After his first bath in more than a year, he lay beneath clean muslin sheets and fell asleep, anticipating his homecoming. Mac slept until after 7:00 when the traffic on the street below woke him.

After a filling breakfast, Lizzie handed Mac a tin of biscuits with ham and a small pone. "You get to eatin', Mac. Put some meat on those bones before I see ya again."

"God bless ya, Lizzie Lee. You're a dear friend. Thanks to you, I'll be back at Shiloh in two more days.

Mac set out for Greenfield. This road was usually well-traveled. He prayed he could catch a ride back to Greensboro with a freighter. If only his luck would hold.

Within the first hour, a freighter approached Mac. Mac attempted to wave him down. The driver refused to stop, and he spat at Mac as he passed. "No Yankee is gonna get a ride from me." The man called back.

"God bless ya, all the same," Mac called to him. He continued to walk.

A bit before noon, another freighter driving four mules pulled to a halt when Mac motioned for a ride. "Where ya headed, Soldier?" A tall, burly teamster drawled.

"Home. Be much obliged if you'd let me ride with ya as far as you go toward Greensboro," Mac answered.

"I can take ya to McCollough's store if you don't happen to be in much of a hurry. I've gotta layover in Jonesboro to pick up some freight tomorrow mornin'."

"Thank the Lord!" Mac's prayers had been answered.

"But only if you don't preach at me all the way."

"I ain't no preacher, Friend. I'm just a happy homesteader who'll be home in two days."

Mac's spirits soared. He sat back, removed his well-worn boots, and sang a good part of the way home.

True to his word, the freighter stopped at McCollough's General Mercantile at 1:00 p.m. the next afternoon. To thank him for the ride on the last leg of the journey, Mac helped the man unload the cargo he'd brought. Mac thanked him and started to leave when he felt the two coins still in his pocket. He stepped back onto the boardwalk and pushed open the door to the familiar store.

"Hello, McCollough. How's business?"

"I'll be. If it ain't MacLayne. I wouldn't knowed ya if you hadn't spoke. Man, we thought you was long dead."

"Not quite. Now that this war's over, I'm more alive than I've been in nearly three years."

"Where ya been all this time? Fightin' in the east? In the north?" McCollough asked.

"Some but mostly just praying to get back to Laurel and my kids."

"Well, I can't believe my eyes. Thought sure you'd gotten your just deserts when they told us you died." Richard Barton walked up behind Mac.

"Hello, Barton. No, I'm still hale and hearty."

"Well, maybe your punishment is more fittin'. If you's dead, you wouldn't have to deal with the shame ya got comin'."

"Barton, I don't want any trouble with you. I'm headed home to Shiloh. The war's over, and I wanna put the arguments and insults in the past."

"We'll see if you can when you get home to find your harlot of a wife in bed with another man and his bastard son at her breast."

McCollough walked between Mac and Barton. "Richard, ain't no call for that. You don't know any of those rumors to be true."

"Dave, everyone in Greensboro and Shiloh knows that boy Laurel spawned last fall belongs to Dr. Cavanaugh. Dang, they may even be married by now."

"Richard Barton, you will take back that slander of my wife. I'll not fight you now because I've only got one goal to reach today. But if you besmirch Laurel's name again, you will answer to me."

"Me? You're the one who deserted her with a house full of kids to feed. She had to find help somewhere."

"Shut your foul mouth. You don't know what you're talkin' about."

Barton swung at Mac, but another man caught his arm. "Leave him be, Richard. The man just wants to go home."

"Dave, please fill me up a couple of bags of whatever kind of candy ya have, whatever this two bits will buy. I haven't given my kids candy in well over a year."

The sun kissed the horizon as Mac walked across the back pasture of his Shiloh home. Even before Mac could see the multitude of pink and white blossoms on the trees, the sweet smell of the apple blossoms wafted across the meadow. His slow deliberate pace became a quick shuffle as he spotted the orchard in full bloom. In the middle of the row, he saw Laurel, her back to him. Just beyond, he saw Andy astride the corral fence, watching Mark Thomas ride Sparky in a circle. Mac began to run toward home.

Laurel turned, concern showing on her face at the sight of the tattered, unshaven, dirty soldier crossing her land. She called out to him. "Do you need something?"

"I do."

"What do you want here?" Laurel's voice shook.

"Don't ya know me?"

Laurel looked at the thin, ragged man who spoke. She dropped the hoe. She gazed into the storm-blue eyes of her husband. "Patrick. Oh, thank you, Father in Heaven. Patrick!" She threw herself into his arms. "Thank God. You're home. I knew you'd come back to us."

"I told you I would. Laurel, I love you. Nothing that's happened in the time we've been separated matters. We are a family again."

Mac kissed Laurel, but she pulled back from his embrace.

"Mac, what are you saying…nothing that's happened since you've been gone matters?"

"I know life's been hard for you. I just want us to pick up from here."

Before more could be spoken, Andy ran to his father with Mark Thomas close behind. The girls heard Andy calling out that Papa was home, and they began to stream out the back door. Mac took Laurel by the waist and pulled her toward the children. They piled into his arms until he fell under the load. Such laughter and joy had not been heard at Shiloh in many months.

After many minutes of hugging, kissing, rolling around in the grass, tousling hair, and patting backs, Laurel broke up the welcome.

"Enough, young'uns. Your papa has to be worn to a frazzle. Let's go in and get him a bite of supper."

Although the MacLaynes had eaten supper already, Laurel put a good meal in front of Mac. The entire family sat around the table as he ate. They shared stories, told of misdeeds of another sibling, and said a hundred times how glad they were to have him home. Mac sat and listened, soaking up every minute of the thing he'd missed most—family suppertime.

As the sun was setting below the ridge, a loud wail came from the second pen. Laurel rose and went to bring the hungry baby to the family table.

"So, this is the young fella the men at Mc Collough's Mercantile told me about," Mac said.

"Didn't you know about him? I wrote a letter to you and sent it to Batesville the week after he was born."

"No, I didn't get a letter after I left Helena. What do you call him?"

"We've been callin' him Macky," Cathy answered.

"That's an unusual name."

"We all like it, Papa," Andy replied.

"Okay. It's a good name, I guess." Mac had a frown on his face.

Laurel rolled her eyes and said, "Of course that's not his legal name. We named him Patrick Matthew. Only fitting that he's named after the two best men he'll ever know."

Mac stood and walked to Laurel's side. "You named him after me?"

"Of course. He's the spitting image of his father." Laurel handed the crying baby to Mac. When Mac took him, Macky stopped crying and stared up into his father's eyes, eyes exactly the same storm-blue color as his own. The baby smiled.

"No doubt he's a MacLayne. Look at those eyes." Mac kissed his new son and then pulled his wife into another embrace.

"Mac, I hate that scraggy beard. I hardly knew you when you walked toward me in the orchard. I think you need to see if you can't find my husband somewhere under all that dirt and hair."

The MacLaynes laughed again.

Well past bedtime, the MacLayne cabin became still and quiet that night. However, when Mac and Laurel retired to their sanctuary with Macky asleep in Mac's arms, a tub of water awaited Mac in the water closet. Laurel had also laid out the scissors and Mac's shaving implements that the colonel from Batesville had returned with Mac's belongings. Mac soaked in the tub for a long time, enjoying the luxury of a real bath. Laurel washed his back and shoulders, as she'd often done in the past. She teased him with a gentle kiss on the corner of his mouth.

"That's the last kiss you'll get until you shed that awful beard."

"When did you get back my razor and soap cup? I thought I'd lost those at Oil Trough."

"Your commanding officer, a man named Livingston, and one your troop, named Josiah Parchman, brought them to me when they came to tell me they believed you'd died at the skirmish near the White River. The younger man, Josiah, said he'd seen your dead horse there. They gathered up your things from the camp and brought them to me when they brought Midnight home.

"My dear Lord, thank you. Midnight is here, safe?"

"Yes, Mac."

"I never dreamed I'd see him again." Mac began to restore his beard to its pre-war shape and trimmed his chestnut-colored hair. "I feel almost human again."

"You look almost like my Mac. You've lost so much weight."

"War is about the worst thing a man can experience, Laurel. Right now, I don't want to dwell on it. In time, I'll tell you whatever you want to know. Now I only want to look at you and think about our future together."

"I understand. Are you well, my love?"

"I'm not injured, but I've seen so much ugliness and senseless waste. I hope I can come back to be the father and husband I need to be. Be patient with me."

"We have so much to talk about. Those men at Greensboro, they told you about the rumors concerning Macky, didn't they?"

"None of that matters. Laurel, I know you. Macky is my child. I never had a doubt. I'd guess he's our Christmas baby. But even if he weren't, I don't care. You are the only woman who can fill my life. All the time I was in Cahaba prison in Alabama, I survived day after day because I had you here waiting for me. I promised you I'd come back. Nothing would keep me from Shiloh."

Laurel walked into Mac's arms. He covered her lips with his as he'd longed to do since he'd ridden Midnight toward Helena to enlist. The lingering, passionate kiss brought both Mac and Laurel to tears.

"Wife, please come lay with me this night. Cradle your head on my shoulder as you do so well. Spoon against me and let me hold you until the sun pours through our window. This night, I need to know we are together. And Laurel, I promise you with a vow as unbreakable as our marriage vows—I swear on my blessed gift of salvation, we've been parted for the last time."

With a final, gentle goodnight kiss, Mac and Laurel MacLayne fell asleep, spooned together in the beautiful old-four-poster.

As a hint of sunlight began to tint the tops of the ridge, Mac pulled Laurel up from the bed.

"Grab that beautiful baby. We're goin' for a walk in the orchard. It's beautiful now."

As they approached the rows of fruit trees, the sweet aroma from the pink and white blossoms filled the air. The gentle breeze caused several petals to drift across their path. Mac stopped and picked a perfect blossom off the limb just above his head.

"You just killed an apple, ya know."

"I remember you said that to me a few years back, the day you became my wife."

"I'm happy you brought this orchard to Shiloh. These seven years of waiting for the promise have been good ones, haven't they?"

"For the most part. The only bad times happened because we were apart. But even in those times, good came from it. Like that first separation…during that time I was with my mother in Maryland, I realized I loved you."

"I don't think much good came out of the past year and a half, Mac. For a year of that time, I feared you weren't coming back. You don't know how close I came to giving up."

"Laurel, look at the self-sufficient, capable woman you are now. You didn't need someone else to carry you through. You didn't know I'd ever return, and I had no way to tell you I was alive. Yet, you let your faith carry you all that time. I had your picture, and every day when I looked at it, I knew you'd be here when I got home. I'd look at your beautiful face, and Romans 8:28 would cross my mind. You kept me goin'." He bent to kiss her.

"Mac, I'm not so beautiful anymore. I'm a mother six times. My skin is brown from the sun. I've callouses from the hoe. I'm not a belle."

"Have you lost your mirror again?"

"Yes. Without you here to reflect my worth, I can't see myself very well."

"Speaking of mirrors, what happened to the one I made for you last Christmas?"

"That's another long story. The Spinster of Hawthorn tried to come back. I'm afraid I used it to chase her away."

"You don't need it anyway. I'll not leave you again. You can always see the love of my life right here." Mac turned Laurel to face him. "Do you see the most valuable asset in this valley?"

"Yes, Love. I always do when you look at me."

Mac pulled Laurel to him. His lips met hers in a tender kiss. Macky squirmed before he released her. "Hold on there, young'un. I'm kissin' your mama." Mac again brought his lips to Laurel's. "I love you so much. Thank God I am home at last."

"I love you." They walked to the end of the orchard in silence. "Patrick, there is one thing I need to tell you. We've been so happy since you got home, I've not wanted to bring up a serious matter."

"What is it, darlin'?" he asked.

"We can't have any more children. When Macky was born, some permanent damage was caused by the surgery. I'm sorry."

"Laurel, I thank the Lord the doctor knew how to save your life. To have saved our new son is just a blessin' on top of a miracle. And he is perfect! We have the perfect family—just the right size. We'd be totally selfish to ask for more when we have so much."

"Thank you for understanding."

"What an added blessing for me. I can make love to you for the rest of my life and never have to worry I'll lose you in childbirth. I seem to remember at least three pretty frightening times I spent considerable time in fear waitin' for a MacLayne to make an appearance."

"Mac!"

"Why Laurel, even after eight years and all our kids, I believe you are blushing."

"Stop teasing. We'd better go back. The kids will be up for breakfast soon."

"Not yet."

They continued to walk. Shortly, Mac sat on their fallen log at Eden. Laurel kissed her new son's baby cheek and nestled him on a mound of moss at her feet. When she returned to Mac, he pulled her to his chest with his arms wrapped around her waist. The sun, rising just above the horizon, cast its golden rays across Shiloh homestead.

"Lord, this place is beautiful. Too often I almost lost hope I'd ever see it again."

"Mac, you'd never lose your faith. You taught me what it is to believe. We survive on hope, and we thrive when we're together." Mac kissed Laurel. She returned his passion.

"Praise God for the miracle of you, Laurel, and the miracle of home. I recited Genesis 49:10 to my men back at Cahaba prison more than any other scripture. I tried to explain what it means to be at Shiloh. I know now I didn't do it for them. I did it for me. It kept me alive. I repeated it a thousand times...'Til Shiloh Come."

"Mac, we'll repeat the verse together as long as we live. Wherever we are together, Shiloh has come."

# *Author's Note*

*The scepter shall not depart from Judah, nor a lawgiver from between his feet until Shiloh come, and unto Him shall the gathering of people be.*
*Genesis 49:10*

Reaching the end of the Shiloh Saga is a bittersweet experience. I have spent a major portion of my time since the fall of 2012 working on some aspect of this project. Now the fifth and final volume of Mac and Laurel's story is complete. Much of the time has been a joy. Some has been a pain. Truthfully, at times I cried. But today, I am finishing this labor of love. I believe it is time to move on to a new tale, if the Lord decides to give me a new story to pen.

Some of my readers have asked me to go on, but I believe my two characters have come to the point in their lives that I had hoped to see them. Laurel has grown up. She knows she can survive and thrive because she is a whole person. She has learned that her faith and the love Mac has invested in her will carry her through whatever life has in store.

Mac too has learned that Shiloh only exists where his family surrounds him. He is not a man who will be satisfied without challenges, but his efforts from this point will be directed closer to home so that he is never far from Laurel and Shiloh. Local politics, community issues, and local hardships will always draw his attention, but Laurel will be by his side. His children will grow up under his watchful care.

Shiloh Church will come together once again. Something so important to both the MacLaynes could not be displaced from their lives permanently. I actually wrote a scene to add to the final book but decided it was out of place in the ending.

I am proud of the amount of history I have been able to use in the back story of these books. Remember the plot is fiction, but when I recounted points of history, I tried to tell the story as realistically and honestly as I was able through the research. I am indebted to many who helped with that research process.

Battles and skirmishes of the Civil War did happen in Arkansas. Today, you can visit historical sites of many of these places, and I did have that opportunity. There is a lovely state part on the site of the Chalk Bluff battles in Clay County, Arkansas. The Fort Curtis site in Helena, Arkansas is outstanding, complete with replicas of cannons and the ramparts inside the earthen redoubts about four blocks from the Mississippi River. The *Sultana* Museum in Marion, Arkansas, is small, but growing. It is filled with memorabilia and historical information about the worst naval disaster in American history. Sadly, few people even know about this event. The docent at the *Sultana* Museum is kind and loves to share her vast knowledge about the site. All of these places would make great day trips for Arkansans who enjoy Arkansas history.

The Cahaba Archeological site in Alabama remains as a symbol of one triumph of the Confederacy and the good that one Godly man can do. In stark contrast to one of the South's greatest shames, Andersonville, Castle Morgan at Cahaba held more than 2,500 Union prisoners at one point in a camp built for 500, and due to the efforts of H.A.M. Henderson, fewer than 150 men died. Thousands died in Andersonville, most due to the sadistic cruelty of the leadership. A visit here would make a great stop on a drive through south Alabama. I enjoyed it immensely. The National Park docents were helpful and very knowledgeable.

For those interested in the research, I will put a bibliography on my website. Please visit it for more information and a few pictures of my research trips after the new year.

# patriciacblake.com

I'll end with my thank you' s…. The Shiloh Saga is complete now because of my wonderful friends and editors. I don't have adequate words to express what they mean to me.... Mary Lee Cunningham, Yevon Prater, Martha Rodriquez, Brenda Thakkar, and Beverly Thompson. I love you, Girls! God blessed me with your friendship and your dedication to 'our' project.

I also thank my readers for your encouragement and support.

A special thank you goes to my family. Like the MacLaynes, I'd never know Shiloh without them.

I offer this series as a tribute to God, Jesus Christ and the Holy Spirit.

*'Til Shiloh Come*
*An Arkansas Family in Time of War*

www.ingramcontent.com/pod-product-compliance
Lightning Source LLC
Chambersburg PA
CBHW070829260626
47170CB00007B/2320